SCHOOLING THE DUKE

SCHOOLING
THE DUKE

Christi Caldwell

For more information about the author:
www.christicaldwellauthor.com
christicaldwellauthor@gmail.com

ISBN: 1944240314
ISBN 13: 9781944240318

PROLOGUE

Wallingford, England
1810

"Rowena, the Duke of Hampstead is here…to see *you*."

Kneeling in the gardens, with the sun burning down on her neck, Miss Rowena Endicott froze. She stared unblinkingly at the pink freesia. The strong scent of those vibrant buds any other time would have been a soothing balm. Not, however, in this instance.

The duke was here to see her? It didn't make any sense. The Duke of Hampstead looked through her at Sunday sermons and hadn't even once since Rowena's family moved here, bothered with so much as a "hello." Why would he be here—? Then the truth slammed into her.

Graham. Graham Linford, the duke's second son whom she had fallen hopelessly and helplessly in love with, who'd gone off to fight Boney's forces. Her stomach turned over itself. *He is dead…*A piteous moan spilled from her lips.

"Rowena?" her youngest sister, Blanche, whispered.

With fingers that shook, Rowena pulled a tenacious weed from the base of the flowering plant and tossed it atop the growing collection of debris. *Do not look at her…if I do not look, she'll go away, and then this moment will not be real…*

Small fingers tugged at the fabric of Rowena's sleeve. "Mama and Papa said you must come inside *now*." Why else *would* the duke be here? Even if her stepfather was the vicar of the duke's parish, there was no reason for a nobleman one step below royalty to pay her a visit. Except for one: *Graham.*

Blanche gave another tug. "Rowena, are you listening to me?"

"I heard you," she said sharply, and her sister recoiled. Even through the panic and terror and agony roiling in Rowena's breast, guilt assailed her. "Oh, poppet," she said softly, gathering the seven-year-old girl in her arms. Born to a different father, her bond and love for this girl was no less than if had all their blood been shared. "I'm sorry. I"—had no reason to give to a small child to explain this crushing pain and fear. Blanche and her other sister, Bianca, were two innocent souls in a world marred by scandal and sin—as Rowena's past was testament to.

Blanche's lower lip trembled. "Are you s-scared? Because Mama and Papa seem scared." Yes, because their family dwelled on lies made of shifting sands, where discovery of Mother's past loomed, a danger that could see them all ruined. All secrets her young sisters didn't know, and would not ever know. "If you're scared, then *I'm* scared, so please don't be."

At that quavering whisper, Rowena brushed a hand over her cheek and mustered a false smile. "Tsk, tsk. You know I'm not afraid of anything." It was just another lie, only this one to protect her siblings. She puffed out her chest and spoke in deep tones. "I am Queen of the Gardens."

Her sister giggled. "Mistress of the Pen."

"Lady of the Locke," she finished the saying she always gave whenever Blanche and Bianca worried. Rowena tucked several brown strands behind her sister's ear. "It will be fine." She spoke those words as an assurance for herself as much as Blanche. Except…it wouldn't.

Graham. Again, she focused on breathing while terror swamped her senses.

I will come back for you…Make you my wife…Not even God himself could keep us apart…

"Roweeeena." Both sisters looked up as Bianca came hurtling forward. Her flame-red hair hung in messy curls down her back. "Mama and Papa said it is very important. They said you need to come now."

It was time. These handful of minutes she'd allowed herself to pretend and keep reality at bay would not erase the duke's presence—or worse, what actually brought him here. Rising to her feet, a lone freesia still clutched in her left hand, Rowena trudged through the gardens, along the graveled path, to the modest cottage they called home.

The door opened, and her stepfather froze. All the color leeched from his cheeks.

"F-Father," she managed to squeeze out, the one word emerging on a weak croak. One of her mother's many lovers, the Vicar Tobias Endicott had been the only man to offer Mother more…respectability and a name…and because of it, the same gift given to Rowena, too.

He held her gaze a moment and the flash of regret and sorrow there ratcheted up the pressure weighing on her chest.

How am I standing? How am I standing, when I know the duke has no reason to visit me, other than Graham?

"Rowena," her stepfather whispered, averting his gaze from her own. "I'm so sorry. I…" Tears filled his eyes. "Forgive me." Yanking off his spectacles, he dusted the back of his hand over his face and stalked off.

Numb from the inside out, Rowena forced her legs into movement, entering through the small doorway. The duke would have had to duck on his way through as Graham had every time he paid her a visit. It was a silly thing to note, and yet, silly kept her sane. It kept her from spiraling out of control into a place of grief and loss.

"M-Mama?" she called into the quiet, as she shucked off her dirt-stained apron. Shifting the freesia in her fingers, she hung up the garment. "M-Mama?" she tried again. Though it was foolish to go a-calling when there were but three bedrooms and two parlors.

"Here." The steadiness of her mother's reply from within the only true home they'd ever known somehow steadied her. It enabled Rowena to continue walking to that room for this hated, unwanted meeting. She stopped at the threshold.

Alongside her mother, the duke stood, his body stiffly held. Several inches past six feet, and powerful of frame, he exuded power and arrogance. His noble roots were further reflected in his aquiline nose, wide, firm jaw—and now, his pursed mouth. He'd the look of a man who'd sucked a lemon, not a man who came to upend her world with grief that would destroy her forever.

Rowena wetted her lips. "Y-Your Grace." She sank into a belated, awkward curtsy.

He gave not even a hint that he'd heard her wobbly greeting.

"Rowena," her mother began, studiously avoiding her eyes. *Just like Papa.* "Will you close the door?"

Feeling much like a person living outside her body and watching the actions of another, Rowena complied.

"My son is dead," the Duke of Hampstead said without preamble.

A keening cry, a tortured sound better suited to a wild animal sailed past her lips. Rowena's legs gave out from under her, and she sank to the floor, rocking back and forth. *NoNoNoNoNo.* She clamped her hands over her ears, attempting to blot out her mother's urgings.

"My *heir*, Miss Endicott," the duke said impatiently, his sharp tones cutting across her misery.

Rowena yanked her head up and blinked wildly. His heir. *Not Graham.* Graham's brother. "The marquess," she whispered, needing a confirmation anyway.

The older man gave a curt nod.

Thank God. On the heel of that was guilt at the relief that brought forth that silent prayer in the face of the duke's loss.

Except, jade green eyes—the color a near-identical hue to Graham's—gave no hint of anything but cool indifference. Her legs still limp from the shock of his announcement, and eventual relief, Rowena shoved to her feet. "I'll not waste anymore time here than I already have, Miss *Bryant*."

She froze. Miss *Bryant?* Rowena gave her clouded mind a shake, and yet the cobwebs remained. The surname she'd been born with, that she'd been instructed to never again use or respond to, the moment her mother had wed Vicar Endicott. Unease skittered along her spine, and she cast a searching look over at her mother.

Her mother buried her hands in her palms and wept.

Oh, my God. He knows. Of course, it wouldn't take much for a duke to look into the true origins of his vicar's marriage from eight years ago. Yet, why should he have? There'd been no reason to question or wonder.

"Graham will someday be a duke, Miss Endicott," His Grace said matter-of-factly, his condescending gaze burning her flesh. "It was one thing for him to bed a village girl..." Mortified heat stained her entire body that he should know about those shared, stolen moments. "But certainly you see that as my heir he can never wed a baseborn miss." Rowena flinched. "You're worse than baseborn"—he flicked a derisive gaze over her once more—"you're a whore's daughter."

The air lodged painfully in her lungs, and she tried to force it out. She dimly registered the piteous weeping of her mother. Their secret had been discovered. Not only her family's but also the pledge Graham had made to her before he'd gone off to fight...*I will wed you, Rowena Endicott...*

She slid into the folds of the nearest seat. "I love him," she said, proud of the evenness of that delivery.

The duke snapped his eyebrows into a steely silver line. "I expect you love him even more now that he'll be a duke."

She gave her head a dizzying shake. "No. It never mattered. It doesn't matter," she rambled, needing him to understand. "I love—"

He held up a commanding hand, silencing her. "Graham will return soon, and when he does, I want you gone."

A dull humming filled her ears. "I'm not leaving." Did that bold challenge belong to her?

Surprise lit the duke's eyes, and then was gone, masked with his icy disdain. "But you see, you will, Miss Bryant." He took a step toward her. "Because if you do not leave, I'll have your father tossed from his position as vicar and your mother's reputation known in every circle and county." With every vile threat, panic grew and grew until she threatened to crumple under the weight of it.

Rowena looked helplessly to her mother. All that would remain after this visit was Rowena...and her family. Her mother loved her too much to make this sacrifice...even if it would save Blanche and Bianca, whose very names meant purity.

Except...Mother hugged herself and looked away.

Rowena sucked in a breath as a slow, dreadful understanding slithered around her mind.

Two years earlier, when her family's cottage had been struck by lightning and the thatched roof caught fire, Rowena had been besieged by nightmares. The terror would come, fleeting and unexpected as that summer storm, and through it, Graham had always been there. When the fear had threatened to cripple her, he'd taken her in his arms, playing games to distract her from the terror until it dissipated.

But there was no Graham here. *He is gone in every possible way, to me.*

And now as evidenced by her mother's silence and father's absence, there was not even a parent to help her.

"If you remain here in wait for my son, I promise all will know your sisters as a whore's daughters. No future will await any of you."

Did he sense her wavering? She wanted to tell him to go to hell. To send him to the devil and with directions how to get there. She wanted to rail at her mother and father for being cowards, complicit in their silence. And yet...she glanced over to the lead windowpanes, to where her sisters played outside. Their laughter carried from the gardens and pealed around the room.

Rowena looked to her mother and their gazes caught. Her mother's blue eyes filled with tears, pouring out her regret and sorrow. "I am so sorry," Mama mouthed.

Those four, silently spoken words, speaking more plainly than had they been shouted into existence: her mother had chosen to save her youngest children. Rowena choked back the sting of resentment, rage, and hurt. What should her parents do? Sacrifice their legitimate children because Rowena, like the strumpet the duke took her for, had given herself to Graham Linford?

"What would you have me do?" Rowena's hollow question, came from a place of logic, and love for the two little girls who deserved far more from life.

"If you'll excuse us?" the duke directed that to her mother, and for a moment Rowena believed there was far more courage and strength in her than she'd ever credited. But then, eyes averted, Mama fled, closing the door behind her, leaving Rowena alone with the dragon.

The duke reached inside his jacket and fished out a page. "You'll take employment elsewhere."

"Employment?" she parroted back, automatically taking the sheet and reading words about her and for her but yet so foreign she couldn't make sense of them.

"I don't want you to return, Miss Bryant. The moment you do, I'll see you not only out of this honorable employment but any future posts. You won't find work except the kind your mother knew in London—on your back." His Grace withdrew his gold watchfob and consulted the timepiece.

She crushed the page in her hands. "Graham loves me." Surely his son's happiness should mean something. And yet, he was a nobleman who'd come here, the day his eldest son died, with the express intention of ridding the village of her.

"Love?" The duke scoffed. "My son loved tupping you and not much more." His jibe struck like a lance to her heart.

Rowena steeled her jaw and glared at him in defiance. "If you believed that, you'd not send me away. It wouldn't matter if he returned and found me still here."

His nostrils flared. "Regardless, the decision is yours. Remain and find your kin homeless without a hope for another vicarship for your father, or take employment elsewhere."

Rowena's eyes slid involuntarily to that page. The inked words ran together in her mind.

Mrs. Belden's Finishing School...Servant...

"I see that we understand one another. You'll depart within the hour." An hour? Panic swelled once more. "My carriage will see you delivered." And with that, he left.

Rowena remained frozen to her seat, with the clock ticking loudly in her ears. In the distance, her sisters' laughter mingled with the cacophony in her mind, punctuated by the click of the front door closing as the duke took his leave. Leave. He'd send her away, from her family, the only family she'd ever known, and more—away from Graham. A tear slipped down her cheek, followed by another and another.

The front door opened, and for a sliver of a moment, hope reared that her mother and father would not make her to do this. *They will*

CHRISTI CALDWELL

fight for me and prove I matter as much as Blanche and Bianca. The soft pitter of a child's footsteps killed that foolish yearning.

Blanche filled the doorway. "He's gone…" Her smile dipped. "What is it?" she whispered, taking a tentative step closer. "You're sad," she observed with an intuition only a child could possess.

I am dying inside. My heart, broken first when Graham left, is dying all over again. "I'm not." Where did that lie come from? Where, when she'd leave behind her family and friends. She choked down a sob. "I-I am overcome with happiness." *Would the ladies of Berkshire who'd taken you under their wing of friendship still feel kindly toward you should they discover the truth? They'll never know.* She steeled her jaw. Not Aldora, not Emilia, not Constance, not Meredith, and certainly not her own sisters. "I'm going to someplace wonderful," she said softly, continuing the stream of lies to reassure her sister.

Blanche widened her brown eyes. "Truly?" She sprinted over. "Where are we going?"

We. Not "you." Except, Rowena had never been more alone than she was in this instance. Cupping her sister's cheek, she blinked through the tears. "It is a secret." One that no one would ever know.

Blanche pouted. "A secret. When can you tell me? When will you return?" As her sister peppered her with questions, a sob stuck in her throat, and she quickly dragged the little girl close. Over her small shoulder, her gaze caught on the forgotten freesia lying on the floor.

"Someday," she promised. "I'll be back someday." When Graham returned, she'd come back. He would marry her, as he'd vowed, and all would be right again.

A knock sounded at the door, sparing her from any further questions, and she and Blanche looked up.

Jack Turner, with his thick crop of blond hair, stood in the doorway ringing his hat in his hands. She, Graham, and Jack had been friends from the moment she'd entered the village, and the sight of him chased back some of the panic cloying at her breast. "Your mother said I should come in and see you," he murmured.

My mother. That coward who'd been unable to meet her eyes. Heart twisting, she patted the top of Blanche's head. "Run along so I might speak to Jack."

Blanche rushed off and stopped beside Jack. "Mr. Turner." She dropped a curtsy.

"Miss Endicott," he greeted with a bow and equal solemnity. Giving him a final wave, her sister left.

Jack lingered in the doorway, his gaze traveling over her tear-stained cheeks. "What is it?" he asked, drawing the door closed.

Unable to speak, she bit her lower lip and gave her head a hard shake. And then the enormity of this day slammed into her. She dissolved into tears. The force of her sobs shook her frame and burned her lungs.

Rowena dimly registered Jack coming close and taking her into his arms. He made useless, nonsensical calming noises that only further increased her weeping. "H-He's sending me a-away," she rasped against the fine fabric of his wool jacket.

His fingers ceased their distracted circles. "He?"

And through the noisy mess of her crying, she explained all, carefully omitting the shame of her family's past that had resulted in her banishment.

Jack held her like that for a long while, saying nothing, and then—"Marry me."

Rowena's ears rang from her own ragged breaths and tears. Blinking, she edged out of his arms. Marry him? This was Graham's closest friend. A young man he'd called brother, and who was forever at his side.

There was an earnestness in Jack's gaze. "Surely you know…" he said hoarsely. Rowena gave her head an uncomprehending shake. After the duke's visit, nothing made sense. "I love you."

The air left her on a hiss, and she recoiled at the depth of that betrayal. Were there any limits to the lack of loyalty this day? "*Graham—*"

"Is gone," he said firmly. "He doesn't matter. He is dallying with French beauties while you are left here with his father who will see you ruined." Jack gathered her cold hands and dragged them close. "I will care for you. Love you. Be a good husband to you."

The gentleness of that offer was contradicted by the fierce glint in his eyes. He offered her stability, security, and yet, she'd sooner carve out her heart with a dull blade than betray Graham. "Oh, Jack," she said softly, giving his hands a squeeze. "I love Graham. You know I could never—"

"You've given him everything," he whispered. "Your body, your heart. I've offered you my name and security, and you'd reject my offer?"

Her heart twisted. He'd been a good friend, and she hated to see him hurt...and hated even more that she'd caused it. "I am grate—" Her words ended on a sharp gasp as he slammed his mouth down hard on hers. Jack swallowed the sound of her protest, thrusting his tongue inside. Reaching between them, he grabbed her breast, squeezing that flesh. Shock and fear made her motionless.

As he dragged her closer, terror threatened to choke off her airflow. Gagging, Rowena shoved at him but he was immovable. She whimpered and caught him hard between the legs with her knee. A hiss slipped past his lips and he jerked away. Writhing in pain, he glowered at her. "You would be lucky to have me as your husband, whore," he spat. Then he froze, blinking wildly.

Legs shaking, Rowena touched her fingers to her bruised lips.

"R-Rowena." He stretched his hand out and she recoiled.

Then shaking her head, she raced from the room. He called after her, his voice wreathed in agony. "Forgive me. I don't know...forgive me," he implored.

Ignoring his pleading, she sprinted from the room...wanting to run and hide forever from the pain of this day—a day of nothing but betrayals.

ONE

London, England
1820

G raham Linford, the Duke of Hampstead, lived a lie, and but for one loyal friend, not a single person knew it.

Society once saw him as a rogue who lived for excess, and now as the reformed duke, driven by rank and power. A man who honored societal customs and traditions. For that and his title alone, he found himself sought after by every last-matchmaking mama in England.

Ultimately, the world was content to see what it wished: a powerful, austere duke, and not much more. That façade allowed him to keep secret the nightmares that had haunted him since the battlefields of Bussaco. The truth of his insanity he intended to take to his grave, once he drew a final and, at last, peaceful breath.

Until now. Now, he very nearly thought of drawing forth that truth and revealing his greatest shame. Before a stranger, no less. Because no lord, lady, or anyone with a jot of sense would entrust a young lady to a madman's care.

Seated before the same mahogany desk his own father had occupied, and his father's father before him, Graham peered at Mr. Dappleton, the solicitor. A man who'd invaded his office with the intentions of foisting a ward on him.

"I beg your pardon?" he stretched those five steely syllables out.

"Guardian, Your Grace." Not taking his gaze from the task before him, Mr. Dappleton shuffled through a leather folio and drew out page after page. "You were named guardian by Lieutenant Hickenbottom."

1

Then, staking a claim on Graham's desk, the man of middling years laid the documents out like a commander on the eve of battle, pouring over his plans. Surveying the documents, the graying solicitor tapped his fingertip in a sharp, staccato rhythm. *TapTapTap*

PopPopPop

Sweat beaded his brow. Mr. Dappleton had requested this meeting for more than a fortnight; a meeting which Graham had neatly sidestepped until now. All memory and mention of the past had the power to yank him under, and Hickenbottom's name alone drew him back to that dark day. *Do not give in to the damning weakness.* His stomach churned. *TapTapTap*

PopPopPop

The blare of cannon fire thundered inside his head. Agonized screams. Men dying around him.

Linford, I've got you, man!

"Your Grace?"

Pulled back from the brink of his waking nightmare, Graham counted slowly to five. In a bid to maintain a façade of calm, he drew forth his watchfob and consulted the timepiece. "You were saying?" he asked in smooth, emotionless tones long perfected.

"I trust you do recall Lieutenant Hickenbottom?"

"Indeed," he said in austere, faintly mocking tones. Even after all these years, his thigh occasionally throbbed from the dull pain of a bayonet, and then being unceremoniously carried upon the back of the very man, in death, who asked a favor of him now. Did he remember him? He peeled his lip back in a cool grin. Yes, one tended to remember the man who'd saved one from certain death, even taking a bullet in the shoulder for his efforts.

"According to Lieutenant Hickenbottom, you would recall the favor he sought of you, in the event of his death." A drunken discourse between two equally inebriated rogues who'd toasted the hell of those days in Belgium, slipped forward. Only, it hadn't been the sole reason for Graham's descent into a drunken state. Rowena Endicott's clear bell-like laugh echoed around the chambers of his mind. The muscles of his stomach seized. Dappleton slid another page across the desk.

Grateful for the diversion, Graham automatically picked it up. He scanned the official-looking document. The document that would see his life invaded and his carefully crafted façade threatened. Setting it down, he pushed it back, and reclined in his seat. "Hickenbottom must have named another guardian." For, drunken pledges aside, even from a dissolute rake, the man would have had the sense to know Graham would make a rotted guardian for any child.

"Lord Tannery. Also dead," the solicitor issued that blunt deliverance with nary a crack in his careful demeanor.

How easily Graham had come to be one of those dissolute lords, consumed by the blaze of his own wickedness. In the earliest days of his return from Belgium, in the darkest corners of his mind where the demons dwelled, he'd clung to the dream of death. In the even further recesses, he'd entertained bringing himself into the only place oblivion would truly be found. Instead, he'd attempted to lay siege to his monsters with the same wickedness that had killed Hickenbottom.

Where he had ultimately shifted course, and sought sanity along the path of respectability, Hickenbottom had been consumed by his own recklessness.

"Given the death of Lord Tannery and the absence of any familial relative, care for Miss Hickenbottom has fallen to you." The solicitor slid another page across Graham's previously immaculate desk. Picking it up, Graham skimmed the sheet.

Modest dowry. Seventeen years old. His gaze lingered on one detail of the girl Hickenbottom would leave to him:

Natural daughter.

Unwanted, the face of another girl from long, long ago slipped forward, a smiling face, with rosy cheeks and emerald eyes. Assaulted by memories better reserved for a crypt, his hand shook. Graham swiftly released the sheet and shoved it across the desk. "This is no place for a child." Nor any man or woman.

Mr. Dappleton nodded once. "I understand, Your Grace."

Ignoring the latter part of the gentleman's statement, Graham steepled his fingers under his chin and leveled the solicitor with a stare. "And what is it you think you understand?" he asked, with a deliberately condescending smile. After two episodes of madness at the then-wicked clubs he'd attended ten years earlier, he had kept it all at bay. His friend, Jack Turner, had helped cover up that humiliation. From that moment on, he crafted the aloof image that allowed him the veneer of sanity. As such, with the exception of Jack, the world only knew the details Graham carefully fed them.

Demonstrating a remarkable composure, Mr. Dappleton lifted his shoulders in a shrug. "She is a bastard." As though Graham were a consummate idiot who couldn't read, the solicitor jabbed his finger in the middle of the page.

Not deigning to look at the man's gesture, Graham's cold tone turned glacial. "I'm well-aware of her birthright. That is not why I'm rejecting the role of guardian."

Mr. Dappleton's gray eyebrows shot up over the frame of his wire-rimmed spectacles.

Of course, this man, and all of Society would rightfully assume that the severe Duke of Hampstead wouldn't want a dead rake's by-blow underfoot. They could not know, at one time he'd given his heart and ultimately would have offered his name to a woman of that same ignoble fate. A pang stuck in his chest. He rubbed at that dulled-by time ache. An ache determined to linger, no matter how much he'd buried thoughts of Miss Rowena Endicott from his memories. *Damn you, Rowena Endicott, and goddamn the resurrection of old ghosts from every corner.* Battling the restive fury her name always roused, he stacked the papers requiring his signature and held them out.

"Your Grace?" the man puzzled aloud.

When he made no move to collect his paperwork, Graham let it go. The papers hit the surface of the desk with a soft thwack. "Let me explain it to you in terms you might understand." Terms that had nothing to do with belittling a girl's worth because of her parentage. "I've no duchess." Not yet. It was a task Jack had been wisely pushing him toward, with the duchy and future of the estates in mind. The Hampstead line, once revered and held of more importance than even his own children's happiness by the late duke, meant rot to Graham. Rather, it was the men and women dependent upon him to whom his allegiance came. "As such, a bachelor residence is not for a young girl." He peeled his lip back. "Surely, even you see that?" The miserable twaddle who'd besmirch Hickenbottom's child.

"But there will one day be a duchess." Redirecting his bespectacled focus to the sheet before him, Dappleton prattled on with his late employer's requests.

And with the man's tenacity, Graham didn't know whether to haul Dappleton by his jacket and heft him from the room, or hire him.

Yes, the insolent servant was indeed right. There would one day be a duchess. Soon. Very soon, to be precise. The papers had already begun to speculate as to which lady it would be. With even more speculations that the young woman was, in fact, Lady Serena Grace. A lady Jack had put forth as a suitable prospect. Daughter to the Duke of Wilkshire. Flawlessly perfect from her manners down to her golden curls. The nineteen-year-old lady had been ruthlessly honest in her desires for him from the moment they'd been introduced.

It is expected that I'll be your duchess, Your Grace...

How very different her avowal from the false ones given him by another. His fingers curled reflexively so hard, he left crescent marks on his palms. He eased his grip.

It was Lady Serena's ruthlessness he appreciated. Society anticipated a power-match between two ducal families, and Wilkshire's daughter had been honest in that very same prospect. After having learned for himself the perils of love, Graham no longer had a heart to offer. Lady Serena would live her life as revered hostess, and he could retreat to the countryside and continue to live his lie. As such, they were a perfect match. Most would consider him heartless for the coldhearted arrangement he sought. As he saw it, he had no other choice.

What he did have were people dependent upon him. Tenants. Servants. And having failed too many at Bussaco, he'd sooner sell what remained of his soul than allow his wastrel cousin to inherit. Mr. Abelard Marlowe, rumored to bugger children and beat servants, would never touch a Linford farthing. "We are done here," he said, unfurling to his full-height.

The solicitor peeked up from his documents, and in a remarkable show of courage remained sitting. "I am afraid we are not, Your Grace." Other than that slightly emphasized word, there wasn't a single apologetic air about the man. Hickenbottom's solicitor may have a condescending view of the girl's parentage, but he was fearless, and that Graham respected. Dappleton tapped his finger on the desk, like he sought to drum his point into the surface. "Lieutenant Hickenbottom's family has adamantly stated they've no intention, desire, or willingness to take her in." By that rote deliverance, these were familiar words, uttered many times to the man. The solicitor paused. "The young lady has nowhere else to go." Had there been more than that blunt reality, it would have been easier to send Dappleton on his way with his official documents.

"He has a sister," he ground out.

"Lady Casterlon," The graying man shook his head. "will not take her."

"His brother, the earl—"

"Stated you are the living guardian, and he'd not take her in, even if you won't."

By Christ in hell.

Tension and terror mingled to set his heart pounding. With the episodes he suffered when the horrors of war unexpectedly crept in, he'd fought for evenness in every aspect of his life. He'd not give over to the mind-numbing panic that came in: one, conceding that Dappleton was indeed correct, and two, facing the intrusion of an innocent young miss underfoot. Struggling for calm, Graham smoothed his features and returned to his seat.

Dappleton pushed the documents requiring his signatures his way once again.

A thick silence descended as Graham grasped the pen from his inkwell. There would be not one but two people with whom he'd now share the sanctuary that had become his home. For this bastard ward was far worse than a wife he could leave to her own amusements. This was a charge and her companion, who'd require oversight. Suddenly, the urgency in marrying reared its ugly head in a whole new, necessary way. Once he was married, the chit and her presentation to Society would fall to the duchess. "See that she and her companion are readied by nightfall." The scratch of his pen, inordinately loud. "I will send a carriage to collect them." He added his last signature. His palms grew moist, and setting his pen down, he laid his hands on his buckskin-clad thighs, brushing the moisture from his skin.

"As you wish, Your Grace."

If it were as he wished, Graham would even now be free of the responsibility of looking after the bastard daughter orphaned by his reckless friend. He bit back the acerbic reply. It was hardly Dappleton's fault that Hickenbottom had gotten himself killed, along with the other guardian. Or that Hickenbottom's surviving relatives were the same propriety-driven, ruthless bastards Graham's own father had been. When Dappleton remained seated, he snapped, "What is it now, man?"

"There is one more issue, Your Grace."

He gnashed his teeth. "Issue?" What else could there possibly be this day?

"There is no governess."

Mayhap Graham was cracked in the head in addition to being mad. "You said the girl was sixteen."

"*Just* seventeen," the other man amended.

A lady in need of a blasted London Season. Fighting once more for calm, Graham reined in his annoyance. "A companion, then?"

"There is no one."

No one.

"No one but the girl, that is." With an infuriating nonchalance, the solicitor opened the small tin of powder, and proceeded to sprinkle it on the documents. "Lieutenant Hickenbottom never bothered with one for the girl."

A young lady on the cusp of womanhood who'd *never* had the benefit of instruction on gentilesse? Graham covetously eyed the sideboard filled with spirits. Years ago, when he'd donned the persona of carefree rogue, he'd have already had a bottle in hand. He grew frustrated: with Hickenbottom for leaving him in these straits and himself, for being a bloody monster unwilling and unable to do right by his now-gone friend. "What am I going to do with a girl without a companion?" he snapped.

"Hire one, Your Grace? Send her on to finishing school? She is your responsibility now."

7

No wonder the insolent blighter had withheld that particular, important piece of information. A bastard, without the benefit of an estimable chaperone.

As the solicitor put together his belongings, Graham entertained the childish thought of shredding those pages and grinding them under the heel of his boot.

At one and thirty years, however, he'd adopted a polished demeanor; he'd not break any more than he already had for this man.

"There is but one more thing, Your Grace," Dappleton said, as he came to his feet.

What now? "I thought you'd said there was…"

The solicitor fished a note out of his jacket and handed over the folded scrap.

Graham accepted it, freezing at the familiar inked writing. A few moments later, Dappleton, folios in his arms, took a bow and left.

As soon as Graham found himself alone, he unfolded the note. His chest tightened.

Hampstead,
If you're reading this, I'm dead. No doubt, through some outrageously wicked act for which I'm solely to blame.

"Indeed," Graham muttered, and continued reading.

You are no doubt also cursing me for leaving you in this sorry state. After all, the last thing a gent needs is a young chit underfoot. This girl, however, is different. I'm fairly certain, she's the only person I've ever liked. And I'm not saying that because she's my daughter. Society will be unkind to her because of her parentage. Keep her under your wing. Teach her the ways of our miserable Society, so that she can find a good bloke, and not someone like her da. I've certainly not done any-thing in the way of preparing her.
Respectfully yours, even in death,
Hickenbottom.

The immediate intention to scuttle the girl off to some finishing school until Graham wed quashed by two paragraphs left by a man he'd called friend. He'd of course known he would marry. Now, the urgency of that boiled to the surface. With a curse, he tossed the page on his desk, and it sailed to a noiseless heap. In the end, he proved lacking in self-control. Hungering for a drink, he stalked to his sideboard and poured himself a glass.

A knock sounded.

"Enter," he called out.

The door opened. "Mr...."

"I met with Hickenbottom's solicitor," Graham's blunt interruption cut across Wesley's announcement. Graham set down the decanter and, glass in hand, strode back to the desk.

"Have you?" Jack murmured when Wesley left, closing the door behind him.

Mayhap if the other man had been present, he'd have had some inclination as to what Graham could do with a sixteen—or was it seventeen?—year-old bastard ward. Without a governess. Or companion. He took a long swallow.

All affability faded from Jack's demeanor. "What did he want?" Since Graham's return from war and his ascension to the role of duke, his friend had stepped in as his man-of-affairs. He'd overseen his business ventures with a military-like precision that had seen an immense rise in his already plentiful coffers. That was not, however, the sole reason he was Graham's only confidante. That loyalty went back to a friendship more than two decades old, strengthened in part by his loyalty through Graham's descent into madness.

Cradling his glass between his hands, Graham relayed the details surrounding Dappleton's visit. When he'd finished, Jack took a seat. "A child," he parroted.

Graham gave a terse nod and tossed back his drink. He grimaced as the liquid seared his throat and set the glass down. At the other man's silence, he looked up.

"The nightmares." Jack's quiet reminder, wholly unnecessary.

The nightmares, as they'd taken to calling them. An image that conjured ghosts and monsters that lurked in the back of a child's deepest fears. And not the reality that was life: of hell and dying and gruesome battles that, thankfully, no child's mind could conjure. "I'm well aware of them." He stretched his legs out before him in an artificial nonchalance, and then laid his clasped fingers on his flat belly. "I require a companion *and* a wife." Not necessarily in that order.

Jack's frown deepened. "Lady Serena won't welcome having a bastard underfoot."

No, most members of the peerage would want nothing to do with a girl of questionable birthright.

Do you believe I'd ever judge you for your birthright, Rowena Endicott? Our hearts were joined the day you entered this village, and nothing will change that...

"Hampstead?"

A fool. He'd been a bloody fool. "Lady Serena will welcome anything for the privilege of becoming my duchess," he said, pointedly ignoring the question in his friend's tone. Marriage to a woman coined the Ice Princess would not only mark his responsibilities to those dependent upon him nearly complete, it would also mark a finality to the chapter in his life that had ever included Rowena Endicott.

Jack snorted but did not refute that claim, either. "As your man-of-affairs and friend, I'd recommend you wed the chit off as soon as possible."

Yes. It was for the best—for him *and* his ward. Graham, so he could maintain his mundane life. She, so she wasn't exposed to his madness. There could be no doubt that Jack's suggestion held a vast appeal. Graham's gaze trailed involuntarily over to the note, Hickenbottom's appeal in death. He sighed. "I'll not rush the girl into marriage to appease Lady Serena—"

"It is the Duke of Wilkshire you should worry after."

"Or anyone," Graham finished over the other man's interruption. "Wilkshire included." The Duke of Wilkshire, in possession of one of the oldest duchies, had been abundantly clear that he craved a match between his only daughter and Graham. That he'd not settle for anyone less than a duke…nor would Lady Serena. In fact, Graham suspected that should the duke know the truth about Graham, he would gladly sell her off for the title of Hampstead duchess, anyway.

Jack's mouth tensed and Graham braced for an additional battle. "As you wish."

Since he had stated his intentions to wed, and identified Lady Serena as his likely match, his friend had been stalwartly committed to seeing an arrangement formalized. And he would. It was time for him to see to those responsibilities. Soon. After his obligations toward Hickenbottom's daughter were fulfilled.

Jack gathered his belongings, and shoved to his feet. "I will put out enquiries and secure a respectable companion for the lady." That offer dangled temptingly before him. As his friend made his goodbye and started for the door, Graham stared at his retreating frame. How easy it would be to let Jack do this.

Allow him to take this on. He oversees all my business, and that is ulti-mately what this girl is.

The distant report of a pistol and an agonized cry pealed in the room with a vividness that sent his body recoiling. "Send me the names of the most respected institutions," he called out sharply. "I'll conduct my own interviews with any potential companion."

Jack wheeled around, surprise stamped in his sharp features. "*You'll* conduct the interviews?"

"Yes, me." The other man was entitled to his shock. Since the episode eight years earlier had nearly revealed him for the madman he was to the whole of Society, Graham had retreated, and Jack had helped him uphold the façade that was his existence. Going about finding and securing members of his staff had not been a task Graham had seen to. "It is my responsibility. Hickenbottom saved my life in that carriage. This is the very least I can do."

Outside of mundane *ton* events, he had gone out of his way to avoid breaks in his well-ordered routine. Placidity had brought some relief from his demons, and there was a value greater than any coin in that peace. It was one thing for Graham to entrust his business affairs to Jack. Until now. The role of guardian had been expressly handed over to him, and he had an obligation to the man who'd saved his life to carry out his last wishes at least.

The other man made a sound of protest. "It is enough that you'll have a ward of dubious origins underfoot. Wilkshire will be a good deal less inclined to formalize any agreement while you're off for the Season conducting affairs you've deemed more important than his daughter."

Yes, he would. Wilkshire was cut out of the same pompous cloth as Graham's late father. As such the duke would hardly take kindly to him abandoning London at the height of the Season. Particularly as his absence would signal a lack of true intent for a match with the Lady Serena. Nonetheless…

"I'll have you coordinate an intimate dinner party with the Montgomery's so they might have the privilege of being the first to meet my ward." That would send a message as loud as a second dance on the connection between their families. "Inform him that matters involving my ward, however, are otherwise calling me away."

"You are certain I cannot find the companion for you?" Jack's persistence could only come from a man who'd born witness to the demons that haunted Graham.

"I am."

His friend hesitated. "As you wish." Jack opened his mouth and then closed it. With a slight bow, he left.

As he wished. It was the second time that day those words had been uttered, and there was so much he wished for. Sanity. Peace. Freedom from pain.

In the absence of those elusive gifts, he'd settle for something within his control: finding the most qualified and esteemed companion possible to shape a hoyden into a lady.

Only then would Graham's debt at last be paid.

TWO

Spelthorne, England
1820

Most young girls lost themselves in tales of beautiful princesses and the dashing princes who saved them. As a child, however, Mrs. Rowena Bryant had possessed an inordinate fascination with dragons. It had been a coincidental interest born of a book given to her as a birthday gift from one of her mother's many protectors.

The book told the tale of fierce, scaled dragons with great enormous wings. Mythical creatures capable of fire and flight. Rowena had studied and scrutinized every page until they'd frayed in the corners and time turned the blank ink gray.

Now, nearly in her thirtieth year, she'd never dreamed she would find herself identified as one. Only, a creature not at all magical and wholly lacking in those fascinating traits that marked them as great.

"Miserable dragon…"

The muted whisper was met with a smattering of giggles. Seated behind a rose-inlaid desk better suited a fine lady's parlor, Rowena snapped her head up. Odd, how time changed even the meaning one ascribed to words. Dragon was the hideous title she'd been afforded by her students. A name jeeringly tossed about to all the women *fortunate* enough to find employment at Mrs. Belden's Finishing School. Rowena frowned her students into compliance.

The girls swiftly schooled their features and returned their focus to the embroidering frames on their laps. She skimmed her gaze over the young ladies assembled before her. All daughters of powerful noblemen, the sixteen- and seventeen-year-old ladies occupied the edges of their delicate chairs. Under her tutelage, the girls had honed their skills as flawless ladies, prepared for their entrance into Society. The irony of it was not lost on her. She, Rowena Bryant, the daughter of a reformed courtesan-turned-wife of a vicar, doling out lessons on propriety and preparing young ladies for a respectable future.

With her students focused on their tasks, she studied them. Wistful memories crept in to when she'd been their age, laughing with friends, dreaming of love, and hopeful for the future. Her students, by their birthrights, would never know what it was to make a life of their own, on their own. They would never be ladies toyed with by powerful noblemen and tricked out of their hearts and virtue. A sad smile pulled at her lips. For a brief moment in time, she had even called women born to the peerage her friends. And, yet, she had been wise enough to withhold the truth of her origins. For the truth would always remain: people such as Rowena could never truly belong.

Except...you once allowed yourself that illusion...

A sharply chiseled face of long ago flashed into her mind's eye. A half-grinning visage that briefly brought her eyes closed. Heart hammering, she glanced around to see if her peculiar reaction had been noted. Her students, seated like little ducks in a row, continued stitching away. Some of the tension left her, and she shoved aside thoughts of *him*. A man whose knavery had seen her future forfeited and found her here at Mrs. Belden's.

Steepling her fingers together, she shifted her gaze to the lead windowpanes. Sunlight streamed through the glass panels and cast a luminous glow upon the floor. There were few options for unmarried women. There were even fewer for the daughters of reformed courtesans. Even knowing how fortunate she was, Rowena wanted more. A wave of longing besieged her to be free of the dreary schoolroom she'd called home for nearly ten years.

If she were, in fact, one of those great-winged, mythical creatures long ago, she'd have taken flight far, far away from this miserable place. Anything to be free of it.

A scratching outside the door snapped her from her reverie. Mrs. Elizabeth Terry, a bespectacled, gray-skirt wearing instructor hired two years after Rowena stood in the doorway. "Mrs. Belden has requested your presence."

The announcement was met with gasps. Gasps, which under most circumstances would have been met with a silencing look from Rowena and Mrs. Terry. Except...Rowena's stomach sank. "A summons?" she asked haltingly, setting off another round of whispers.

An instructor at Mrs. Belden's Finishing School never wished to be summoned to the headmistress's office. *Particularly* when one was in the midst of delivering a lesson. Time had inevitably proven all those summoned mid-lesson by Mrs. Belden inevitably were sacked or removed from their posts.

That truth held her frozen, unmoving, wide-eyed, while her charges stared back with a befuddlement to match her own.

Mrs. Terry nodded slowly. "Immediately."

You ungrateful, foolish chit. This is fate's punishment for your moment of ungratefulness.

"Oh, God," she blurted, and her words, wholly lacking in decorum, sent up further gasps amongst the five students. Of course, she was one of the instructors who had worked here the longest. She was the most favored of Mrs. Belden's employees and, oftentimes, was feared by the students. Rowena certainly never did anything so outrageous as to blurt or gasp or stand and gape. And certainly, not blaspheme. Both of which she'd now done for the better part of several moments.

The young lady in the matching gray skirts better fitting an abbess than an impoverished miss-turned-instructor cleared her throat. "She said not to dawdle," Mrs. Terry urged, and then dropped her eyes.

But not before Rowena saw the flash of regret in their depths. *I am being sacked.*

Oh, God. Of all the blasted times for fate to be listening to her yearnings, it had chosen the bloody worst.

Through the quiet, a loud flurry of whispers went up, and the other instructor made another clearing noise. Rowena sprung into

15

motion. She turned to face her students, and the girls promptly fell silent and turned their gazes downward. The lack of spirit from the sixteen-year-old ladies set guilt turning in her belly. *I did this. I have instructed countless ladies on avoiding eyes and silencing their voices.* Then, what had her fiery spirit earned her other than a banishment from Pembroke, a broken heart, and the title of dragon at Mrs. Belden's, as all instructors were invariably titled?

"I will return shortly, and we will renew the lesson on acceptable behavior for soirees and other small fetes." The irony not lost on her—she, former hellion and mischief-maker—instructing anyone on deportment and decorum. "You may resume your embroidering until I return." *If I return.* The obvious truth hung in the air. Rowena knew it. And the ladies scrambling to open their small leather books no doubt knew it too. And reveled in it. Everyone knew a dragon was feared, reviled, and scorned.

Panic spiraling inside, Rowena strode from the classroom and stepped out into the corridor. Mrs. Elizabeth Terry stood in wait. With crimped red curls and wide green eyes, she'd long earned nasty side-comments from their students. There was not, however, a more loyal woman in the school. As such, she'd been the closest Rowena had to a friend since her girlhood days in Wallingford.

"She might not be sacking you," Elizabeth said, as soon as Rowena stepped into the hall. "You're flawless and impeccable. Her finest instructor."

Rowena was also a whore's daughter. Surely, despite her greatest hopes and efforts, it was a secret that could not stay buried forever. A secret she'd entrusted to no one. *I'm going to be ill.* Had an angry former student discovered the truth and sought retribution on one of the dragons? "She does not summon anyone unless it's for a sacking, Elizabeth." That reminder came out surprisingly even.

Elizabeth chewed at her lower lip. She did not, however, refute her correct claims.

They'd made it no further than halfway down the hall when the loud whispers from inside her classroom met her ears. At one time, the unkind words of rightfully hateful students had struck painfully inside.

She'd gone from beloved daughter with friends and family to despised instructor. Now, the fury and pain of those cold glances and snickering words about spinster dragons had dulled somewhere along the way…

And mattered not at all.

What mattered were her security and her place in this wholly uncertain world. Hands shaking, Rowena slowed her footsteps and unfurled her tightly clenched palms. *Where will I go now?* Returning to her *family* would never be an option.

I am going to marry you, Rowena Endicott.

Is that a question?

She slowed to a stop, as that long-buried voice floated to the surface of her memory. She'd not allowed herself to think of him in years. Whenever he slid into her thoughts, she'd easily buried him away. A task that hadn't always been easy, to bury thoughts of the man who'd once been friend then lover…and then nothing at all. But eventually, she'd banished the memory of Graham Linford to the far recesses of her mind, so the pain of that long-ago betrayal could heal.

Mayhap it was the uncertainty roused by the headmistress's summons that rekindled the horrors of a similar summons of long ago. Rowena stared unblinkingly at the end of the corridor ahead. She was no longer the cowering child intimidated by a title, dominated by a powerful duke. In the time since she'd established a new life inside the finishing school, she'd shaped herself into a strong, capable woman in charge of her own fate. If she were sent away this day for some imagined failing by the miserable woman who ran this institution, then she would go out into the world with her experience as an instructor and begin again. Just as she'd done before. She could begin again. Panic churned in her stomach, making a mockery of her confidence.

Rowena started as a soft, reassuring hand settled on her shoulder. Elizabeth gave a slight squeeze.

With that truth and the other woman's unspoken support fueling her, Rowena squared her shoulders. "It will be fine," she said softly. "Go see to your tasks." She'd not see another in Mrs. Belden's potential bad graces because of her.

Her friend lingered. "You're certain?"

Forcing a smile for the younger woman's benefit, she nodded. "I've long been in Mrs. Belden's favor. Surely I cannot fall so quickly out of it." That assurance was made as much for Elizabeth as for herself. Yet, any woman employed in this hallowed institution with a brain in her head knew that to be false. Mrs. Belden was as fickle as the day was long.

Elizabeth briefly gathered Rowena's hands in an emotional display that would have seen her sternly warned by the headmistress. She released them and started reluctantly down the hall, pausing to cast a final searching look at her.

Rowena kept her lips turned up, straining those muscles. But as soon as Elizabeth disappeared around the corner, she let that false expression of mirth go. Drawing in a deep breath, she resumed her forward march. For all the heartbreak life had thrown at her, hadn't she ultimately prevailed, triumphing over cruelty and finding herself on her own two feet? Albeit with the *help* of a now-dead duke. Oh, how she abhorred a Society where she had so little control over her fate and future. She wanted a life where she dictated the course. Not because a nobleman interfered on her behalf or against it, but because of who she was—a bastard.

If you're sacked for your mother's sins, you'll have no place awaiting you but one on your back. Returning *home* was never an option. She'd been cast out with the same expediency the Lord had banished Lucifer, and Rowena had learned from that moment that she'd only herself to rely upon.

Bile stung her throat. She stopped outside the hated door and, as she'd been told from her first day as an instructor, took a slow, steadying breath, battled back nausea, and scratched on the panel. Like a bloody cat. If she'd ever run this, or any school for young ladies, her employees and charges would all give an appropriate, unapologetic knock.

"Enter." The headmistress' frosty, curt reply penetrated the paneled door. Schooling her features, Rowena stepped inside. She flexed her palms to still the trembling.

The older woman sat behind her desk as she always did, scribbling away at a page inside a leather folio. Rowena often suspected the gray-haired headmistress took her meals and spent her nights in that very chair: the throne of her small kingdom. Was that the fate of all women who ascend to the rank of headmistress? She would be contented with happy students and a lifetime of security.

"Close the door, Mrs. Bryant," Mrs. Belden ordered, not taking her gaze from the book that commanded all her attention.

With still unsteady fingers, Rowena promptly closed it behind her. She'd learned early on that you didn't speak or make a move until orders were directed specifically to you. It was a lesson handed down the day she'd arrived, a girl forever separated from her family—scared, miserable, and nursing a broken heart. Now, with this unexpected summons raising the possibility of her being sacked, she searched the headmistress for a hint of knowing.

"You may sit," the older woman said, at last setting down her pen.

It was an offer that spoke volumes about Rowena's exalted position as first instructor. All the others, the instructors included, were made to stand. Surely if she'd been found out as a whore's daughter, she'd not be invited to sit before the decorous harpy? With smooth, practiced steps, she crossed the floor and slid onto the edge of the stiff, wooden chair.

The older woman sat back in her seat and laid her arms along the sides of her chair. Silence stretched on as she scrutinized Rowena in an assessing manner that sent panic spiraling once more. *Oh, God. She does know.*

When she was first sent here with letters of reference from the Duke of Hampstead one year after his son had gone to war, Rowena had moved through each day, breath held for the damning discovery. Not only had she given her virtue to a nobleman's son in the grass like a common whore, but she'd also shared the blood of one of those shameful women. With each passing year, that fear had receded so Rowena, in her own mind, was left with the sins of her failings and weaknesses. *She'll not sack me. I have been good and loyal and have broken no rules.*

Not any that the woman was aware of—or, at least not at the school.

And, yet, the headmistress had a reputation for disdaining any employee who became too comfortable in her post. *Comfort makes sloppiness* was the charge they were each reminded of.

Mrs. Belden slowly removed her glasses, and then folded and set them on the immaculate surface of her desk. "The day you were brought here, I judged you as I do all. I found you wanting." And there had been much to find wanting. An eighteen-year-old woman with eyes swollen from too many tears shed, cowering and unable to spit out her own name without stammering. "In my experience, when an older nobleman brings me a woman, she is either a by-blow or a lightskirt."

Rowena went still. *Oh, God. She knows.* "Mrs. Belden?" she asked evenly, and her palms grew moist just like that. One utterance from her, and she was transformed, once more, into that scared child she'd been.

"I was instructed to give you employment. A girl of eighteen," she scoffed. "A promise that you'd one day become instructor." That is, after all, the hollow pact that had been struck. Rowena's virtue, her name, and her family's security for honorable employment in the Surrey countryside. The extent of a duke's power, even after all these years, staggered her still. To make a woman such as Mrs. Belden take in an unknown, few questions asked, all because of a man's title.

Then again, the world of the peerage had always been as foreign to her as a country she'd never visited but often wondered and read about.

"Countless women have come to me seeking employment in this honorable institution." A place where young girls' spirits went to die. "And countless more have been turned away. It requires a special woman to work here," she said, leaning forward in her chair. Her words rang with more emotion than Rowena recalled in all her years working for the miserable harpy. "A woman incapable of emotion and feeling." Yes, that was the person this headmistress and the students saw in Rowena. For all her failings, she'd been a master at shaping herself into someone different than the girl she'd been—a woman who now felt little and hurt less. It was far safer that way. "It requires a woman of strength and honor. You have proven yourself to be the best of any other to come before you."

"Thank—"

20

"It was not a compliment, Mrs. Bryant," Mrs. Belden snapped out. "You know the rules on compliments." Yes, they were reserved as pretty endearments for gentlemen to woo an unquestionably genteel lady, so she might become a *dutiful* bride. Distaste filled her mouth at those words Rowena had been forced to utter to girls in her care.

There was a special place in hell for women who would encourage others to dampen their spirit, all to preserve one's own security as she had done.

The woman tightened her mouth and sat back suddenly in her seat. "Alas, you are the best," she said, reaching inside the pocket of her apron and pulling out a kerchief. "And do you know what the problem is with being the best?"

Invariably everything was some manner of test with this woman. "What is that, Mrs. Belden?" she asked, because invariably the woman would always be the one with the answers.

"The problem is," the woman repeated, leaning forward, her chair groaning under the weight of that slight movement. "Noblemen require the best. And the needs and wants of the peerage matter most."

Rowena bit the inside of her cheek hard. That truth had been handed down years earlier, at the hands of the Duke of Hampstead and his son. There were no further lessons required from this woman.

The older woman pursed her already pinched mouth. "Yes, the desires of a nobleman come before even this institution." With that, she looked expectantly at her.

"They come before all," Rowena at last managed to utter. The headmistress was too arrogant and blinded by her own self-importance to ever hear the biting sarcasm in her retort. But then, no one in these hallowed halls, including the head dragon of them all, would ever hear or see anything less than dignified from her.

On a sigh, Mrs. Belden dusted the rims of her spectacles. "Precisely. It is why your services are required elsewhere." She paused and looked Rowena squarely in the eyes. "A powerful nobleman who has been named guardian to a young…*lady*." By the sneer on the woman's lips, she found the young girl in question wanting. "Regardless, the lady requires a companion."

21

The muscles of Rowena's stomach twisted. Surely this was some mad jest. And yet, in all her years here, this cold, unfeeling woman before her had never revealed a hint of a grin, smile, or giggle. And with that, the façade of demure lady was cut out from under her. Rowena surged forward in her seat.

"What?" she blurted for a second time that day. Panicky questions ran frantically through her mind as with but a single exchange, the well-ordered existence she had singlehandedly shaped for herself was thrown into tumult.

"Mrs. Bryant," the older woman said in clipped tones. At any other time, Rowena would have dropped her gaze in a demure rendering of the lesson handed to her students. Not now. Not when presented with the prospect of being shipped off and sent into a world where she didn't belong. Nor ever aspired to. *His* world. That difference between them had seen her entire existence ripped asunder.

"My apologies," Rowena managed in even tones.

"As I was saying, your services have been requested." Not hers, specifically. Rather, the best instructor. After all the years she'd worked to cement her position as the first instructor to preserve her place, now she'd be sent away for it. "However, the gentleman wishes to interview you, and determine your worth. If he approves, you are to depart for London."

"London," she squawked. The place where Graham Linford, the new Duke of Hampstead, had years earlier set himself up as rogue, and then, by the papers' reports, as an austere, powerful, and coolly aloof duke. Just like his father. Her lips twisted in a pained rendition of a smile. Then could there have been any other fate for him? The searing words he'd inked on a sheet of vellum served as a forever reminder of what came in loving and dreaming beyond her station. "How old is the girl?" she asked, when she trusted herself to speak.

"Seventeen."

Not a girl, then. Rather, just one year younger than Rowena herself had been when she'd been forced to leave her family and friends and the only true home she'd ever known. She pressed her eyes briefly closed. But life was and always would be vastly different for a lady of seventeen and a courtesan's daughter of a like age.

22

Now she'd be forced to return to London. A place she'd not been since her mother and stepfather packed her up and made for the country to begin a new life. As a young girl, she'd been euphoric when they'd put the busy, unkind streets behind them. She'd vowed never to return. And why should she have wanted to? She and her mother had been derided by those powerful lords and ladies they passed shopping and during jaunts to the park.

Yet once more, the proverbial rug had been tugged out from under her feet. Only this time, she'd be plunged directly *into* that cold, unfeeling world. A place inhabited by Graham. *I am going to throw-up.* Rowena made a desperate bid at self-preservation. "Though I am"— *horrified*—"flattered, Mrs. Belden, I have no ego and recognize that each instructor in your employ is possessed of equal skill, logic, and character." In short, they'd had the spirit knocked out of them, just like her. "Surely it would prove problematic to remove me from my role and fill it with a new instructor. Would it not?"

It was a futile bid. And yet, by the furrowing of the older woman's brow, a practical argument. And the headmistress was nothing if not practical. Hope blossomed in her breast.

"I do largely agree that all my girls are of like accomplishment, I also see you've risen above in your capabilities. Otherwise, you'd not be first instructor," the headmistress pointed out needlessly. That position had presented the possibility of greater stability and a larger salary. Now her experience would be used against her. Mrs. Belden folded her hands primly on her desk. "I am not illogical, Mrs. Bryant." Rowena's heart kicked up a beat, as with that single utterance hope was restored. "I'll allow him no more than a year of your services." *Oh, God, a year?* It may as well have been an eternity plus a day. "His Grace was very specific in—"

Another bloody duke. Those men with their inflated sense of self-importance and arrogance who ruled the world.

A knock sounded at the doorway and the headmistress was interrupted. "Enter," Mrs. Belden called out, climbing to her feet with a stiff elegance.

Rowena followed suit and dipped her head with the deferential respect she'd believed herself incapable of years earlier. God, how she despised these pompous nobles. All of them expecting the earth to halt its movement and people to drop their eyes and dip their curtsies. She firmed her jaw. Though, there was one noble she despised above all others. And as long as she did not ever again have to see the Devil Duke of Hamp—

"His Grace, the Duke of Hampstead," the servant introduced.

And all her years of smooth grace flew out the proverbial window, Rowena spun about with such speed she knocked the delicate chair over where it landed with a loud crack. Her heart thundering, she ignored the shocked gasp and words of recrimination from Mrs. Belden and the servant setting the chairs to rights. Rowena's eyes remained fixed instead on the towering, dark duke now coldly assessing her.

In all her remembering of this man, he'd been frozen in time as the lean, easily smiling gentleman of his youth. A dull humming filled her ears. This broad, towering bear of a man with his chiseled features and powerful muscles straining the fabric of his elegantly cut garments belonged more on an ancient battlefield than in a headmistress's office. The jagged scar that zigzagged down the right portion of his face started at the corner of his eye and ended at his chin.

She focused on breathing. Nay. She'd merely misheard the servant. This fearsome gentleman bore no hint of the man who'd stolen her heart, won her virtue, and then left without giving her another thought. She was going mad. Hearing things. Imagining him, even when she'd schooled herself in all the ways with which to forget.

"Mrs. Bryant?" the headmistress barked, snapping Rowena to attention.

Then, the gentleman smiled, dimpling his left cheek. Graham's smile, only harder, wiser, angrier.

He'd promised to return. And he had.

Only, eleven years too late.

THREE

Long ago, Graham had become master of his emotions—over nearly everything and everyone.

Or so he'd believed. Until this very moment. His heart hammered like the beat marked upon a drum through long marches across the European countryside. It pulsated inside his confused mind until his fingers twitched with the need to gouge his eyes and drive back the vision of her. For despite his mastery of emotion, there was still this one.

The one who'd refused to relinquish her hold, so he might shape himself completely into a wholly unmovable duke. It was surely why he saw her before him even now.

He stared unblinkingly, willing her gone. And yet…she remained. Miss Rowena Endicott stood before him, like a thief caught with her hand in a lord's purse. As she should, the miserable little chit. She'd been the dream that had sustained him through countless battles. Her whispered words of love had given him the strength to kill, to avoid being killed, because ultimately at the end of his life he'd have traded his eternal soul to return to Wallingford and see her once more. His gaze went to the long, graceful column of her throat, as it moved spasmodically; that slight movement the only indication she was effected by his presence here now. How many times had he touched his lips to that satiny soft skin? He should want to wring that beautiful flesh. The faithless, feckless deceiver.

For in the end, she'd been careless with her words and flippant with her heart, choosing another when he had been off fighting to survive and return home to her. And in the end, whom had she chosen?

25

A man who, by her placement now here as instructor, had left her in dire straits.

He waited until his heart resumed a normal cadence. *This* was the woman the old headmistress would have serve as companion to Miss Hickenbottom? If he were capable of laughter, this moment crafted by the fates would have been the time for it. "Mrs. *Bryant*," he said, icing his greeting with a ducal arrogance his father would have been proud of.

Most women averted their eyes out of deference to his station. Rowena stared briefly back. "Your Grace," she returned, sinking into a flawless curtsy.

Then, she'd never been like most women. She'd been spirited and unapologetic.

The headmistress passed a probing look back and forth between them, and Rowena hurriedly lowered her gaze to the floor. Could the older woman see the years of history between him and her most-esteemed instructor? If she knew all the ways in which he had made love to this tall, Spartan beauty, she'd expire from shock. And yet... it was Rowena's reaction that gave him pause. That uncharacteristic hesitancy that defied everything he knew about her.

Mrs. Belden reclaimed the chair behind her desk. "Will you please sit, Your Grace?" Unnerved by that change in Rowena Endicott, he sat. The fawning deference in her employer's request and Rowena's silence matched everything he'd come to know from Society.

As a second son bound for the military, he'd previously evoked little interest in anyone, his own father included. Most spares would have chafed at being dismissed in favor of an older brother. He, however, had reveled in the freedom it permitted him.

I could never want a duke or a lord, Graham...I only want you...

Tension crackled in the room as he settled his larger frame in the delicate shell chair better reserved for the young ladies called before this cold harridan. Of all the bloody instructors, this was the one suggested him. Oh, how the fates must be rubbing their hands with mocking glee.

"Mrs. Bryant?" the headmistress inquired.

Rowena stood stock-still with such a remarkable calm, he wondered if he'd merely confused the always laughing girl of his past with this serious-faced creature. Rowena Endicott would never have been one to move with those precisely measured steps and perch on the edge of her seat with her back straight enough to rival a military man. He peered at her through deliberately hooded lashes. Those thick, burgundy-streaked brown tresses, however, could belong to no other.

"Your Grace," the tight-mouthed headmistress began, "I must praise the devotion and dedication that has brought you here seeking my finest instructor." She motioned to Rowena the way Cook made a selection of roast at the market. "I thought you might interview Mrs. Bryant and determine her suitability."

Wanting to rouse some response from the still creature, Graham turned his lips up in a sardonic grin and faced Rowena. She stared straight ahead, at the wall behind the headmistress. An honorable man would feel some compunction at the lady's silent distress. It was there in the hard press of her lips and the muscle ticking at the corner of her right eye. At one time, he would have sooner lopped his arm off than hurt Rowena Endicott—now Bryant—in any way. *This is the woman Mrs. Belden thought fit to serve as companion to Ainsley?*

This creature before him had not a hope or prayer of taming his spirited ward. As such, it would be easy to decline her services and find another. Yet, why was he more bothered by the woman she'd become? He sought to elicit...some reaction. For it grated that she should be this cool, removed creature when inside, she'd thrown him into tumult. "I concur, Mrs. Belden. An interview is in order." He stretched out that pronouncement and, if possible, her back went all the more straight: a proud, regal carriage befitting a queen. He took an unholy glee in the idea of putting questions to her before Mrs. Belden and breaking that remarkable calm. Already knowing, in the end, after all that had come to pass, he'd never set foot outside this institution with her at his side. He craved calm in his life, and Rowena Endicott had always roused in him too much emotion for her to ever be safe.

27

"It is not every day a duke enters my esteemed institution, himself seeing to the task." The headmistress tapped her desk once. "It speaks volumes of your honorable character."

Rowena dissolved into a fit of coughing. Graham leveled a hard stare on her splotchy red cheeks and shaking frame. "Are you all right, Mrs. Bryant?" Rowena of old would have pointed her eyes at the ceiling and challenged him.

At her immediate failure to comply, the headmistress frowned. "Mrs. Bryant," she chastised. "His Grace has spoken to you."

Graham pondered her. Who was this new laconic woman before him?

"F-Fine," Rowena belatedly rasped out through her strangled fit. "I am fine." If looks could kill, she'd have smitten him dead with the fire in her eyes. At that familiar spark of her spirit, some of the tension left him, and he puzzled through her reaction.

What was the reason for her outrage? Did she believe he'd reveal their love affair from long ago to this woman and shatter her reputation as unblemished instructor? He might despise her with everything he was, but he was not such a bastard that he'd share their past with this woman or any other. That she believed he would set his teeth on edge.

Furthermore, why should she question his honor when she'd been so flippant with her words of love? How little they'd *truly* known each other.

"Very well. Now you may ask Mrs. Bryant your questions to determine her worth."

Had he not briefly dropped his gaze, he'd have failed to see Rowena dig a claw-like grip into the edge of her seat. That was the spirit he recalled. A once intrepid, unapologetic young girl, free with her thoughts. This was a woman capable of the role of companion: fearless, unrepentant, strong. Such a person could easily transform a lively girl into a model of propriety and face down the ruthless members of Society. And for the first time since he'd entered the room, he entertained the possibility of bringing Rowena Bryant back as Ainsley's companion. He started. What madness was this, even *considering* hiring the woman before him?

Finding strength in her unease, he leaned back, and laid his palms on the arm of his chair. "How long have you been an instructor here, Mrs. Bryant?" How long since her husband had kicked up his heels and left her in this sorry state? Damn that question for flitting forward in his mind. And God how he despised himself for caring that there had been a Mr. Bryant.

"I've been an instructor nine years."

Graham's careful mask of indifference slipped. His mouth fell agape, and he forced himself to promptly close it. She'd been married but a year, and then widowed young. She would have been just nineteen. Far too young for widow's weeds. His chest tightened. How quickly she'd fallen in love with another, and then lost all. Why did he not relish that truth? *Because I once loved her. Because I would have cut out my own heart and handed it over to secure her smile.* A sad smile pulled at his lips. Yes, he'd been that foolish.

"Mrs. Bryant has provided instruction on everything from embroidering to husband hunting to painting."

A snort escaped him. Rowena was a girl who'd rather spit at a man than pay respect to his title. It was not, however, that detail enumerated by the headmistress that earned his derision. "You are skilled, then, in the matters of husband-hunting, Mrs. Bryant?"

After all, she'd garnered not only one promise of marriage from him but another from the bastard who'd actually given his vow before God. Unlike Graham's pathetic romantic promises atop a hill while the sun set.

Rowena glared at him. "I'm particularly skilled in recognizing faithless bounders who've only dishonorable intentions and guiding a lady toward respect and devotion."

He went still. Surely the lady wasn't...she hadn't...by God, was she calling into question *his* honor? "You speak freely of respect and devotion," he rebutted. "I trust those are important sentiments to you?"

"They should be important sentiments to everyone." Her chest rose and fell quickly, at odds with her even tones.

"Indeed, Mrs. Bryant," Mrs. Belden said with a proud nod. "As you can see, Mrs. Bryant is skilled in helping a young lady make the most advantageous match. She is also quite skilled with watercolors and sketching."

He forced his gaze to Rowena. "Are you, Mrs. Bryant?" She was. She'd delighted in sketching his likeness so many times in the fields of Wallingford when they'd snuck off together.

"I am merely proficient," she said tersely.

Mrs. Belden tittered like a proud mama. "Such modesty on Mrs. Bryant's part. She instructs her students on compositions of floral arrangements and bowls of fruit."

Bowls of fruit and floral arrangements? Apparently, with time's passage, Rowena had become, at best, a shell of her once-spirited self. As if in proof of that very realization, she avoided his eyes. "And is that what you see as most important, Mrs. Bryant? Making the most advantageous match?" If so, the duplicitous chit must have regretted the moment he'd returned from war, heir to a dukedom, when she'd already found herself married to...to...a Mr. Bryant. If Graham hadn't already paved a path to hell with his actions on the battlefield, he did so in this moment, wanting to kill an already dead Mr. Bryant.

"No." That solemn declination pierced the quiet.

"Mrs. Bryant?" the headmistress squawked. "Of course—"

Not taking his gaze from Rowena, he held up a staying hand to the older woman. He pressed her with his eyes to speak in defiance of the headmistress intending to silence her.

"For me, it is not the most advantageous match my charges might make, but rather, their ability to see through schemers and rogues with pretty endearments and dishonorable intentions. It is important that my students look past a title, and see the strength of a person's character, else they be deceived."

Graham furrowed his brow. That honest answer, that had nothing to do with the love they'd once shared, momentarily flummoxed him. It also marked her an ideal guide for his charge.

"A wonderful answer, is it not?" Mrs. Belden's frank statement came, devoid of any pride or emotion.

"Indeed," he said, looking once more to Rowena. She'd not meet his gaze but rather the headmistress opposite them. "Leave us," Graham coolly ordered.

Rowena promptly stood, dropped a curtsy, and then started from the room.

"Not you, Mrs. Bryant," he called over his shoulder.

The lady staggered to a stop and wheeled around, questions parading through her expressive eyes.

It was a testament to the distinguished headmistress's aplomb that she gave no outward show at his ducal arrogance and abruptness. She moved around the desk and with smooth, elegant steps, and took her leave. The echo of her retreating footfalls indicated the lady had moved no more than five paces. Heightened senses were just one of the proverbial gifts he'd returned from battle with.

Graham stood. "*Mrs.* Bryant," he drawled mockingly, and a guilty blush stained the lady's cheeks. She'd always possessed that creamy, white skin prone to burning and blushing. Once, he'd found it endearing. Now, it just served as an unwanted reminder of their past together. And her treachery. He walked slowly forward, circling the lady, and with his every slight movement, her shoulders came further and further back. "The late *Mr.* Bryant left you dependent to work. Tsk, tsk. Poor form of him."

"Is this part of your interview?" she shot back with a show of her old spirit.

Graham smirked. "Indeed, it is."

Her mouth tightened, drawing his gaze to her tense lips. "What do you want?" She paused and added, "Your Grace."

That bold confidence, that undaunted strength momentarily knocked him off-kilter, reminding him of the young lady who'd moved into his father's parish and stolen his bloody heart. His stomach muscles clenched, and he damned himself for having ever been so weak.

It was only the careful mask he'd donned and the secure walls he'd resurrected about his heart and body that kept him carefully emotionless in this instance. Graham folded his arms across his chest. "Why,

31

what do you expect I should want with you?" He layered a wealth of meaning to those words and the lady promptly dropped her gaze to the floor, in a wholly uncharacteristic way.

God help him, he preferred her snapping and hissing to this subservient instructor routine.

"Nothing," she said quietly. "I expect you'd want nothing with me."

And several years ago, he would have wholeheartedly concurred. After returning from fighting Boney's forces on a litter, a breath from death, he'd discovered her gone. He'd sworn the last thing he wanted or needed in life was Rowena Endicott.

She'd been his Achilles heel. His Delilah. It was why he should call back Mrs. Belden and ask for another. And yet…he studied her. This woman, who by her birthright shared more with Miss Hickenbottom than any other seemly instructor who could be paraded before him. Other possible candidates for the post who'd barely concealed their disdain for a bastard charge. Rowena may be a widow now, and the finest instructor at Mrs. Belden's Finishing School, but she would always be the girl who'd haltingly told him the truth of her parentage. It was why, even as he wished to send her to the Devil, not a single instructor in this entire school suited more. With slow, precise movements, Graham tugged free his immaculate white gloves. Rowena watched him, a guardedness in her eyes. "I require a companion for my ward."

The wariness deepened in her features, settling in the mistrustful eyes she now studied him through. The tangible loss of the innocence she once had held him momentarily frozen. Life had made her a cynic, too. "And of all the companions, you wish to hire me?" Healthy skepticism coated her inquiry.

Actually, no, he didn't. The moment she'd stepped inside this office and unsettled his already precarious world, he'd vowed to turn her away and demand another, more suitable instructor. A companion whose lips he'd not kissed. Whose thighs he'd not lain between and been welcomed with such warmth. His body still burned with the memory of her throaty moans as they'd found surcease in one another's arms.

His resolve to hire her, despite their past together, weakened. It would be sheer folly bringing her into his household. She would serve as a daily reminder of his greatest hopes and most painful heartbreak.

She gave him a questioning look, and he searched for a curt rejection for the lady's services. Words that would not come. He'd responsibilities to a girl that mattered more than his own weakness.

"Aren't you the best, *Mrs.* Bryant?" he asked instead. He drifted closer, and the lady squared her shoulders all the more with an erect bearing any military commander would be hard-pressed to emulate. Graham lowered his lips close to her ear, and the scent of primrose that clung to her skin wafted about his senses. Just like that, he was sucked deep within her snare, her hold as strong as it had been all those years ago, as an electric charge surged between them, punctuated by her audible inhalation of air.

Yes, even as a girl of sixteen to his eighteen years, there had been an explosive passion between them.

Rowena took a hurried step away from him. "Come," she scoffed "with my"—she stole a glance at the doorway, and when she returned her focus to him, spoke on a hushed whisper—"reputation, you would want my sullied self near your charge?"

At her grating condemnation, Graham struggled for calm. Never had he judged her as inferior because of her birthright, and once he'd promised to give her his name. That reminder lanced at his chest, still, all these years later. For even had he returned a whole man, he could have never truly made her his. As such, it shouldn't matter that she'd not waited for him...and yet, it had mattered. Mattered still. He neatly tucked his gloves inside his jacket. "You are the best, though, aren't you?" he countered, instead. "Hmm?" he impelled when she still said nothing.

"What would you have me say?" her question emerged faintly breathless yet coated with an anger she had no right to. "If I were to agree, it would reek of an arrogance of which only a duke could aspire." He narrowed his eyebrows. God, she was as insolently clever now as she'd been then. As a duke's mere second son, he'd been captivated by her wit. As a man, hardened by battle and seasoned by her betrayal, he ached to know her in his bed once more. "If I disagree, it would either ring of false modesty, or worse, seem as though you've cowed me with your ducal pomposity."

And despite the shell of a man he'd existed as for the past eleven years, Graham's lips twitched in a rusty smile that strained the muscles at the corner of his mouth.

Damning that revealing expression of mirth, he firmed his lips into an unyielding line and refocused himself on the sole reason for his being here. For ultimately, it was not about his past with this treacherous lady before him, but rather a vow he'd made Lieutenant Hickenbottom. It was ultimately about his ward. And more…she shared more with Rowena than she would any of the other stiff, celebrated companions Mrs. Belden would send him. "As you stated, you've been an instructor here for ten years?"

"Nine," she corrected.

"My ward is spirited," he continued over her interruption. "Romantic." Graham dipped his lips close to her ear once more. "In short, everything you are, Rowena Bryant."

"If that is the reason you'd employ me, then find another. I am no longer those things, Your Grace." Your Grace. Not Graham. Not "my love." Simply "Your Grace." He should be grateful for the natural barrier erected between them; and yet, he wanted to strip his title from her lips and replace it with the husky whispered endearment she'd once made his name.

I am a bloody fool.

"I do not care what you are now," he lied. "I care about who you once were." The lady flinched and disgust coated his mouth at the bastard he'd become. "My ward has no grasp of propriety or decorum. She'll need to be schooled before she makes her Come Out, and you will serve admirably as her companion." Withdrawing his gloves, he turned on his heel, but her sputtering pulled him up short.

"What if I say no?"

Graham clasped his hands at his back, bringing her gaze unwittingly to the broad expanse of his chest. "You won't say no."

Rowena tipped her chin up at a furious angle. Fire flashed in her brown eyes, momentarily sucking the breath from his lungs. God, she was breathtaking. "Because you believe no one would dare defy a duke?"

He looked her over, allowing him to assess her in ways he'd resisted since he'd entered the room and seen her standing before the head-mistress. Willowy, narrow-hipped, and tall as she'd always been, there was more of a generousness to her breasts than there had been when she was a girl. His mouth went dry with a hungering to explore this new, mature, still-bold Rowena. "Because you were never one to refuse a challenge, Rowena," he murmured, laying command to her name for the first time in eleven years.

"Is that what this is?" she demanded tightly.

"No," he said taking a step toward her. In the first remarkable crack in her façade, she retreated, stumbling over herself in her haste to be free of him. Fear sparked in her eyes, but in an instant, it was gone, and had he not witnessed that same flash in too many terrified stares on the fields of battle, he'd have, mayhap, missed it. His annoy-ance with her spiraled now, for altogether different reasons. "This is employment, and you are capable of serving as a companion and, as such, I'd have you care for my charge." Graham pulled out his watch-fob and consulted the timepiece. "Mrs. Belden?" he called.

The patter of footsteps filled the corridor and, moments later, the headmistress ducked her head inside. "She will do." Rowena's teeth knocked loudly together. "Please see her belongings readied."

Without sparing her another look, the headmistress stalked off.

Tossing her hands in the air, Rowena made a choking noise. "You ordered my belongings packed? The insolence of you, Your Grace," she hissed.

He arched a single eyebrow. "Do you intend to refuse me?" Her silence served as her answer. The headmistress would turn her out for failing to take on the *illustrious* assignment. "I did not believe so." He made to leave once more.

"Is that all?" she called out, the high-pitched tenor of her husky voice cascading over him, rousing in him an unwanted hunger. God, how he despised this need for her still. "You will not even tell me any-thing about your ward? Her name? Her interests?"

He'd have to be deafer than a post to fail to hear the reproach there. No doubt she took him for one of those unfeeling, diffident noblemen. In this she would be correct. "There will be time to discuss my ward in our carriage ride to London."

She widened her eyes to the size of saucers. "*Our* carriage ride?" she choked.

Graham forced his lips up in a slow, emotionless half-grin. "Rest assured, Mrs. Bryant, we will have countless hours to discuss my ward... among other things." He paused. "We leave within a quarter of an hour. We introduce the girl to Society in three weeks."

"Society?" she echoed. Her mind raced for a horrifying moment that went on forever. What if her path again crossed with the women she'd briefly called friends? What if they discovered just how far she had fallen? Her stomach churned. *Don't be silly...It's been more than ten years.* Why, it was likely they'd not even noted she'd one day gone from Wallingford. Rowena's own family hadn't made a single attempt to contact her over the years.

"A formal dinner," Graham elucidated, slashing through her maud-lin musings. "A musicale. Balls and soirees." Events meant to ease Miss Hickenbottom's way into a cold Society.

She shook her head. "But I cannot..."

"Do you find yourself unable to serve in the role?" he dared.

Rowena pursed her mouth. "No, Your Grace," she said curtly, dem-onstrating that intrepidness lived within her still.

With the faint thrill of victory, Graham turned on his heel and left.

FOUR

W hen presented with the option of dancing with the devil in the fiery flames of hell or sharing the confines of a carriage with a man who'd broken her heart years earlier, Rowena would have invariably chosen the former.

As it was, the prince of darkness handily absent, she was left with an altogether different one or, in this particular case, a duke of darkness. She huddled against the interior wall nearest her, attempting to make herself small and invisible. It was an impossible feat when this new, all-powerful Graham's frame swallowed the much-needed space inside the elegant, black barouche.

Eleven hours in a carriage. With one stop at an inn along the way. At the inn, she'd not need to see him or speak to him. In the carriage...well, mayhap he'd tire of the closed quarters and take to his mount as any polite, respectable gentleman would. At the very least, mayhap he wouldn't speak—

"You are a good deal more laconic than I recall," he observed, stretching out his legs. Their knees brushed, and she damned the quickening of her heart. Foolish, foolish body's response to him. Then again, a body cared not for long buried hurts.

"I am a good deal many more things since we last saw one another." More Bitter. Wiser. Stronger. "Your Grace." She placed a slight emphasis on those two words, raising an unnecessary reminder of the great gulf between them.

As a duke's second son, the divide had been great, now it may as well have been the width of the Atlantic Sea.

"Indeed, you are." By the dry bite to his words, she could venture precisely to what manner of things he referred. None of those things were kind or flattering.

...I could lose myself in the pools of your eyes and drown happily without ever a regret.

God, what utter rot and rubbish she'd allowed to fill her ears and rule her thoughts. In doing so, she'd become everything she'd never wished to be: her mother—a nobleman's plaything. Only, in the greatest irony, her mama, a reformed courtesan, had found love with a vicar. Whereas Rowena had given her virtue, heart, and soul to a man merely toying with her affections. And in so doing, she'd secured a powerful enemy in his now-dead father, the late Duke of Hampstead—God rot his soul.

When her mother had warned her of the perils in loving a nobleman's son, Rowena had scoffed with the arrogance only a naïve girl was capable of. Graham was unlike the man who'd fathered her. Or any of the others to serve as her mother's protector, until she met the vicar. Rowena had trusted one of those powerful peers—and lost. Not only her heart, pride, and happiness, but her family who'd had no choice but to send her away. At the duke's orders.

All the age-old hatred had burned strong in her heart.

Her bitter smile reflected back in the lead windowpane, Rowena shook her head. How naïve she'd been...believing words of love and talk of marriage could have swayed the late Duke of Hampstead in his efforts to separate her and Graham. If possible, the all-powerful duke had known even less about love than his son.

No, she'd dipped her toes into the world of nobility and been so burned, it was a place she never, ever again wished to be. Not as a servant. Wife. Widow. Or anything else.

Rowena pulled back the curtain and stared out at the passing countryside. Seeing the green meadows and rolling hills, she could almost imagine herself in Wallingford, making that long, miserable journey alone in a different carriage at a different time, a scared, lonely child.

Taptap-tap-taptap-tap...

The grating staccato of that incessant beat cut across her useless musings. He was trying to get under her skin. The same way he'd reentered her life and stolen her anonymity at Mrs. Belden's, Graham sought to rob her this time of calm.

I am no longer an impulsive girl. I am no longer an impulsive girl.

Taptap-tap-taptap—

"Must you do that?" she snapped.

Tap. He paused. "No, 'Your Gracing' me now, Rowena?" Once more, he boldly commandeered her name. She curled her toes into her boots. Why did his gruff whisper set off this wild yearning inside her, still? "You are even bolder than you were as a girl of sixteen." And then promptly commenced his incessant drumming.

"Cautious," she said between tight lips. He stopped his beating. "I am even more cautious," she clarified. Learned at the hands of his iniquity.

"Ah." He leaned forward, his broad-muscled frame shrinking the space between them. "But wherever is the fun in caution?"

That husky whisper wrapped in seduction and sin belied the gentle, charming gentleman he'd once been. In his place was this older, cynical, wicked lord who thought the world was his due and the ladies around him were a pleasure for the taking. Her ire stirred, a frustration that this was the man he'd become…and that her belly still danced and fluttered at a mere hooding of his thick, black lashes.

"Some of us are not afforded the luxury of *fun.*" She peeled her lip back in an involuntary sneer. "Some of us must hold sacred and honor our reputations." It was all a lady had between respectability and a life of sin upon one's back.

His chiseled features, set in a mask, gave little indication as to his thought. "I daresay, I see how you've attained your reputation as most-revered instructor. But I do wonder…" He dangled that bait, the lure as great now as when they'd parried with word riddles and puzzles at the copse on his father's properties. Nay, his properties. They were now Graham's.

Those same green meadows she'd cried herself to sleep thinking of when she'd first arrived at Mrs. Belden's. The same ones that, if she closed her eyes and dreamed just so, she could draw forth from memory.

He leaned forward once more, and the red velvet squabs of his bench creaked under his shifting weight. "At one time, you would have asked me what I wonder."

At one time, she would have done a whole host of other things, all that would have ultimately found her in his arms with his lips on hers. On the heel of that, cool logic was restored and the memories of old were extinguished like the flicker of a once-bright flame. Schooling her features into the dragon mask she'd donned and perfected in her time at Mrs. Belden's, Rowena faced him squarely. "Perhaps this is the ideal time, Your Grace, to tell me of your ward and discuss your expectations of me as her companion as well as my expectations of you, as my employer." That last part was added as a pointed reminder to the both of them that, ultimately, that was all she was. Which was a good deal more than what she'd once been to him.

He narrowed his eyes, and she braced for his jeering contradiction of her orders, but he slowly leaned back. "Very well," he said, stretching out those two syllables with a frostiness that could only come from a duke. He may have been the spare to his brother, Monty, but Graham spoke and moved with the ease of a man born to that position. Her heart tugged with regret for the young man he'd been and whom he might have grown into. "Her name is Ainsley. She is spirited. Wild. Romantic."

Just as she had been. "Very dangerous combinations," Rowena said evenly.

"Then, it is a combination you would know very well." Her stomach muscles clenched reflexively, but she'd be damned if she gave him any indication as to how that barb struck.

"And a gentleman thought the illustrious Duke of Hampstead to be the ideal guardian for such a girl?" It had taken but a handful of readings of those gossip columns long ago to glean that Graham had returned a conquering war hero and shaped himself into a rogue, whom widows and ladies vied for with equal fervor. Until, by the words reported in those gossip pages, he'd become the proud, austere duke who'd sown his last oat, and become a model of the late Duke of Hampstead. *Then...he was always that man. I was just too blind to see it.*

"Hardly," he snorted, tugging off his gloves. He stuffed them inside his jacket, revealing long, tanned fingers. "I was the second. The first chap had the bad form to up and die on the girl."

Who was this aloof, unfeeling man? Did his ascension to the title of duke alone account for the change that had overtaken him? "How rude of him," she drawled.

"Regardless, I find myself guardian and eager to turn her over to someone else's care." He paused. "Yours."

How ruthless he was. How coolly methodical he was about a young lady's future. What a master he'd always been at prevarication. He'd presented himself as teasing, gentle, kind, and loving. In the end, he was always this privileged lord before her. "And is there no Duchess of Hampstead to oversee the girl's education?" She held her breath.

"There is no duchess."

Why did the tension in her chest ease at that four-word revelation? He was one and thirty years, and yet, he remained unmarried. *Bah, foolish twit.* She forced her lip back in a sneer. "Ah, of course, you are too busy carousing and womanizing to be bothered with a wife or charge underfoot." That stinging rebuke came before she could call it back.

He smiled a slow, seductive, and tempting grin that Satan himself could not so perfectly emulate. "Miss Bryant, I am far too old for carousing." Graham winked.

She opened her mouth and closed it, and then heat slapped her cheeks. Of course, he'd not refute the womanizing portion of her charge. The bounder. "Mrs."

He cocked his head.

"If I am to remain in your employ, I am to be referred to as Mrs. Bryant. Otherwise, my reputation will be in question." And all an unwed lady had was her reputation.

"Ahh," he whispered and damn her for the butterflies that were set to dancing, yet again, inside. "And your position as instructor is so very important to you?"

It was the best she could hope for. Unless, she wished for a life of sin like her mother. "It is all I have," she said quietly. "Young women without the benefit of a husband..." *I will return to you. Make you my wife...* That long-ago pledge whispered around her memory. Fool that she'd been, she'd failed to see that had he truly wished her to be his forever, he would have given her the benefit of his name long before he'd left.

"Rowena?"

She snapped to. "Young women without the benefit of a husband or employment find themselves with no security and even more uncertain futures." Or whores like her mother had been.

Graham studied her for a long moment, and she remained motionless under that frank perusal. Then, he layered his arm over the back of his seat. His biceps strained the fabric of the garment. "What of Mr. Bryant?"

It was a statement, devoid of any inflection, perfect for a military man who'd ordered men about the battlefield. Long ago, with his falsity and defection, she'd given up on the dream she'd carried for a loving husband and chubby-cheeked babes with his jade green eyes. He wouldn't know that. He saw, just as the world saw, what they were content to believe her to be: a proper widow.

"Tell me of your devoted husband," he drawled.

"If your questioning pertains to my employment status, then it should have been asked prior to our leaving Mrs. Belden's. If it does not, then you should refrain from asking it," she rebuked, cursing the widening grin on his face. Damn him for finding amusement in this.

"Tsk. Tsk. I expect you wish we'd married before I went off to fight. Who would have thought my brother would up and die while I was away, no less? Imagine, *you* could have found yourself a duchess."

He may as well have slapped her across the face. *Say nothing. Say nothing.* He merely sought to bait her. Odd, she'd failed to see the deliberately cruel streak he carried. His father's blood ran strongly through his veins. Rowena focused her attention on the passing countryside and damned her gaze as it found his in the windowpane. His mocking smile reached his eyes. She curled her toes into the soles of her serviceable boots so hard her arches ached. His father's loathsome face flashed to her mind. "And I expect you find yourself fortunate not to have been saddled with a lowly vicar's"—and reformed courtesan's—"daughter so you might *nobly* carry on your roguish ways."

"Been following my pursuits?" At the triumphant thread to that question, she gritted her teeth.

It did not escape her notice he didn't counter her charges. Of course, her status as lowly vicar's daughter had always mattered to him. He'd simply done a masterful job of concealing it until he'd no longer had a need. Rowena angled her shoulder away from him. She'd already said too much.

Any other moment, the confines of a carriage would have commanded all Graham's focus. The closed-in walls brought him back to another place, another time, when he'd been injured on the Peninsular and the carriage carrying him had been attacked. The sharp report of pistol balls striking the conveyance and finding mark in two of the men riding with him. The stench of gunpowder permeated his senses and forced him to relive the moment of helplessness where he'd been too weak to steadily wield a weapon. While his brothers-in-arms battled the enemy. It was a never-forgotten horror that revisited him in too many carriage rides.

That staccato tap that so grated on Rowena's nerves, however, also had become a calming mechanism he'd developed over the years. A distractionary measure that moved his mind from the fields of Bussaco and into that steady beating he could control. It was just another demon he had slayed, and for it, he prided himself on his calm and composure. His entire life, however, was an artful façade he'd taken on to conceal his madness and demonstrate restraint.

Yet, here he sat, a man who avoided all hint of strife, deliberately baiting her. Then, her hold had always been great over him. It was not her fault. It was his folly.

His weakness for her had once been so great, he'd have turned over the English flag to Boney's forces if she'd but asked. It was a frailty he'd spent years despising himself for.

Never had he hated himself more than he did in this moment. God curse him, he cared that she'd thought of him. For with her barely restrained fury and telling words, she'd revealed herself as clearly as the sun rising on a clear summer's day.

He hated his own inherent weakness that he should care or that truth should matter in any way. The memory of Rowena Endicott had sustained him through countless battles when he'd fought death and dying on the fields of Italy and Belgium. He'd written her more god-damn letters than all the words his miserable tutors had demanded of him for the course of his life. And not once had he received a return word from her.

Even so, lovesick fool that he'd been, Graham had clung to the dream of them. From every field he'd marched through to his near-death atop a mountain in Portugal, spared by the grace of a merci-less God and Lieutenant Hickenbottom, she'd sustained him. Those aching wounds had seen him returned to England on a litter, where he'd existed in a murky state. In those days, he'd alternated between begging for death and aching to see her once more.

Only to, at last, go in search of her and find her parents unable to meet his eyes, apologetic. She'd married another. He'd stood, staring at the door they'd all but closed in his face, numb and broken from a pain that no bullet or bayonet had managed to inflict.

And yet...

For her treachery, even with all the lies and heartbreak, that she'd thought of him turned him, once more, into that silly young man pick-ing bluebells in a meadow with her at his side.

Why had she followed any of his pursuits if she'd not, in some way, cared for him? Had it been regret that she'd not waited for that coveted role of duchess? "Did you follow my pursuits in those scandal sheets, Rowena?" he murmured when still she said nothing.

Her mouth tightened. "I found more important uses for my time than reading anything about you." Found more important uses. A slight distinction, but a telling one. The lady hadn't denied his charges.

"If it is any consolation, I never had a woman after you that could comp—"

44

Rowena shot a hand out, catching him hard on the cheek. The peal of her slap rang loud in the carriage, punctuated by the steady roll of the wheels. All the color leeched from her face and she yanked her palm back. "I…"

A wry grin formed on his lips as he rubbed the wounded flesh. God, the lady could pack a blow. Prior to his leaving, he'd given her skills with which to use to protect herself in his absence.

Then, with the smooth, precise movements that had surely earned her the reputation as Mrs. Belden's leading instructor, the lady squared her shoulders and smoothed her hands over her skirts. "Your father was a monster." He stiffened. The late duke had been hard and condescending in every way. "He disdained all but those of your exalted stations. And you, Your Grace, prove the demonstrator that an apple does not fall far from the proverbial tree."

He flared his nostrils. That likening to his bastard of a sire stung worse than her earlier, impressive blow.

Rowena continued, her cheeks flushed. "You command my fate, but I'll not be baited and jeered at every turn simply because I'm in your employ." She twisted the blade of guilt all the more.

Where his father had been a cruel employer, treating those in his employ as objects more than people, Graham had vowed never to be that man. "Forgive me," he said quietly. "You are, indeed, correct." He'd invited her back into his life look after the young lady in his care. Not to needle and hurt, as she'd done.

Rowena eyed him suspiciously. What had placed that world-wariness in her eyes? Then, she nodded slowly. "We were discussing your ward."

His mind raced. Had they been? Once again, her unyielding grip remained over his logic. "Ainsley's father and I fought together. She is illegitimate." He stared at her for a long while.

Rowena angled herself so they faced each other directly. An understanding dawned in her eyes.

"The young lady has informed me she is proficient on the pianoforte," he went on. "I'll have a recital arranged with the leading members of the peerage. Society will be unkind. Her father, in his living,

45

was a dissolute rake who buried himself in a bottle after returning from war. He left quite a scandal with his passing—"

Rowena held up a staying hand. "It is not my place to hear the girl's family history from you, or for you to tell it. Her past will not affect my judgment or treatment of her. She is simply a young lady, and that is how I will see her. If she chooses to confide her familial circumstances, then that is for her to determine."

It was why, despite the volatile history between them, he'd employed her. Appreciation stirred. An unwanted, dangerous softening at that character.

"Has the lady had any governesses?"

He shook his head. "Never." None? "According to the girl, her days were rather solitary."

Emotion suffused her saucer-round eyes. "What a very sad existence."

Then, wasn't all of life truly miserable for everyone?

"And what of my responsibilities, Your Grace?"

God, she was magnificent. Any other companion, would have kept their deferential gazes permanently at the floor. Rowena seized hold of the discussion of her charge, regard for his title of duke be damned. When that is all ladies of the *ton* had seen, her honest responses to him made him feel more like the man he'd been before he'd gone to war and had his life ripped asunder.

"Graham," he said quietly.

Four lines creased her adorable brow.

"There is no reason for us to stand on formalities. Graham will suffice."

She frowned. In the hour since they'd been together, her lips had turned downward more than they had in the three years they'd known one another. "That would hardly be appropriate, Your Grace. I am a mere servant…" She'd never been a mere anything. She'd once been his everything. "…and my actions will be subject to scrutiny."

It was the right answer. The correct one. And wanting both his life orderly and his charge transformed into everything decorous and polite, he should applaud her reply. He should. Instead, this deference to societal opinions set his teeth on edge. "Damn Society's opinions."

Rowena held up a gloved finger. "Ah, but complete freedom of your actions and decisions are liberties only afforded dukes and royalty. Lesser people"—she flattened her lips—"must follow the dictates laid out, or we are destroyed."

Her somber words ended in hushed tones that barely reached him, leaving a chill in their wake. Those words suggested she knew very well about the personal destruction she warned of. He'd not allowed himself to think of her outside her perfidiousness. Now...for the first time, he wondered what her life had been like these past years. Who had been the bounder who'd betrayed her and seen her working in a miserable finishing school with an equally miserable headmistress?

"We were once friends," he said softly. "As such, certain liberties are permitted." Once friends. Friends turned lovers. And lovers turned enemies. He braced for her tart denial. Instead, an aching smile hovered on her too-full lips.

"Friends." She spoke that word as if testing its veracity and meaning. "That was a lifetime ago. And you were not a duke." No, he'd not found himself destined for that miserable rank until Monty had perished of a wasting illness while Graham was off fighting.

I am heartily glad you aren't a duke, else you would be one of those stuffy, monocle-wearing boys who'd never be friends with a vicar's daughter.

The memory of her bell-like laughter rang around the chambers of his memory as real now as it had been all those years ago. "No," he agreed. "We were children." It had been the last of his innocence. "Now we are a man and woman capable of our own decisions, and I'd have you call me Graham." He didn't know why it should matter if she called him Your Grace, You Bastard, or Graham Linford...it just... mattered.

The lady warred with herself. She wore that fight in her expressive eyes.

Sensing her weakening, he pressed. "Unless you are otherwise too fearful of the connection it reminds you of?"

Rowena knitted her chocolate-brown eyebrows into a single line. "It reminds me of nothing, *Graham*."

With her slightly crooked front teeth, she worried the flesh of her lower lip, bringing his gaze downward to her mouth...and God help him, a potent surge of lust went through him as that subtle, seductive gesture drew forth the taste and feel of those lips, known too long ago. "Nothing?" he whispered, rolling that word in a seductive caress. He leaned forward and Rowena's breath caught loudly. "Not even the feel of my hand on your skin...?" He brought his hand slowly about her nape, giving her time to pull away...and yet she did not. She remained frozen, heat pouring off her slender frame. "Not the feel of my lips as I caressed you here..." He shifted his head and hovered his mouth beside the sensitive skin where her neck met her ear.

"No." Except her denial emerged as a raspy, hungry plea.

"Not even the taste of my lips as we made love?" And with a low groan, Graham covered her mouth with his. She stiffened in his arms, briefly battering her fists against his chest. He gentled his kiss, and Rowena curled her fingers against the fabric of his jacket. With every touch of his mouth on hers, fire built between them until they met in a primitive mating of two people who'd spent more years hating one another than loving. Dragging her across the carriage onto his lap, he never broke contact. He slanted his mouth over hers again and again, and as she twined her fingers in his hair, he thrust his tongue between her full lips. She met his kiss with abandon. Their tongues danced in a bold thrust and parry. Heat spiraled inside him. Roused all the oldest hungers he'd ever known for this woman. "Rowena," he moaned into her mouth.

She wrenched away from him. Her cheeks flushed and horror slowly filled her eyes, replacing the thick haze of desire in their depths. In her haste to escape from him, she stumbled off his lap and crashed to the floor of the carriage. He reached out to help her up, but she slapped at his hands.

"No," she said sharply, scrambling awkwardly to her feet. She rushed into her seat and huddled in the corner. She eyed him like he was more monster than man. "That is not to happen again. I am not that woman anymore." She'd never been that woman. She'd been only his. She'd come to him, a virgin, and together they'd learned the wonders of one another's bodies. "And I am in your employ."

Had she removed the gun from inside his boot and shot him through the chest, she could not have landed a more vicious blow. It had been no secret to the villagers, servants, or lords and ladies of Society the late Duke of Hampstead had a wicked proclivity for bedding the women on his staff. Graham had vowed never to be that man…and, once again, Rowena proved how weak he truly was.

"Forgive me," he said hoarsely. "When I sought your services, it was never my intention to…" He grimaced. His neck heated, and the flush traveled up his cheeks. "You may rest assured I will not put my hands upon you again, Mrs. Bryant."

And mayhap he was more the bastard his father had been. For giving her that pledge, he'd never regretted uttering any words in his life more.

FIVE

With a lover, a woman knew every intimate detail about a man. Long ago, after Rowena gave herself to Graham, she discovered the light mat of curls upon his chest. Those soft tufts, that, as she'd listened to the beat of his heart, had tickled her cheek. She'd known the taste of mint and ginger on his breath. Each discovery of those small but intricate details had made up a tender composite of a person that not even time's passage could erase.

He still snored.

She'd not remembered that about him—until now. Such a detail about Graham Linford, the Duke of Hampstead she'd gathered long ago, curled against his side, with the stars twinkling overhead, and the world unknowing of where they were or what they did.

Rowena dropped her chin into her hand and, with the benefit of his slumber, studied him in his repose. How very odd to know those intimate details: the birthmark just below his navel, or that cinnamon made him sneeze, and to not truly know a man in any way that truly mattered. His closed eyes twitched and she stiffened. But then another bleating snore escaped him, filling the carriage, and proving he slept still. This time, she abandoned her study of him and stared outside at the countryside. Thick, gray clouds rolled overhead, blotting out the earlier spring sun.

He'd kissed her.

Following Jack's attack in her parents' cottage, the memory of his punishing mouth as he'd groped and grabbed at her, haunted her still long after that dark day. That violent assault, on a day when her life

50

had been forever changed, had overshadowed the beautiful embraces she'd shared with Graham. So much that Rowena had ceased to believe she could ever know a man's kiss without feeling that suffocating panic. She'd been wrong—yet again. For Graham had gentled their embrace, rekindling all the oldest yearnings and desires she'd carried for him and his touch. His kiss, however, had not been the tryst of young lovers they'd shared countless times years and years before, but rather the soul-searing, toe-curling kiss of a man who hungered for her. It had roused that same forbidden desire inside her.

In the lead windowpane, her gaze snagged on her visage and the wanton creature with too many strands of hair hanging about her shoulders stared back in damning testament to her weakness for him. She slid her eyes closed. Mayhap she was the whore his father had accused her of being. After all, a reformed courtesan's blood ran through her veins. Surely that is why it had been so easy for her mother to send her away because ultimately she'd seen her daughter had fallen and followed the same wicked path. Rowena had not allowed herself to think of the parent who'd foolishly thought she could carve out a life of obscurity for all her family in the countryside, just as she had deluded herself into believing that love was real. And that dukes' second sons could love and marry those scandalous descendants.

Her heart buckled as the clutch of pain she'd believed herself immune to reared once more. Could a woman ever truly move on after one's lover had set her aside, and one's mother turned her out? She bit her lower lip. *Damn you, Graham Linford. Damn you for making me believe…and worse for making me remember how desperately I wanted that dream of us.*

Swallowing back a ball of regret, she grabbed the small, industrial bag at her side. Made of a thick cotton, it was not the satins or silks of a lady's reticule but rather a stark, purposeful bag. Fishing around the drawstring sack, she pulled out a book.

Proper Rules of Proper Behavior and Proper Decorum. She gave her head a disgusted shake. All valuable lessons, but by the saints preserved, what person could ever take a book with such a bloody foolish title seriously? Rowena opened the well-read, aged book that often brought her a much-needed distraction. Her gaze lingered on the now-yellowed, folded scrap. That hated note. Purposefully stuffed within these very pages as a marked reminder of her station and her suffering.

Biting the inside of her lower lip, she yanked out the missive and buried it in the back of her book. Out of sight...but forever in her mind. And she began to read.

All ladies must adhere to essential rules of behavior. It is the only...

She swallowed a sound of frustration. How could she think of anything or anyone except the towering bear snoring away on the opposite bench? The man she'd given her virginity to in the fields of bluebells with the stars twinkling on as their witnesses. "Focus," Rowena muttered under her breath. She returned her gaze to the inked words and began again.

All ladies must adhere to essential rules of behavior. It is the only...It is the only...

It is futile...

With a sigh, she set her book aside. Not taking her gaze from him, Rowena reached carefully inside her bag. Her fingers collided with metal, warm for its placement inside, and then she folded her palm reflexively about it. She slowly withdrew the heart-shaped locket attached to a small chain. She let it dangle from her fingers, and it spun in a slow, sad half-circle back and forth. It was no grand bauble a noblewoman would don, but to her, it had once been more cherished than the Queen's crown.

Now, it bore the marks of time. The clasp long since broken. The heart pendant as tarnished as the organ that beat in her breast. She popped open the clever latch and stared at the small tendrils of hair trapped under each side, protected by glass. His midnight lock alongside her own drab brown strand.

For years, she'd succeeded in burying the memory of Graham. Whenever the pain of losing him had left her incapacitated with the force of her tears, drawn close in a miserable heap, she'd pulled out this very piece. A gift given in love. A gift her mother had scolded her for taking with a warning that ladies did not receive gifts, and only wickedness was attached to them.

In the end, her mother, who'd spoken from life's experience, had proven right. Graham's gift had become a talisman of his deceit and deviltry. Handed to her on the front steps of his country estate with a note, and the end of her grand illusions on love.

Rowena closed the locket, the faint *click* muffled by the rumbling carriage wheels and Graham's occasional snore. In those times when he'd trickled into her thoughts, and she'd suffered the agony of his betrayal all over again, it had been easy to kick ash upon the memory of him—nay, of them—by taking out this very piece. He emitted a bleating-broken snore, and heart jumping, Rowena quickly shoved the pendant back inside the bag.

But this, this was an altogether new impossibility. Now, forced into his company, into his carriage, and then his household, there would be no hiding. She briefly pressed her eyes closed, and allowed memory after memory to parade through her mind. This time, she did not bury them but punished herself by reliving those darkest days. Learning he'd returned home from fighting Boney's forces soon after his brother's death. The seemingly endless carriage ride from Mrs. Belden's, and the terror that had filled her breast at risking her security at Mrs. Belden's, all to see him. And then, in the end, he'd not even deigned to let her into his foyer. He'd given her one final note, care of his father. A note so unlike all those beautiful lines and verses he'd written her through the years but succinctly marked in his elegant, bold strokes.

I would have married you...on nothing more than a lie. In dallying with a vicar's daughter, I lowered myself beneath my station. However, you are no vicar's daughter, Miss Endicott. You are a whore's daughter, and as such, there can be nothing respectable in marrying you. If you desire a place in my bed, however, it is yours...

Bile burned her throat, and she swallowed back nausea. That moment on his stone terrace, as vivid now as it was all those years ago. She blinked back the dratted sheen of tears that misted her eyes.

Tears she'd not let fall for him and what had come to be. For as broken as he'd left her, Graham's desertion had also made her stronger. Through his unfaithfulness, she'd grown and matured. She was no longer a weak child, huddled in the corner of a mail coach, afraid to so much as move. Rather, she was a woman grown, with her own mind, shaped by her past. And determined to own her future. There were no longer grand illusions of love and family. No, her dreams were altogether different. Stability and security, and a life of respectability—unlike her own mother's dreary start.

A whore, like her mother, she would never be. Reaffirming that vow, Rowena picked up her copy of *Proper Rules of Proper Behavior and Proper Decorum* and proceeded to read.

A soft whimpering cut across her musings and she shot her head up. Silence reigned, with the only break in the quiet the beginning stirrings of a storm whipping wind at the carriage walls. Frowning, Rowena retrained her focus on her small leather volume.

All ladies must...

An eerie, agonized moan ricocheted about the interior of the conveyance and, heart thundering hard against her ribcage, she swiveled her gaze to Graham.

Braced against the carriage wall, he thrashed his head back and forth. His arms twitched as though he fought some dreamed of demon, and she wanted the sight of his suffering to not matter. He did not matter. Why did that mantra inside her head feel like the greatest lie?

"Nooooo..." A deathlike plea tore from his lips.

Rowena bit down on the inside of her cheek, drawing blood. A metallic tinge flooded her senses. She would feel pain at the sight of any man's suffering, and Graham's was no different. She told herself as much in a silent litany. She was a bloody liar. He mattered still, all these years later. With his effortless ease in believing the worst of her and abandonment of all they'd shared, she cared for him. What nightmares did he battle? What evil had he faced on those fields of battle? Society had hailed him as a hero, and yet, some heroes were born of horrendous deeds and painful acts.

"Your Grace," she said quietly, setting her book alongside her on the bench.

Graham jerked, and then his thrashing grew more frantic. He shot a foot out and caught her hard in the shin. A sharp hiss ran through Rowena's teeth as pain radiated up her leg. Despite all that had come to pass between them, she could not allow him to suffer, if even just in his dreams.

Ignoring the throbbing of her lower leg, she slid onto the bench beside him and touched his tense forearm. The muscles jumped under her palm. "Your Grace," she repeated, this time more loudly.

A cry exploded from her when he surged sideways and pinned her against the wall of the carriage. Her chest heaved violently, in time to the frantic pounding of her pulse, as Graham stared at her through vacant eyes. A chill rippled along her spine. For the dazed blankness in his gaze, she may as well have looked into the face of death. He curled a hand about her throat and he squeezed, cutting off the scream that formed. She scrabbled and scratched at his fingers, attempting to yank free, damning her ineffectual efforts. Stars danced behind her eyes. "G-Graham," she managed, pleadingly.

And at last, the use of his name drew him back from whatever hell had gripped him.

Graham eyed her the way he might a foreign species of insect, and then he abruptly released her. Rowena sank against the side of the carriage and choked. Sucking in great, gasping breaths, she borrowed strength from the side of the wall and, at last, forced her eyes open. Her gaze collided with his.

The remnants of the tortured demons that had haunted his dreams lingered still. Gooseflesh dotted her skin. "Rowena." By the gruffness of his agonized whisper, it may as well have been him who'd had hands wrapped about his own throat. "I'm so sorry…" He gasped out. "I thought…I believed…" He continued to ramble, his incoherent sentences laced with horrified regret and shame. He stretched trembling hands out and then swiftly yanked them back. "I apologize, Mrs. Bryant," he said, his eyes glittering as he glanced frantically about.

A portentous howl echoed through the countryside as the storm hovered in the spring air, an ominous threat that matched the darkness inside the conveyance.

"It is all right." That assurance emerged hoarse from the strain on her throat. "It was just a dream." A nightmare. It had been a nightmare. She touched his coat sleeve.

He wrenched his arm away. "It was no dream," he thundered, and she cowered. This barely restrained, volatile man bore no hint of the affable grinning boy who'd once been her friend and lover. A muscle ticked at the corner of his eye, turned nearly jade green from the emotion pulsing there. Then he recoiled, and he blinked wildly.

In this moment, she might have been a shadow upon the wall, for his gaze bore right through her.

Then, he went still. Blinking slowly, he glanced around before settling his eyes on her. Hunched against the side of the carriage, she tried to steady her trembling limbs. He stretched his arms toward her, and despite herself, despite knowing the hatred he carried for her, knowing he would never *intentionally* put his hands upon her, she flinched.

As if burned, he dropped his arms. "Rowena." That gravelly utterance emerged as an entreaty from tense lips. He recoiled and then slapped his still shaking palm to his mouth. "Forgive me. I'm so sorry. I thought...I..." Then with a tortured moan better fitting a just-felled creature drawing its final sweet breath of life, Graham shot his arm up and rapped hard on the ceiling. The carriage rolled to a slow stop in the middle of the old Roman road. He shoved the door open. Wind whipped inside the carriage, tossing Rowena's loose tresses about her face. "My apologies," he said with his usual cool. With that, he jumped outside and slammed the door in his wake. A moment later, the carriage resumed its gradual rumble forward, before continuing at a quick clip.

She sat there motionless long after he'd gone. That volatile reaction and his secret demons proved without a doubt how little they'd known of one another, then...and how even less they knew of one another now. Just as life had forever changed her, surviving away from home at the cold, loveless Mrs. Belden's institution, so, too, had he been changed, in ways she'd naively not allowed herself to think of.

His nightmares were his own. His past belonged to him and someday to the woman he'd eventually take to wife.

Dukes, even tortured ones, married illustrious ladies. They did not marry whores. They did not marry the daughters of whores. Nor did Rowena aspire to the role of his wife, or for that matter, wife to any man. She'd learned the perils in relying on anyone other than herself. Her parents, Jack...Graham—all had left her with an indelible lesson. She'd not be so foolish to again entrust any part of herself or security to another. No, she would come and fulfill the terms of employment he laid out in whatever macabre game he sought to play and, ultimately, leave.

Despite his nightmare-gripped attack, his kiss, however, had proven his unyielding hold over her, still. Rowena touched her gloved fingertips to her lips, the memory of that embrace burned through the fabric. It recalled past kisses that had stirred a wicked desire inside. A dangerous yearning which had led her to throw away her virtue and risk her future. Now she'd been forced to enter his employ. How could she survive and hold on to her preciously guarded strength and control where Graham was concerned?

Only, if she were being truthful, at least with herself, she could admit she'd never been strong where Graham was concerned. Since the moment she'd spied him in the village, a girl new to Wallingford, she'd been captivated. And his hold was just as strong all these years later.

Rowena drew in a deep breath. Except, she was no longer a naïve young miss seeing love and romance in the world around her. Now, she was a woman grown, who'd been stung by a *gentleman's* falsehoods... and despite the demons that haunted him and her urge to see him safely through, she'd do well to remember that.

No good had ever come out of her relationship with Graham Linford. Nor would it ever.

SIX

Later that evening, seated in the corner of the Fox and Hare Inn, Graham stared into the bottom of his empty tankard. Rain pinged against the leather windowpanes in steady torrents.

The sharp beat echoed like gunshots in his mind.

...By God, you'll never hold them back...leave me...just leave me... Moisture beaded on his brow, and he pressed his fingertips against his temple to drive back the nightmares.

"More ale, my lord?"

Yanked back from the precipice of madness, Graham looked up. The innkeeper Martin smiled benignly back and lifted his pitcher. "Ale?" he repeated. Incapable of words, Graham nodded. The other man poured his tankard full and shuffled off.

Since he'd return from fighting Boney's forces, he had been a man hunted by the ghosts of the lives he'd taken and the soldiers who'd given theirs saving his worthless one. Those crimes were the reason he fought the war's hold still, all these years later.

Now, Graham's life had been upended, and he'd be forced to share his home and life with not only a charge but the one woman who earlier that afternoon had seen past the composed façade he presented to the world. For all that had come to pass...for all the vitriol and resentment, she'd attempted to offer him calming assurances.

He tightened his hold on his drink. She wore the marks of his fingers on her neck and with her rasping breaths, she'd sought to calm *him*. The evidence of that goodness when presented with the beast he'd been to her since he'd arrived at Mrs. Belden's, left him shamed and humbled. What would she say if she knew what he'd really become?

58

For her romantic spirit, she'd also always been clever. As such, that quick wit would have surely resulted in her declining a position in a madman's household should she know the full truth.

He'd spent years hating her. Despising her for that forsaken vow she'd made to love him and only him. She hadn't even cared enough to respond to a single note he'd written her. He'd been carried home weaker than a babe to find his brother dead and Graham on the cusp of death himself. Through it, she'd sustained him but she refused to even pay him a visit in friendship. When he'd managed to climb out of bed, the first place he'd gone was to her family's cottage, and just like that, every hope and happiness he'd ever known had been shattered. Not even gone a year and she'd married another. That ruthless, fickle creature she'd proven herself to be was at odds with the stoic woman who'd sought to soothe him earlier.

A rusty chuckle rumbled from deep in his chest. *Friendship.* He'd been so pathetic where Rowena was concerned, he would have taken even that scrap from her.

Graham sipped his drink. For years, he'd hated her faithlessness. For marrying another. The cold reality was her marrying Mr. Bryant had been for the better—for her. Had she waited for him to return, he could never have made her his wife. And it had been selfish of him. For even as he with his madness couldn't have ever married her, he'd at least wanted to know that her love was true.

"Do you need your tankard filled, my lord?"

He glanced up at the innkeeper's wife and mustered a return smile for her. "Your husband recently refilled mine. Wonderful stuff," he lied for her benefit. It was sour enough to burn a hole in a man's belly.

She grinned. "You're one of the kind lords."

And guilt twisted away at his belly. Would the old woman think the same if she knew he'd spent the better part of the morning trying to bait and taunt the only woman he'd ever loved? The old woman dropped her voice to a whisper. "The ale, it's rotten stuff, though." She stole a glance back to where her husband mopped down another table. "My Martin, however, thinks it's wonderful, and I do not have the heart to tell him otherwise." Her eyes twinkled. "But then, isn't that the way of life? You hold close a secret if it means sparing the other person hurt."

He forced a return smile and then desperate to turn the discourse to anything other than love and loyalty, Graham held his tankard out. The woman hefted her jug, and with shaky fingers, tipped it, filling his glass to the brim. "Thank you…?"

"Martha."

Martha and Martin. Two people, who went together, even in names. How did fate so perfectly join some couples, while wreaking havoc on other mismatched pairs who were never meant to be?

"Is My Lordship hungry? I've made fresh bread…" She sniffed at the air as the scent of burning permeated the taproom. Jug in hands, the woman shouted for her husband and went tearing for the kitchens.

Martin snorted himself awake. "Who…what…?" Then climbing with difficulty to his feet, he started for the kitchens.

Graham stared after that happy pair a moment and, giving his head a bemused shake, took another drink. How odd. He'd one of the oldest titles in the realm. A status that placed him a smidgen below royalty. He'd vast holdings. Unlimited wealth. And he did not know a jot of the happiness the old couple had.

The sound of groaning floorboards pulled his attention to the darkened stairwell at the front of the room and he glanced over. A thrill of awareness went through him; the same volatile charge that had been there since the day she was fourteen, and he seventeen, noticing things about his one-time friend he'd really no place noticing. The shape of her lips. The curve of her hips. That same day, he'd kissed her and nothing had been the same since.

Yes, some things never changed. And yet, other things did.

With the benefit the darkened shadows afforded him in the corner, Graham took the opportunity to study Rowena without her notice. Where once she'd moved with an excited spring in her steps, now she picked her way about with the same care he'd practiced navigating enemy fire on the battlefield. She clutched a small book close to her chest and looked about the room. Again, he sought the girl of his past who'd been vibrant and lively. Had it been the loss of her husband that had left her broken? The amorphous face of a nemesis he'd never known danced around the chambers of his mind. Swallowing back a vile bitterness, he drank deep of his ale.

Ultimately, Rowena found him with her gaze. He held her stare, expecting her to look away. Alas, the same spirit he'd long loved and admired remained as strong in the lady. She bowed her head in greeting. Graham lifted his glass in a silent toast.

With that, she surveyed the room before claiming a spot at the stone hearth where a fire blazed within. She sat like a princess upon her throne, with her back to him. That wordless but powerful request for privacy rang louder than a shot in the silence.

This is what we've become. Nay, this was what they'd always been. Strangers.

But this was worse than the agony of her defection. This was the agony of...nothing. No words. No exchanges. No...*anything* from a woman he'd once bared his soul to and for.

Graham took another long, much-needed swig of his ale and welcomed the fiery sting of the bitter brew sliding down his throat. *Get control of yourself, man.* There was but one reason for Rowena's presence in his life and that was to serve as a servant in his employ. What had come to pass and what was never to have been didn't merit—not any longer. As a boy it had mattered more than anything. As a man now past his thirtieth year, old resentments no longer signified. He sought for the stoic, ducal control he'd perfected where he needed no one and wanted even less.

The quiet rumble of thunder sounded outside. Rowena jumped in her chair. The book she held sailed from her fingers and landed with a solid *thwack* on the table. The lady still feared the thunder. Graham briefly closed his eyes, damning the fates for that reminder. Odd, a person not only clung to the old fears that had once dogged them, but with the passage of time, acquired new ones as well. Not allowing himself to dwell on the fact that her comforts and peace of mind were no longer his affair, he shoved to his feet. Tankard in hand, he started over to the scarred, wooden table she'd claimed.

Rowena looked up, surprise paraded across the planes of her face.

He jerked his chin. "May I?" he murmured, already pulling out the seat opposite her.

She opened and closed her mouth like the trout they'd plucked from the river, searching for air. Another rumble of thunder shook the foundations of the establishment, and she hurriedly nodded.

I fear nothing when I am with you, Graham. His lips still burned with the feel of her whispered words against them from long ago.

Rowena dropped her gaze to her book, and he took in her bent head. Inevitably time changed them all. He'd learned that lesson most clearly on the fields of battle with his friends-in-arms shot down around him and strangers dying at his hands. Had her change to this silent, subdued woman been a slow one? Or had it been a gradual, painful death of her spirit?

The faint marks at her throat drew his eyes and reminded him of his own transformation. "Are you all right?"

Picking her head up, there was a flash of understanding that glinted in her brown eyes. "I am fine," she assured him once more. Yet again, she sought to provide him an undeserved solace. He tried to reconcile that with the fickle woman who'd so quickly found another in his absence. She wet her lips. "You didn't hurt me."

He gave a small, sad chuckle. "You were always a rotten liar, Rowena Endicott."

...Why could my mother not be bothered to give me a second name...?

She gave him a weak smile. "And you were always far too clever with words, Graham Marshall Francis Linford."

I promise our babes will have outrageously long names like yours, Graham Marshall Francis Linford.

Their babes. Had he never gone off to fight, and had his brother never died, even now they could have a passel of children—a family of eight like they'd wished. A babe. Anything other than the meaningless, lonely life he now lived. One that would soon be filled with an equally cold wife and a requisite heir to fulfill his responsibilities to those depending on him.

Unable to meet her life-hardened eyes, he dropped his gaze to the table.

Lightning cracked noisily, casting a streak of bluish-white light through the dirtied windowpane, shattering his maudlin thoughts and her fleeting calm. Rowena gasped, her skin blanching. She'd been forever changed...and even all these years later, the sight of her fear gutted him worse than the bullet shot into his left thigh at the Battle of Bussaco. *It matters not. Her demons are her own...*

"What are you reading?" the quiet question left him before he could call it back.

He sought to distract her. The same way she'd always known him so well; his soul a mirror of her own in some ways, she knew he sought to divert her attentions from the storm.

Why did he have to unsettle her like this? The baiting and harshness were easier than this gruff concern. Concern that contradicted the aloof stranger who'd forced her from Mrs. Belden's and back into his life and into a world in which she didn't belong.

Why should he even care if I'm scared or worried...or...or anything? And no matter that on the morrow they'd return to being aloof strangers; for now, he was the friend from long ago. She hesitated and then slowly turned her book around. Rowena braced for his mockery.

"*Proper Rules of Proper Behavior and Proper Decorum,*" he murmured. She sought to make out anything in his emotionless tone.

He'd always been teasing and charming. Where all the young women and ladies in the village had courted the favor of his brother, the future duke, she'd never given a jot for that useless title. Rowena braced for a jest.

That did not come. His face a carefully schooled mask that revealed nothing, he collected the volume from her, drawing her eyes to his right hand. A vicious scar marred the center of that once perfect appendage, this jagged flesh highlighting the truth—he was no longer that coaxing boy and she was no longer that always-grinning girl. "It is not a gothic novel," he said. His was more a matter-of-fact observation from a man given to ponderings.

"No. It is not," she confirmed. Long ago, she'd ceased reading those tales. Those silly tales of love and good triumphing over evil had served as nothing more than a mockery for the reality that was life. "Work hardly permits a woman the luxury of time to read for pleasure." She settled for a safe, false explanation.

"Is that what this is? Material you are expected to read for your employment?" He lifted his gaze. His penetrating stare could pierce her every secret and unspoken regret.

"It is all that is available for us to read." Her words came haltingly. Was this another game he played with her?

"Us?" He lifted an eyebrow.

The dragons. "The instructors," she clarified. Women seen as an extension of the dreadful Mrs. Belden and hated for it. A coolly, emotionless woman Rowena had morphed into these years. She balled her hands into fists, and she battled back regret at the way life had turned out for her. Of course, she should be only grateful. Whereas her mother had been passed around from protector to protector, Rowena had been spared that ignoble fate. The duke had seen her cast out of the folds of her family, and she'd lost every remnant of her once-happy existence. But he hadn't seen her suffer the fate of a whore. What a horrid liar she was even in her own mind. Bitterness soured her mouth. For this childless and husband-less existence had never been the one she'd dreamed of. She tamped down a sound of disgust with herself. How wholly selfish and ungrateful, not being content with security and secretly yearning for more.

At Graham's silence, she stole a sideways peek at him. Instead, he continued to wordlessly turn the pages of her book. What did he think of the words there? Those tedious lessons designed to drum all spirit out of a woman and make her into a refined, emotionless figure?

The Graham of her youth would have pressed her with questions. Mayhap teased her for the silliness inked in those pages, and they would have both dissolved into laughter. This new life-hardened, older version of himself said nothing but rather periodically flipped those pages in a distracted manner. The hated note pressed into her hands long ago, slipped onto the table, whispery soft in its descent. They froze. At once, they looked at it. *Oh, God.* Heart racing, she shot her hands out and rescued the page from his vision and tucked it into her lap. Surely a man who'd so easily discarded her wouldn't recall that long-ago note. A letter now aged by time. If he did, what would he make of her carrying it around, all these years later?

He narrowed his eyes but did not press her for details on that yellowed scrap. "Your Mrs. Belden's sounds like a miserable place." Her Mrs. Belden's. Ironically, it was the only place that had truly belonged to her. A place where young ladies' souls went to die. Students and instructors alike. An establishment filled with strangers, whose very presence there ensured Rowena's security. But security did not always happiness bring.

It is a miserable place.

"And yet you remain on there?"

Rowena stared unblinkingly at his immaculately folded white cravat. Had she spoken aloud? She trailed the tip of her tongue over the seam of her lips, picking her way carefully around her words. "There are not many options"—outside of whoring oneself—"for a young woman without noble connections." Even less for a reformed courtesan's apparently equally wicked daughter.

…You could return home…

As soon as the notion slipped forward, she started. Where had the foolish idea come from? Once upon a lifetime ago, she'd entertained the thought of again seeing her parents and sisters. With the passage of time, she'd accepted the truth—they'd never truly seen her as a member of their family. She'd too much pride to go back to the people who'd turned her out. Nor had they made so much as an effort to welcome her back. Rowena gave her head a slight shake, shoving unwanted memories to the side. No, she was not so much the fool that she'd ever trust anyone but herself again.

Graham folded his arms and, in an effortless move more befitting the carefree lad he'd been, he kicked back on the legs of his chair, hooding his thick black lashes all the more. "Your family could not have taken you in after your husband passed?" Her fictional husband.

Rowena dropped her hands to her lap and balled them so hard that her nails left crescent marks upon the flesh. "Is that a question?" she dodged.

"An observation."

Of course, Graham, as a duke, would know all. Not all. That ugliest sin kept from him, the one that had seen his father shatter her. It was a fragile secret that his miserable father had taken to his grave. Or had he?

"I see your family when I return to Wallingford Castle."

For a second time, the *parents* who'd betrayed her, the life she'd left behind, forced their way back into her thoughts.

Oh, God. His casual statement ripped a jagged, vicious hole inside her heart that left her aching and numb. That he should see her kin when she remained nothing more than a stranger to them. A mother. A stepfather and two younger sisters who may as well have shared all her blood for the depth with which she'd loved them. It was what had made leaving them possible. Even so…that selfish, small part of her wished her parents had fought the duke for her. Wished they'd put her before their family's security. But she'd never mattered to anyone in that capacity: not the mother who'd birthed her. The lord who'd sired her. The stepfather who'd called her his daughter on a lie. And not Graham.

"I…" Words stuck in her throat, melding with the agony of pained regret and love. "Do you?" Was that hoarse, ragged whisper her own? Lightning cracked close to the Fox and Hare and, for once, she did not hear that always terrifying sound, fixed as she was on Graham's words.

"At Sunday sermon." He paused. "When I attend." He grinned, and her heart caught, as he was momentarily transformed into the dashing boy who'd won her heart. "I recently saw them at the village fair. I'd been observing the festivities." As any benevolent lord would do. "Your sisters were speaking to an old gypsy woman…" He continued speaking, his voice coming as if from down a long, muted corridor.

She'd relegated the memory of her mother and two younger siblings to the far-flung corners of her mind. Not thinking of them. Not drawing forth memories. In that place, they remained forever young, frozen in time, unaging versions of their innocent selves. But they were not. Bianca and Blanche would now each be young women, seventeen and eighteen...The same Rowena had been when she'd been sitting with friends, giggling about gypsy's tales and lore. She swallowed hard. Only, her sisters had no doubt avoided the wicked path Rowena and her mother had once traveled. Were they even now happily wedded to kind gentlemen from the village? Her heart pulled with that hope for them.

Mayhap Graham was even crueler than she'd credited, and his purpose in joining her was to flay her open and leave her even more exposed and broken than he had before. Rowena leapt from her seat so quickly, her chair scraped along the hardwood floor, noisy in the quiet inn.

Stopping mid-sentence, Graham looked questioningly up at her.

"I have to go," she rasped, and gathering her book and stuffing the note inside, she spun on her heel and did what she should have done the moment she'd spied him sitting in the taproom: she fled.

SEVEN

His tankard empty and forgotten, Graham remained in the tap-room long after Rowena left. Steepling his fingers under his chin, he stared into the high flames dancing inside the hearth.

When he'd gone off to battle Boney's forces and learned firsthand the harsh reality of war, Rowena had been the person he'd clung to. As friends were cut down around him on the battlefields, he'd fought through the gripping agony of loss by thinking of her face. And when he'd slayed his first victim with a bayonet to the throat, sobbing and screaming, it had been the hope of seeing her again that had given him the strength to end that man's life—and all the countless others he'd killed thereafter.

The moment he'd learned of her perfidy in her parents' cottage all those years ago, he'd taken his leave of them, bitter and broken. He'd descended first into a bottle, and then further and further into debauchery in the arms of countless whores and mistresses. None of the scandalous parties or wicked women had done anything to dull the pain of losing Rowena. In a bid to drive her from his memory he'd shredded all hint of morality. Carousing, drinking in the most dangerous ends of London. Until one of his moments of madness had seen a nameless whore with a swollen cheek and terror in her eyes. He'd stumbled from that room, and with the help of Jack, his one loyal friend, found his way home. It was the last time he'd relinquished control of his emotions or taken a woman to his bed. Every decision he'd made for the past eight years had been logical and clearly thought out.

Until now. With Rowena's reemergence, all the oldest hurts and regrets and resentments stirred, challenging the life he'd made for himself. It no doubt accounted for the moments of madness he'd suffered not once, but twice in her company.

Not for the first time since he'd required Rowena return to London with him, he doubted the wisdom of that decision. By her very presence, she threatened his need for placidity. But against his better judgment, he'd demanded she take the post of companion, and now his turbulent mind was paying the price for that rashness.

Rain beat down a heavy torrent on the roof of the Fox and Hare Inn. Steady rivulets struck the lead windowpanes with a noisy pinging like sharp nails being driven into the glass.

What was that note tucked between the pages of her book? At first, he'd believed it was nothing more than a letter from Mrs. Belden. The pain that seized her features before she'd gone told a different tale. As a man with secrets, he well appreciated that every person battled their own demons. Yet, his fingers had still twitched with the need to yank the book from her fingers and read the words she'd so desperately sought to protect. What words were written there? Had they been penned by Mr. Bryant and Rowena had therefore kept them close? An unwanted, seething jealousy twisted around inside. *You bloody fool...*

"Another ale, my lord?"

Graham started, and looked from the indicated tankard to the always grinning innkeeper, Martin, who held a cloth in hand. "No. Thank you." Pushing back his chair, he stood.

Dropping a bow, Martin set to work wiping down the scarred but immaculate table. Graham made his way abovestairs, the wood stairs groaning loudly in the nighttime still. He started down the narrow corridor, briefly pausing beside a door. Her door. His jaw flexed as resentment flooded him that she should know rest when his thoughts ran amok with questions and regrets.

Giving his head a disgusted shake, he found his rooms and closed the door quietly behind him. Shucking off his jacket, he laid it neatly on the lone chair. His cravat came next. With meticulous, precise movements, he unfolded the stark white satin and set it atop the seat. The young man he'd been before he'd gone off to war, he would have thought nothing of tossing the garments into a messy heap or even sleeping in his travel-worn clothes. From across the small, cramped quarters, he caught sight of his reflection. The cracked and dusty mirror did little to conceal the austere features and stiff set to his frame that was very much his father's. Graham stared at himself. This is who he'd become. This is the cool, emotionless figure he'd worked so desperately *to* become. And he'd do well to remember the need for that rigid control. Seeking out the bed, he sat and removed his boots. He lined them up with their sides touching against the bed. It was those little measures of control that grounded him.

Graham reclined on the lumpy mattress and closed his eyes, eager for sleep so he might be free of Rowena Bryant.

Drip. Drip. Drip.

Bloody hell. At that incessant trickle he opened his eyes. In the darkened space, he stared at the ceiling. The lone candle cast shadows about the room and highlighted the water pooled in the far corner of the Fox and Hare's *finest* rooms—as the proud innkeeper had referred to them.

He shifted the pillow under his head, all the while considering that growing water stain on the wall. Where most noblemen would have sneered at the accommodations, Graham had spent too many years with the hard, muddy earth as his only mattress and rain-soaked garments his only protection from the elements. No. It was not the state of the rooms or his miserable mattress that kept him from sleeping. Nor the nightmares that haunted him too often.

Rather, the grief that had contorted Rowena's face, just before she'd hastened away from the taproom and raced up the stairs that kept him awake, still. At one time, there had been no secrets between them. She would have turned to him and shared whatever silent trouble that weighted her, just as he would have shared with her. When he'd entered Mrs. Belden's and demanded she be hired as companion to his ward, he'd gleefully relished the reality of her having no choice but to enter into his household and squirm as he forced her to confront her own treacheries. And at last, with her in his life, he could put the memory of her to rest. Purge her from his thoughts and retake mastery of the heart she'd ravaged eleven years earlier.

What he'd not accounted for was this tender regard for her that had existed since the moment they'd spit in their palms and shook on a pledge of forever friendship to the day he'd lain her down under the stars and claimed her virginity in an act of love.

A rolling thunder rocked the countryside and he turned his head, looking toward the wall shared between him and Rowena. He strained his ears. Mayhap she slept.

His senses, heightened on the battlefield, and the paper-thin walls between them did little to mute her faint whimpering. Graham dragged his hands over his face. Why could she not be sleeping? Why could she not be peacefully resting, so that he did not have to lay in the opposite chamber joined by a thin wall knowing and hearing those telltale sounds of her fear?

She is not my responsibility. She is nothing more than a servant in my employ.

She was also the woman who when he'd been off battling Boney's men had not bothered to write him a single note. The same woman who, for the years of friendship between them, hadn't even had the decency to tell him to his bloody face that in his absence she'd come to love another. Instead, she had left him to find out from her parents and his loyal friend turned man-of-affairs.

Then, his heart always had been weak for her.

A streak of lightning illuminated the room in a soft blue light. He automatically turned his head toward her chambers. Rowena's low moan filtered into his room.

With a curse, Graham gave up on the hope of a *peaceful* slumber. He swung his legs over the side of the bed and climbed to his feet. The floorboards shifted and groaned in protest as he stalked over to the faded white plaster that separated him from her. Spreading his arms, he propped his palms on the walls and leaned his forehead against the cool surface.

Another flash of light spilled through his chamber window, followed by a sharp crack that struck close to the inn.

He pressed his lips into a hard line and knocked his forehead silently against the surface, listening to her whimpering as it pierced the walls. After her treachery, he'd believed nothing could bring him peace in life except to know Rowena Endicott suffered. What he'd failed to realize, until he'd forced her back into his life, was that her suffering still had the power to gut him. Graham sank to the floor. "Are you all right?" he called, not for the first time that day.

Silence met his inquiry and, for a long moment, he thought she'd feign sleep. "I am all right, Your Grace."

Your Grace. "Graham," he reminded her, frustration turning over inside him that she continued "Your Gracing" him. Silence met his request, stretching on, indicating she'd either not heard or had no intention of replying.

His brother and father's passing had marked the death of his existence as just Graham Linford. From that moment on, lords and ladies and servants, at last, saw him. And yet, they hadn't. Not truly. They saw one of the oldest, most distinguished titles and carefully averted their gazes in reverence. Unlike Lady Serena who wanted nothing but to be his duchess...and who, one day soon, would be. Therefore, Rowena's deference to his title shouldn't matter. It didn't matter. In fact, this new, older, quieter, more serious version of Rowena Endicott fit more precisely into the life he'd carved out for himself: a life of calm, order, and logic. The demons he battled made calm more crucial to his existence.

Wind howled and battered the window, throwing the rain at an odd angle into the lead pane, and battling back his own disquiet, Graham shoved to his feet. A rumble of thunder shook the foundations of the inn. He briefly closed his eyes, and then his gaze was drawn back to the plaster between him and Rowena. Another faint whimper penetrated the thin wall. That sound hinting at her restraint.

She does not want my help. She does not want my help. She had been abundantly clear with the whole "Your Grace" business.

Graham dusted a hand over his eyes and returned to his spot on the floor. "Turning to face your opponent on a dueling field and finding your gunpowder is wet," he called quietly.

As soon as the nonsensical offering left his lips, he cringed. When she was a young girl on the cusp of womanhood, during one nasty summer storm, he'd invented a game in which they took turns providing something far more terrifying than a bolt of lightning. It had been an attempt to distract her until the tempest had passed. It had been so long. Countless years since they'd last played. She probably no longer remembered. Giving his head a hard shake, Graham started for his bed. He made it but one step.

"Sailing in a skiff with a hole and having to abandon the boat when you cannot swim."

His chest tightened as he came slowly back and wandered over to the spot he'd previously abandoned. Graham slid down into a seated position and angled his head sideways toward the wall. "Throwing a rock at a tree and accidentally knocking a beehive to the ground."

"Oh, that is a splendid one."

His lips twitched. She may as well have been the rosy-cheeked young lady, clapping her hands excitedly at his cleverness. Through the quiet, he fixed on the rain striking the roof. "Have you been defeated so quickly?"

"I am thinking. I've not played this game in…" Either the wall ate away her words or she allowed them to trail off. When had been the last time she'd played their game? Had it been with the lover she'd left him for, the man who'd ultimately abandoned her? Not for the first time since his return from war, he allowed himself to think about the nameless stranger who'd made her his wife. Had he been kind to her? Had he known the places to tickle her until she was breathless and snorting with laughter?

Lightning streaked through the window.

"Visiting an ancient ruin and finding a banshee following your movements." Her high-pitched words ran quickly together.

He shoved aside thoughts of the man who'd called her wife. "Riding through the countryside and finding your horse is, in fact, a kelpie."

She laughed, the sound clear and bell-like. In that instance, she may as well have been the sixteen-year-old girl curled against his side. "You cannot use Celtic lore, after I've just used one."

Graham cupped his hands around his mouth. "Different lore," he said, waggling his eyebrows, forgetting until he did that she could not

73

see, forgetting the space between them—the tangible and intangible gulfs.

They remained in silence, with the rain trailing off to a quiet, gentle stream, until it ultimately stopped altogether. He looped his arms around his knees and dropped his chin atop them. For in that moment, he was no longer Graham Linford, the Duke of Hampstead, and she Mrs. Bryant, widow, and now esteemed instructor at Mrs. Belden's, but rather, they were Graham and Rowena—as they'd always been.

"Graham?"

Her quiet voice brought his head up. His heart kicked up its beat. "Yes?"

"Thank you."

What had he expected her to say? What *was* there to say or offer? Useless apologies and explanations that would change nothing for either of them? His purpose in finding her whereabouts and bringing her to London had been one-fold: to have her serve as companion to a young lady shunned by all.

Sitting here, with her sharing the rooms next door, he readily admitted the truth that bringing Rowena Bryant to London might prove more perilous than any battle he'd ever faced.

He banged the back of his head silently against the wall.

EIGHT

The following morning, the sun shone with a blinding brightness through the dirty lead windowpanes. But for the occasional noisy gust of wind, the storm that had raged the countryside the night prior may as well have been nothing more than a nightmare.

Except, the midnight conversation with a man she'd spent years cursing for his faithlessness had been so very real it had stolen all sleep in ways no nightmare ever could.

Eyes swollen from her lack of rest, Rowena now sat on the same chair before the hearth she'd occupied yesterday afternoon with a plate of—she glanced down at the cracked porcelain plate and peered at the contents—of…of something that might or might not be fried eggs. She squinted. Well, if she were the wagering sort, she'd bet the coin she had that it was the roast vegetables from last night's meal fried.

The innkeeper's wife spoke. "Are you enjoying your potted beef, my lady?" Her question brought Rowena's head shooting up.

Potted beef? Puzzling her brow, Rowena reexamined her plate, and then lifted her gaze to the older woman. And it was fortunate she was not the wagering sort or she would have lost all her hard-earned coin. "Quite," she said, and forced herself to take a bite, smiling around the salty piece of meat. She forced her jaw to move, grinding the tough bit of beef. Picking up her napkin, Rowena dabbed at her lips. "It is splendid," she said, the lie coming out easily. Her mother, once one of the most sought after courtesans in London had flourished in the countryside, away from London, but she'd been a rotten cook. For the lousiness of this kindly woman's food, it was wonderful for the connection she felt to it. "Please, you may call me Rowena." Years of employment in Mrs. Belden's had stripped her of the identity she'd had as a nobleman's by-blow, leaving her a servant like so very many others. "I am not a "my lady," I am a mere Miss—*Mrs.*," she swiftly corrected. Approaching nine and twenty years, there was no longer anything missish about her. "And I'm employed by the duke."

The old woman, stained rag in hands, shot her eyebrows to her thinning hairline. "A duke," she murmured, sliding into the chair across from Rowena.

Yes, an all-powerful, coldhearted duke. Only, he was not the manner of man who announced that lofty position to innkeepers. Instead, he was one on the opposite end of a wall, distracting her from her fear of the storm in a move that was anything but coldhearted. "Yes, he is a duke, and I am a servant in his employ." Her cheeks warmed. "A companion for his ward," she hurried to explain, lest the woman believe her one of those indecent sorts instead of a woman who shared the blood of one. "There is nothing romantic at all between us," she added that last part for her benefit more than for the older woman.

Martha reclined in her chair and layered her arms along the wood. "I have seen the way that gentleman looks at you and you him. There is everything romantic in the way you watch at one another."

Rowena's skin burned ten shades hotter, and she damned her creamy white complexion that revealed those telling blushes. "You're wron—"

Martha leaned forward in her chair and the seat creaked in protest to the shifting weight. "My dear," she whispered, dropping her elbows on the table. "I entered this taproom last evening when you were speaking to the gentleman to offer you bread and ale, and God Himself running around my inn could not have interrupted your exchange." She finished her statement with a wink.

Then, that is how it had always been between her and Graham. When they were together, the world had ceased to exist except for them.

Martha settled a wrinkled hand on hers, patted it, and then, humming a discordant tune, slowly stood and resumed wiping down the tables. Alone once more, Rowena absently picked up her fork and pushed it around the questionable contents of her plate.

At one time, the woman would have been correct in her speculation about her and Graham. No longer. When he was at war, she'd written him note after note after note. Not a single one had been sent by him in return. She had been so delusional then she'd alternated between dread that something had befallen him and useless assurances to herself that his time and efforts didn't permit him the luxury of letter writing—even to the woman he'd vowed to wed upon his return.

In the months that had passed, the niggling doubt had grown. If he'd loved her and intended to make her his bride, why had he not done so before he left to fight Boney's forces?

At the end of the proverbial day, it was his father who ultimately severed the thread between her and Graham. His heir dead and Graham now elevated to that exalted position, the ruthless duke had ordered her gone or her family destroyed.

And even through that, allowing him to send her off like a shameful secret, hidden away at Mrs. Belden's, Rowena had clung to the hope. The hope that someday when he returned, that she could go to Graham, and he would be the hero she'd painted him to be in her mind. For the agony of being ripped apart from her family, she'd sustained herself with the hope of meeting him once more and hearing from his own mouth how much she, in fact, meant to him.

"I've not come to see you...I've come to see Graham..."

"I was instructed to give you this..."

With that perfunctory announcement, his father had turned over a note—in Graham's distinct hand. His non-looped joins of slightly slanted letterings hadn't contained words of love but rather an offer to make her his mistress. And a curt dismissal from his estate if she declined. In the end, she'd been fortunate to leave with a promise from the duke to preserve her post at Mrs. Belden's if she vowed to never darken their doorstep again.

That pledge had been far easier to give than the first she'd made him. For with that one, every last hope she'd carried for Graham had died a swift death.

Rowena stared blankly down at the crisply burnt eggs as nausea churned in her belly at the remembered shock and agony of taking that note in Graham's hand and discovering the truth. How easily he'd treat her as a doxy, not even to be spoken to or with—unless she bedded him. That pragmatic transaction, conducted through his father, demonstrating the same ruthless precision of Graham's note.

With trembling fingers, she set her fork down. Odd, for all the strength she'd prided herself on these years, for all the walls she'd built about herself and the assurances she'd made that, were she ever to see Graham again, she'd feel nothing more than an icy indifference. How wrong she'd been. Seeing him and reliving memories that were as fresh now as they'd once been reopened wounds she'd thought long-healed.

As if summoned by her ruminations, heavy footfalls sounded at the stairway and, moments later, Graham ducked slightly and entered the dark taproom. His gaze briefly landed on hers. Her heart thumped wildly. His cropped, midnight hair slightly damp hinted at a man who'd just finished his morning ablutions. Those gleaming strands accentuated the sharply chiseled planes of his face, lightly scarred on one cheek, but even more masculinely beautiful for it. A knowing smile danced at the corner of his lips, and he lifted his head in acknowledgement. Her body went warm at being caught staring, and she forced herself to return a slight, aloof gesture before attending her dish once more.

She braced for his approach as his footsteps neared, and then an inexplicable rush of disappointment assailed her as he continued walking.

His voice reached across the taproom. "Your accommodations have been exceptional, Martha," he praised. He referred to the old woman by her Christian name. Unlike his father, the vile Duke of Hampstead, who would have never dared address a servant. Nay, he'd never so much as look at one. She tried to make sense of the incongruity. The boy, Graham, who'd teased her in the gardens knew the names of servants and the pigs she'd named in her family's pen. The man who'd returned wouldn't even deign to meet a person outside his rank. Rowena curled her fingers. But then, even with his title of duke, he was always the charmer. And how very skilled he'd been at the game of pretend. Her ears picked up the dialogue between the still-conversing pair. "Allow me to thank you for your service and…"

"Surely you understand he cannot, given his eventual ascension to a duke-dom, marry one of your station."

Rowena glared at the all-powerful duke. "I don't care what you have to say about it. I am here to see Graham."

"My son asked I give you this."

Her skin burned with the weight of that heavy sack being placed in her palm. And had she been able to cry still, all these years later, this would have been the moment for those blasted drops. Alas, she'd shed her last tear the day she'd stalked off with that coin and note and hadn't mustered a single drop since.

"Mrs. Bryant." Graham's deep baritone slashed into her musings, and she slowly picked her head up. Unlike last evening, when he'd asked permission, now, he simply slid into the seat across from her.

The old innkeeper immediately shuffled over with a plate. With a smile for them, Martin set the dish down and moved on, leaving them their privacy.

A privacy she did not want. Not with this man. She cast a covetous glance at the doorway, eager to begin the journey. And then what? *I am a companion off to chaperone a young lady during her London season.* Would she again see the friends she'd left behind without so much as a note over the years to explain her absence? Or mayhap they'd not even truly cared that much, either. Her chest squeezed as her past continued creeping forward, threatening the fragile security she'd acquired. Rowena stole a peek at him. Sipping from his coffee, Graham passed a bored glance about their surroundings.

He was a model for cool aloofness, wholly unfazed by her presence, and she'd wager a man incapable of ever being daunted. Then, that had always been Graham. He'd been one who inspired confidence but always managed a smile. Or he had. The grim set of his mouth hinted at an older, more cynical figure. Had his time fighting been the cause of that change? Or had it been something else?

His gaze collided with hers. Cheeks burning, Rowena hastily dropped her stare to her plate. In a bid for nonchalance, she forced her mind to the present, thinking not of regrets of old but rather the task that lay before her. She took a small bite of unflavored eggs and chewed. How long would it truly be for a duke's charge to make a redoubtable match? Six months, at most? Until the end of the Season. As such, Rowena would endure, at most, one-hundred and eight days in Graham's household. She would offer tutelage to his ward, and he would carry on his ducal affairs. Their paths would only cross when she apprised him of Miss Hickenbottom's progress or accompanied him and his charge to *ton* events—where ladies no doubt clamored for the title of duchess.

An unwanted jealousy stirred low in her gut. She forced down the tasteless eggs.

Martin came forward, and she gave silent prayer for the old man's interruption. He filled Graham's glass.

"My thanks," Graham offered, smiling at the innkeeper.

It was petty and small and all things awful of her, but she despised this show of niceness for servants. Having schooled young ladies *below* Graham's lofty station, Rowena had been subjected to their derision and mockery. Yet, ever-charming, Graham spoke so easily to this older servant of the weather and the morning fare with the ease of a man talking to one of his same station. It was nothing more than a crafted façade that she herself had been so deceived by years earlier. And she hated that all these years later that same *false* regard was responsible for the admiration glittering in the old man's eyes. She gritted her teeth, the damning *click* resonating loudly.

Graham looked to her, a question in his eyes. She hastily averted her gaze and filled her mouth with a heaping spoonful of egg. The last thing she desired were questions of any kind.

He made a clearing sound, and she reluctantly looked up. "The carriage is readied."

She gave a slight nod, confirming she'd heard that announcement but something in his gaze froze her.

"Given my"—Graham skimmed the empty taproom and, even though finding it empty, dropped his voice to a quiet whisper— "episode yesterday afternoon…" He grimaced. "I will not impose my presence on you in the carriage. It is yours." The haunted glimmer in his eyes bespoke an altogether different gentleman than the carefree one who'd been chatting with the innkeeper.

She'd spent years wishing his life was as miserable as her own. Some of the fight went out of her. Despite her resentment of him, she never wanted to see his suffering. Not like this. Not in any way. "I'm not afraid of you, Graham." Not in the ways he worried about. "And I do not fear a carriage ride with you."

With a methodical precision, he continued as though she'd not spoken. "When we arrive in London, we'll have limited dealings." Which was as she preferred it, and yet…limited dealings? Rowena furrowed her brow. She would serve as companion to his ward. As though he followed the silent path her thoughts had traveled, he went on. "My days are primarily spent overseeing business affairs. My evenings are spent at *ton* functions." A pang struck. How very…empty his life sounded. *Not so very unlike mine…*She pushed aside the jeering reminder. "All dealings with my ward are handled by my man-of-affairs." He paused, and then added almost as an afterthought, "Any questions regarding the girl or concerns or questions, you will speak to Jack."

She jerked, feeling like he'd run her through. "Jack?" she echoed dumbly. Perhaps there was another. It was a common name. Even as she knew those hopes to be futile.

"Turner," he said casually. "I trust you remember Jack?"

Any other moment she would have fixed on that slightly jeering edge. Now she could hear nothing past the buzzing in her ears as he casually spoke about that *gentleman*. Another friend from long ago. They'd been so close, Jack had given them the name, "*Les trois Mousquetaires*." Cheerful, boisterous, and clever, he'd treated her no differently when she'd revealed the truth of her birth to him and Graham.

Until, he'd forced his kiss on her, proving precisely the manner of man he was. The bitter irony of it not lost on her in this moment. Graham had cut her so easily from the fabric of his life, and yet, remained friends with the same man who'd attempted to woo and win her in his absence. What would Graham say if he learned of that truth? As soon as the thought slid in, she scoffed. No doubt he wouldn't care. A man who'd had his father hand her a note with an offer to make her mistress was hardly a person who'd much bother with actions of a then twenty-year-old Jack Turner.

To give her trembling fingers a task, she forked another bite of egg into her mouth. The food sat heavy and flavorless on her tongue. Yes, Graham and Jack's friendship had carried on, while everything that had ever existed between her and Graham had been so easily thrown aside. She swallowed past the bitterness clogging her throat as reality intruded and washed away the shared intimacy of last night. The lie his father had forced her to fabricate. And, a young *widow* who upon his return from war, had rushed to see Graham, risking her post at Mrs. Belden's, he'd repaid that devotion by offering her nothing more than a place in his bed. On the heel of that came a slowly dawning realization: *does he know my past?* Did Graham's father break his oath and share the truth with Graham? If the world discovered she was not just a bastard but a whore's daughter, she'd never find respectable employment again. One whisper of the truth and the rug of security under her feet would be yanked free with no hope of employment.

Fighting back the fear swirling in her mind, Rowena drew in a deep breath. No. For, even with her bastardy, if Graham knew the whole truth, he'd certainly not force her into the post of companion to his ward. She instead focused on the immediate crisis within her control. She'd be damned ten times to Sunday before she answered to Jack. "No." Even she had her limits, and no demands Graham, Mrs. Belden, or God himself that challenged them would she blindly adhere to.

Graham paused, his glass halfway to his mouth. "I beg your pardon?"

She tried to determine any hint of emotion within that query, but he was an icy mold of his father just then. And that stark reminder gave her strength. "You've required I leave behind my post and serve in your household." His shoulders stiffened. Did he have qualms in hearing the truth stated aloud? Mayhap he did have a conscience after all. "*I* will set out my own terms of service, Your Grace." Rowena held her breath, braced for a seething fury. Instead, the ghost of a smile hovered on his lips. She squinted. Or was it merely a trick of the dim lighting?

Setting down his glass, Graham leaned back in his chair. That slight shift brought their knees touching under the table, briefly stealing her breath. *Don't be a silly girl where he's concerned...I am a woman...It's merely a leg. A long, heavily muscled—*

Graham winged a dark eyebrow.

She spoke on a rush. "You're the girl's guardian. Any questions I have, any matters requiring discussion, needs that must be met, I answer to you. No other." And certainly not Jack Turner. She'd sooner crawl across glass on bended knee to beg her parents to take her back than ever have any dealings with Jack again. The threat to her past would never go away, but this would be some small mastery over her future. Rowena angled her chin up, daring Graham to deny that claim.

He dusted a hand over his chin, contemplating her through thick, hooded lashes. Then, he let his hand fall to the table. "I should think you'd want as little time with me as possible, Mrs. Bryant."

Mrs. Bryant. She welcomed that barrier he willingly kept in place with that formal address. Her mind, however, raced with the seeds of questions contained within his inquiry. For the truth was, under any other circumstances, he was indeed correct; she didn't want anything more to do with him. Graham threatened her security and thrust all the oldest doubts and fears back to the surface. He, however, aside from the nightmare that had gripped him in the carriage, had never lifted a hand to her in violence. Nor did she believe he ever would. He was cool, unfeeling, and rigid, but not cruel in the way Jack had proven himself to be.

"Mrs. Bryant?" he prodded, leaning forward in his chair.

"You have a responsibility to Miss Hickenbottom," she said, settling on only one of the truths. "It was not Jack Turner who received guardianship...but you." At his silence, she made a desperate appeal. "If you do not agree with my terms, I can always return." She'd be spared from all possibility of any additional people learning the lies she'd built her life on. "Mrs. Belden will gladly see you with another instructor who—"

"No," he said brusquely, killing that fledgling hope. In a bid to spare herself Jack's company, she'd only traded one devil for the slightly less dangerous one. "It will be you." There was an air of ducal finality in that pronouncement that stirred both annoyance and unease.

What game did he play? Why was he so insistent that she be the one? Was it about a need for control and mastery over her?

Unnerved, Rowena shoved to her feet. "There is nothing further to discuss, then." Not now. Talks of her charge would come later, when she had regained control of her thoughts. With the stiff, practiced movements Mrs. Belden expected of her charges and instructors, she inclined her head. "I will leave you to your morning repast...Your Grace," she added, maintaining that much needed protective wall.

He frowned, the jagged scar at the corner of his mouth whitening at the movement. She dropped a formal curtsy and, turning on her heel, started for the carriage.

The sooner she arrived in London and began work with her charge, the better it would be for all involved. No. The safer it would be. For, then, Graham would be drawn back into his ducal responsibilities, and she would be the mere servant in his employ, and everything would resume just as it had been for the past eleven years.

And, then, she would be free of him, at last.

Except, as she allowed the liveried driver to hand her up, why did it feel as though she'd never truly be free of Graham Linford?

NINE

S he'd not spoken in the nearly two hours since his carriage had pulled away from the Fox and Hare Inn. Nay, to be precise... *they'd* not spoken.

In their time apart, Rowena had become...silent. She cloaked herself in a quiet that was safe for Graham's peace of mind, and beneficial for the model she'd set for Ainsley Hickenbottom. In several fleeting moments, she revealed glimmers of her former spirit. Prior to their departure, she'd put demands to him that since his father's passing, no single person, not even Jack, had dared to. She'd given him an ultimatum. In the crystal windowpane, his grinning visage reflected back. The first real smile he'd managed in...more years than he could remember.

His smile slipped. He craved a dignified, steady existence, so why did he want to see the lively Rowena unafraid to go toe-to-toe with him and not be the stoic stranger across from him? Shifting his focus from the passing countryside, Graham studied her now. Seated with her body stiffly held, Rowena's attention was reserved for the small leather book at her nose. The only sound in the otherwise silent carriage the rumble of the wheels and her periodic turn of a page.

The same thick tension that had blanketed the conveyance yesterday morn when they'd departed Mrs. Belden's remained as heavy today. If possible, even more so. It was as though there had been no shared discourse in the taproom about her family and the exchange between the wall had never happened. Which was as it should be.

The lady had been, in fact, correct. Who Rowena had transformed into, and what he had become—a mad-monster—had no bearing on her presence in his life now. She would serve the role of respectable companion and him, her employer. It was a mutually beneficial role grounded in logic, precisely as it drove Graham's every decision. Which is why he could not suffer another break in control and do something as outrageous as kiss her. *Even as I wanted to do so much more...*He thrust aside that mocking reminder dancing at the back of his mind. He'd become many things since he'd gone off to fight: a killer for the king, a detached, unfeeling lord. But even *he* had some scruples.

While they'd been living, his father and brother had both made a habit of bedding maids and servants in their family's employ. Graham had only been filled with loathing for *gentlemen* who'd take their pleasures with members of their staff. He'd vowed to never follow in the steps of either reprobate. As such, his and Rowena's shared past mattered not when presented with the role she now served as companion to Miss Hickenbottom. To touch her again put him in the same ranks as his lecherous kin, and it also defied the careful role of impassive duke he'd cultivated over the years. She was off-limits in every way. That reminder rang like a litany in his head.

A gust of wind knocked hard against the carriage, distracting him from his musings. The conveyance lurched, and with it the contents of Graham's stomach.

Hold tight, men...it's going down...

Graham drummed his fingers. *Taptaptap-tap-taptaptap-t—*

Rowena swiftly lowered the book. "Must you do that?" Annoyance danced in her eyes.

Yes, he really must. He battled back nausea and proved himself a shameless bounder, for cracking the wall of her indifference was vastly safer than giving in to the nightmares. "Forgive me," he murmured. She narrowed her eyes on his face. Did she seek the veracity of that apology? With a quiet grunt, she returned her attention to the book in her lap.

Her upside-down book. That endearing truth chased away the darkness tugging at the edges of his mind.

At the intent manner with which she devoted her attention to that page, a grin pulled the muscles of his lips up. His scar protested the strain of that unfamiliar movement. He swiftly smoothed the expression of mirth, making his face a careful mask. "You have an additional talent since I last saw you, Rowena," he dangled.

As though a rod were being inserted in the lady's spine, her back straightened, and she lifted her flashing gaze. "What—?"

Graham motioned to the small leather volume held in her hands. She jerked her gaze down and color exploded in her cheeks in an enchanting blush. Hastily, she flipped her book right-side up. Her eyes threatened to bore a hole through those pages. They did not, however, move.

Again, another smile pulled. She peeked over the top of her copy and then swiftly returned her gaze to that miserable tome. And he was left once again with the wind buffeting against the carriage. It swayed violently—

Taptaptap-tap-taptap—

Rowena swiftly snapped the book closed with a firm click and set the volume onto the bench beside her. "Have you become such a bored nobleman you must spend your time annoying me? Can you not ride outside as any polite gentleman would and allow a young woman, a young woman in your employ, the right to your carriage?"

"I was injured," he said quietly. His own shock stared back at him, in her eyes, and a dull heat climbed up his neck. His cravat suddenly tight, Graham tugged at the silk fabric. Where in blazes had that admission come from? It was a detail she, of course, would have known about him had she been there when he'd returned, broken and a day away from death. By that point, however, she'd already been married—one, two years?—to a man he'd never met. A man who'd not been besieged by madness, and one step from Bedlam.

Rowena opened and closed her mouth repeatedly. "What?"

Reclining in his seat, Graham gestured to his left thigh. "During battle, I was shot through the leg." He grimaced recalling the sharp pain that had brought him flying over his horse where his fall had been softened by the pile of dead soldiers stacked upon one another. That agony nothing compared to the bayonet plunged into his thigh by a Frenchmen who'd brought his blade back for another final thrust.

A blow that, had it not been for Hickenbottom, would have ended him. Absently, he rubbed the tight muscles of his thigh. That particular injury had landed him in a miserable field hospital fighting to retain his leg and his life. And in fate's mocking irony, his brother had succumbed to a wasting illness that very same week. That news had seen him plucked from the Continent and returned home to convalesce. His throat tightened, as all the oldest horrors whispered forward.

"Graham," she whispered, and that soft utterance brought him back from the brink. Her skin leeched of color, Rowena touched quivering fingers to her lips. "I knew you were…" She let her hand fall to her lap.

"What did you know?" he asked curiously, more than half-expecting her to decline answering.

"I knew you were injured." She'd known, and yet, she'd not come. Bitterness burned through him. Her gaze grew distant as she dropped her eyes to his leg. "I did not know how badly. That it causes you h-hurt still." That slight crack in her voice had the same affect her tears always had on him. The kind he'd cut himself open for if it would spare her that hurt.

That evidence of her caring moved something in his chest. For even though she'd broken her promise to him, he'd once loved her more than any other. The sight of her suffering would always cut him to the quick. He grinned wryly in the more familiar, empty expression of forced humor. "It hardly hurts." He lied for her benefit. The twisted and mangled flesh where the bullet and shrapnel had shredded him made him wholly useless in ways he'd always been in control.

A sad smile pulled at her lips. "You're a rotten liar, Graham Linford," she said, tossing back those familiar words they'd teased each other with as children long ago.

"Yes, well, it doesn't hurt nearly as much as it did when I"—his mouth hardened—"first returned."

With a handful of words, the barriers of their past went back up.

She angled herself toward the window and he believed she intended to end their discourse, but she simply fiddled with the red velvet curtain. "How little we know of one another anymore."

He scoffed. "Come, Rowena. We never truly knew one another," he taunted, wanting her to give him the fight he desired. So he could heap every deserved accusation upon her ears and damn her for the schemer she was.

Alas…she sat primly, hands folded upon her lap silent. Once again, she embodied the perfectly grim companion who, because of that hardness, would fit splendidly in his household. And damned if he did not want to shake that rigidity from her, too.

Refusing to let her determine the end of this volatile discourse between them, he leaned forward. "Tell me," he stretched out those two syllables. "Were you happy when I was gone?" When she met that with nothing more than a mutinous glitter in her eyes, he persisted. "Was Mr. Bryant," she flinched. "a devoted husband?" he asked, not knowing from whence the question came but needing to know the answer. Had there been happiness before life had found her cheated of a husband and forced to work in that cheerless finishing school? He was filled with resentment for both the failed Mr. Bryant and her for having ultimately chosen that unworthy bounder who'd left her reliant upon her role as instructor.

Fire lit her eyes, and he reveled in that glimpse of the Rowena Endicott of his past. "He was far more devoted than any gentleman I knew before him."

He jerked as that barb struck a mark. "He did not see you well-cared for, though, did he?" It was petty and cruel, this need to castigate her.

She lifted her chin a notch. "I don't require anything that any gentleman can give me, Graham. I have employment. I teach young ladies full of hopes and dreams. I've found my own security. What more could I want?"

I want at least five babes…

That was what she'd wanted. Graham wished he might have been the man to give her those dark-haired children with her fiery spirit. But that right had belonged to another and could have never belonged to him. He stared vaguely at the opposite carriage wall, as wonderings about her late husband knocked around his mind. In their short marriage, Mr. Bryant had not given her children, but he'd known both Rowena's heart and body in ways that made Graham want to gnash his teeth like an angry beast.

"What of you?" she began hesitantly, and where his inquiry had been intended to punish her and himself, Rowena's emerged calmly as if they were two friends discussing a past. "Have you been happy?"

He'd not known a single moment of peace or happiness since he'd marched off to war. Her face reflected in the windowpane revealed her tightly closed eyes. He wanted to spew lies about the grand time he knew in London as a duke. There had been countless widows and miserably married ladies to warm his bed as well as endless nights of entertainments. "I—"

The carriage lurched sideways, and his hoarse shout blended with Rowena's cry. Jolted from her seat, she flew forward, landing hard against his chest. She folded her arms about him as the carriage skidded and careened through the rain-slicked roads, and with every slide of the wheels, he was dragged deeper and deeper into the past. He clenched his eyes as his ears rang with the ping of bullets striking the conveyance. Penetrating the wood. Cutting down the men who'd saved him. Rowena gripped him hard, pulling Graham from the edge.

Then the carriage came to a jarring, miraculous stop.

Silence descended, punctuated by the heavy falls of their mingled breaths. She layered her cheek against his chest, and their hearts matched in a like, panicked rhythm.

With a curse, Graham ran his hands over her arms. "Are you hurt?" he asked as he continued his search lower down the curve of her hip. That searchingly intimate gesture seemed to penetrate her own fog. Rowena hurriedly pushed herself from his lap and scrambled onto the opposite bench. "Fine. I am fine." Was that faint, breathless quality of her whispered words a product of fear? Nervousness?

"Your Grace?" the driver called, that much needed reminder that they were not, in fact, alone. And that his driver had very nearly ended them on a muddied country road.

"By God, Hickley," he thundered. "There had better be a goddamn highwayman with a gun pointed at you to—"

"Sheep, Your Grace."

Graham yanked back the velvet curtains. More than fifty of the creatures bleated loudly as they picked their way slowly over the old Roman road. A long stream of curses that would have shocked a weaker woman left his lips.

It would appear they were stuck.

They were to be stuck here, then.

Fate was a cruel master with a vicious sense of humor that would not quit where she and Graham were concerned.

Leaning around him, Rowena glanced over his shoulder to the enormous herd blocking the road. "Sheep, indeed," she said under her breath.

The driver pulled the door open, spilling sunlight into the conveyance. "Aye, Your Grace. We'll not be going anywhere, any time soon." By Graham's darkening expression, he was as pleased as Rowena with the sudden change of their circumstances. At least they were of a like opinion on that matter.

"How long?" Graham's terse question raised a grin from the older servant.

"If I knew such details, I'd not have lost a heavy purse to the old innkeeper last evening."

While Graham and his driver proceeded to discuss the remaining course of the journey, Rowena squinted and stared out into the bright morning sunlight at the lush green earth slick with yesterday's rains. Hickley and Graham's voices grew distant as a memory trickled forward of her and Graham as they'd sat atop the stone wall around her family's modest cottage.

A sad smile played on her lips. When her mother married the vicar of the Duke of Hampstead's parish, Rowena, for the first time had left London and found a home in the countryside. Every aspect of the green meadows and blue skies had fascinated her. She'd traipsed through the hills, exploring everything and anything. It had been one

91

of those joyful summer afternoons laying within a field of bluebells that two boys, Graham and Jack, and come upon her. They'd become the first friends she'd ever known. One of those boys would ultimately become her lover and sweetheart.

How many times had they lain on their backs in the sunlight, picking shapes out of the clouds, and when the night sky rolled in, searching for shooting stars on which to wish? In the end, it had all been taken from her. She looked over at Graham. This perplexing man who alternated from gently inquiring about her past one moment to surly stranger the next. Her smile fell as melancholy swept her.

The driver's high-pitched squeal slashed into her useless self-regret. "Gah." He darted away, so quickly the cap tumbled from his head. The older servant abandoned that garment as four more sheep idled over to inspect the offending hat.

Her lips twitched, and she cupped her hands around her mouth. "They are not dangerous," she reassured the servant. Generally docile, they spent most of their days eating, and when they weren't eating, they spent the remainder of their days grazing...and sleeping.

"You're the only girl I know who'd prefer a sheep to a dog or cat."

"And you know so many girls, Graham Linford?"

"Only one who matters."

Her skin pricked with the heat of his gaze. Did he remember that moment of long ago? Or had he relegated her to the same place he had all the women who'd warmed his bed? She gripped the strings of her reticule in a painful hold. Yet if she hadn't mattered to him in even some small way, why should he show such vitriol when speaking of the husband she had fabricated for her security? Carefully avoiding his gaze, she gave thanks as Hickley dashed back and retrieved his cap.

"Well?" Graham urged his servant.

The older man jammed his cap back on. "I suspect we'll be here a couple of hours, at least, Your Grace." He spoke with an air of finality. "Though there really is no saying..." That reminder hung ominous in the conveyance.

Again, pushing back the curtain, Rowena shielded the sun from her eyes and attended the large flock, grazing in the middle of the road. Of course, a gentleman and a servant who'd not had experience with sheep and other livestock would not think of shepherding those creatures. She fixed on the sheep. Moving livestock was far easier than sitting here with Graham, having the bandages ripped from old, never fully healed wounds. A duke and his driver could sit here and wait for a flock to pass. She, however, had little intention of waiting until more than fifty creatures decided to graze in some other field. After all, it was one thing to be forced to take up residence in Graham's house for the whole of a year. His townhouse was surely one of those massive, sprawling homes where he would have little interactions with a servant in his employ. It was, however, quite another thing to be in the confines of this suddenly cramped conveyance, delving back into those days he'd returned from war when she'd been a relatively new employee at Mrs. Belden's. Missing him. Loving him. Desperately needing distance, Rowena grabbed her small woolen sack and shoved the door open. Stepping down, her heels immediately sank into the thick mud, soaking her ankles.

Yanking first one boot from the dense earth, she took an awkward, lurching step forward. Her bag dangled and twisted in a back and forth half-circle as she waded through the sea of sheep. They dispersed in opposite directions.

Graham fell into step beside her.

She gasped and slapped her bag against her chest. How did a man so broadly powerful move with such stealth? His driver moved forward with all the enthusiasm of one marching to the guillotine, and Rowena gave thanks for his company. Company that would spare her from any further explosive discussions of the past.

"There is no need," Graham assured the older servant, stopping the man quickly in his muddied tracks. "Mrs. Bryant and I are quite adept at tending sheep." Her heart tripled its beat. Why must he be so amiable with servants and his staff? That contradictory sentiment so at odds with the man who'd reared him, and the final letter he'd given her. Then the significance of his words registered.

He remembered.

For his seeming aloofness and his absolute lack of regard and loyalty all these years, he'd recalled those innocent exchanges of long ago.

After the servant had wandered back to the carriage, Graham shifted his piercing focus back to her. "Tell me, Rowena," he said, his baritone hushed. "are you still skilled with livestock?" There was a faintly teasing quality to that inquiry that startled her. As an all-powerful duke, she'd believed him incapable of that sentiment. His father certainly hadn't possessed anything but a requisite ducal coldness.

"It was two sheep," she murmured, brushing her palm along the soft, downy back of one sheep. Hope and Faith. Silly names, given by a silly girl. Her hand curled involuntarily. Startled, the ewe bolted sideways. Yet Graham remembered her beloved sheep. Remembered that she'd been hopelessly enchanted by those two south down sheep in her family's paddock. Why should he, a man who'd not given another thought to her after he'd left, recall that? And yet, talk of livestock and shepherding a flock of sheep was far safer than any mention of her earlier admission...and their past.

He clapped his hands, and a handful of the docile creatures wove a path to the edge of the lake.

Unabashedly, she studied him as he shepherded the flock, deepening her consternation. "You don't strike me as a gentleman who would take to driving sheep through a muddied road, Your Grace." It was a scandalous act that the late duke would have sooner lopped off his hands than take part in. He would have required the driver, regardless of that man's fear, see to the task before ever muddying his boots and hands.

Not bothering to look at her, Graham patted the top of a fawn-colored ewe, and the creature bolted off. "I fought soldiers over the Continent," he said dryly. "Sheep certainly do not scare me, Rowena." Rowena, not Mrs. Bryant. How easily he commanded her name, and yet, in this instance, even with the past a dark barrier between them—it felt right.

94

She paused in the middle of the road to look at him. The sheep parted around her and continued their slow grazing path forward. "I did not presume you'd be afraid of them. I thought it would be beneath you." *Just as I was. Nay, just as I will always be.*

Graham looked up from his task. The sunlight heightened those flecks of gold dancing in his eyes. "I became a duke, not a pompous bastard." He followed that with a wink that sent her belly flip-flopping. That slight intentional twitch of his dark lashes marked him more man than aloof nobleman.

She gave silent thanks when he abandoned his teasing and resumed his efforts. While she worked, Rowena, from the corner of her eye, took in his every step. Periodically, he'd brush his hand gently over a nearby sheep and those notoriously skittish creatures lingered for an additional stroke. It was a tangible reminder of the ease he had always been in possession of with her, and any man, woman, or child of any station or status.

Not another word was said as they worked silently together side-by-side to clear the sheep.

They continued herding the flock, making a path for the carriage to pass. And for any passerby who might have happened upon them, they may as well have been any married couple. He, with his jacket since removed and his shirtsleeves rolled up, and she with her cloak and jacket tossed aside. Her throat convulsed as a longing she'd thought not only dead but safely buried stirred in her breast. For that was what she'd wanted not only for herself...but for them. A life together. She'd been so blasted naïve she'd not acknowledged that her past would always have been a barrier between them. That whether he'd been born a duke's first, second, or fifteenth son, she would have never been a suitable wife for him. Now, if she returned with him she risked not only the agony of resurfacing old memories but the peril of her past being discovered.

Then what will I be? What became of such a woman, then? Nothing that was proper.

While she wrestled with unwanted regrets and old aches, he strode forward, quietly clapping his hands and dispersing the flock. Rowena moved along more slowly behind him, guiding away the stragglers hovering on the roadside. Until, at last, the road was cleared. Pressing her hands to her lower back, she arched the muscles, stiff from two days' traveling and now their efforts in the fields.

"You've done it, Your Grace," the driver called from the distance, lifting his joined hands together in salute. He pulled the door open and waited.

Graham mopped his damp brow with the back of his forearm. "I must attribute the credit to Mrs. Bryant," he returned.

The driver's reply was lost to her as she lingered her gaze on that open door. Even in the distance, the sun gleamed brightly off the lion crest emblazoned on the black lacquer carriage. That same seal etched on the note written by Graham's father...and then, when he'd ascended to the role, Graham himself. That gold mark of his wealth and power, a reminder of who she was and all the reasons she could not serve on his staff. Nay, did not want to serve on his staff. Somewhere between the reality that had slammed into her and him joining her in the field, she'd accepted the folly in working for him. She had worked so hard to become the dragon, and with every argument...every slight grin or caress or embrace, he was singlehandedly tearing that away.

As Graham shrugged into his jacket, Rowena wandered over to the small boulder she'd rested her belongings on and picked up her cloak. Draping it over her arm, she reached for her bag.

"Rowena," Graham, began quietly, and there was no hint of the earlier camaraderie with the servant thirty paces away. "We should—"

"I should not come with you, Graham." He abruptly stopped. "With my..." She grimaced. "...Past, it is not a place I should be." It was the safest excuse to give him. One that neither revealed the weakening effect he still had on her nor made mention her shameful past. "Your charge deserves a more respectable companion." Her secrets would always be a threat that lurked. And yet...why did it feel like the reason she gave him was one of the grandest lies she'd ever told?

"Of course you can," he said gruffly, starting back for the carriage. His tone and dismissal indicating he considered the matter at an end.

Why must he be so tenacious in this? He was one of the most powerful men in all of England…Why should he not find another? "I have no place chaperoning your ward," she persisted. "You know that. I am asking you to let me return to my post and resume my life." *Please.* Because then she could forget how he'd always caused a dangerous fluttering in her belly and a more perilous one within her heart.

"Do not be foolish," he said brusquely, the cool veneer of duke back in place. A muscle twitched at the corner of his eye. "I know no such thing." He closed the distance between them; his rapid movements kicking up gravel. "It hardly matters to me that"—her heart knocked hard against her ribcage—"you're illegitimate." He didn't know. That much was clear in the absence of those words. "I'd not judge Miss Hickenbottom for her parentage, and I never did you."

Rowena worked her gaze over his face. "Why, Graham? Why, of all the women you can hire would you ask me—?"

"Because you are the best—"

"Bah, the best," she interrupted, waving a hand about. Why did he truly want her there? Was it to mock her? "You are a *duke*," she said with an achingly painful laugh. "Dukes hire the finest, nobly connected individuals." He opened his mouth. "And do not tell me it is because your ward is a bastard. No one would dare refuse your employment."

Just as I had been unable to. The words rang as clear as if they'd been hurled at him.

The muscles of his face briefly contorted. Did he feel guilt? Good. He should, for forcing either of them to feel *anything* again. "The nobles without heavy pockets send their daughters to finishing schools. The instructors who work there are respectable women, but not noble ones, who are down on their luck."

"Is that what you were? Down on your luck?" At the harsh quality to his deep baritone, her insides knotted.

Rowena's body burned ten degrees warmer. She wasn't the self-pitying sort. That useless sentiment had gotten her nothing through the years, and she'd resolved to never give over to it. "Do not sidestep what I'm saying."

"And do not disparage yourself," he said somberly, and she jerked.

"I'm not." Only the protestation felt weak to her own ears.

Graham gathered her hands, and gave a slight squeeze forcing her eyes to his. "You look at yourself, Rowena, and see nothing more than your parentage. You see your birthright and find yourself wanting because of it." Damn him for being in this instance more than a faintly mocking nobleman.

What did he know about what it was to go through life an outcast because of circumstances of one's birth? "Not me," she gritted out. "Society would find me wanting should they know." She wrenched her hands free. It was and would always be the way of their world.

"You are far more worthy than any other woman, regardless of station," he continued, relentless. "Do not decline the position for that reason."

She damned the quickening of her heart. For just now, he was the same young man she'd confided partial truths to, who'd not judged her, then...and who didn't judge her now. What fool did he take her for?

Graham sighed, and looked past her shoulder for a long while before speaking. "If you wish to return to Mrs. Belden's, I will order the carriage around and seek a new woman for the post."

She started. He would do that?

Noblemen had proven themselves singularly focused on their own wishes and desires. His offer defied everything she knew of those powerful peers—himself included in that mix—until now.

He offered her everything she'd wanted since he'd reentered her life. So why did the prospect of returning to Mrs. Belden's leave her hollow inside? "It would be for the best," she said hollowly. Were those words for her benefit? Or his?

Graham gave a curt nod and glanced about, settling his gaze on those sheep they'd worked together to clear from the path.

Rowena fiddled with her drawstring bag. Those letters she'd carried for the whole of her adult life practically burned a hole through the worn fabric. *Go. He's offered me freedom. Take that gift.*

She started when he settled a large hand briefly upon her shoulder in a fleeting contact. "We were once friends." They'd been so very much more than that. He shifted his gaze to hers. Those green depths wiser and older than they'd been—eyes befitting a man who battled demons now. "I do not expect we can ever go back to…the way we once were, and I understand you moved on with your life long ago."

Moved on. Bitterness stung her throat like acid. He spoke as though the decision had been hers, when the truth is since she'd drawn her first breath, she'd been without any power—any power except for that which she'd shaped for herself at Mrs. Belden's.

Again, life had taught her a healthy wariness. "What do you want?" she asked guardedly.

"You can leave, if you wish. Return." *And never see me.* That hung unspoken, as loud as if he'd shouted it into the barren countryside. Yes. That was what she wanted. Didn't she? "I have no right to ask you for any favor." But he'd ask it anyway. "Miss Hickenbottom has not…" He sighed. "She's not had an easy time of it." A rake's by-blow, it would only become worse once she entered Society's unkind fold.

I was that girl he speaks of. As a small child whispered about when she'd visited Hyde Park with her mother. And then as a young girl with a mother who'd married, Rowena had found herself on the outskirts of even her own family. She felt a weakening and fought it. Damn him. Damn him for making this not about him, or her, but another person—one treated with the same unkindness she herself had known.

"I ask that you meet her," Graham compelled. "If you enter my household and decide you no longer want the post, you are free to leave, with a two-thousand-pound severance."

Rowena choked. "Two thousand pounds?" For simply meeting the girl? At his nod, her mind raced. She could secure a small life of anonymity away from the world. Away from her past as a courtesan's daughter. Away from the drudgery of working in miserable Mrs. Belden's employ. It was a small fortune that would see her cared for forever.

It was, however, still money Graham would pay over, however, for services she'd never rendered. Part of her wanted to say damn her pride and take the funds and get herself off to the life of obscurity she craved. Yet—Rowena closed her eyes briefly. She'd always had too much dignity.

Had he uttered anything else…about their past, his faith in her abilities, or praising platitudes, it would have been easier to board that carriage and order him to return her to Mrs. Belden's. But he hadn't. He'd issued nothing more than a request, with his charge's best interests in mind.

Why had she always been weak where he was concerned?

"I will meet her."

Her own shock was reflected back in his eyes. He gave a juddering nod. "Thank you."

As they began the slow trek back to the carriage in silence, she couldn't help the pebble of unease in her belly that said she'd made a grave mistake where Graham was concerned—yet again.

TEN

They arrived in London late that afternoon.

Following a bath and a change of garments, Graham had immediately sought out his office where he'd since buried himself in his ledgers and correspondences. Over the years, work had brought him an empty—albeit vital—succor. In shaping himself into an austere duke with a rigid control over his affairs, he had discovered a peace that he desperately clung to. One that he'd had a tenuous grip on these past days since Rowena's reemergence.

Now, in his own home and removed from her, he welcomed the serenity that came in attending his ducal affairs. Here, in the quiet of his offices, reviewing reports of his landholdings and business ventures, his mind was clear. There were no demons. There was no remembered suffering or loss. There was no Rowena. There was simply the mindlessness that his responsibilities brought. Muscles stiff from, first, a long carriage ride, and then his stillness these past hours, he rolled his shoulders, attempting to bring a normal bloodflow back through his arms.

This was where he found his strength.

Snapping his ledger shut, Graham reached for the tall stack of correspondences that had been lain upon his desk, awaiting his return.

He scanned the invitations to various balls and soirees. As a duke's son and now a duke himself, there'd never been an absence of requests. He was not so arrogant that he didn't see that even with his title the *ton* would be waiting to sharpen their teeth on Hickenbottom's daughter. With that in mind, he made two piles: *Safe Events with Somewhat Benign Lords and Ladies*. And the *Ruthless Others*.

Graham tossed sheet after sheet into the stack of declinations.

A long while later, every single missive had been filed and organized so that two distinctly different ones existed side by side.

With his thumb and forefinger, he measured the heap of rejections, and then reducing the wide stretch of his fingers, took in the much smaller acceptances. Doors would be opened to his ward, but there could be no denying that Ainsley Hickenbottom would also face great unkindness.

...Society would find me wanting should they know...

Rowena's words spoken in the countryside whispered around his mind. She'd known Society's cruelty. Had been made to feel less worthy, but it was as she'd said...Society was the one bearing that opinion of all those born on the other side of the blanket. It was the way of their world. And, by God, how he hated the world for it. For her... and now Hickenbottom's daughter. It served as a reminder of why no other companion could or would ever do for the girl. Rowena would understand those struggles in a way no other could.

If she stays...

He had put to her a generous offer that could see her gone tomorrow if she so decided. As much as he resented the truth...he needed her here—for Ainsley. Even if having Rowena back in his life tried him in ways that only the battlefields of the Peninsula previously had.

Absently, he picked up the deeper stack of invitations, those sheets of vellum heavy in his hand. Until now, this manner of guests and events were the only ones he sought out: emotionless, ruthless peers who would never look past the cool façade he'd perfected.

Now, he'd be drawn into an altogether different sphere: smaller affairs, intimate ones with lords and ladies with dubious pasts and a propensity for niceness for it. Or as Society deemed it: weakness. In their world, it was all the same.

A knock sounded at the door, and his gaze immediately swung to the doorway. *Rowena.* The same surge of anticipation he'd always known where she was concerned rushed through him. "Enter," he called out, tossing the stack down. It hit the surface with a noisy thump.

The door opened, and his butler filled the entranceway. Disappointment chased away that earlier excitement. His butler, and another person, Lady Serena's father.

"The Duke of Wilkshire to see you, Your Grace."

Belatedly, Graham climbed to his feet. "Wilkshire."

Wesley backed out of the room, leaving the two dukes alone. Nearing his seventieth year and in possession of a monocle and crop of silver hair, Wilkshire fit in every way the image of a duke…right down to his crisp, condescending tones.

"Returned at last, have you?" The other man stalked over and, uninvited, settled his lean frame into an open seat.

Graham reclaimed his chair and fixed a deliberately cool grin on his lips. "Come to verify with your own eyes, Wilkshire?" He intended to marry the man's daughter, but he'd certainly not make apologies for seeing after his responsibilities toward Hickenbottom's daughter. Who, with Rowena's help, would be flawless and escape some of the scathing criticisms against her.

Lord Wilkshire snorted. "My sources are reliable enough that I'd not bother to waste a visit unless I was certain of your presence."

Something else had brought the man, then. Of course. Wilkshire never made any move without deliberate intent. Even the formal arrangement he'd been working through with Jack had demonstrated a military precision, grounded in business and devoid of emotion. It was why their families—Graham's future betrothed included—were ideal matches, in every way. "The *ton* has been remarking on your absence."

Graham leaned back and settled his palms along the arms of his chair. "The *ton* remarks on everything." A fortnight. It had been a fortnight since he'd retreated to oversee to far more important matters than societal events.

Wilkshire dipped his eyebrows in the only visible show of his anger. "They do not, however, remark on anything unfavorably about my daughter. Until now."

No, Society wouldn't have. A Diamond of the First Water who'd only made her Come Out after a year mourning the late Duchess of

Wilkshire, she'd been heralded as the *ton's* leading beauty and the most heavily dowered, sought-after debutante. As cold as she was mercenary, she was Graham's perfect emotionless match.

Why did that suddenly turn his mouth sour?

"Nothing to say, hmm?" Only Wilkshire could make a casually spoken question emerge as a frosty command.

"I've had matters to attend to with my ward."

"The bastard," the duke opposite him supplied. As though there could be another ward. As though Ainsley's parentage needed to be inserted into their discourse.

Society would find me wanting should they know...

This was why Rowena had spoken as she had. Not solely because of her own self-confidence but because of men like the one before Graham now. His fingers curled reflexively into the aged leather, leaving crescent marks upon the fabric. "Why don't you say what it is that's brought you here," he said in frosty tones.

"I'm here to determine whether your business is more important than a potential match with my daughter."

With the old duke's frequent use of "my daughter," Graham sometimes wondered if Wilkshire even knew the lady's name. Then, a single word in that statement registered. *Potential match.* Nothing formal had been agreed upon. No contracts signed. Rather Jack and the duke had entered into discussions the way they might any business dealing. Which is what Graham's someday marriage with Lady Serena would be. He'd accepted that as fact...wanted it to be. Didn't he? He fought the urge to dig his fingertips into his temples and rub the deuced ache that niggling of doubt caused.

"What, nothing to say?" Wilkshire snapped. "Every damned lord in London wants to wed my girl." He crossed his ankle over his opposite knee. "And I'm not pleased with any business you've deemed more important than her."

"All my business is of equal import, Wilkshire." Graham stretched those syllables out in icy tones. "I'm methodical in *all* my dealings." In that regard, a marriage of convenience would be no different than any other of his pursuits.

Lady Serena's father stared on through that quizzing glass, and then grunted. "It is why I approve of you." He smiled coolly. "And because you're a duke." The older man rose. "I'll assure my daughter, then, that your intentions are still the same."

There was a question there. Graham attempted to force out a confirmation in the affirmative. No words, however were forthcoming...or by the duke's next words, necessary. Wilkshire stood, and Graham followed suit. "Now that you've returned, my daughter intends to host a card party as a way to meet your..." His lip peeled back. "ward."

Any other moment, one of those mundane affairs would have been ideal for him to attend. The idea of bringing Ainsley and Rowena into that household to face that derision set his teeth on edge. "I will be looking forward to the invitation," he offered instead.

On that, Lady Serena's probing father took his leave. That brief, curt meeting speaking volumes about the duke's expectations and also his limitations.

Whereas prior to his departure for Spelthorne he'd been of a like mindframe, now he felt a healthy annoyance: at Wilkshire's high-handedness and the speed with which he sought to push the match.

It is what I want. If I wed Lady Serena, I can be rid of Rowena and all Ainsley Hickenbottom's care would fall to my wife. It was a suitable conclusion for all parties involved.

Except Ainsley.

And now me...

Unnerved by that taunting voice, he forced himself back into his chair. What rubbish. "Of course, I don't care either way," he muttered under his breath. Restless, he grabbed the small pile of events he'd attend with Ainsley...and Rowena.

"Have you gone and sacked your man-of-affairs?"

The stack slipped from his fingers, and Graham shot his head up. His ward, Miss Hickenbottom, stood in the doorway, her skirts tied up, revealing her breeches and work boots. Graham said a silent prayer of thanks for Rowena's presence. Though she still had not committed to the role. Where he craved control, the unconventional chit before him robbed him of any order. *I have to convince her that being in my household and working with a troublesome charge is preferable to life at Mrs. Belden's.*

The young girl arched an insolent eyebrow.

"Miss Hickenbottom," he greeted, coming to his feet.

Uninvited, his ward shoved her heel against the heavy wood panel, and it shook in the frame. Graham jumped at the sudden bang. His mouth went dry. *It is just the door…It is just the door…*

"I thought you were off seeing to roguish business," Miss Hickenbottom said cheerfully skipping over, and that clear chipper sing-song penetrated the hell pulling at the corner of his thoughts.

"My…?" He instantly clamped his lips closed. His roguish days were long, long behind him, and regardless, any topic pertaining to a rogue, rake, or scoundrel were never fit discussion for a lady—regardless of age.

"That is what I called it when my father would leave," she explained, as though schooling a child on a too-complex principle. His ward flopped into the seat and sprawled one leg over the arm of her chair. "Visiting, you know, brothels. Bordellos. Gaming hells. Those." She swung her dusty boot back and forth.

Graham tugged at his cravat. "I am no rogue." He had been, bedding wicked widows and unhappy wives, all eager for a tumble with a *war hero* turned duke. And all because he'd been so broken with Rowena's perfidy. Agony sliced at his heart.

"My father said every gentleman is a rogue."

Usually, a bother he knew not what to do with, now his ward proved a diversion from the turbulent emotions rioting inside him. No doubt Hickenbottom was smiling from his grave at the hoyden he'd left Graham. Couldn't the other man have provided the girl with even a modicum of propriety? If Rowena weren't committed to leaving before, the absolute hopelessness of the task he'd set her would certainly be the death knell. Then again, if anyone could guide the hoyden, his wager was on her. "I was not at a gaming hell." He neatly avoided mention of those other scandalous places no young girl should know of. "I was—"

She stopped her abrupt swinging, and leaned forward in her seat. "What are you doing?" Before he could respond, she grabbed his pile of invitations and flipped through them. She paused mid-shuffle. "So who is the Duke of Wilkshire?"

The coolly unaffected Duke of Hampstead's cravat went tight. He gave it a tug.

"Well?" Miss Hickenbottom prompted. "Never tell me?" she supplied when he wasn't quick enough to speak, which was all and fine as he didn't have a suitable reply. "Two powerful dukes who intend to cement their power over the peerage by your marrying the miserable blighter's equally miserably daughter." His perceptive ward burst into laughter.

This was how every exchange went with this young person who'd invaded his household. She would enter in a whirlwind. He would sit, neck burning, speechless through her questioning. She would leave, and he would go on with his business, praying someone would come and deal with the girl. Except today. Now, she remained.

Ainsley abruptly stopped and wiped tears of mirth from her eyes. "Egads, I was correct, wasn't I?"

"I don't intend to discuss my personal affairs with you, Miss Hickenbottom," he said in curt tones meant to ebb the flow of her questioning, which would have effectively quieted anyone else.

She wrinkled her nose. "You're in a surly mood." He was always in a surly mood. "More than usual," she added, perceptively having read his thoughts. Then, narrowing her stare on his face, she probed him further. "Does this have to do with the fancy piece who arrived in your carriage earlier this afternoon?"

Graham choked on his swallow, gasping for air. "I assure you, she is no fancy piece." Just a companion, whom he desperately needed to speak to before introducing her to Miss Hickenbottom. A person needed to be prepared for her hoydenish spirit. If one could ever truly be prepared. "She is a lady," he settled for.

His ward released an inelegant snort. "Undoubtedly."

He frowned. Years earlier he'd have been deserving of that skepticism. He'd not been a man given to emotion and ill-decision since. "She is to be your companion."

Miss Hickenbottom ceased swinging her leg and settled both feet on the floor. "Truly?" Her hazel eyes formed saucers. "You found one who'll brave the post?" she asked, waggling her eyebrows, but he'd survived enough battles on the Peninsula that he'd come to note the details of all around him. She'd been lonely. It was there in every desperately eager feature on her rounded face.

I was lonely. Until you, Graham Linford.

Rowena's long-ago whisper against his lips caused a dull ache in his chest. Had that loneliness driven her into the arms of another man? Or had she always been that fickle with her heart? Those questions continued to flood his consciousness in a way that could only be perilous for his sanity. So why not let her leave as she wished? Why ask her to stay? Because of Ainsley. And yet, why did that only ring partially true? He cleared his throat. "I will coordinate a visit on the morrow after Mrs. Bryant has rested. Now, I am..."

His ward resumed studying his notes. With a boldness not even the queen would have dared, Ainsley hurled them at him. They fluttered noisily about, scattering the surface of his desk and disrupting the stack of rejections. He quickly set to organizing them.

"Hmph," she muttered, as he worked.

Hmph, what? Withholding the questions...but really..."What?" he asked brusquely.

"I just wouldn't have taken you for one who'd tolerate another duke making demands of you." So she'd been listening at the keyhole. Should he expect anything else of her? "Is she to be your bride?"

Good God, why had he given Rowena the remainder of the day off? Why hadn't he insisted that she meet her charge and keep her close? Yes, the sooner he was married off to Serena and his ward was married off to any respectable gentleman, the sooner he could resume living in a logical, well-ordered existence.

"I've matters to attend." Graham stood. "If you'll excuse me?" he said quickly.

Alas his obstinate ward remained seated. She gave her head a slight shake.

Bloody hell. He reclaimed his seat. Dropping his elbows on the surface of his now-cluttered desk, he leaned forward. "All right. I trust you haven't come here to discuss my marital affairs. What is it?"

She matched his pose. "Turner's been by the past two mornings looking for you."

Which was not uncommon. Since Jack had witnessed his fits of madness, he'd become protective. And though he appreciated that loyalty and friendship, Graham chafed at having his every move scrutinized and questioned. "And?"

The girl hesitated...when there was nothing ever reluctant about her. She reached inside the cleverly sewn pocket along the front of her gown. Ainsley tossed a folded sheet of vellum in front of him. "He brought this."

Graham puzzled his brow. Picking up the officious document with its cracked seal—a broken seal indicating his private correspondence had already been read—he unfolded it. And he gave thanks for the mask of indifference he'd perfected over the years. His stomach sank.

"I didn't want to go to Almack's anyway," Ainsley assured him, sprawling back in her chair.

He didn't know how much he believed the girl. What he did know, however, was the importance of that introduction to Society. An introduction she'd been denied by the *esteemed* hostesses, Lady Jersey and Lady Sefton and distinguished others. Those bloody arbiters of a lady's fate. Clearing his throat, he neatly folded the page and set it down. "Miserably dull affairs anyway." Ones that even he, with his desiring of an orderly existence, hadn't put himself through. Not for the first time, selfish bastard that he was, Graham damned his late friend. Life had been vastly safer and more preferable when his only worry was the image he presented to the world, and the only events he sought out were the ones that maintained his reputation of aloof, austere duke.

"Oh, undoubtedly," Ainsley concurred, again swinging a leg back and forth.

"Consider yourself fortunate."

"Regardless of Almack's, you now have a companion." Rowena. His stomach tightened. How very odd and wrong to speak of her as though she were nothing more than a servant in his employ. But then, wasn't that what she was? "And we'll begin introducing you to Society." Beginning with Lady Serena's intimate card party.

"That really isn't necessary."

Absolutely it was. If he wanted to go back to the routine that was his life where he wasn't forced to confront the memories of his past—or worry after Ainsley's future. Where he could simply exist in a cold, emotionless state. That was why her entry into Society was so damned important. Not wishing to further discuss in any depth, way, or form Ainsley's exclusion by the leading patronesses of Society, not when it stirred a dangerous anger that could never be good for his calm, Graham inclined his head. "If you'll excuse me? I've matters to attend." Which wasn't an untruth. With his landholdings, and the sizeable number of tenants and staff dependent upon him, there were always responsibilities he had to see to.

Ainsley hopped up. "Oh, very well, Duke. Until tomorrow."

Until tomorrow. Those words lingered after she'd gone.

For now, there were people, people outside of Jack, that he had to share his home with…Ainsley—Rowena. People he had to speak to and worry after. And feel things about. A cold sweat beaded on his brow.

Picking up his brandy, Graham took a much-needed drink. He'd survived war with the French. Surely he could manage to muddle through this.

ELEVEN

Rowena's steps fell silent upon the carpeted halls as she followed the butler Wesley for her meeting with Graham.

By rights, she should be well-rested. After their arrival yesterday afternoon, Graham had allowed her the remainder of the day to herself. She'd welcomed a warm bath in her new, extravagant chambers... chambers vastly fitting a duke's esteemed guest and not a courtesan's daughter-turned-finishing school instructor. She'd enjoyed a meal that was not over-salted and under-seasoned like Cook's at Mrs. Belden's. And after having moved livestock across the English countryside, she should have been suitably fatigued.

Except, last evening, sleep had eluded her. Rest had been impossible. Instead, she had lain in the grand, gold silk-papered room, contemplating sharing the walls of this Grosvenor Square townhouse... with him. She'd buried all thoughts of Graham Linford in the far recesses of her mind, battling back those infrequent musings when they would sometimes surface. She hadn't wanted to think about him and his inconstancy, or how he'd broken her heart. The only purpose in thinking of him had been to remind herself why she needed no one and why it was far safer to trust no one than let anyone in.

Somewhere between the moment she'd lain upon that massive four-poster bed, staring up at the mural overhead and the moment she'd been summoned for a meeting with Graham, Rowena had accepted the truth: she could not accept the post. She could not remain here. Being around Graham forced her to remember old hurts and feel the ache of loss, as though it were new.

Nor would she accept that small fortune he'd offered for simply meeting his charge. Not if she wished to have her pride, and in a world where one had so very little, such a thing mattered.

The butler guided them down another long corridor. "It is beautiful, is it not?" Wesley said with the pride of ownership. He gestured to the fresco paintings and pale-robin's-egg blue satin wallpaper finer than any fabric she herself had ever owned, let alone had adorn her walls.

"Indeed," she murmured. None of this had ever mattered to her, however. As a girl, Graham's connection to wealth and privilege had been a barrier that, even in her youth, she'd spied and hated. Hated because it marked them as belonging to two different worlds.

"And it is to be your home, now, ma'am," Wesley said with a wide-toothed smile.

Her home.

This place was never destined to be her home. A whore's bastard daughter and a duke's son...they may as well have been born in entirely different universes. Her lips pulled in a sad smile as she stopped alongside a family portrait of the three Linford males. Those all-powerful lords whose aquiline noses and noble brows served as a testament through time of their origins. Unlike her, whose own mother had been between two lovers at a given time period and, as such, had never been able to say with any certainty who had sired her daughter. Rowena fisted her hands tight, hating how the circumstances of her birth still had the power to hurt. Hating...

Her gaze snagged on Graham's father. She took in the vile, loathsome figure sneering down at her even in death. The late Duke of Hampstead who, with his son, had shattered her existence and cut her off from the people she'd called family.

A family that had so very easily let her go.

Ripping her eyes away from his hateful stare, she studied Graham memorialized upon that oil painting back to when he'd been commissioned to the Royal Guards. He stood, resplendent in the crimson of his military attire. How would their lives have been different if he'd not gone to battle Boney's forces? She stretched a hand up and grazed her fingertips over the gleaming black Hessians.

You will hardly have a use for me when you return a war hero.

You are all I want, Rowena Endicott...

In the end, what a liar he'd proven himself to be. How many widows and unhappily wedded women had he had in his bed? And why did that truth still rip at her insides? She turned her attention to the two foils in that painting, taking in the harsh, emotionless painted planes of his late father and brother's faces. There were too many old hurts between them...and any polished instructor would do as well for Graham's charge. They needn't suffer through the pain of the past.

She could not stay here.

Not for him. Not for two thousand pounds or any pounds. Not to try and put her demons to rest. Because as she'd said, there could be no undoing a lifetime of hurt.

"Mrs. Bryant?"

Gasping, she wheeled about to the forgotten servant.

The young butler stood patiently, smiling. With his affability, he was so very different than the butler who'd greeted her on the steps of Wallingford Castle all those years ago. Servants wouldn't have been permitted the luxury of a smile in the late duke's employ. "Forgive me," she said, her cheeks burning hot.

"It's all a bit overwhelming." Wesley lowered his voice to a whisper. "The majesty of it all?" He followed that with a wink.

Content to allow him his erroneously drawn conclusion, Rowena forced a smile. "It is."

Without waiting to see if she intended to follow, Wesley marched with military precision to his employer.

Hastening her steps, she rushed to keep up, all the while training her gaze on the servant's back. After they'd cleared the sheep from the road, Graham had handed her inside the carriage, and then ridden his mount the remainder of the journey. She'd not seen him since. Nor after this meeting would she see him again. A vicious pressure weighted on her chest, and she fought the urge to rub that peculiar ache.

She did not want to be in this townhouse. She did not want to be beholden to Graham for her position. The only place she wished to be just then was in a return carriage to Mrs. Belden's so she might set her off-kilter world to rights, and then present herself once again as *The* Mrs. Bryant, first instructor at Mrs. Belden's Finishing School.

Now, with the kind-eyed butler guiding her through the palatial townhouse, she swallowed down a frustrated groan. The butler came to a stop outside an opened doorway, and her belly knotted. *Stop this. I am a dragon. I am a fearless instructor who thrives off propriety and survives on respectability.* Rowena brought her shoulders back.

"Mrs. Bryant," he announced, and setting her facial muscles in a mask, she entered Graham's office. She braced for that same powerful regret and pain that had filled his eyes earlier that morn. He picked up his gaze briefly from the work commanding his notice and not a hint of emotion glittered in their depths. He motioned her forward.

Had she imagined the night at the Fox and Hare Inn and the ensuing discussion along a muddied Roman road? The man before her, in a neat black jacket and crisp white cravat, bore no hint of a duke capable of smiling or one who'd willingly converse with a person of her station. How was it possible for him to present two very different faces to the world?

"There is no need to hover at the doorway, Mrs. Bryant. I assure you, I've no intention of biting you."

At his booming voice, Rowena jumped. And God help her for being the shameless wanton that she was, Graham's words conjured forbidden memories of long ago. Back to when he'd nipped and suckled at the sensitive flesh of her neck. Marking her as his. Laying claim to her. Stroking—

Graham lifted his head again and winged an eyebrow upward. She rushed over with a lack of decorum that would have seen her sacked by Mrs. Belden, and then abruptly stopped. Rowena eyed the two leather seats before his massive mahogany desk. He flicked a hand, and she promptly perched herself on the closest chair, and then set her book down on the edge of his desk.

"Gra—Your Grace," she swiftly amended. "I've come to speak to you about the post."

"My ward will be along shortly." Her stomach sank. She didn't wish to meet his ward, the young lady he believed to be so much like her. Didn't want to find a reason to stay. She had, however, promised to at least meet his charge. "Wesley will be collecting her. I will perform the introductions, and you will then be permitted to meet with the girl."

Some of the tension drained from her frame. "Of course, Your Grace." How neatly he'd shuffled her back into the role of servant and how grateful she was for the safe, comfortable station into which he placed her. It would be all the easier to decline the request he'd put to her.

He resumed scratching away at the ledger in front of him, pausing periodically to dip his pen into the crystal inkwell. The sharp, swift strokes of his pen melded with the long-case clock ticking away across the room. How very in control he was. Collected. Master of every moment. Unlike Rowena. With each click of his pen-tip striking paper, her nerves stretched and stretched, fraying to the point of breaking. "The girl, as I mentioned, is spirited." Graham continued writing, not deigning to so much as look at her. "Her father entrusted her to the care of a fellow soldier." His fingertips froze, and he stared unblinkingly down at the page.

Rowena waited dutifully in silence.

"He was a good soldier, a better man, who upon his return, lost himself in drink. Stumbled down the stairs one night and broke his neck." She gasped and he held her stare. "I tell you this so that you are prepared for some of the gossip she'll face. It is why it is imperative that she adheres to propriety. She needs to demonstrate impeccable deportment. Conduct herself in an exemplary manner."

His concerns and goals were no different from any of the other powerful nobles who'd enlisted the aid of Mrs. Belden's instructors. Yet...this was wholly different. Rowena stared in abject befuddlement at the man across from her, this stranger who with a curt enumeration demonstrated both pomposity and stodginess. "Should I also instruct her on the *proper* way to chew?" she asked masking all dryness to that acerbic reply.

He resumed writing. "I suspect she knows the rudimentary formality of dining. But you are indeed, correct. In order to be safe, it is best that she be instructed in how to conduct herself at formal dining parties."

With an ever-growing incredulity, she watched as he scribbled several sentences upon the page. *Safe?*

"There is also the matter of her wardrobe. Despite her elegant gowns she insists on donning breeches."

Some of the shock and disappointment with Graham's transformation to stuffy duke was masked by a new kind of surprise. "Breeches."

He nodded once. "Indeed." He made another note on the sheet. "The girl is free with her words and thinks nothing of sharing her thoughts and opinions in the moment."

"And it matters so much to you that she conceals that part of herself?" she asked cautiously.

"I'm concerned that the girl conducts herself in a way that she does not attract further scandal and gossip."

While he sprinkled drying powder upon that ink, and then gently blew on the page, annoyance roiled in her belly. *I am a dragon. I am upright. I am...*"Ainsley."

Graham looked up from the page, a question in his eyes.

"You continue to refer to her as the "girl" but never mention her by name," she said crisply. "Her name is Ainsley." The solitary figure he described, who'd never known a mother's affection or a governess' care, should be known by her Christian name.

He shoved to his feet with a languid grace that momentarily held her spellbound. "I assure you I do know the girl's name." He handed over that sheet.

Rowena studied the brief notes he'd made—a list—with an enumeration of all the ways he sought to change his charge. She dimly registered his movements as found his way to the sideboard. Those inked words, however, held her immersed. *Demure. Quiet. Reflective.*

116

In short, passionless. *This* is the manner of woman he wished Miss Hickenbottom to become?

The tinkling clink of crystal touching crystal filled the room. "Given you're both…" He paused mid-pour.

"Bastards?" she offered up, without inflection.

"Of like spirit," he neatly supplied, "she will benefit from your guidance. To your earlier question as to why I'd upset your life and force you to London, I know the g—*Ainsley* is wholly unprepared in the ways of the *ton*. Her father was a rake and a drunkard." He returned the decanter to the sideboard with a loud *thunk*, a remarkable crack in his icy veneer. "I received a note indicating she was denied entrance to Almack's."

The air left Rowena on a whoosh, and she lowered the sheet to her lap. His ward, even with her connection to him, had been coldly slighted by Society. Then, should any cruelty by the peerage surprise her?

"Which is fine," he said tightly, turning back. "The lady doesn't require their support."

Did he seek to convince her of that? Or himself? Poor Graham. So unaccustomed to being shunned in any way by Society, what must this experience be like for him? "Have you provided instructors for the young lady?"

"Jack has coordinated the finest. You'll oversee her lessons. We've been issued an invite by the Duke of Wilkshire to an intimate card party. It is essential you see Ainsley prepared."

A muscle ticked at the corner of his eye, holding her riveted. It was a subtle but telling movement. Rowena shoved slowly to her feet and took several steps closer to him. "It matters to you so much how she is received and treated?" She damned herself for caring about that mark of his character.

He shoved out of his elegant repose and wandered closer with lazy steps befitting the rogue those papers had once purported him to be. "You think me a monster, don't you?" he countered in those teasing tones of long ago. Only now an edge of ice underscored them.

She gave her head a dizzying shake, dislodging a curl from her tight chignon. "I never said as much."

"Ah," he whispered, capturing that errant strand and tucking it behind her ear. "You didn't have to." *I always knew you too well...*That meaning hung clear. He lowered his head slightly, and when he spoke, his breath, tinged with brandy and chocolate, fanned her lips. "I'll prevent her from any cruelty as long as I'm able."

Those somberly spoken words devoid of the earlier brevity, however, posed even more quixotic than the sweet yet masculine scent caressing her flesh. For it had been vastly preferable...nay, *easier*, when she'd taken him as an austere duke unknowing of his ward's name and eager to be rid of her. The evidence of this powerful nobleman who, in fact, worried after her, held her momentarily flummoxed.

His gaze darkened, and then fell to her mouth. And God help her, staring at his own lips, her body burned with the memory of them on her, everywhere. Heat pooled in her belly. He dipped his head lower, and on a shuddery sigh, she tilted her head back.

Footsteps sounded at the front of the room, and they looked as one. A diminutive lady with frizzy brown hair and freckled cheeks looked unapologetically back. Curiosity spilling from her saucer-shaped eyes, she alternated her focus between Graham and Rowena, before ultimately settling that stare on her. "Hullo," she greeted, startling them into movement. They jumped away from one another. Liquid droplets splashed from the rim of his snifter and littered the floor.

Skipping forward, Miss Hickenbottom skidded to a stop beside Rowena and stuck a palm out. "You are?"

With his spare hand, Graham motioned them to the two winged-back chairs opposite his desk. How was he so blasted calm? "Miss Hickenbottom, allow me to introduce you to your companion, Rowen—" The young lady's eyes went wide in her face.

"Mrs. Bryant," Rowena swiftly amended, placing her fingertips in the girl's.

With a mischievous sparkle in her eyes, Graham's ward enthusiastically pumped her hand.

"Splendid to meet you, Mrs. Bryant. It will be lovely having a friend about. Hampstead spends most of his evenings in his private suites," the young lady confessed as the unlikely trio settled into their seats. "Unless I search this one out"—she jerked her chin at him—"I've been left," she dropped her voice, "to my own devices." Ainsley winked. "Not always a bad thing, is it, though?"

At the scandalous admissions tumbling from the girl's mouth, a laugh bubbled up from Rowena's lips. When was the last time she'd laughed? That expression, nay, any hint of emotion—happy, or otherwise—had been discouraged at Mrs. Belden's Finishing School. Smiles were to be gentile and practiced. Laughter, never anything more than a polite giggle...but how very wonderful it felt to simply smile again.

Aware of Graham's gaze on her, she schooled her features. "His Grace has brought me to meet you, to see if we might suit."

"Oh, we'll suit," Miss Hickenbottom said, following that assurance with another impish wink.

Speechless, Rowena took in Ainsley Hickenbottom with her skirts tied up and breeches showing. Barely an inch above five feet, she had the diminutive form of a child and not a woman about to make her Come Out. And she knew with just one look that Graham was wrong; Ainsley Hickenbottom was far more spirited than she had ever been in all her wildest girlhood years.

He clasped his hands before him. "Miss...*Ainsley.*" At that deliberate effort to use the child's name, a warmth suffused Rowena's chest. This was the boy who'd welcomed her to the village and earned her friendship. "I should be clear that in summoning you both here, I want to ascertain that the post is one Mrs. Bryant in fact wants."

Oh, blast him. She smiled through her teeth. Must he be so...so... *direct?*

"Ahh," Miss Hickenbottom said, her shoulders slumped, that slight, detectible sag so at odds with the lively girl who'd skipped in like she owned this very office. "I see."

I see. Two words Rowena had thought and uttered throughout the whole of her life. Every time children had dashed away from her in the park, to when her nursemaid had insisted she not bother her mother while she was entertaining a visitor.

This is why Graham had asked her to come. Not because he sought to humiliate or shame her. Not because he wished to make her an indecent offer and renew their previous love affair.

It was because of this young lady.

It was also why Rowena could not go. No matter how much she wished it. No matter how much it would gut her and break her apart inside being constantly forced to relive the pain of what had once been. Once upon a lifetime ago, she had been this girl, and all that had pulled her from her lonely state was a village boy whom she'd met. A boy, who happened to be a duke's son. And from there, a whole world had opened to her. She'd found another friend in Jack and young ladies of Berkshire's most distinguished families. How quickly it had all been yanked away.

She pushed aside the nostalgia. "I assure you after a brief meeting," she began softly, "I'm very excited to guide you through your Season." Those words, taking Rowena, herself, by surprise. Miss Hickenbottom yanked her head up quickly, knocking her cap askew. With the shock that flared in the girl's wide eyes, Rowena found herself, for the first time since Graham's reentry into her life, welcoming the post. "If you'll have me, that—"

"Yes," the girl interrupted with a toothy grin. She reached for Rowena's hand once more and gave another firm shake.

"It is my expectation that your evenings will be filled," she said, when Graham's ward released her hand, "so, you shan't be…uh, left to your own devices." Rowena turned to her employer. "Isn't that correct, Your Grace?"

"Indeed," Graham confirmed.

At her pointed look, he started. "I've received a number of invitations. Dinner parties. Soirees." Ainsley made an exaggerated yawning noise.

Rowena cleared her throat. "But I expect His Grace will also coordinate a visit to the theatre and Vauxhall Gardens," she neatly put in, ignoring the sharp look Graham slid her.

Ainsley clapped excitedly with a young girl's lack of artifice, confirming Rowena's read on the young woman. "When will we attend?"

"Soon," she supplied earning another glare.

"About bloody time," Ainsley mumbled and fixed a glower on her guardian. "Tucked away here, I had no hope of ever finding a swan."

Rowena exchanged a mutually befuddled look with Graham. "A swan?"

"I'm sorry." The girl let out a beleaguered sigh. "A *muted* swan. You're correct. Entirely matters which kind of swan."

When Rowena was a girl of fifteen, she and Graham had joined opposite hands and swung about, counting each time they circled around, until they'd collapsed in a dizzying heap upon the lush, Wallingford grass. Speaking to this peculiar, if garrulous, charge felt a good deal like that. "I'm afraid I do not follow—"

Ainsley hurled her hands high. "The muted swan. Magnificent creatures. They swim beak to beak. Why," warming to her topic, the vibrant child stuck a foot out, "the males even help with nest-building and watching over the eggs." She pursed her mouth. "Though, if you ask me, any decent male, swan or the human-kind, should help care for his partner." Clever girl. Ainsley jabbed a finger in the air. "And, of course, they mate for life."

Rowena choked on her swallow and, from the corner of her eye, caught the growing horror in Graham's chiseled features.

"Therefore, I want a swan someday."

When Graham had shown up and all but forced her into his employment, she'd been filled with a resentment at his manipulation of her life. Now, with this innocent, effusive girl before her, and knowing the coldness and unkindness she would face, Rowena would rather be no other place—particularly at Mrs. Belden's.

How am I going to return to that lonely, miserable place where no one knows me and all hate me?

121

"Yes, well, I promise to prepare you so that you may find your... uh...swan, Miss Hickenbottom," she said softly with another smile.

"Splendid," the girl said with a clap of her hands. "And, please, you must call me Ainsley. Horrid enough being saddled with a name like Hickenbottom that I shouldn't have you going about calling me by it." Rowena opened her mouth. "Not unless you intend to be one of those nasty sorts of companions I've heard about."

Every student who'd entered her classes at Mrs. Belden's had hated her from the moment they'd set eyes on her. Revered and feared, each instructor was thought of as a dragon and nothing more. "I don't—"

"I do not take you for one of those mean sorts," Ainsley assured her, patting her hand. They shared a smile, and then the girl looked to Graham. "I take it we are concluded with our introductions? I've a book to finish reading."

Most other lords or ladies would be horrified and offended by the girl's lack of artifice and grace. Rowena found her an endearing image that reminded her of the girl she'd once been.

"Of course, you may return to your..." Graham's words trailed off as Ainsley gave a parting wave to Rowena and then skipped out, slamming the door in her wake.

Well. The girl was a veritable whirlwind. Except, as with all whirlwinds, they eventually settled, and when they did, all that remained was the scattered dust.

"The theatre?" he said as soon as they were alone. "Vauxhall?" His voice emerged a garbled growl.

"She needs to know some cheer, Graham." There would be cruelty enough that Ainsley should find joy where she could.

"She needs to be polite. She needs—"

"If you're so clear on what the young lady needs then perhaps you should see to her edification and I can return to Mrs. Belden's."

That effectively silenced him.

"I see we are understood." Rowena dipped a flawless curtsy. "If there is nothing else you require, Your Gr..."

Graham stalked slowly toward her and all words went out of her head as he stopped beside her. Heat rolled off him in waves, momentarily blotting thought and reason, so all she was capable of was breathing in the deeply masculine scent of his sandalwood soap and the hint of brandy that clung to his breath. "Thank you, Rowena."

It was on the tip of her tongue to point out that she'd not accepted the post for him, but rather a child, more like her than any other girl she'd taught in her ten years at Mrs. Belden's. The words, however, would not come. For part of her had accepted the post for who Graham was. A man who, given his elevated status could have easily turned the task of finding a companion over to a man-of-affairs. The late duke certainly wouldn't have lowered himself by meeting with a companion and a child. And he'd certainly not have tolerated a girl in breeches and dusty boots anywhere near him. He, however had…and it knocked loose another desperately needed defense against him.

"You were right," she said, taking a step away and putting a safer distance between them. "She is a remarkable young woman." Society would kill her spirit. It was inevitable. But mayhap, she could help her retain some of that inner joy and strength.

Rowena dropped a curtsy. With his gaze searing a place in her back, Rowena took her leave, praying she'd not made another mistake where Graham Linford, the Duke of Hampstead, was concerned.

It is about the girl. Focus on the girl.

Drawing in a breath, she registered Graham sliding back into the leather folds of his seat, as she left his office and went in search of Miss Hickenbottom. Rowena paused at the end of the corridor and looked first right, then left.

"In here."

At that exclamation, she wheeled around. Miss Hickenbottom stood with her head peeked around the corner of an open doorway and motioned her forward. "Miss Hick—"

"First," the young lady began sticking one finger up. "I thought we'd already agreed I'm simply Ainsley because of the whole horrid Hickenbottom business." Rowena's lips turned up in an involuntary smile. "Second, I'm not one of those miserable sorts of ladies. Can't afford to be." She paused. "I'm a bastard."

A kindred warmth unfurled inside for this girl who was more alike to her than different. It was not the first time Ainsley had reminded Rowena of her birthright. It was that defensive, dare-the-world-to-mock-me look Rowena had perfected as a small girl in London whispered about by maids and servants. She wandered over. "We are more than our birthrights," Rowena said, her words ending on a gasp as Ainsley shot a hand out and wrapped fingers around her wrist. She tugged her inside.

"You know of it." The young lady's words were more of a statement of observation than a question.

Rowena wetted her lips. She'd been listening in on her and Graham's exchange. "I do," she said tentatively. How much more had she heard? Her mind raced, as she desperately tried to recall that intimate discussion. She should feel suitable horror and terror. A passing servant, a word back to Mrs. Belden, and the carefully crafted lie she had lived all these years would come crashing down about her like a sugar castle in a rainstorm. Oddly, there was something freeing in owning who she was. In a move that would have seen her sacked by Mrs. Belden and any other respectable employer, she hitched herself up onto the table beside her charge, a girl only a few years younger than the age her sisters would now be. "I do know something about it," she confessed, freed all the more with the truth. "Though my mother eventually married a vicar, I didn't always have a comely papa." The miserable blighter, alive still, had washed his proverbial hands of his offspring after he'd tired of her mother.

"Oh, there was nothing comely about my papa," Ainsley said, flashing another one of those troublesome smiles, which quickly faded. "He was more a friend who spent most of his nights out drinking and whoring, his days sleeping, and the other times, telling me outrageously bawdy jests. We did get on great, though," she said wistfully. "It has been lonely without him."

What a peculiar life this young lady had known. And Rowena would wager, given those handful of stories she imparted, that this one's girlish innocence had never truly existed. She covered her charge's hand with her own.

"Mr. Miserable believes a bastard can't ever become a lady."

Rowena had heard that same, ruthless opinion more times than she could recall in her eight and twenty years. It still did not stop her from wanting to pummel the nose of the gentleman speaking ill of Ainsley. "Who is Mr. Miserable?"

"Hampstead's man-of-affairs."

Of course. Jack Turner. Unease brought Rowena's eyes briefly closed.

He doesn't matter. He is dallying with French beauties while you are left here with his father who will see you ruined…

What would he think of her reemergence? For the first time the extent of her peril in being here, with both Jack and Graham knowing of her past, settled around her brain, spreading fear through her like a fast-moving cancer.

"Must say I was quite pleased when Hampstead insisted on finding me a companion on his own." Ainsley grinned. "I'd no doubt his man-of-affairs would have brought me back a cruel sort." She pulled herself onto a nearby side table and swung her legs back and forth in an innocent manner better fitting a girl of seven than seventeen. "Do you know him well?"

Her mind went blank and then raced.

"My guardian, that is. I saw the look pass between you," she said with such matter-of-factness Rowena choked. "I saw the way he watched you." There was a wistful, far-off quality to those whisper-soft words. "I'm fairly certain he was about to kiss you when I interrupted."

Rowena glanced about, desperate for escape. She'd been far too confident in her abilities these years. Nothing had or ever could have prepared her for Graham's quick-speaking ward.

"Is the duke your swan?" Ainsley asked curiously.

"Is he my…?" And her mind recalled the romantic young lady's talks of swans and forever partners. "No," she exclaimed as heat burned from the roots of her hair down to her toes. At one time, he'd been.

"We knew one another briefly as children. I'm now merely a servant in His Grace's employ," she settled for weakly.

Ainsley peered at her through narrowed eyes. Did she seek to gauge the veracity or Rowena's assertion?

She went still under that scrutiny.

"Hmph," her charge observed with far too much acuity for a lady who'd obtained her information at keyholes. "Regardless, I think you and I shall get on well."

Some of the tautness seeped from Rowena's toes. This was safe. This relationship of instructor to student was familiar territory she'd danced within for years. Only...the easy smile on Ainsley's lips that met her pretty brown eyes was...real, when, in the past, other young ladies had only looked at Rowena as a dreaded dragon. "I believe you're right," she added softly. For as long as she was here. Then she would be free to return to Mrs. Belden's where she'd promptly forget the time spent with Graham Linford, the Duke of Hampstead.

Liar.

The young lady hopped down. "I'm..."

At the worried lines creasing Ainsley's brow, her curiosity stirred. "You are?" Rowena gently prodded, climbing off her perch.

"I'm a bit worried about the coming weeks. The duke intends to introduce me to Society," she clarified. "But there is the whole bastard-business, and—" The young woman firmly clamped her lips. For all Ainsley's bravado and beautiful show of confidence, she worried still. Because, ultimately, daughters born on the fringe of Society well knew the cruelty that existed for anyone outside that respected sphere.

"You will be marvelous," Rowena promised, hating that she made a promise she could neither keep nor ensure. The disdain directed at her, a girl of seven, was still as fresh as it had been all those years earlier. Graham's was a ruthless world. It was a place where station and rank mattered, and where ladies were deemed outcasts just because of their parentage. "Come." She held her elbow out. "Let us cease worrying and go prepare for your first introduction to Society."

Excitement replaced the earlier worry and Ainsley looped her arm through Rowena's. They made their way from the library and started down the corridors. "One of the benefits of having a lax guardian is they do not insist you don those dreaded whites or ivories, and I've plenty of freedoms."

Only, Rowena had once possessed plenty of freedoms. Now, to school a young girl in being cautious with what one did with those freedoms.

TWELVE

R owena's proficiency with her students at Mrs. Belden Finishing
School had earned her the vaunted post of head instructor.
She'd been so feared by the students, revered by the other instructors,
and respected by the headmistress that she'd truly come to believe
herself truly an accomplished instructor.

Until now.

After almost ten years working with young ladies, she came to
appreciate her own infallibility.

"But it doesn't make sense." That beleaguered complaint was followed by an exaggerated sigh. Abandoning her efforts at walking with
a measured gait, Ainsley hurled herself onto the ivory upholstered
sofa. The scowling girl draped her legs over the arm of that chaise,
rucking her skirts about her knees. Rowena winced. "Why does it matter *how* I walk?"

Why, indeed.

After an hour practicing gait and posturing and positioning,
Rowena resisted the urge to dig her fingertips into her temples. For if
she were as skilled as she'd believed, she would have suitably answered
Ainsley the first time...and not ten questions later. Alas, she had spent
so much time following the script of Mrs. Belden's lessons that she'd
ceased to think for herself. "It shouldn't matter," she finally said, vali-
dating the girl's frustrations. For they were shared and real. "And yet,
just as there are men and women"—like Rowena herself—"who must
work in order to survive, there are certain rules that guide Society and
should be adhered to."

"Would I truly wish to call those people as friends if they'd be so stuffy in their judgment?"

Ainsley spoke with a child's simplicity Rowena had once possessed. She looked around the elegant white and gold parlor. It had been three days since she had begun schooling her charge in lessons on deportment and ladylike pursuits. In that time, she'd demonstrated the same frustration Rowena had over the years at the strictures binding women to such staid, purposeless endeavors.

"You wouldn't," she conceded, "yet, sometimes it is not about friendships." Frustration roiling inside at her own limitations, she looked around Graham's vast library. With its soaring ceiling and wraparound shelving of books, it had the look of the Temple of the Muses, that place she had so loved to go as a girl, before she'd begun to note the way women yanked their skirts away from her and Mother as they walked by. Remembering back to the day they'd bumped into the vicar, who became Rowena's stepfather, she drifted over to the shelf. With numb fingers she tugged the nearest volume free and fanned the pages, absently.

…We will always know security and love, now, Rowena…We are going someplace safe. Someplace wonderful…

In the end, she'd been the only one who'd been without that someplace safe and wonderful. Her chest squeezed; and yet, at the same time, she welcomed that pain for its valuable reminder. One she desperately needed with Graham back in her life: trusting others was perilous. Ultimately, she'd only herself to rely on…and it was and would always be safer that way.

"Mrs. Bryant?" Ainsley asked hesitantly, with that astuteness she'd demonstrated since their first meeting.

"Do you wish to know the truth, Ainsley?" she asked quietly, as she turned back to face her charge.

The girl swung her legs to the floor and scooted closer to the edge. "Always."

May she always feel that way. "It is good to never betray who you are, but who you are is not defined by how you walk. Life is hard and"—she touched her gaze upon the young lady's delicate features—"I expect you know that as much as anybody. Mayhap more. Life is filled with uncertainties and dangers and struggles, and if one can make life easier for oneself by doing these"—she waved her book about—"small things to conform that ultimately don't matter, that doesn't make one weak." It made one a survivor. "It makes you resourceful." Just as she had been.

That resourcefulness had saved her life. It had kept her from a fate upon her back as the plaything of a powerful lord...whether it was Graham, Jack, or any other nobleman. A whore was a whore was a whore, and a woman who could rise up and find altogether different circumstances than those was a woman of strength. "Then it makes it vastly easier to convert one's energies to the ones that truly do matter.

Ainsley wrinkled her nose. "So, I should change?"

"No. Yes. *No.*" Speaking to her charge felt a good deal like running in circles to chase a tale that wasn't there.

The young lady scratched at her confused brow.

Battling a frustration at her inability to wholly articulate what she sought to convey, Rowena set aside the book in her hands. "I do not want you to change who you are," she said at last, in a truthful utterance that would have sent even an unflappable Mrs. Belden into a fit of the vapors, and only after she'd sacked her. "But you can retain who you are in here." She tapped her hand to her chest. "It doesn't mean you have to approve of the gossips or the unfairness in social station, but you can hold onto who you are and prove that being spirited and free-thinking does not preclude you from knowing about and respecting Society's expectations of who you are in here." She briefly touched her head. "And here"—she touched her chest once more—"is what people should see...And if you only flaunt societal conventions, they won't ever be able to look past that to see who you are."

Ainsley folded her arms and grunted. "Then, I think I shouldn't care what they believe."

No. She shouldn't. That truth slammed into Rowena. This child had more courage and strength than she did—or ever had. She who'd always longed to find acceptance in Society…an acceptance that would never be forthcoming.

Ainsley flipped onto her belly and, scrunching her brow, reached under the sofa. She muttered under her breath, and then—"Aha." Her eyes lit. She dragged a leather book out and sat up. Her spirited charge handed the leather tome over.

Accepting it, Rowena skimmed the title: "Da Vinci." She looked up. "You enjoy art, then," she said, relieved. They could move on from the exact way to walk. This was a safe pursuit Rowena was familiar with. One the *ton* approved of.

"No. I hate it." The young lady spoke with such candor that as a companion Rowena should be despairing. Instead, a smile tugged at her lips. How easy it was to smile around this girl. There was a refreshing realness to her that had long been missing in her own soul. "I found this book by chance when I first moved into Hampstead's household," Ainsley explained. "It was the first one I took off the shelf." She plucked the copy from Rowena's hands. Her face riddled with concentration, she fanned the pages, and then stopped abruptly. "Here." She turned the book back over.

Rowena searched the dog-eared page, and then paused as she read.

"He was a bastard," Ainsley said needlessly with the words all right there. She proceeded to tick off on her hands. "He was left-handed, and he never received a formal education." She paused, giving Rowena a pointed look. "He wrote backward, Mrs. Bryant. *Backward.*"

Rowena returned her attention to the book and proceeded to flip through those bent, well-read pages. All those facts, marked off by the girl, in this very volume. As well as other details she'd underlined in a charcoal pencil…about flight and a moveable bridge. Graham had said there was no child like his ward. He'd greatly understated the uniqueness that was Ainsley Hickenbottom. Affection filled her for the unconventional lady who would challenge both her and polite Society.

"Would you like to study these concepts?" Gesturing to the peculiar flying machine and anatomical images of men, Rowena turned a question that would have set most ladies to blushing.

131

Ainsley dragged her legs close to her chest and looped her arms around them. "Oh, yes." Her charge was a bluestocking. She smiled. How very refreshing this girl was from so many of the others who'd entered her classrooms. Her smile withered. *But then, I was tasked with killing spirits, and that's just what I did. Turned spirited girls into dull, lifeless versions of myself.*

"And do you know what else?"

"What is that?" she asked, unnerved by the truth of what she'd done these years...or rather, the truth of what she'd *not* done.

"Everyone remembers Da Vinci hundreds of years later. We still have books about him," she said, motioning to the volume in Rowena's hands. "He is remembered. I would rather be remembered than well-liked." She held a hand out.

Rowena eyed her fingers.

"I'm going to teach you how to skip, Mrs. Bryant."

"I know how to skip," she said instantly. As a girl, she'd taught a hopelessly incapable-of-skipping fifteen-year-old Graham those fanciful movements.

I bet a duke's son has never done something so senseless as skip.

Laughter had pealed from her lips over the Berkshire countryside as he had gone through those awkward, lurching steps. Her gaze slid to the door. And, now, he'd become one of those somber, duty-driven peers.

Rowena gasped as Ainsley grabbed her hand and tugged her to her feet. Stumbling, she quickly righted herself. "Then it should be easy to try again. First, we must rearrange the furniture, Mrs. Bryant?"

Curling her toes into her soles, Rowena made a sound of protest. "I don't—"

"Uh-huh, Mrs. Bryant." In the greatest of role reversals, her charge wagged a disapproving finger. "I'll allow you to teach me your dull, boring steps if you let me school you on skipping."

Ladies walk with small, precise, genteel steps. A lady who walks with noble grace finds a noble husband.

Rowena worried the flesh of her lower lip. Should word reach Mrs. Belden that she had done something as indecorous as not only skip but encourage it in her charge, she'd be sacked without a single reference to account for more than ten years of honorable service. She nodded slowly. "Very well, Ainsley. Deliberate steps and *then* skipping it is."

Ainsley studied her through narrowed eyes. "Agreed." Grabbing Rowena's fingers, she pumped them once.

"Shoulders back, chin up, steps measured," she guided, demonstrating those very movements.

Brow furrowed in concentration, Ainsley took several stiff, awkward ones of her own. "You're very good at this, Mrs. Bryant." That pronouncement emerged as an indictment more than anything.

Another smile tugged at Rowena's lips.

"But you aren't always miserably stiff like Hampstead."

Rowena missed a step and quickly righted herself, damning the way her heart skittered at the mere mention of his name. Bringing herself back about, she started a slow walk back the other way.

"Oh," she said, striving for nonchalance. "Is he truly miserable?" She'd born witness to his cool, ducal demeanor, but she had also seen glimpses of a man who smiled at servants and teased and sought to calm her fears through a threadbare wall.

Ainsley's gaze concentrated on the opposite wall; she didn't even bother to look over. "Not like Turner, mind you. Just formal. *Ducal.*" Yes, Graham had ascended to the title as though he'd been the one born to it. "He's dreadfully dull in that regard."

There were many words Rowena would have ascribed to Graham Linford through the years: ruthless, unfeeling, bastard, but never, even with the passage of time and the veneer of powerful nobleman fair glistening off his personage would she have ever dared to call him...dull. A desire to know more about the man he had become in her absence. Had the loss of his once-exuberant joy been a product of the war? His ascension to the dukedom? Or a combination of the two?

"You have many dealings with him, then?" Rowena ventured hesitantly.

"Pfft." Ainsley took another measured step. "Hardly. It's how I know he must be dull." She startled a laugh from Rowena, and as that mirthful expression echoed loudly off the walls, she clamped her palm over her mouth.

"You know, it is quite all right to laugh, Mrs. Bryant," Ainsley admonished, adjusting her strides as she started back in the opposite direction. "Mayhap that is why you and Hampstead once suited."

"We don't suit," Rowena said quickly, all amusement now gone. How could the young lady, a stranger of three days, know that they'd had a deep past together. "We never suited. He's merely my employer, and I'm—"

Her charge continued over her rambling protestations. "He doesn't leave his office except to visit his boring clubs and attend his dull affairs. But you, Mrs. Bryant?" She looked over, a sparkle in her eyes, and stopped her awkward strides. "There is hope for you yet." She held her fingers out. "And now we skip."

Graham shrugged into his midnight black, double-lapel jacket. Waving off his valet, Smith, he buttoned the garment himself, and then held a hand out for the stark white cravat. He accepted it with a word of thanks. Looking in the bevel mirror, he went through the motions of knotting the white fabric.

Years earlier, when he'd fought off death and the agony of Rowena's abandonment, he'd reentered the world of the living; losing himself in the inanity of it all. Or he'd tried to. For some of that time, he'd overindulged in drink, bedded eager widows and beauties, and visited the most dangerous hells in London. Through it, he'd failed to fully vanquish his demons.

They were always there. Always lurking. As Jack had aptly reminded him.

As such, he'd come to abhor making an appearance before Society. Be it the balls he was never without an invitation to or the club engagements with Jack, the opportunity of a misstep was always present. The chance that the nightmares would come and the whole world would bear witness to his weakness.

For the first time, however, he was eager to be free of the once-safe walls of his townhouse. His need to escape the one place that had been his sanctuary had everything to do with a five-foot, eight-inch lithe woman who'd occupied his thoughts since they'd arrived three days earlier. One whom he'd taken care to avoid. It had been abundantly easy for him to focus all his days on meetings and his evenings at *ton* events while Rowena remained behind, schooling his ward.

And through his work, thoughts and questions would sometimes creep in. If life had continued along a different path, she'd be guiding Ainsley not because she was a servant in his employ but because she was his duchess.

If she had waited for him.

If he hadn't gone mad.

So many "ifs," and there could be no going back.

"Is there anything else you require, Your Grace?"

A decanter of brandy, and a second one behind it. "No. That will be all."

As the door closed, signaling Smith had left, Graham re-fixed his attention on the man reflected back at him. He'd delayed this inevitable meeting with Jack since he'd arrived. Giving over the tasks of organizing Ainsley's debut ball and the formal dinner party with Wilkshire and Lady Serena, he had successfully put off news of the companion he'd hired. It couldn't be avoided any longer.

With that, he took his leave of his chambers and started through his house when a bright peal of laughter made him freeze. That free, unfettered expression of happiness went through him, drawing him forward down the opposite corridor. He'd dwelled these past years in a self-imposed darkness, embracing his solitude and solemnity. His life, by design, was as he wanted it: passionless, quiet, organized.

When was the last time there had been any hint of mirth in this house? Now, the sounds of that lightness suffused a corner of his darkened soul. He stopped outside the library, hovering on the edge. Rowena and Ainsley's muffled voices were periodically punctured by another round of snorting laughter. Graham layered his forehead against the cool plaster as another raucous round of amusement broke out from that room. It had been so long since he'd heard or taken part in that joyous mirth. So long, that he'd once believed he'd not even recognize it were it to slap him in the face.

He was wrong. Standing outside with Ainsley and Rowena conversing, he very much did recognize the sweet sound of that happiness and, God help him, he wanted to forget his plans for the evening. Forget his responsibilities and those dependent upon him. Forget Lady Serena and her equally-determined father, and just join in the simplicity on the other side of that door. Rowena's bell-like laughter, as pure as it had been in the countryside of Wallingford, drew him. He stepped inside the doorway and all the air was sucked from his lungs.

Hand in hand, she and Ainsley skipped enthusiastically across the large, and recently rearranged, library. Her skirts whipping wildly about her slender ankles and her hips deliciously swaying, the sight of her held him as enthralled as when he'd first been discovering her lying in a sea of wildflowers, gazing up at the cloudless summer sky.

Transported back to that moment, he drew in a slow, agonized breath, aching for—

"We have an observer, Mrs. Bryant."

Graham's carelessness was a misstep that would have seen him killed in the Peninsula. He cursed as Ainsley's pronounced whisper held him trapped. Silence fell inside the parlor, and he briefly contemplated a hasty retreat in the opposite direction. Alas, he'd never been one to walk away from a literal or figurative battle.

Forcing a smile, he stepped deeper inside the room, his graze trained on Rowena. Her cheeks flushed from her earlier laughter, her eyes sparkling with that same mirth, chipped away the years of jadedness that had clung to her since they'd been reunited. She was, once more, transformed, into the hopeful, starry-eyed girl who'd entered the village and stolen his heart. His pulse quickened. This is how she should be...always. How he'd wanted to remember her, and how he wanted her to remain. "Miss Hickenbottom. Mrs. Bryant," he greeted.

Eyes lowered, Rowena worried at her lower lip. "Your Grace. We were…I was…" She had the look of a child caught with her hand in the biscuit jar, and God, if she wasn't more endearing with every blush and hastily averted look.

"There is nothing to worry about, Mrs. Bryant," Ainsley reassured. "It's just Hampstead." Just Hampstead. Since he'd ascended to the rank of duke, he'd existed as nothing more than that hated title. How he preferred the simplicity of how this child saw him.

"I didn't take you as one who'd listen at keyholes, Your Grace."

That suspicion-laden charge turned his attention from Rowena. "No," he concurred, and then waggled his eyebrows at his charge. "Then, mayhap there hasn't been good reason to be listening at keyholes before now."

His ward's eyes formed round moons, and then she burst out laughing. "By God, Mrs. Bryant, who would have thought it? Hampstead *does* have a personality." He had. Once. Long ago. Before battle. Before betrayal. Before it all.

Rowena said something quietly for the girl's ears, and Ainsley wrinkled her nose.

Graham took in the room.

"We moved the furniture," Rowena murmured, a guilty flush on her cheeks.

"I see that." Sofas since shoved against the far back wall. Side tables neatly placed alongside chairs. It was a disorderliness that would have enraged the late, well-ordered duke, who'd not tolerated a hair out of place of the maid's chignons or his breakfast routine at all interrupted.

"We were…" Rowena tried again. "We were…" From the corner of his eye, he detected her fingers nervously plucking at the fabric of her brown skirts. She should be adorned in sapphire hues and bold purples, not these dark, dreary colors meant to dim her beauty and light. "I'll see it righted." Did she think he'd sack her for having shoved his furniture about? Worse, what did it say about the existence she'd likely lived? And not for the first time, he damned her bastard of a husband for entirely different reasons. For having seen her reduced to this sometimes hesitant, oft-worried woman.

137

"Come, Mrs. Bryant," he rebuked. "Do you believe I'll take you to task for something as mundane as moving the furniture?" But, then, how little they knew of who and what the other had become.

Rowena spoke into the quiet. "We were working on a lesson."

"Yes," Ainsley said with an emphatic nod.

His interest stirred. "What manner of lesson, Mrs. Bryant?"

"Uh..." the lady glanced down at the tips of her slippers, and then beyond his shoulder to the door, like one calculating her odds of darting past him to freedom.

"*I* was teaching Mrs. Bryant how to skip." Ainsley's pride-filled declaration brought his head swinging back and forth between student and teacher.

He should be horrified. Only...with that innocent admission, images were conjured of a carefree Rowena, just fifteen, skipping with wild abandon through the bluebell fields of Wallingford, before he'd overtaken her and rolled her under him, both of them dissolving into laughter. A pressure weighted at his chest. "Mrs. Bryant already knows how to skip." Did she recall those happier times? Or had anger for him blotted out all those once-wonderful memories?

"Yes, she said as..." Ainsley's words faded, and she angled her head. "You know that, do you?"

Graham blinked slowly, and he tamped down a violent curse. If Lieutenant Hickenbottom had possessed a jot of this girl's sense, the fool would be alive even now.

His ward was like a starving pup with a bone. "You said Mrs. Bryant knows how to skip, but how—?"

"Walking," Rowena blurted, effectively silencing the girl.

Graham and Ainsley looked to her.

"I was instructing Miss Hickenbottom—"

"Ainsley," the young lady corrected.

"On how to walk." Rowena coughed into her hand. "Come, Ainsley," she insisted. "It is late. We can resume our lessons on deportment tomorrow." The girl's groan of disappointment matched the sentiment that held him locked to his spot in the parlor. "His Grace has far more important events to see to this night than discussions of my

138

rather horrid skipping abilities," she neatly slipped in, rescuing him from further probing on his far too-astute ward's part.

He locked gazes with Rowena. "Mrs. Bryant," he murmured.

"Your Grace." She sank into a flawless curtsy, and gave Ainsley a slight nod.

The girl sighed, and then dropped a version of something that might or might not have been one of those deferential dips.

And reluctantly Graham took his leave of the pair. His footsteps echoed down the empty corridor, and then…

Another round of laughter went up, trailing after him. He paused and looked longingly over his shoulder. The austere, unsmiling visages of the previous Dukes of Hampstead glowered on, disapproving even in death. With a sigh, he continued across the foyer.

A short while later, he found himself striding through the familiar room of White's. The chandeliers cast a deceptively bright glow upon the famous floors. Patrons of the distinguished club dropped bows and called out convivial greetings. He tensed his jaw. Then, the peerage was always welcoming of a duke. A young lady—Rowena, Ainsley—were not the fortunate recipients of a like kindness. Graham reached his table where Jack now consulted his timepiece. He yanked out a chair.

His friend looked up with some surprise. "Goodness, you look more dour than usual," he said with his usually drollness when Graham sat.

A servant rushed over with a bottle of brandy and two glasses. Waving him off, Graham saw to pouring two snifters. He pushed one toward his friend and claimed the other for himself. Delaying mention of Rowena, he asked after the formal business he'd assigned to the other man. "How goes the planning for Ainsley's ball?"

In an un-Jack-like manner, his friend tightened his mouth. From the moment Graham was named guardian, the other man had done little to hide his disapproval with the entire situation. "The invitations have been issued." That admission came as though dragged from him. "You're asking much if you expect Wilkshire to embrace your bastard-ward with open arms."

Friends since they'd been the second- and third-born sons to nobles, they'd forged a bond as children. Their jocular relationship had always been faintly competitive but built on a deep, abiding loyalty. However, there were moments Graham couldn't sort out where Jack's coldness toward Ainsley had come from.

"Pfft, come, Jack." Swirling the contents of his drink, he leaned back. "Wilkshire would walk across hot embers for the title of duchess for his daughter." He eyed him over the rim of his glass.

Jack made a sound of disgust. "The young lady is deplorable. You'll have no hope of her making a match in her current state."

There was no doubt his ward would someday set the *ton* abuzz... for all the wrong reasons. Until, she was learned in the ways of polite Society, and even then, Ainsley Hickenbottom would charge an uphill battle in earning a place in their ruthless midst. Still, Jack's callous opinion of the girl grated. "You weren't always a stodgy bore," Graham pointed out. "We were more like the lively Miss Hickenbottom than the tiresome boys our brothers were."

With a snort, Jack took a long swallow, finishing off his drink. "We also had manners. That girl..." His clever gaze narrowed. He'd always been perceptive. "What is it?"

Ignoring his question, Graham poured him another snifter. The other man would need it when he revealed the reason for their public meeting. Once closer than the Three Musketeers, after Jack had discovered Rowena's deception, he'd burned with a palpable hatred whenever her name was mentioned. "I found a companion for the young lady," he said at last, rolling his glass back and forth in his hands. "She is the ideal woman for the post."

"Did you?" Jack gave a pleased nod. "Very good. Now you can focus on finalizing an arrangement with Lady Serena. Which—"

"It is Rowena."

That single name dropped a charged, heavy silence between them. His friend sat back slowly in his chair, the leather groaning in protest. The same shock that had filled Graham when he'd stepped into Mrs. Belden's office now reflected back in Jack's furious eyes. "What?" he breathed.

"It is Rowena," he repeated.

"Rowena?" Jack echoed.

Graham nodded.

And then Jack froze. He tossed his head back, laughing.

"There is no jest," Graham said in solemn tones, instantly silencing his friend.

"I don't understand."

"I hired Rowena."

"No," Jack gritted out. "I don't know what she said or how she's attempting to wheedle her way back in your affections, but I'll not let that viper hurt you again."

He stiffened at that vitriol directed against her. Yes, she'd betrayed him, but she'd still also begged out of the post and taken it on anyway to aide Ainsley. Still, it had been Jack who'd stood beside him when Rowena had left him shattered, and he was deserving of his loyalty for that. "She didn't want the post, Jack." He proceeded to explain all, and withholding details about the passionate kiss they'd shared and the intimate nighttime exchange in the midst of a thunderstorm, he shared everything from their unexpected reunion.

When he'd finished, Jack sat in silence while the din of chattering guests carried on around them. "It is a trick. Nothing more," he finally said, through tense lips. "She's merely pretended she doesn't wish to be here, and she's going to seek a place back in your bed and in your heart and—"

Graham held a silencing hand up. "There's no pretending. I know her."

A violent hiss escaped the other man. "You *know* her? You know her, you say? You knew her so well you believed she'd wait for you? That you trusted she'd not marry another and would be by your side when you were battling death?" Graham went motionless through Jack's diatribe. He couldn't very well expect after every vile word he had uttered about her treachery that Jack would welcome her trustingly back into their fold. When he'd finished, his friend lifted his glass in mock salute. "You were always weak where she was concerned."

He glared at the other man. "This is not about weakness," he said, shifting his gaze about the club. Grateful he'd not had this meeting in

141

his townhouse where Rowena and Ainsley might have born witness to Jack's biting hatred.

"Hampstead," he began in gratingly placating tones used by past tutors. "I understand you set out to find the ideal lady for Miss Hickenbottom because of your friendship with that gentleman."

Graham set his jaw. That *gentleman,* as Jack flippantly called the late lieutenant who had saved his worthless-until-now life. His sole, living friend, however, made that bond out to be nothing more than two rogues who'd shared drinks and a promise for Ainsley's future. "This goes beyond that," he said with finality. The matter of Rowena's presence here would not be debated.

His friend latched onto that. "Then, if this is about locating a suitable companion for the girl, *I* will find one. But, if this is something more—"

"Ainsley will need Rowena. They share similar pasts and struggles."

"If the lady does not wish to be here, then allow her to return," he continued, ignoring Graham's pointed reminder. "See if she is so compliant when you present her with the option she so craves."

Graham picked up his glass. "She will be Miss Hickenbottom's chaperone," he said, infusing his words with a deliberate air of finality.

"Do not do this," Jack pleaded. "Send her away. If—"

"It has to be her."

"Hampstead, think, man." Did Jack sense his wavering? "For her history alone, she should be sent back." Jack leaned closer, erasing all the space between them. When he spoke, he did so on a hushed whisper that barely reached Graham's ears. "Should Society learn of her parentage it will cause a scandal. A scandal which Miss Hickenbottom certainly does not need, given her own dubious beginnings."

He eyed his man-of-affairs. When had the other man become so boorish that he'd disparage two young women because of their birthright? "Her origins never mattered. Nor does it matter to me now. Rowena *will* serve as Ainsley's companion," he said with ducal tones his father would have been hard-pressed to fault. "Have I made myself clear?"

A muscle jumped in Jack's jaw. "Abundantly. If you'll excuse me?" he said tightly, setting down his glass. He made to rise, and then stopped. Some of the fire had left his eyes, replaced instead with concern. "You might interpret my reservations about Rowena as snobbish, and yet, I saw the hell she left in her wake. She broke you." Graham said nothing. After all, what was there to say to that truth? "Have you forgotten Lady Serena?"

"I know my responsibilities, Jack," he said tightly. His sole purpose was to find a dignified, boring, steady, consummate hostess wife who could hold Society at bay so he could retire to the country and retreat from everything that threatened to steal his control.

"Given your…circumstances, there can be nothing with Rowena."

God, the man was relentless. He clung on with such tenacity, talking Graham out of something he already knew could never be. For reasons that included both her faithlessness and his own need for a safe, passionless existence. And now she was back in his life, forcing him to remember the past and feel…anything, when he'd succeeded in feeling nothing for so long. His patience snapped. "I do not require a lecture or a lesson. I do not want anything with her." Why did it feel as though he sought to convince himself?

Jack reeled, his expression stricken. "Forgive me. I spoke solely of our friendship. I will leave you, then." With jerky movements, his longtime friend stood and stalked off.

Long after Jack left, Graham sat nursing his brandy.

The other man had responded to Rowena's presence with a volatility he'd expected. After all, Jack had witnessed the heartache and suffering Graham had known at her betrayal.

For his earlier annoyance, his friend had been correct. Having Rowena close was perilous. No good could come in being with her. Doing so brought forth memories of what had been, and what might have been.

Silently cursing, Graham stood, and abandoned his clubs for the evening. With the late-night hour, his house was certain to again be quiet and free of the chaos Ainsley had unleashed on his existence. At least until the morrow.

THIRTEEN

A insley was not ready for London's Polite Society, and standing in Graham's marble foyer in wait for the younger lady, Rowena didn't believe as much because she doubted Ainsley's capabilities... but because the *ton* could never, would never know what to do with a woman of her spirit.

Having worked with her, dined with her, and sat together simply conversing, she had come to the conclusion: his ward would never be the decorous-driven, demure miss he sought.

That desiring on his part, for Ainsley just served as further testament to the stranger who'd returned from war. Rowena would have never sufficed. Her heart gave a little pull at that. When he'd become heir to a dukedom, his obligations and responsibilities had shifted. The girl she'd once been who'd laughed freely and run wildly through the hills of Wallingford with mud stains on her hem and her hair whipping about her cheeks could have never found herself as his duchess. He'd known that.

It hadn't been until he'd methodically run through his expectations for Ainsley that she herself had at last realized it. Realized after more than a decade of her life had passed just why that fate and future had been impossible. When Graham Linford inevitably took a bride, she would be the model of every attribute he sought. A woman who was refined and straitlaced and...respectable. And the truth would always remain that Rowena would live and eventually die as the perfect dragon, but she would *never* be respectable.

The muscles of her throat worked as every age-old shame rose to the surface. She would always be a bastard, and worse...a whore's daughter. But she'd not have had any man who'd not loved her with all her flaws and faults, anyway. She'd deserved more then, and she did just as much now.

"How very serious you are, Mrs. Bryant."

At that low murmur, she gasped and spun about. A fluttering started low in her belly, as she caught sight of Graham. Standing at the doorway, he epitomized both a ducal strength and masculine beauty. The midnight fabric of his jacket and breeches accentuated muscles better suited to the cobblers and stable masters who'd worked in the Berkshire countryside than a nobleman of vast wealth and influence. "Your Grace," she forced herself to say as he came over. Rowena smoothed her palms over her brown woolen cloak. Her own garments stood out in stark contrast to that station divide that had always been there.

A servant rushed to greet him with a black floor-length cloak. Waving off any help, Graham shrugged into that heavy satin fabric. As he latched the clasp at his throat, the sapphire lining peeked out. The interior part of that elegant garment finer than *anything* she'd ever donned.

Rowena remained motionless, hands folded before her.

As the footman melted into the shadows, Graham lingered his gaze briefly on her hands. "Where is the skipping and exuberant laughing woman of our last meeting, Mrs. Bryant?" he commented, drifting closer.

She forced her feet to remain planted to their spot. She drew in a deep breath, and the masculine hint of Bay Rum that clung to him flooded her senses. *Do not let him rattle you. Do not let him...* "Given your statement of preference for orderliness and propriety, I expect this should meet with your approval." She glanced around at the Doric columns and frowned. "Nor is a foyer generally the ideal surroundings for skipping. Hardly enough space with all the inconveniently placed pillars."

Graham froze, and then tossed his head back on a laugh, that expression hoarse and rusty as though foreign. The sound of it, muddled her senses, and she stared on as his stone-cold features softened.

145

This was the Graham of her past, and as his eyes glimmered with amusement, she saw traces of who he'd once been. And mayhap, in some ways, still was.

"Ah," he whispered, placing his lips close to her ear. Her flesh tingled from the caress of his breath upon her. "But you were meant to be laughing and blushing and skipping, Rowena. Queen of the Gardens."

Her heart hitched.

"Did you think I should have forgotten the girl who ruled the gardens, pens, and locke?"

"Yes," her voice emerged tremulous. Why should he remember those details about their time together? "Actually, I—"

"*And* he laughs, too," Ainsley called out, voice booming. "Hampstead you are full of surprises."

Rowena jumped back.

Together, they looked up to the young lady at the top of the stairwell. In pale blue satin skirts and butterfly haircombs, Ainsley Hickenbottom was transformed into an elegantly attired English lady. Not a single person this evening would dare look at the lady and see anything less than—

She hitched her hip on the stair rail.

Rowena and Graham surged forward. "No."

Ainsley pointed her eyes at the ceiling. "Here I thought with your earlier laughter you were both capable of a bit of a jest." With a spring in her step, she sprinted down the remaining stairs. She jumped from the second one, her satin slippers noiseless when they struck the marble.

Graham frowned and looked pointedly to Rowena.

Another footman appeared with a muslin cloak that he helped Ainsley into.

She narrowed her eyes. He expected primness from his ward, did he? Deliberately misinterpreting the reason for that intense glint, she turned to her charge. "Curtsy to His Grace, Miss Hickenbottom."

"Oh, blast. Yes. Of course." Ainsley sank into a somewhat less sloppy gesture. "Shall we?" she suggested, and the butler came forward, drawing the door open.

146

Ainsley skipped ahead to the waiting black carriage. Graham fell into step beside Rowena, matching her smaller, measured movements. "Society is going to rake her through the bloody irons," he gritted out.

Was he upset with her for not adequately instructing his ward? Or worry about how the girl would be received? "Because she skips, Graham?" she said from the side of her mouth.

"Yes, because she skips. And because she curses and laughs freely and—"

"And this from the same gentleman who only just now spoke to me of doing those very things," she shot back.

His mouth opened and closed. Good. Let him be flummoxed. "It is entirely different."

They reached the carriage when that sputtered reply left his usually every composed sentence.

"Because she's a duke's ward."

His cheeks flushed red. "Hardly. I wasn't insinuating…I didn't mean to suggest…"

Rowena made to accept the waiting footman's hand, but Graham gave him a pointed stare, and the crimson-clad servant backed away. Graham shifted, angling his tall frame to cut their exchange off from Ainsley's view. "You insist that she should be spirited and passionate, and yet you'd bury those parts of yourself."

"Yes," she said emphatically, giving a nod. "Because some of us do not have the luxury of that zeal and innocence. I'd protect her." *As I wasn't protected.* With that, she slipped around him and climbed without out assistance inside the carriage. She took up the spot beside Ainsley.

A tense silence ensued between them, when he'd claimed the spot on the opposite bench, and the carriage started forward. Ainsley's discordant humming filled the quiet, and grateful for the young lady's presence, Rowena looked outside.

The rub of it was, Graham had been right in his question. Except, he couldn't understand. Not even if she explained it to him every day in every way she knew how.

She would deliver lessons to help guide Ainsley on societal expectations. She'd help her to understand the unkindness she'd face by not conforming. But she would not drill those lessons into her, beating out all hint of her spirit. She'd done that to too many students over the years. Shaped them. Shaped herself. Ainsley had the same joyous spirit Rowena had once been in possession of…but the girl also had something more, something she had never had: the support and connection to nobility behind her. With that combination, Ainsley could… and should be anyone she wished to be.

After an interminable ride through the busy London streets, they arrived in front of a pale yellow stucco Mayfair townhouse. Graham made his exit, handing down his ward. Rowena froze briefly in the doorway, staring at the home. This was a side of London she'd never been part of. Not in this way. Stepping down with the driver's assistance, she followed along at the requisite seven paces behind a nobleman as Mrs. Belden had advised. With every step that brought her closer, she focused on every lesson she'd delivered. Yet, somehow, although she'd instructed women who'd grace these halls, this was an altogether different experience. It was the ultimate reversal of roles, where Rowena now belonged to their world.

Graham glanced back. The full moon's glow illuminated his scowl. She frowned. What reason did he have to be upset now? He said something to the young lady on his arm, and then doubled back to Rowena's side. "I haven't hired you to be a subservient in my employ," he said in hushed tones. "I'll not ask or expect you to walk behind me or Ainsley or anyone, as though you're lesser, Rowena."

The sharp anger and indignation there lost to the meaning of his words. She paused, mid-step and then forced herself to complete the stride. That command he gave wholly at odds with who his father had been and whom she believed him to be, and it only threw her into further confusion. "Who are you, Graham Linford?" she whispered, frantically searching his face.

"Are we clear?" he demanded, ignoring her question.

She gave him a long look. "I cannot walk beside you, Your Grace." She deliberately invoked his title. "Not here. Nor at any of these events. Not without raising questions and earning whispers, and that Ainsley does not need." His green eyes pierced her, and the strained white lines at the edges of his mouth hinted at a man prepared to fight her. "You know I'm right," she said quietly. Then, he stalked off to where Ainsley waited.

They were admitted a moment later. Entering another marble foyer, Rowena waited in the wings while Graham and Ainsley were divested of their cloaks. As more an afterthought than anything, another footman came over and collected her coarse brown wool one. Turning it over with a murmur of thanks, she immediately fell into step behind the pair as they were escorted through the dark hardwood floors of their host's home.

"I confess, Hampstead, a card party is the perfect first event for me to attend," Ainsley praised. "Of all my skills I'm most proficient in hazard, whist, and faro."

From several steps ahead, the butler choked.

Graham winced, sending Rowena a desperate glance. Her lips twitched. *She will be fine,* she silently mouthed. They turned the end of the corridor, and the loud hum of conversing guests spilled out into the hall. A moment later, he and Ainsley were introduced to the small assembly. Rowena escaped an introduction...and notice. After all, a companion of nearly thirty years in dragon skirts would hardly *be* noticed by the Duke of Wilkshire's esteemed guests.

"Hampstead."

That booming voice, which stank of arrogance and power, could only belong to another duke. "Wilkshire," Graham confirmed a moment later with a bow for the monocle-wearing lord.

Introductions were performed, and as pleasantries were exchanged, just like that Rowena was alone within a nest of hornets, trying to emerge unscathed. Rowena wandered over to the corner of the parlor and settled herself into one of the Hunzinger folding chairs where a snoring matron sat, a pug on her lap.

With all the room's attention trained on the recently arrived duke, Rowena used their distraction to study Graham, so wholly in his element as he performed introductions between his ward and the other noble guests. He moved and spoke with an ease that could only come to one born to his station. She stared on wistfully as guests bowed and preened, seeking his favors. Who would have imagined when she'd first met him all those years ago, and fallen so desperately in love, that this was the future that awaited him? Had she known, had she the foresight to see he'd been just one brother away from that esteemed title, she'd have recognized their fates could never have been as one.

I wanted him as he was...

A duke's second son, who didn't give a jot about whether people were refined or mettlesome. She wanted him...as he'd been outside a short while ago. Challenging the social divide that required she be relegated to a place behind. Urging her on to laughter. Now, he waffled between two very different people: one who was coolly indifferent and unfeeling...and one who still caused her heart to miss its beat.

He motioned for Ainsley to join one of the tables of whist going on. Instead of claiming a seat there, or at any of the others, Graham stood at his ward's shoulder, protective, watchful. By his steadfast positioning, his message of support rang clear for the roomful of guests and, God help her, Rowena lost a piece of her heart to him all over again. That devotion marked him different from the other lords and ladies present...and from even the man she'd now taken him to be.

Her skin pricked with the feel of being studied. Which was peculiar as it was silly to think possible, and yet—Rowena did a cursory search of the room. An elegant gold satin-clad lady seated at a piquet table stared back at her with bald curiosity. There was something vaguely familiar about her, and yet even as Rowena scoured her mind, she took in the magnificent sapphires draped about the stranger's neck and glittering in her gold curls. She exuded wealth and privilege, and as such, was one who'd never mingle with the likes of her. *And yet...why is she staring at me still?* Rowena's palms grew moist as the oldest fears that were never far from her resurfaced. The flawless English beauty's attention was recalled by her partner. Some of the tension left Rowena. Of course the woman didn't know of her or her secret. It was silly to think anyone would...or remember the famous courtesan's daughter who'd left London years earlier. Why, Graham himself didn't seem aware of that secret she kept. Now she wondered what would he say to that discovery. Would he be the unrepentant man who expected her to make apologies to no one? Or would he cast her out as his father and her own family had?

A sharp, familiar snorting laugh slashed into the din of the activity, and Rowena instantly found Ainsley. She'd said something that had brought a blush to the cheeks of the gentleman next to her and a frown from the lady on the other side. Ainsley glanced in her direction, and Rowena met her smile with one of her own and a slight wave. Her charge gave a cheerful wave.

No matter what Graham wished, she'd not stifle the girl.

Ainsley's table settled down into a quiet play. Again feeling that stare trained her way, Rowena looked immediately to the source. Near an age to her years, the lady couldn't have been a student. She searched her mind for a memory of the woman with dark curls and flawless white skin. Unnerved, this time, it was Rowena who looked away and froze.

Graham stood conversing with another guest, and yet something in their positioning, and the young lady's determined smile suggested she was not simply any other lady. Rowena had never been the proud sort, with a taste or even appreciation for elegant fabrics and fine gowns. Dresses and clothing were simply a matter of necessity and, as such, they served a functional purpose. Seeing Graham alongside the delicate English beauty, a woman attired in a soft satin pink gown trimmed in diamonds along the daring décolletage, Rowena felt her first dose of envy. The Duke of Wilkshire joined the pair, and then led them to a small table where he joined them for a game of loo.

Rowena sat motionless, afraid to move, afraid to breathe, afraid to so much as blink. For when she did, she would have to give in to feeling the white-hot, unwanted envy snaking its way through her. Ugly, vicious, searing envy. It was one thing accepting that a future between them had been an impossibility. It was an altogether different thing to have it play out before her like a Drury Lane production.

It was too much. Needing a moment to separate from this and restore herself to the dragon she was, Rowena pushed to her feet.

"Escaping?" that dry observation put an immediate cessation to her hope for escape. Tall, blond, faintly bored, and dangerously handsome, the man bore every mark of a rake and rogue that she'd ever warned her students away from. He raised his half-empty port glass to his lips and sipped. "I must say I certainly cannot blame you. Miserably dull affair."

She wetted her lips, struggling to evoke every lesson she'd given her students should they be presented with this very situation Rowena now found herself in.

Seeming content to carry on without a word from her, he gestured to the snoring matron. "Lady Aberney has the right of it, I'd say." He followed that with a wink.

A laugh burst from Rowena's lips, and she instantly closed her mouth. Scandalized she glanced about. Alas, the guests were otherwise engrossed.

"Worry not. They won't see you here," he whispered. "Too pompous to look to the corner." He dropped his voice to a low whisper. "It's why I've taken to hiding out at these very spots." The gentleman with his blond curls, dropped a bow. "Lord Morgan Montgomery, the Marquess of Midleton."

Lest she offend the gentleman, Rowena fought back a smile.

Glass dangling lazily in his fingers, Lord Midleton folded his arms. "Yes, well, there is some consolation knowing I'll someday inherit a dukedom and break up the stream of "M's" my parents saddled me with."

Giving up all her best attempts at serenity, Rowena laughed.

"And *that* is the first honest reaction from anyone this entire evening," he said on a grin. "Except for perhaps that one," he nudged his chin, and Rowena followed that gesture to where Ainsley sat.

All mirth gone, Rowena stiffened her shoulders. Whether he'd intended that statement as an intentional or unintentional slight, she'd not keep smiling company with one who'd speak of her charge in any way. "If you'll excuse me, my lord," she said stiffly. "It's hardly appropriate for us to converse, given no formal introductions have been performed, and my status here as "that one's" companion."

Instead of being affronted or chagrined, he flashed her another even, pearl-toothed grin. "The companion?"

"The same."

"I see," he said, with mock solemnity. "And I'm the son."

She winced as something he'd said earlier registered. Praying she was wrong…Hoping…"The Duke of Wilkshire's?" Please let her not have insulted the host's son.

"The same."

Oh, well drat and double drat.

"Rest assured, Miss…?"

"Mrs.," she swiftly corrected.

"Rest assured, Miss Mrs."—Her lips turned up in another reluctant grin—"I didn't mean any slight against the lady or insult. Mine was a mere observation made after an evening of absolute tedium."

Rowena would have personally characterized it as a study in self-torture, and though she conversed with the duke's son *sans* a formal introduction being made, she briefly welcomed the diversion from her own earlier melancholy. "Bryant," she said at last. "Mrs. Bryant."

Graham made a show of examining his hand. His winning hand. All the while, from over the top of those cards, he studied Rowena and Lady Serena's brother, Lord Midleton, and he seethed inside.

Bloody rogue. The bloody, rotten rake. One of Society's wicked-est lords, recently returned from the Continent, what business had he speaking to Rowena…and what tales did he regale her with to earn her endearing blushes?

Another one of Rowena's laughs filtered through the noise and reached his ears, and decided it. He tossed down his cards. "I fear whist has been unkind, though the company kinder," he said to Lady Serena who looked up with surprise in her pretty blue eyes. "If you'll excuse me?"

"But you've only just partaken in four hands, Your Grace." Her perfect bow-shaped lips formed a moue. "I would be so very disappointed if you left now." She brushed her right hand over his in a bold showing.

That cloyingness hadn't bothered him before. It had merely hinted at a woman with ruthless designs on his title.

Another one of Rowena's bell-like laughs cut through the noise, and he tamped down a growl, warring with himself. Battling the propriety and logic that said to remain with Lady Serena and this unpleasant seething inside to find out just what Lady Serena's rake of a brother was saying to Rowena to bring her to that unfettered laughter. In the end, rescue from making that decision came from the unlikeliest of places—or in this case...people. Ainsley stepped up to the table just as Lady Serena began to deal the cards. "You owe me a game of piquet, Hampstead."

He opened and closed his mouth several times.

Lady Serena frowned. "His Grace was just partaking in another match of whist."

"Given that you've not yet dealt, I expect this would be the perfect time for me to steal him away," Ainsley boldly challenged.

Outrage blazed within his card partner's blue eyes.

Graham intervened. "Lady Serena." He gathered her fingers and placed the requisite kiss upon her hand. "If you'll excuse me? It has been a pleasure."

On that, he and Ainsley started for an empty table where they settled into the seats across from one another. "Wilkshire's furious," she said quietly as Graham began to shuffle the thirty-six cards.

"Lady Serena?"

"Enraged," she supplied happily, cutting the deal for that hand. She turned over the low card and proceeded to deal each set of twelve cards into groups of four.

Graham's gaze crept beyond her shoulder, past a handful of other gaming tables, to where Rowena stood conversing with Lord Midleton. He narrowed his eyes. What in blazes were they talking about? And why did she have that damned smile on her lips and blush on her cheeks, those expressions she'd once reserved for him. And the sight of Wilkshire's affable son charming her, he was filled with an unholy urge to stalk over like a primitive beast and knock the damned grin from his lips.

"He's a rogue, you know."

"I do," he answered, automatically, and then registering what he'd admitted to, his neck went hot.

"He's been eying Mrs. Bryant since we arrived."

"He h—" He immediately cut himself off. How in blazes did the girl see so much? And it begged the terrifying question…what else did she see? Careful to avoid her astute eyes, he drew four cards.

"My father was a rake," she explained matter-of-factly, taking two cards for herself. "Dangerous fellows for an innocent lady."

Indeed. Graham looked over to where Rowena stood conversing with Lord Midleton. It didn't matter whom the lady spoke with. Her role in his household was strictly of a purpose of serving as Ainsley's companion. As long as she conducted herself in a respectable manner above reproach, she could freely converse at any *ton* event they attended.

Only, he lied to himself. It mattered. Mattered very much, and sitting here, in Wilkshire's parlor, he confronted these ugly, volatile emotions: burning fury, jealousy, resentment. All of which went against everything he craved.

He'd shaped himself into a dull, emotionless lord to avoid feeling anything. It was why he'd selected Lady Serena as his future betrothed. Having Rowena here—in his life—was proving as perilous as fighting on those battlefields of the Peninsula. Rowena brought out who he was before, and it scared the hell out of him. At the same time, it gave him hope…and made him despair of ever being that person again.

Jack is right. It is dangerous having Rowena close.

Which left him with what alternative? To allow her to return? Or to endure the volatility of yearning, jealousy, and regret all to help his ward?

"Your play," Ainsley said, slashing into his musings. She tipped her head sideways over to Rowena's corner. Blinking slowly, he again found the tall, dark-haired woman who he'd spent years hating.

Graham noted the double meaning to Ainsley's words.

His play.

In the days since he'd been reunited with Rowena, he had lost all control over the chessboard that was his life, and he despised it. Damn Jack for having been correct. By letting Rowena back into his life—nay, insisting upon it—he'd threatened the carefully constructed world he'd built for himself.

Thwack.

A loud crash ripped through the noise of the parlor…*by God, they're coming. The damned French are advancing…*Heart thundering, Graham jumped up. Wild-eyed he searched for the approaching enemy.

"Don't pretend you don't hear me, Hampstead." That sharp cry mingled with the rapid fire of bayonets in his mind. Why were they calling him, Hampstead? *"I have had enough, Hampstead."* That second angry shout brought him reeling briefly back. Ainsley stood before him, arms planted akimbo. "Do you hear me, Hampstead?…I am talking to you…you vowed we'd attend…"

His ward's rapid demands emerged muffled, intermittently going in and out of focus. Graham blinked slowly. What was she saying? What…? Sweat beaded on his brow. Then like a swarm of angry bees, the guests assembled around Wilkshire's parlor began whispering. His stomach lurched, as he was jerked back to the moment. *Oh, God.* Horror creeping in to every corner of his numbed being, he glanced about the room—to the sea of observers staring back at him…Lady Serena with her hand to her gaping mouth…and Ainsley. His world was spinning. He stood there at sea.

It had happened. Publicly this time, when he'd taken such care to conceal his demons. Sweat beaded on his brow.

The whispers became rampant, growing into full-fledged discourse as the lords and ladies began talking in earnest. *I'm going to be ill.* Battling between madness and horror, Graham fought for control, when Rowena stepped before him, the only person in the room wearing a smile. It was a false one, tense, and deliberate, but it pulled him back from the edge, and he found a lifeline in that mark of her courage.

"Your Grace, Miss Hickenbottom was merely pointing out the previous engagement you'd accepted an invitation to." *Previous engagement?* Graham clenched his eyes briefly shut, searching his mind. When he opened them, Rowena gave him a long, meaningful look. She's attempting to disentangle me from this humiliation. Just as Ainsley had with her outburst. Shamed and grateful all at the same time, he gave a slight, deliberate nod for Rowena.

"Other engagement," he dimly registered the Duke of Wilkshire's sputtering.

Rowena looked to Ainsley. "Your elbow," her faint whisper spoken through her still smiling lips, jolted him.

He hastily offered his arm and escorted the girl from the room.

After a painfully long trek and wait, they found themselves outside his carriage. Waving aside the driver, Graham helped Ainsley up and reached for Rowena.

Worry wreathed her delicate features and spilled from her eyes, but there was something more there, too.

Please do not ask questions. Please...

With not a single word spoken, they made their way through the London streets. As soon as their somber trio arrived at his townhouse, Graham marched quickly ahead of Rowena and Ainsley. From behind, he heard her quiet words for Ainsley. He lengthened his stride, his office, that sanctuary of reason, beckoning.

The soft tread of delicate but determined footsteps indicted she followed close. He rushed inside his office and made to close the door. "Graham," she called quietly and put her hand out.

He wanted to spit, snarl, and sneer. To close the door in her face. Except...she'd called him Graham. He held the door open, and without hesitation, she entered.

The rapid pace she'd set for herself had knocked several dark brown strands loose. They framed her ashen face, highlighting saucer-round brown eyes.

Only, what was there to say?

She took a step closer, and he flinched. "After you left...when you'd gone off to fight..." His body went whipcord straight at that unexpected beginning. "When I was alone." She'd been alone. Is that why she'd turned to another? "I found myself in need of employment." He listened now, his ears trained on every word that fell from her lips. With each word uttered, he learned far more about her than he had in more than ten years' time. "I was away from you...my family..." She drew in a shuddery breath and looked down at the tips of her slippers.

Graham stared at the glorious crown of brown tresses, strands another man had wound his hands through. "Mr. Bryant?" he supplied, this time without malice.

Rowena lifted her head slowly, and blinked: once. twice. A third time, befuddlement gleaming in her eyes. And then—she nodded frantically. "After all of that loss…"

I wasn't lost to you. If you'd waited. Yet she hadn't. Mayhap she'd had no choice. It was a thought he'd not allowed himself to think in more years than he could remember. He fought back the questions, listening to what she imparted.

"I shut everyone out, Graham. The other servants." Oh, God, she'd been a servant. "The instructors. The students. I didn't want to talk to them about any part of myself. Now"—clasping her hands at her back, she leaned against the paneled door—"Now, I wish I hadn't. I wished I'd let someone be there because, in being alone, all one has is their memories…and silence…and that, I have to believe is more terrifying than letting someone in."

His throat bobbed spasmodically. He couldn't get the words out. Couldn't share the reasons for his collapse that night. "Thank you… Mrs. Bryant." In a bid to protect himself, he built up those barricades.

Rowena stiffened. "Forgive me. I will leave you for the night…Your Grace." With a flawless curtsy, she swept from the room with a regal elegance the queen herself couldn't muster.

As soon as he was alone, Graham unleashed a stream of curses. Hurt, frustration, anger, despair all broiled within, and letting out a roar, he shoved the ledgers off his desk, clearing the surface. They landed hard on the floor, a haphazard tangle of pages and leather that bore a marked resemblance to the chaos that his life had become.

What was happening to him? Everything he'd worked for, everything he'd sought to be—collected, reserved, unfeeling—had been singlehandedly destroyed by Rowena. She'd made him feel again; and he had paid the price of his control for it. And now she'd seen the darkest weaknesses of his mind and sought to placate him like a damned child.

Restless, he skittered his panicky gaze about. It collided with his sideboard. Marching over, he grabbed a bottle, carried it to his desk, and sat—determined to get himself, for the first time in seven years, well and truly soused.

FOURTEEN

She should be sleeping. She should at the very least be sitting quietly in her chambers reading or evaluating the week's activities planned with and for her charge.

Sleep, however, proved impossible. Lying on the four-poster bed more comfortable than any mattress she'd so much as sat on in the course of her life, Rowena stared overhead at the mural of an English country landscape. The fire's glow cast eerie shadows upon the frolicking sheep and pastel blue skies there, turning the tableau into something macabre.

Graham's struggles were not hers to worry after. Nor could he have been any clearer when he'd coolly addressed her by her surname that he'd no interest in her beyond the role she served within his household. The moment he'd departed for war and turned her away, he'd cut her from the fabric of his life in all the ways that mattered. She lived here now as nothing more than a servant in his employ, a companion to his ward, whom when wedded, would mean her return to Mrs. Belden's.

"Miserable Mrs. Belden," she whispered into the quiet.

The flames snapped and hissed in the hearth in an intangible agreement.

Not unlike Ainsley who referred to Jack Turner in those like terms. That was precisely how Rowena had, in her mind, referred to the merciless headmistress, when she'd arrived at that cold, lonely school. Mrs. Belden's, that place devoid of warmth and love and laughter—and she'd been forced there because of her connection to Graham.

She flipped onto her side and grabbed the book laying open on the nightstand. Tugging free the letter written long ago, she read. Though reading was no longer necessary. She'd had those words inked in her mind for more years than she cared to remember. She trailed her fingertips over the hated sentences there, back to when Graham would have made her his whore, when he wanted nothing more of her than that.

With the suffering brought into her life by the Linford family, why should she care about the haunted glint in his eyes—the terror, the horror, and shame—as they'd fled the Duke of Wilkshire's card party?

Because I care about him, still.

Being here, with him, in his household didn't lessen the truth of the love they'd once shared—it only heightened it.

Her mother, her stepfather, Graham...they may all have easily snipped her from their lives without another thought, but when Rowena loved, she did so deeply. It was why she'd been able to walk away from Blanche and Bianca and the fields of Wallingford. Because when one loved, one wanted to take away a person's struggle and suffering. One did everything in one's power to ease any hurt and ensure the happiness one could.

Love wasn't conditional. For if it was, she'd now be sleeping like a babe who'd just finished a bottle of warm milk, Graham's earlier outburst buried under the peace of her own slumbering.

A faint knock sounded at the door. Shoving herself to an upright position, Rowena hurriedly stuffed the missive inside her book, and snapped it closed. *Graham.*

Hating the charge that went through her at the mere thought of his name, Rowena jumped up, grabbed her wrapper. Sprinting across the room, she shrugged into the garment just as another knock ensued. She pulled the door open. "Oh." An inexplicable disappointment swamped her. Her charge stared impatiently back. "Ainsley," she belatedly greeted.

"You don't look like you were sleeping," she observed, sweeping inside with the air of one who owned the guest chambers.

Rowena peeked out into the empty hall, and then pushed the door closed. "Is everything all right?" she repeated.

Ainsley plunked herself down on Rowena's bed, perching herself on the edge, dangerously close to her book and letter. "I'm sure the gossips will have a good deal to say about that in the morning."

She didn't pretend to misunderstand. "Yes. They undoubtedly will," she said gently, coming over, and taking a spot alongside the young lady. Following Ainsley's wild display at the Duke of Wilkshire's they'd not spoken of the scandalous outburst. Rowena was not so oblivious or naive, however, to fail and realize just what had prompted that show. "You did that to help His Grace."

The younger woman lifted her one shoulder in a little shrug. "Better me than him. They were always going to talk about me, anyway. Nothing he, you, or I could do about it." Any other lady would have been shedding copious tears and bemoaning the unfairness of their cruel Society.

All these years, Rowena had prided herself on her strength...for having survived when most women would have crumpled. How wrong she'd been. This bold, fearless, and undaunted lady before her was far braver and stronger than she had ever been, or ever would be. And what was more, she moved through life with spirit and a smile, anyway.

Humbled, Rowena searched for some suitable reply, when Ainsley spoke suddenly and unexpectedly.

Ainsley hesitated, and then, eyeing her warily, demanded: "You are one of Hampstead's friends, are you not?"

Rowena automatically nodded. For everything that had come to pass, he'd been her first friend and lover, and he would always own a place in her heart.

The young lady scooted closer. "And you witnessed him tonight." She had. Rowena's heart flipped over with the pain of his suffering. Ainsley edged back on the mattress and drew her knees up to her chest. "My father suffered the nightmares," she confided, looping her arms around her small limbs. "After my father's nightmares, when he came through, he'd drink heavily and shut himself away in his offices."

Rowena listened on, filled with pain for the late father and Ainsley's suffering. She covered the girl's hands with one of her own.

"The night he…" With a somberness Rowena hadn't seen in the young lady, Ainsley stared down at her toes peeking out from under the hem of her nightshift. "fell, I was walking the halls. I heard a thunderous bang. It was the worst sound ever, Mrs. Bryant," she whispered, the hissing flames from the fire marred her tortured face in shadows.

Knowing Ainsley needed to speak these words, even as Rowena selfishly didn't want to hear them or consider the suffering this young lady in fact had endured, she sat in silence.

"It wasn't a normal sound." She sucked in a shuddery breath. "Not the sound of a man who fell down the stairs."

Oh, God. And despite the assurances Rowena had given Graham she proved to be a liar, once more. Tears pricked behind her lashes. She blinked furiously not wanting to give Ainsley those useless expressions of sorrow.

"Do you know what I'm saying?" Ainsley asked in solemn tones.

"I do," she whispered. God, she did. He'd taken his own life, and his daughter had been listening the moment he did so. She remained in awe of who this young woman was. How had she maintained her cheer and spirit?

"Yes, well." Ainsley cleared her throat and scooted herself to the edge of the bed. "As you're a friend, I thought you might…look after Hampstead."

And then her meaning became clear. Their eyes locked, and at the same time, a gooseflesh dotted Rowena's flesh. *She is worried Graham will find that same fate.*

"He was in his office. Drinking," Ainsley said, eerily following her unspoken thoughts.

She forced a smile for the young lady's benefit. "You don't have to worry," she said softly, taking Ainsley's hands in her own. "His Grace will not…do anything that might harm himself." She was certain of it. "You should rest," she said, climbing to her feet. Her charge followed suit.

Ainsley nodded, and then darted from the room. She closed the door quietly behind her, and was gone.

The moment she'd gone, Rowena let her false smile fall. Grabbing her book, she threw herself back on the bed. Of course Graham wouldn't harm himself. Ainsley's fears came from the loss of her own father. Furthermore, Graham had been eager to be rid of her. That much had been clear. Rowena popped her book open...and attempted to read.

Ainsley's veiled warnings, however, blotted out her earlier confidence for the girl. With a sigh, she climbed to her feet. Book in hand, she made her way from her rooms, through the darkened halls, until she found herself outside Graham's office. She pressed her ear against the panel. An eerie silence lingered.

She creased her brow. Shifting her book under her arm, she pressed the handle and dipped her head inside.

"Mrs. Bryant?" Back presented to her, Graham stood at the hearth, staring downward. Somewhere during the night, he'd discarded his jacket and boots, and this rumpled version of him tugged at her heart.

With more reserve, Rowena entered and closed them in once more. "Your Grace."

Graham shot a glance over his shoulder. A derisive tilt on his lips, he took in the book in her hands. "Seeking out an early morn read?" That slightly jeering question gave her a brief pause.

Setting her thin disguise on the rose-inlaid table at the door, she ventured forward. "I didn't know what to think," she confessed with absolute honesty. At his silence, Rowena found her way cautiously over to him. She stopped at his shoulder. "You've nightmares, too," she spoke into the quiet. Nightmares, as he'd taken to calling her panic during the summertime storms.

His muscles strained the fabric of his white lawn shirt. He nodded, an empty chuckle rumbling from within his chest. Graham raised his glass in salute, and then downed the contents. "What can one expect of a madman?" he asked in his rigidly perfect ducal tones.

Rowena followed his jerky movements, as he set the glass down with a hard *thunk*. The quake of his fingers hinted at a man hurting. Is that how he saw himself? As a madman? "You are not mad, Graham," she said softly, drifting closer.

He settled his palms on the edge of the mantel, that subtle shift of his body. Was his a deliberate move, to keep her out? As one who'd held everyone at arm's distance, she well knew the power that came in protecting oneself from hurt. From feeling...*anything*. "What do you call it, then?" He directed his question to the flames. "What do you call it when a man's control snaps, and he's transported to another moment. Another moment so dark it leaves him sweating and shaking and incapable of rational thought?"

In those earliest days, when she'd returned to Mrs. Belden's with a purse and a note from Graham, sniveling in her lumpy bed at night, she'd cursed him to the devil. Wished him to know pain like the one he'd inflicted. How wrong she'd been. The sight of it wrenched her heart in two. She laid a palm on his shoulder, and the muscles bunched under her hand. "I call it being human, Graham. It does not make you weak or insane to think of what happened. It makes you a very real man, who hurts at the suffering he's seen—"

"And caused," he rasped, spinning around. Rowena braced her legs, refusing to retreat.

"It was war," she said simply. "You did not create that conflict...but you helped to end it."

He dragged a hand through his hair, and then glanced about. The fire illuminated the volatile glint in his eyes as he turned and stared blankly into those crimson depths. "Do you want to know the truth?" he asked with a vagueness that raised the gooseflesh on her arms.

Rowena nodded, and yet selfishly she did not want him to reveal those words that would let her into any more of his darkest horrors.

"In the first year I returned home, the pain was so great I willed myself to die."

Agony lashed at her heart. "Oh, Graham," she said on an aching whisper, stretching a hand out.

"I came home, and there was shrapnel still in my leg. It became infected." A humorless laugh escaped him, wreaking havoc on her already hurting heart. "By rights, I should have been dead. At the very least, I should be without the leg."

Her heart crumpled. "I did not know," she said softly, gripping his shoulder. The heat of his skin penetrated the fine lawn.

His eyes slid closed. "*You* were the hope that sustained me."

Feeling burned, she dropped her arm to her side. She tried to follow that unexpected shift. "Me?" she asked on a faint echo, his admission making no sense with the man who'd so callously turned her away.

He gave her a hard smile. "For years, I had no fewer than twelve thousand questions for you. I spent more years hating you than loving you." Her entire body jerked, and he may as well have run her through. "Resenting you. Wanting to know why. Wanting to know how a person who'd been, first, my best friend and then my lover could so easily forget me. Some days, I told myself you were a fickle, flighty creature like every other societal miss."

Rowena held her body so taut she feared she'd break.

"Other days, I told myself you did it for self-preservation. As one who did all to survive, I understood that." Graham scraped a hand over his face. "Do you know what I found? The truth I denied until I arrived at that miserable finishing school and saw you in that office."

She shook her head slightly trying to compare that broken man he described against the one who'd turned her away with nothing more than a note.

He opened bloodshot eyes. "I don't hate you. I could never truly hate you." Her throat moved. "I hated myself for not being enough for you. I hated you for not having bothered to write me a single note when I'd written you every night I wasn't in battle." While he carried on, she stared back at him unblinking. *He'd written me?* She shook her head but the cobwebs remained. "The truth is you saved me. Through those ruthless days on the fields of Portugal and Spain, to the nights I lay in terror for the coming battle, it was your face I saw. I was fighting to return to you." She pressed a palm to her mouth as she tried to rationalize his drunken admissions. "The dream of you sustained me, Rowena. And for that, I will be forever grateful." He again closed his eyes.

Through her confusion, she tried to think, to form words, to breathe. At last, she drew sufficient air into her lungs to form just three words. "I wrote you," she whispered, hugging herself tight. "It was you who never wrote me."

He blinked slowly. "What?" he asked, that one-word utterance wrapped in befuddlement.

"My notes. I wrote you every single day." There was a panicky tremor to her slowly increasing voice. "Every single day," she repeated. "Would you tell me you never received one of them?"

Graham's mouth moved but no words came out. Then, he slowly shook his head.

"You lie," she whispered.

Confusion marred his features. "I never received anything from you." There was an accusation there.

And that was when, she had confirmation of a truth that had only come to her after all these years. He'd never received her letters. Now, his defection made sense in ways it never had, could never have before. It was why she'd received but one note from him. A note that contained an ugly part of his soul she'd never believed existed. Then, they all had darkness in their hearts. Ultimately, however, he'd believed the absolute worst of her. Doubted her loyalty and love...and had sent her away for it. "Oh, I assure you, quite possible," she said on a bitter, broken laugh. She leveled him with shattered eyes. "*You* were the one who never wrote me."

FIFTEEN

You were the one who never wrote me...

An odd humming filled Graham's ears as he sought to make sense of Rowena's denials and her charges. "I did. I wrote you whenever I was—"

"I only received the one note from you," she interrupted.

"One?"

She nodded.

Graham looked about his darkened office. "*You* didn't...I..." He faltered his way through incoherent words, unable to string a single thought together. The dream of a letter from her had sustained him through hellish nights, when the screams of dead and dying had echoed over the battlefields.

Either Rowena was a consummate liar, which was certainly possible...or she'd never received his letters. He pressed his fingertips against his temple and rubbed, cursing the episode at Lord Wilkshire's that had left his mind jumbled, wishing he could make sense of her pronouncement. He shook his head.

She nodded.

Impossible. He'd been gone for more than two years, and in that time, he'd received not a single missive outside the one sent by his father after Alistair's passing. A niggling of unease whispered around his mind with the dark seeds now planted. Graham looked down into the flames leaping in the hearth. His fingers trembled at his side, and he flexed his palms to still that quaking. He tried again. "I don't under—"

168

Rowena met his gaze squarely; a hurt accusation in their brown depths. "*I wrote you every day,*" she said softly, searching her eyes over his face. Her fingers curled in the fabric of her skirts. "At the end of each week, I would lace one of my ribbons around a stack of letters and send them on to you. By the candle's glow in the dead of night, when my family slept on, I would kiss those pages." A bitter, broken laugh left her lips. "And I never received a word."

She'd written him. His throat worked. He'd seen the truth in her eyes: the shock, the horror. "Who would intercept them?" his voice emerged a gruff accusation. "Who would field all your missives?" Who would want to see him in abject misery?

Rowena drew in a shuddery breath. "Someone determined to keep us apart." Her voice broke. "Your father," she whispered. Her stricken gaze met his. "It was your father. He despised me."

A charged tension filled the room, punctuated by the occasional hiss of the fire.

He lowered his eyebrows, seeking to make sense of the murky waters she'd thrust him into where all his certainties over the years were thrown into question, challenging long-held facts that had shaped deeply-burned resentments. "My father did not discourage our friendship," he puzzled aloud. The late duke had shown him little attention. Until Graham had been named heir upon his return from Portugal.

Another hoarse, humorless laugh burst from her lips. "Of course he did not. Not while you were merely his spare. Why should his second-born son not be tupping the starry-eyed village girl so eagerly spreading her legs?"

Graham whipped his head to face her. "Do not say that," he said sharply. He fixed a glare on her. He'd not have her disparage herself. Not now and certainly not in memory of what they'd shared.

"It's true, though, isn't it?" she persisted, misunderstanding the reason for his order. Rowena took several bold steps toward him. "Before your brother's passing, what use did your father have of you?"

None. His father had no use for his second son. It was a fact that had chafed for the small boy he'd been. Then the new vicar had moved into the village with his wife and young daughter, Rowena. His life had become full—until he'd gone to war and found her gone.

She dusted a hand over her face. "It hardly matters what you felt in those days, Graham." Her voice rang with fatigue and frustration. "Your father ordered me gone."

His entire body jerked, and he backed slowly away from her, he gave his head a frantic shake. "No," he whispered because if there was truth to those few words, then that would mean she'd not left him but had been forced away. It would mean that all these years he'd spent hating her had been for sins that belonged to another: his father...*And me.*

Rowena hugged herself in a lonely embrace. She continued as though he'd not spoken, as though his world was not ratcheting down around him. "I was in the gardens." Hers was a threadbare whisper, laden with the agony of remembered suffering. "The day he arrived..." Her lower lip trembled. "I believed you were dead. Why else would the duke come to call on me?" An acrimonious laugh belonging to an older, more cynical woman split her lips. "How naïve I-I was," she rasped out. "That a duke would ever call on me for any such reason." The gleam of tears in her eyes turned them into crystal pools of despair that struck worse than any bullet or blade to lance his flesh. "That would have meant I mattered in some way."

He shook his head, not wanting her to go on. For if her words were spoken in truth, then it would mean that his life these years had been nothing more than a lie orchestrated by his merciless father. *I'm going to be ill.* "What did he want?" he asked hoarsely.

She eyed him cautiously, with a lifetime's worth of mistrust in her eyes. She expected him to doubt her. "He ordered me to leave. If I didn't..." She briefly closed her eyes, and that visible sign of her grief ravaged him. "He would see my father removed from his position as vicar."

Her words had the same affect of a carriage slamming into his chest. Graham concentrated on his slow, ragged breaths. He drew on every lesson in control he'd mastered these years, and forced himself into a semblance of calm. "When did you...?" *Leave.* His voice emerged garbled to his own ears, and he struggled through a tight throat. Except, by her admission, she'd not gone...not willingly. He had to say it. He had to breathe the truth of her admission into existence, so then mayhap he might process everything she'd revealed. "When were you forced to leave?"

Her spine stiffly erect, her shoulders squared, Rowena possessed the regal bearing, far greater than any duchess or queen. She notched her chin up. "You'd been injured. Near the time your brother died." Of course. His father would have always been thinking of the title. She grimaced. "He could not risk that you would return and possibly wish to make me your wife." Possibly wish? It had been Graham's *only* wish. Every word was a lash upon his soul, and he took the stinging, sharp pain of it, and through his tumult, she continued in a stoic calm. "He promised to see the world knew who…" Her voice grew soft, and he strained to hear. "…*what* I was." *A bastard.* It had been a detail Rowena had confided in him, and somehow, his father had found out her past.

Then, the late, all-powerful duke had known all. The ruthless, rank-driven ways that had forever driven his now-dead father, who controlled Graham's world, even in death.

She looked down at her clasped hands. "He gave me fifty pounds and a carriage ride to my new post."

A post as instructor for pampered, privileged ladies. "Was there even a Mr. Bryant?" he asked with a faint imploring. Needing to believe that even as she'd been wronged, that there had at least been one man who'd not failed her, when he had wronged her in every way.

Rowena shook her head. "There was only ever you," she said softly.

"Stop," he pleaded, holding a hand up, trying to process. To make sense of the words she spoke. Because it would mean everything had been a lie. It would mean Graham had spent the better part of his adult life hating the only woman he'd ever loved for imagined crimes. His stomach pitched, the same way he had when he'd marched upon his first battlefield into a sea of screams and cannon fire, with the report of pistols dulling his hearing. He dug his fingertips hard into his temples.

She wandered over to the window. Blankly, he followed her every movement. The slow, careful strides. The stretch of her hand as she brushed aside the velvet curtains. "He gave me fifty pounds." Fifty pounds. *Like she'd been a whore.* Bile burned his throat. "He saw me set

171

up with employment at Mrs. Belden's Finishing School, as long as I did not ever come near you, again. My parents were promised fifteen pounds monthly, until his death."

Fifteen pounds monthly. One hundred and eighty pounds for the course of a year. That was the rate with which a parent would betray one's own daughter. Nausea broiled in his gut. How could her voice be so steady when, with every utterance, she sent him into a muddled tumult? "You were at that miserable school because of him," he whispered to himself. *Nay, because of me.* He thought of that cheerless, stilted institution he'd plucked her from by chance. A place where she'd been stifled and hidden away like a secret shame.

"No," she said with sadness infusing that denial. "I was there because of *us*. Because we could never have been, and he knew that, just as you returned and also knew it." She directed that last piece out onto the streets below.

"That is not true," he whispered. He would have slain the devil himself for her. *But that isn't altogether true. Eaten alive by resentment and jealousy, I hated her all these years...* That voice whispered tauntingly around his tortured mind.

She whipped around. "You were just like him."

He recoiled, burned by the venom in her eyes. "No." And yet, unwittingly, by her revelations, he had been.

Skirts whipping about her ankles she stalked over. "Future dukes don't wed the daughters of whores," she jeered. "You said as much, yourself. You and your father," she reminded him. She stormed to the front of the room. Graham surged forward on his heels, to stop her flight.

Except—

Rowena grabbed her book off the table and marched over.

She tugged out a single note and hurled it at him. The sheet caught and twisted and turned a silent path to his feet. His gaze went to her tightly-clenched fingers, drained of blood, to the page. "What is this?" Numbly he retrieved the vellum and, unfolding it, skimmed words written in his hand. All the air left him on a swift exhale. He frantically ran his gaze again over the words.

...I would have married you...on nothing more than a lie. In dallying with a vicar's daughter, I lowered myself beneath my station. However, you are no vicar's daughter, Miss Endicott. You are a whore's daughter, and as such, there can be nothing respectable. If you desire a place in my bed...

Everything from his too large "R's" and barely closed "E's" had been masterfully created. Graham lifted stunned eyes to hers. "I did not write this," he breathed. Surely she must have known all that had ever mattered was their love for one another? Why should she have known that? What truth had she had of that?

Clutching her book close, she jabbed at the page. "Your father gave it to me when I tried to come to you."

"You came to me?" For his father's threats, she'd braved all, anyway.

"And you had him turn me away with a note. It is in your hand, Graham." There was a high-pitched quality to her timbre that suggested the thin grasp she had on her control.

"I know," he said hoarsely. "But I did not." He balled the page in his hand, and the aged vellum crunched loudly. "I would never..." For on that note contained details he'd never even known about this woman before him. Details that would have never mattered to him but would very much have to the late duke. "I didn't write this," he repeated, holding it out. "I could never say those things to you." His gut clenched like he'd taken a blow to the belly. Not even when he'd hated her beyond all reason could he have uttered a single one of those vile words etched in time.

The small leather volume slipped from her grasp and tumbled to the floor with a soft thump. "You did not know..." She wetted her lips. "About my mother?"

That tentative question gave him pause. When she'd revealed the truth of her birthright, she'd mentioned a mistake in her mother's past that had resulted in her birth. "What about your mother?"

For a long while, she said nothing, and he believed she intended to say nothing more on it. Then, she straightened her shoulders with the regal bearing of any queen. "My mother was a courtesan."

Her revelation slammed into him with the weight of a fast-moving carriage. He reeled back. Numbed. The world unmoving. And through it, he tried to pick his way around what was real and false. She had kept that detail from him? Why?

Rowena flattened her palms against her skirts, but not before he detected the faint tremble there. "She had a string of protectors, one of whom sired me. It was a truth I kept from you." She angled her chin up.

Her revealing eyes glimmered with a challenge. *Why…she still believes I'll condemn her now for that.* Then, although her reaction chafed, he thought of the ruthless lords and ladies who'd take apart a lady because of the very truth she now imparted. To Graham, however, her birthright had never mattered. Only she had. To utter that now would smack of the greatest lie.

In her failing to come to him when he'd returned, all the words his father had uttered, confirmed by Rowena's absence and reiterated by her mother's admission. It had shattered him in ways that the wound he'd suffered on the battlefield never could have. It was why his father would never have allowed a union between them.

He gave his head a dizzying shake. Why had her mother not confided in him when he'd gone to her? "It does not make sense. I saw your mother. As soon as I was able, I went to your cottage." The memory of that day flitted across his thoughts. The stark fear in the lovely woman's eyes. The uncharacteristic somberness of Rowena's two young sisters. "She told me you'd gone. Told me you found another."

Tears welled in Rowena's eyes, turning them into brown pools of despair. She blinked back the crystalline drops.

"Why would she do that?" he cried. To protect the Hampstead title at all costs, his father would have resorted to great evil. But there was Rowena's own mother and stepfather. Surely the whole world had not been in collusion against them.

"What should she have done, Graham? Defy the duke who threatened her family?"

The blade twisted all the deeper. "Your mother put the well-being of your father and sisters before your own?" His voice emerged sharper than he intended, but he could not soften his fury. So many had wronged her. The late duke. Her family. And worst of all...him.

"No," she said quietly, and he went still. Rowena touched her palm to the middle of her chest. "*I* put the well-being of my sisters before my own. What fate would await us if your father saw us cast off his properties? What would become of Bianca and Blanche?"

Her sisters. *What about you?* But isn't that how Rowena Endicott had always been? Putting everyone else first? Which is why her simply forgetting him had been anathema to all he knew of her and about her. A strangled half-sob rumbled in his chest. For if her words were spoken in truth, then all these years he'd spent hating her, the time he'd spent wondering why she'd chosen another, all of it would have been nothing more than lies handed down by his father and perpetuated by her mother.

Graham backed up a step, and his legs knocked against the sofa.

Through his unsteadiness, Rowena stood there calm, cool, wholly unaffected. Only, the sadness seeping from her brown eyes belied that mask she donned. He closed his eyes briefly, trying to sort through the facts and fiction that were his life.

It had all been a lie. Nausea broiled in his belly, and he fought to keep from casting up his accounts at her feet. He'd spent years resenting her when, in fact, he'd been the faithless one of their pair. He'd wronged her. Doubted her. He'd owed it to her to search for her, find her, and sort through these details...long, long ago. Not here, not now, and not because he'd hired her as a servant in his employ.

He swiped a hand over his face. And as the sad irony slammed into him, a broken, empty chuckle rumbled deep in his chest. His father had sent Rowena away to keep her from him...but the moment he had left for war and returned a madman, she'd been forever out of his reach.

"He fed you every lie needed to keep us apart, Graham." Her accusatory eyes met his. "And how easily you believed him." With a sad shake of her head, Rowena left her book and that hated note...and was gone.

SIXTEEN

A ny other day, Graham would have been focused on the gossip columns now resting on the edge of his desk. His public display and Ainsley's attempt to help him save face were splashed upon the front pages for the world to see.

Now, he was closeted away in his office, those sheets sat forgotten. A bottle of brandy and untouched glass rested at the corner of his desk. Ledgers and folios covered every other spare surface. Head bent, he attended the neat ledger before him, pouring through countless months of accounting, searching those lines for secrets contained within, just as he'd been doing since Rowena's revelations a few hours earlier. Figures kept by the late duke's man-of-affairs, who upon the miserable bastard's death had been immediately replaced with the only man he'd ever trusted. He skimmed row after row, and then stopped. One inked sum commanded his notice, freezing him.

Graham trailed his index finger over one line. It was not an exorbitant sum. It was not a figure that would have given anyone pause should they stop and review the ledgers of one of the wealthiest families in England. A fifty-pound mark, recorded on the 29th of September, 1810.

That was the money paid Rowena. To leave. To go away, like a shameful, dirty secret his father had sought to bury. Like Judas, collecting that bag of silver, her parents had accepted a pittance, sacrificing her for their family. She'd been his everything. She'd been the dream that sustained him. The only woman he had, and would ever, love. And they'd sent her away—on a lie. Snarling like a wounded beast, he grabbed one of the already studied ledgers and hurled it against the wall. It sailed to the floor, with a noisy *thwack*.

…What should I have done, Graham? Defied the duke who threatened my family…?

His hand trembled. How matter-of-fact she'd been. She'd simply put her younger sisters' happiness before that of her own, and went on to make a new life for herself. Only, it hadn't been a bag of silver. It had been fifteen pounds, paid monthly, until the duke had kicked up his heels and gone on to meet the devil as he deserved.

Graham dragged over another. He proceeded to flip through the pages, purposefully scanning dates as he went. Then he found it. An entry for fifteen pounds. No markings. No initials. No names. And yet, he knew. With a growl, he turned the page so quickly, he nearly tore it, as he searched a month later for another and then another.

With every confirmation of that seemingly innocuous entry, frustration built inside at what that amount had concealed from him all these years. He tossed aside the book. His fingers twitching with the restless energy thrumming inside him, Graham grabbed another ledger, and turned to the far end of the book, settling on the date his father had died. That would have been the last date of payment.

Grabbing his snifter, he downed the contents in one long swallow and grimaced at the trail it burned in its wake. He set it down hard.

He looked like hell, and he didn't need a mirror before him to tell as much. A night without sleep, after he'd discovered his whole damned life was a lie would have that effect on a man.

His gut churned.

…He fed you every lie needed to keep us apart…

For the hell of it all was that Rowena was correct, and no matter what excuses or explanations or apologies he might make, the truth remained: he'd been unfaithful to her—in every way a man could be unfaithful to a woman. Grief went through him, and he squeezed his eyes shut.

A knock sounded at the door, and his heart kicked up a hopeful beat. Graham surged forward in his chair. "Enter."

His butler entered, quashing those futile sentiments. *Did you truly believe Rowena has a reason to seek you out?* "This arrived a short while ago, Your Grace." The servant came forward and placed an officious scrap of vellum on his desk.

He took in the familiar seal of the Duke of Wilkshire. "Thank you, Wesley." He ignored the page, neither caring nor curious about the contents of that note. Three weeks earlier, it would have been all that mattered. It would have been formalizing a contract and seeing to his ducal responsibilities. Everything changed. "Wesley," he called out.

The servant immediately turned back.

"Mrs. Bryant and Miss Hickenbottom?"

His butler inclined his head. "They are in the ballroom for the young lady's dance lessons, Your Grace."

Some of the tension eased. "Of course. Thank you," Graham murmured. *Did you expect she would have left in the dead of night?* Which she was most certainly entitled to have done. She'd owed him nothing. He'd deserved even less. Yet, she'd come anyway—originally at his insistence—and then agreed to stay for Ainsley. He was humbled by her honor. He'd never been worthy of Rowena Endicott. He clenched his eyes tightly shut. And she'd lost all because of her association with him.

How did a man and a woman go on from here? How did they act toward one another?

Shoving to his feet, Graham abandoned his office and went in search of a woman he had no right to seek out. He paused at the base of the marble foyer. The faint strains of a violin filtered from the ballroom. He paused, and then of their own volition, his legs moved, carrying him close to that haunting melody.

"*Non. Non. Non, il est un-deux-trois...*"

"I cannot understand you," Ainsley's sharp tone carried to Graham's ears, and he stopped in the doorway. His ward stood in the arms of a tall, wiry gentleman with thickly curled golden strands. The young lady glowered up at the stranger.

What in blazes? The pair and Rowena singularly engrossed in the lesson, Graham used their distraction to slip inside the ballroom, and take up position behind the towering Doric column.

"Is this a bloody French lesson? Or a dance lesson?" Ainsley demanded. "Because it really shouldn't be both, Fargand."

"It is both," Rowena confirmed from the edge of the dance floor. The lady stood with her back to Graham, but from her gentling tones, her attempt to stymy a conflict between instructor and student rang clear.

Ainsley deepened her scowl for the handsome gentleman. "If you count in English, then mayhap I'll master the steps. If you can count in English, that is. Can you?"

The beleaguered dance instructor muttered something under his breath, which earned him a stomp from Ainsley. A gasp slid through the man's teeth.

Rowena clapped her hands once. "Ainsley…"

"I know. I know. We do not stomp on the toes of our partners. *Deliberately,*" the lady added as an afterthought.

Rowena motioned for the bespectacled man seated with a violin poised at his shoulder to resume playing. As the strident chords soared through the ballroom, Graham used her distractedness to study her. Her back in profile to him, she displayed the proud regal bearing of a woman better suited to the title queen than companion. So very different than she'd been when he'd taught her how to waltz through the quiet countryside in the early morn hours, when the sun had first peeked over the horizon. She'd moved with such zeal and exuberance he'd been lost in that freeing joy. His own life prior to her entry all those years ago had been stilted and cheerless. He'd been born to parents who saw little use of him beyond his rank as spare. Two people who'd been so fixed on hosting formal affairs and honoring their placement as Society's leading peers that there had been an absolute and total lack of joy—until Rowena.

Graham searched, aching to see a hint of that childlike happiness, but then, how did one retain any hint of it when life proved the ugliness in people's souls and saw one ruined for it? He leaned the side of his head against the pillar, mourning everything his father and her family had killed.

Then, she began to tip her head in a slight beat to the rhythm. And he froze. That jaunty back and forth tilt held him riveted, and he was momentarily transported.

You must teach me how to waltz, Graham Linford. I must know how...

They'd danced in wild circles until they'd tumbled to the earth, and then he'd made love to her there with the sun beating down on their bodies and the birds chirping their summertime song. As a girl, Rowena had been pretty. As a woman, she'd developed a sophisticated beauty. His breath hitched with a hungering to again know the feel of her in his arms.

"*Non, non, non. Il est un à trois comptage. Ne pas*—ahh," the dance instructor cried out, bringing Graham back. Flushed, the gentleman promptly released Ainsley. "She stomped me. Again. I cannot work under zees conditions, Madame Bryant," the man bemoaned, throwing his hands in the air. Abandoning his charge on the dance floor, he hurried over to the chair alongside the violinist.

Rowena sprung into movement. "She is a new student," she protested, while he continued to stack his pages into a neat pile.

"She is a hellion."

Graham scowled. He'd instructed Rowena to advise his ward on matters of propriety and decorum, and yet hearing the dance instructor's condescending opinion of Ainsley's spirit set his teeth on edge. He took a step forward to intervene on behalf of his charge, but then stopped. "She is spirited," Rowena countered. "And I believe that is to be commended." She had been so very much like the girl she now ardently defended. It was a spirit that she would have passed to her own sons and daughters. A pang struck his chest.

"The girl does not want to learn." The instructor gathered his belongings. He motioned to the violinist, but Rowena shot a staying hand out, freezing the bespectacled man. Swallowing loudly, the violinist promptly sat.

Smart man.

Monsieur Fargand made to step around Rowena, but more determined than any battle-hardened commander Graham had served under, she stepped into the flustered instructor's path, blocking his retreat. "She *does* wish to learn. Miss Hickenbottom simply requires a..." She paused, and he could all but see the wheels turning in her mind. "Different approach to instruction."

The dance master hesitated. Yes, then Rowena had always possessed the ability to talk the legs off a table. Reluctantly, the flushed gentleman moved his gaze over to his wayward student. "Is zees true?"

"I do," Ainsley said solemnly.

"See," Rowena said in gentle tones better suited for calming a fractious mare.

"Just not from a French frog," the stubborn lady added.

Rowena slapped a hand over her face.

Shock rounded the instructor's eyes, and sputtering, he took advantage of her momentary distraction and bustled off. The man stalked past Graham and marched proudly from the ballroom.

Quiet descended over the ballroom, broken only when Ainsley spoke. "I am sorry, Mrs. Bryant." The threadbare quality of her apology, so at odds with the lively lady who'd upended his household and saved him from solo humiliation last evening, brought a frown.

Rowena settled a reassuring hand on her charge's shoulder. "It is fine," she said gently.

"Hampstead will no doubt be furious."

He stilled. That is what she believed. That he'd take her to task for the judgmental dance instructor? *Then, why should she not?* Hadn't he given both Rowena and Ainsley to believe that very thing?

Disquieted, he strained to hear Rowena's answering reply. Whatever muted assurances she gave or did not give, were lost to the distance separating them. At that incorrect supposition on the child's part, his frown deepened. It was the image he'd sought to perfect for the world: aloof, frosty, unfeeling duke. Anything to keep the world at bay, and to keep his secrets his own. Standing here, on the fringe of a meeting between Rowena and his ward, he found he did not want to be that cold, desolate figure he'd been. Donning that false persona had not rid him of the demons haunting him. It had not cured his madness. Last night had been proof of that. No, his aloofness had only left an even larger void inside.

"I assure you, I am many things, none of which is furious." His voice boomed around the soaring room, and with like gasps, companion and charge looked to him. Strolling forward, Graham stopped before them. He searched Rowena for a hint of expression after her revelation last evening. Her thoughts. Anything. But she was stoic, divulging nothing in her carefully composed features. When the two ladies said nothing, he folded his arms. "Well?"

"We are without a dance instructor," Rowena explained in her headmistress tones. "Monsieur Fargand has tendered his resignation." She spoke as one delivering an announcement to an employer. *That is what I am.* He scowled, and the lady's explanation abruptly trailed off.

"It is my fault." Ainsley waggled her fingers. "Though, I did deliberately stomp his feet." The lady stared up, a challenge in her eyes.

Graham folded his arms at his chest and looked between them. "Good."

Companion and charge cocked their heads in like angles.

"I'll not have a condescending dance master instructing my charge." Or Rowena. If the blighter hadn't stormed off, Graham would have happily sacked him. Smothering his amusement at their muted shock, he held an elbow out for his ward. "May I?"

Ainsley looked at him as though he'd sprung a second head. "May you what?"

Over the girl's head, Rowena's mouth parted in slight shock, and then her wary eyes turned soft. The deep tension receded in his chest, leaving in its place a remarkable lightness. With the exception of Jack, whose friendship at best had dissolved into a more businesslike, perfunctory relationship since Waterloo, he had been largely alone. There was something so freeing in this shared connection with Rowena and the girl Hickenbottom had charged to his care.

"Dance," she said gently, taking the girl's hand. "His Grace is going to show you the steps." She paused. "In English, Your Grace."

Graham. I want to hear my name fall easily from your lips.

He wanted to strip away all rank and divisions between them, so it was just them, once more, as they'd been.

Casting him a long, dubious look, Ainsley at last placed her palm on his shoulder.

"The posture is the most important of your positioning," Rowena guided from the edge of the floor. "You do not want to slump as you dance. Lift your elbows," she murmured.

The young lady drew her shoulders back and moved into the directed position.

Rowena motioned to the violinist, and the man scrambled to raise his instrument and proceeded to play. "Now, right foot back," she called softly, as Graham led Ainsley through the steps. "Together. Side—"

"Why does the lady have to go back?" the lady groused, her brow scrunched in deep concentration. "I'd much rather Hampstead be the one having to dance backward."

Graham chuckled, and that mirth ended on a grunt as Ainsley stepped on his foot. "My apologies," he murmured. Since she'd been placed in his guardianship, he'd worried about her entry into Society, how she'd be received. How to tame her so she was accepted by at least some of the peerage. After last evening, he'd accepted the truth: there would be no taming this one, and he found he'd rather that she hold onto that part of her spirit.

"Now back on the left and side on the right and..."

Ainsley stumbled, and with a frustrated shout, she stepped out of Graham's arms. "I need to see it."

At their questioning looks, she slashed a hand at them, and then motioned to the dance floor. "I need to see it before I can attempt it. Well?" She clapped her hands. "On with it, then. Show me the steps, Mrs. Bryant."

Graham held out his arm. "Shall we, Mrs. Bryant?"

After everything she'd revealed to Graham last evening, she'd not known what to expect. Mayhap to be tossed out for withholding the truth of her origins. Mayhap a reserved distance.

She'd certainly not expected him to request a dance. An altogether different apprehension gripped her.

Shall we?

"Shall we what?" she blurted.

"You do know how to dance," Graham prodded, his silken baritone washing over her.

Rowena clasped her fingers at her throat. As a girl, there had never been a functional need for her to learn the waltz, quadrille, or any other country reel. Yet, she'd wished to know how, and it had been him who'd taken her in his arms and guided her through each step and movement. Patient. Teasing.

When she was an instructor at Mrs. Belden's she'd overseen the lessons conducted by some of the most prominent dance masters.

But, now, Graham stared expectantly back, urging her to dance those once beloved steps. She let her arms fall to her sides. Coward that she was, regardless of whether or not it would help Ainsley, she didn't want to step into his arms and accept with that onslaught of memories those motions would unleash. Not after last night, when they'd both learned that everything had been an orchestrated lie. For there could never be a path forward and participating in these interludes of pretend would only delude her into false trust once more.

"I cannot." It had been so long since she'd last completed a single dance step. Not even at Mrs. Belden's. And the only partner she'd ever known had been this man before her.

"I don't understand," Ainsley said, scratching at her brow. "You do know how to dance, don't you?"

"Yes. No. Yes." At the girl's deepening confusion, Rowena drew in a slow breath. "Yes, I do know the steps," she said evenly.

Ainsley clapped her hands enthusiastically. "Splendid. Well, then, Hampstead," she said, tilting her chin at the floor. "Get on with it."

"I cannot," Rowena blurted. Not without risking memories of a past she'd spent so long burying. A past that every moment in Graham's presence was slowly unearthing, leaving her confused and aching for everything that could never be. "Miss Hickenbottom and I were to visit Hyde Park for an art lesson, Your Grace."

Ainsley's horrified groan echoed around the ballroom. The young lady splayed her arms before her and dropped her head atop those folded limbs. "First, lessons on walking. Curtsying," she cried. "Then dancing and forms of address and now *this*?"

Despite the strain between she and Graham, Rowena hid a smile. Her charge's spirit was infectious, however. She folded her hands before her. "Da Vinci once said art lives from constraints and dies from freedom."

Grumbling, Ainsley picked her head up. "You are using my Da Vinci against me, Mrs. Bryant. Not well-done of you."

Mayhap not, but it was resourceful.

"I'd much rather see Hampstead's attempt at a dancing lesson," Ainsley unhelpfully supplied.

With guardian and ward seeming in dangerous collusion, Graham brought his arms back into the elegant position: regal, relaxed, and beautifully poised. How graceful he'd always been. Somehow, there was a new, even more refined elegance to his confident movements. Her breath quickened. "I daresay Hyde Park and art can wait until Miss Hickenbottom has a suitable lesson." He glanced at Ainsley. "I promise you, Mrs. Bryant was fortunate enough to take dance lessons with one of the finest instructors in all of England."

"Was he French?" Ainsley called back curiously.

"He was impossibly arrogant," she supplied for him, earning a dangerous half-grin from Graham.

He settled his firm palm at her waist, and the heat of it sent delicious chills through her. "Undoubtedly," he murmured in solemn assent, as she placed her right in his and the other on his shoulder.

The violinist struck his bow to the strings, and they began to dance. She briefly closed her eyes. The sandalwood scent of him filled her senses as their bodies moved in time. During the lessons she'd overseen at Mrs. Belden's, Rowena had allowed herself to look at those sessions as nothing more than a chore. Just one more task and responsibility her future depended on. It had been far easier to view those dance classes in that capacity than to mourn all she'd lost. Not only her family and Graham...but the simple joy of dancing just to dance.

Oh, how she'd missed the joy in these steps. From the instant he had schooled her, laughing and joyous, through her first waltz, she'd been captivated by those movements, the thrill of it only deepened by his arms about her.

Faster, Graham. Faster.

"There is no shame in those backward steps," Graham called over to Ainsley, slashing into Rowena's memories of her girlhood urging.

Rowena glanced over at Ainsley keenly watching and tapping the tip of her boot to the one-two-three pattern. And Graham. She stole an upward peek. He was, as always, reserved and calm. In complete control, so at odds with the tumult running amok in her breast. But, then, he grinned, and her heart skittered a beat. She didn't allow herself to fix on the regret and sadness spilling from his eyes but rather on this dizzying moment.

Graham increased the speed of their steps, and the violinist hurriedly matched his playing to those quick strides.

Her breath hastened. *He remembers.* Why must he show those glimpses and glimmers of who he'd been?

From the edge of the dance floor, Ainsley clapped wildly and laughed. "You are indeed a far better dance instructor than—"

"Mr. Turner to see you, Your Grace."

They stumbled to an abrupt halt, and the violinist cut off his playing with a discordant hum of his instrument.

Jack Turner.

Silence blanketed the ballroom, thick and unending. Several inches past six feet, with a lean frame, the wan, blond-haired gentleman in the room bore but traces of a hint of the boy from her past.

He stared back at her, opening and closing his mouth as though he'd stumbled upon a ghost.

"Hampstead, your man-of-affairs is here, interrupting our fun." And just like that, Ainsley effortlessly cut the tension in the room. The girl followed that admonishment with an insolent curtsy.

Graham was the first to move. He hurriedly released her. "Jack," he called in greeting.

Slowly pulling his gaze from Rowena, Jack glanced over at him. Confusion lined the hard planes of his face. "You were late for our meeting," he said finally. "I thought you'd had another..."

An awkward pall of silence descended among them that not even the usually loquacious Ainsley could break.

Rowena smoothed her palms over her brown skirts and sank into a curtsy, feeling much like a player on a Drury Lane stage without her lines. "Ja—" Ainsley flared her already hopelessly wide eyes. "Mr. Turner," she swiftly amended. The girl was too astute for anyone's good.

With an icy nod, Jack tersely greeted her. "*Mrs.* Bryant." There was a condescending sneer to that slightly emphasized word that she'd have to be either deaf or a dullard to miss.

Graham stepped between them. "I'll be along shortly, Jack." The other man turned with jerky movements and exited, leaving them alone once more. "If you'll excuse me?" He sketched a bow for each lady. There was a wealth of emotion in his eyes as he held her gaze. "Mrs. Bryant," he finally said. "Miss Hickenbottom." With that, he left.

Alone with her charge, Ainsley seethed. "I despise that man."

The instructor-like response would be to take the girl to task for her unkind words for Graham's man-of-affairs, in front of the violinist, no less. But in being away from Mrs. Belden, and in this household, set free from those constraints by first Graham and now this girl, she instead moved closer. Twelve years ago she'd have staunchly defended Jack to the death. Now, he was nothing more than a stranger. With a slight incline of her head, Rowena dismissed the balding, bespectacled violinist. He hopped to his feet, stuffed his instrument in his case, and darted off.

Memories slid forward of a long-ago day, when Graham had first been off to war. Jack's visit to her family's cottage. The unyielding power of his embrace as he'd forced a kiss on her... *You would be lucky to have me as your husband, whore...* She exhaled slowly. The frantic desperation as real now as it had been that moment. It had been solely a kiss, but the glint in his eyes, the barely restrained emotion there, had hinted at his darkness. That had been the last she'd seen of Jack. "Has Mr. Turner done something to insult you?" Rowena asked Ainsley cautiously.

"Every time I see him."

"What has he…" *Done.* "Said to offend you?" she asked cautiously. Still, the tension remained in Rowena's entire being.

"He's offended *everyone.* Me. Wesley." At Rowena's questioning look, she clarified. "Hampstead's butler. His valet." Ainsley paused. "Hampstead."

"His Grace?" Surprise pulled the question from her.

"*Especially* His Grace." Ainsley slashed the air with her hand. "Don't go here. Don't go there. Musn't be near people. Mustn't have any friends."

Questions whirred around Rowena's mind, and she landed at no answer that made sense. "Why mustn't he have friends?" What kind of miserable existence would Jack have Graham lead? And in the name of friendship, no less? *Should I really be surprised given his disloyalty when Graham was off fighting?*

"Turner's convinced Hampstead he's mad."

She reeled. "What?"

Ainsley nodded. "Mad. Corked in the brain. Not right in the nob."

Rowena tried—and failed—to get words out as the pieces of a puzzle she'd put together over the years reassembled themselves. By his cold, hard exterior, she had been of the immediate opinion that Graham had shaped himself into an unfeeling duke after he'd found himself heir to that title. By what Ainsley shared now, and what she herself had witnessed on their carriage journey from Mrs. Belden's and again at the Duke of Wilkshire's card party, there was far more to Graham's icy veneer. Was that why he'd never married? "How do you know this?" she ventured carefully.

Ainsley snorted. "Mrs. Bryant, I've been here with not even a companion underfoot. It took but two conversations between Hampstead and Turner to know." She proceeded to tick off on her fingers. "One, His Grace has episodes. Two, Turner thinks he's mad, and three, he's managed to *convince* the duke he's mad."

What a cross the war had given him to bear. And how she despised it was a pain that would always be with him.

"And, now, Turner's pushing Hampstead to wed a miserable, cold, unfeeling lady who wants nothing more than his title."

That brought Rowena's head snapping up. "What?" The word emerged on a breathless exhalation, dulled in her own ears by her suddenly pounding heart.

"Lady Serena. Wilkshire's daughter." The flawless, golden beauty playing a game of whist with him and the duke. All the breath stuck in Rowena's lungs, frozen and painful. "I'm certain the schemer wants nothing more than his title." Her charge firmed her lips and her eyes blazed with fire. "She is not his swan, Mrs. Bryant. Wholly unnatural and wrong for a person to go about marrying anything other than their swan."

"Indeed," she said, her voice faint. He was going to marry, and by Ainsley's admission, he'd already selected the very woman he'd make his future duchess. That nasty, seething jealousy reared like a serpent inside, poised to strike.

"Mrs. Bryant, are you all right?"

No. The concerned inquiry, followed by a touch on Rowena's forearm, brought her attention to the girl.

She forced a smile. "Fine," she assured her. She had no place sitting here chatting with her charge about Rowena's employer. "Come," she urged, standing in a noisy rustle of taffeta skirts. "We agreed to an art lesson in the park."

Ainsley eyed her warily. "And you promise it doesn't involve anything French?"

"You have my assurance." She waggled her eyebrows. "For today, at least."

With Ainsley's laughter echoing from the high ceilings, Rowena and her charge started from the ballroom. While Ainsley prattled on with a flurry of questions about the manner of artwork she preferred and despised, Rowena's thoughts wandered.

Whom Graham married, and whom he considered friends, and how he lived his life were not her affair.

Yet, with every step, that silent assurance rang hollow.

SEVENTEEN

Having Jack stumble upon him dancing with Rowena was certain to elicit the other man's shock. What Graham was wholly unprepared for as he entered his office was the visceral rage.

"What is the meaning of this?" Jack said by way of greeting, as soon as he closed the door.

No one else would have dared such an insolence in his presence. This, however, was Jack; a man he'd known since they were boys of seven, who'd also seen and stayed with him when he'd been reduced to tears and terror—over Rowena...the nightmares.

"Jack," he drawled in icy tones that raised a dull flush to the other man's cheeks.

His friend gestured to the books scattered about the desk.

Momentarily taken aback by that focus on the books and ledgers and not the earlier meeting with Rowena, Graham motioned to a nearby chair. "Please, sit."

The other man had been as grounded in his hatred as Graham himself. So much so that he'd done everything to quash talk of the woman they'd once called friend.

But, then, Jack had been unwittingly deceived, too.

Strolling over to the sideboard, Graham set to work pouring himself a glass of brandy. Snifter in hand, he carried it over to his desk and sat.

"What in blazes is going on with you, Hampstead?" Jack unleashed. "What transpired in Wilkshire's parlor in front of all Society has been written about in every scandal page. I spent the morning fielding angry questions from the duke about your intentions for his daughter." He laid his palms on the one spare space on Graham's desk. "I spent my morning assuring him that despite your lack of attention for his daughter that you intend to move forward with a formal arrangement." His mouth tightened. "Only to come by to visit after last night's fit"—Graham flinched at that shameful reminder—"and find you…" He leaned forward and dropped his voice to a whisper. "Dancing with her? And your desk in disarray. My God, man, what is *happening* to you? I don't even recognize who you've be—"

"We were deceived, Jack," he interrupted, and the other man ceased talking mid-speak.

A sound of impatience escaped him. "Of course we were. That is the point I sought to make."

"*Not* by Rowena," Graham clarified.

Jack hooded his lashes. "I don't understand," he said carefully.

It had been foolhardy to believe Jack would be so willing to welcome her within their fold. Taking a deep breath, Graham proceeded to tell him everything Rowena had revealed. When he'd finished, the hard planes of Jack's face remained set in an unforgiving mask.

"I don't believe her. She was a liar and a schemer and—"

"I saw the note, Jack," he said impatiently. "It was in my hand." A letter forged by his father to keep them apart.

All the color leeched from his friend's cheeks. Jack brushed a shaking palm over his mouth. Then he let it fall to his lap. "Listen to yourself, Hampstead. She has neatly fed you lies, and you've so easily believed them, because you want them to be real," he said with an earnestness that met his troubled eyes. "I understand that. She always had a hold on you. The lady is attempting to wheedle her way back into your affections."

Fighting his exasperation, Graham grabbed a ledger and stood. "Look at this." He held the book out.

"What?" Jack asked, not even looking at the aged leather record kept by the late duke's man-of-affairs.

"*Look* at it." He forced the book into the other man's hands.

Muttering to himself, his friend took it with all the enthusiasm of one being handed a burning coal. Jack skimmed the page, and then glanced at him over the top of the ledger. "What am I looking for?"

Graham tipped his chin. "The thirtieth of September."

Returning his scrutiny to that page, Jack moved his gaze down the column—and then froze.

"There is an unmarked column, with nothing more than a monetary value," he said, reclaiming his seat. "A fifteen-pound sum." Fifteen pounds each month is what they'd sold their souls and their daughter's life for. Burning with the need for liquid fortitude, Graham grabbed his glass and took a swallow.

Several lines creased his man-of-affair's brow, as he puzzled over that same portion of the ledger. "Perhaps your father's last man-of-affairs was sloppy. Perhaps he was in a hurry and failed to make the necessary notation—"

"Rowena's parents received a monthly payment for their cooperation." He set his glass down hard. *And their silence.* Loathing filled him for the woman who'd given birth to Rowena, who'd so easily abandoned her to the cold world.

What should she have done, Graham? Defied the duke who threatened her family...?

Filled with a restiveness, he grabbed another book. He shoved it over. "Take it."

Reluctantly, Jack swiped the ledger off the edge of Graham's desk. "The thirtieth—"

"I see it, Hampstead," his friend said curtly.

If that were the case, then, why could the other man not truly see? Because Jack had lived more than a decade believing a lie. Graham had naively failed to consider just how difficult it would be for the obstinate man to set aside a lifetime of wariness where Rowena was concerned. To give his fingers something to do, he picked up his glass and rolled it between his palms. "She doesn't wish to be here." *And I do not want her to leave.*

Jack thinned his eyes into narrow slits. "As I told you when you returned with her. She sees a way to become your duchess. This is all part of her scheme," he said at last, returning the book. "There are no markings as to where those funds went."

Graham stared back incredulously. "Surely, you are not indicating that Rowena knew the precise amount paid her family, and then that same sum should be marked each month in my father's old ledgers?"

"I know you were always weak where she was concerned," Jack said bluntly.

Graham fell back in his seat. The other man believed Rowena's was nothing more than a ruthless game, orchestrated by a clever schemer. *I would have believed that very thing about her a short while ago.* But everything had changed. Just as she said, however, he should have believed in her, regardless of those notes.

At his silence, Jack hardened his mouth. "I understand you wish to return to the way we were as children." He held Graham's gaze squarely. "But we are no longer children, and we can never go back." *We can never go back.* But mayhap they could begin again. His friend pulled his shoulders back. "Find another companion for the girl."

Battling down the furious energy inside, Graham took another drink. If Jack hadn't stood beside him through the darkest times in his life, he would have tossed him out on his arse long ago. "I've already told you, the matter is settled. Rowena is staying."

"What are you on about?" Jack cried, slamming his fist against his palm. The pulsing intensity in his eyes hinted at the thin grasp of control he had. "This is me," he entreated. "*Me*, Hampstead. I know you; a man who has gone out of his way these seven years to avoid people is not a one to go about dancing in a ballroom or caring after an unwanted ward…unless there was another reason."

Fury rippled slowly inside. An unwanted ward. Only, that was how Graham had viewed Ainsley since the moment she'd been placed in his care. Everything had changed, however…since Rowena.

Releasing a sigh, he set his glass down. It was wrong to bait the one man who'd attempted to help him all these years. A man who'd urged him to hide himself away and cut off emotional ties to all people. Only, Rowena, however, had helped him to see that he was no monster. He was just a man scarred by life…and they all wore different marks. "I cannot marry her."

Jack scoffed. "Of course you can't. Nor should you want to."

"You misunderstand," Graham corrected.

Understanding dawned in his friend's eyes. He jumped to his feet. "What?" he asked, his voice coated in shock.

"Lady Serena...I cannot marry her." He knew that now. Mayhap he always had.

"Because of Rowena." It was a charged statement, nonetheless Graham nodded, confirming his friend's supposition. He didn't believe he'd ever earn her forgiveness or be deserving of her, but neither could he form a ruthless match with a woman he didn't love. Not even to fulfill his responsibilities as duke.

"But...but..." Jack shook his head. "I don't understand."

"I love her," he confessed somberly. Shock briefly froze him at admitting that aloud after years spent squashing his emotions. "I never stopped loving her," he murmured to himself. Even as he'd told himself he hated her, inside he'd always known that.

Jack sputtered. "But she betrayed you."

"Why can you not see the truth, Jack?" he asked impatiently. "Why, when I've shown you proof of my father's crimes. She was your friend, too."

A choking, barren laugh left the other man's bitterly twisted lips. "She was *never* my friend."

At the vitriol there, an icy chill rushed along his spine. Graham slowly stood and clasped his hands at his back. He'd already given Jack more than he owed on the matter of his future. "We're done here."

The rapid rise and fall of the other man's breath matched in time to the ticking clock atop his mantel. "And what of Lady Serena?" Jack said at last.

Guilt needled at him. Granted, he'd never publically courted the lady, and only partnered her in the requisite sets at various balls, but Jack had spoken with the young woman's father to ascertain the amenability of a courtship. "There was no formal suit," he said at last. "And I'll not marry where my heart is not engaged." He said it. Those handful of words counter to everything he'd professed these years. Rowena had shown him what it was to laugh and feel again, and he'd not live the cold, empty existence he'd lived these twelve years without her.

"And will you marry Rowena?"

"I don't know." Didn't know if he could ask her to brave a life with him. Didn't know if he had any right to try and begin again, even if she was. "I just know I cannot marry Lady Serena."

Giving his head a disgusted shake, Jack spun on his heel, and stalked off. He slammed the door hard behind him, leaving Graham alone with the silence echoing around his office.

Now, to convince Rowena that he was, in fact, a man worthy of her.

EIGHTEEN

Rowena had not seen Graham since yesterday's dance lesson…or if one wished to be precise, since Jack had arrived.

Seated at the breakfast table, she chewed at her lower lip. Was it business that commanded his notice? Or had everything they'd learned yesterday meant nothing at all?

She gave her head a shake. *Do not be silly. He is a duke. I am his servant.* He'd made her no promises, nor did she expect or want them. To open herself to love again would be folly. Most especially a love for him. Another betrayal at his hands would only destroy her. She hated the life that was stolen from the both of them, and the friendship they'd once shared. Just as she hated the reality that there could have never been more with him. And that he'd found the distinguished young lady he would take to wife. Her insides twisted in vicious knots. *Stop.*

Snap.

Rowena blinked slowly.

Seated at the opposite side of the table, Ainsley snapped her fingers. "Mrs. Bryant, I was speaking to you."

"Speaking to…?" A rush of mortified heat climbed Rowena's neck and spilled onto her cheeks. She sat up in her chair. "Forgive me," she said weakly. *I was woolgathering about my employer.*

Ainsley eyed her again for a long moment, with far-too-perceptive eyes. "Yes, well, I asked how we would begin *today's* lessons."

There was a hopeful glimmer in the young lady's eyes that hinted at a woman very much tired of lessons on decorous behavior and acceptable speech. In truth, Rowena herself would scream if they went through the motions of those miserable curtsies once more. "I thought we might make another visit to Hyde Park and discuss the values of art." Those man-made gardens were the closest she felt to the English countryside…and that trip also helped get her free of this townhouse and escape Graham's nearness. "and then after we've finished, we can review Society's rules of polite discourse," she said in feigned nonchalance.

"Is this because Hampstead is worried about my recital?"

Rowena swallowed a sigh. Of course her charge would hear that latter part above all else. She opened her mouth.

"What am I worried about?"

Rowena gasped as that deep baritone slashed across their debate.

Graham stood in the doorway. *He is here.* In his fitted fawn breeches, sapphire jacket, and black hessians, he was a study in masculine elegance. At the heated gaze he trained on her, all doubts faded to an afterthought. Her body burned hot from the tips of her toes to the roots of her hair with the memory of his touch.

"Hampstead," Ainsley piped in, and then with her teeth, tugged at a piece of bread. Flakes broke off and scattered about the white linen tablecloth.

Yanked back from her wicked thoughts, Rowena cleared her throat and stood.

Tossing down her nearly devoured bread, Ainsley hopped up. Her chair dragged noisily along the hardwood floor. "Hampstead," the young lady repeated.

Modeling a curtsy for Ainsley, Rowena kept her focus trained on her charge. Sighing, Ainsley sketched another one of those rusty dips.

Graham bowed, and then gestured for them to sit. After he'd made a dish at the sideboard, he carried his plate over and claimed the chair closest to Rowena. "Well?" he prodded, as he snapped a white napkin open and placed it on his lap. "What am I purportedly worried about?"

"Your introducing me to your stodgy friends," Ainsley replied. "And my lack of ladylike skills."

Rowena's heart tugged. The young lady worried about disappointing him. She wore that fear in her defensiveness.

Graham leaned back in his seat and accepted a cup of steaming coffee from a servant. "I assure you, I'm not at all worried." It did not escape Rowena's notice he didn't take umbrage with the girl's description of the guests who would grace his table. That and his confidence in Ainsley recalled all the reasons she'd first given her heart to this man all those years ago.

Still, the skepticism stamped on Ainsley's face painted her disbelief louder than any words.

Rowena steered them back to the original focus of their discussion. "I was speaking to Miss Hickenbottom about the value of art," she explained as Graham blew on his drink. Her charge sent her a grateful look.

"Of which there is none," Ainsley piped in.

"There is, however, value in having an enlightened mind."

At Graham's solemn reply, an unexpected show of support, Rowena flared her eyebrows. He gave a slight, imperceptible nod that, had she not been looking, she would have missed. His meaning, however, clear—she had his support, even if he didn't wholly agree with the merits of an art lesson, given the girl's upcoming entrance into Society.

"Perhaps we *should* prepare for your upcoming recital after all, then," Rowena suggested, deliberately wheedling. "I've still not heard the songs you've prepared—"

"I'll take the art lesson," Ainsley groused. Her cheeks colored, and she jutted her chin out mutinously. "I've already told Hampstead he needn't worry about the recital. I can sing." Ainsley favored Graham with a hard look. "And play the pianoforte proficiently."

Rowena chewed at her lower lip. Even with the girl's insistence of those respective skills, whenever Rowena suggested they prepare for the gathering, she met it with a fierce opposition and evasiveness.

Ainsley shifted in her seat. "What?" she asked, looking between them when they both said nothing. "I do have *some* ladylike skills."

"I didn't doubt your skill." Graham lifted his glass. "Your father often talked of his love of the pianoforte."

Ainsley scrambled forward in her seat; her gaze imploring. "Did he?" That desperate question came from a woman clearly hungry to know anything about the man who'd left her behind.

Across the table, he held his ward's eyes. "After battle, he would often regale us with song. He often said he missed his piano more than he did any per—" His remembrance immediately cut off and a dull flush marred his neck. He coughed into his hand. "Mrs. Bryant?" he directed at Rowena, and she stared questioningly back, "I would see Ainsley perform several arrangements for our guests, in memory of her father."

It would be an effort to, more than anything, demonstrate to the *ton* that Ainsley Hickenbottom was as accomplished as the ladies whose parentage was not in question. "Of course," she assured him.

"I-I'll decide which songs I perform in his honor," Ainsley's voice cracked. "As such, there are no further ladylike lessons required." She scowled. "Including God-awful watercolors and paints."

Her charge brought them neatly back to the original matter at hand. "Given Ainsley's appreciation of Da Vinci, I thought we would take lessons in Hyde Park later this morning."

"Oh, thank the bloody Lord."

The breathless blasphemous prayer filling the breakfast room after her announcement had them, as well as the smartly uniformed footmen stationed at the walls, coughing into their hands, burying laughter.

Graham made little effort to hide his amusement. With a half-grin, he waggled his eyebrows in silent challenge.

She thinned her eyes into little slits. He found this amusing. The miserable blighter. Either oblivious or uncaring of the response she'd earned, her charge shoveled food into her mouth, as though she'd been told she was sitting down to take her last meal. No help forthcoming from Ainsley's powerful guardian, Rowena redirected her efforts to guiding the girl. "We do not curse," she gently reprimanded.

"My father did it all the time." Ainsley spoke around a too-large bite of eggs.

"Indeed, he did," Graham supplied—unhelpfully.

The girl attended her plate once more, and Rowena paused to glower at Graham. *Behave,* she mouthed.

He winked.

She furrowed her brow, befuddled by this…new…and yet older version of Graham Linford. Where was the pompous, unsmiling duke? And who could believe that she'd prefer him, in this instance, that stodgy ord. Gritting her teeth, Rowena stamped her foot silently under the table.

"What was that tapping?" By the teasing glint in his eyes, Graham knew damn well what that blasted tapping was.

"I didn't hear tapping," Ainsley put in, glancing around.

"It is because there was no tapping," Rowena exclaimed, and two pairs of eyes swiveled to her. Her cheeks burning, she forced herself to calm.

After Graham had turned her away nearly ten years earlier, she'd resolved to never again feel. She'd prided herself on the control and mastery she'd managed over her emotions…only to take breakfast with a teasing Graham and his precocious ward and find herself vastly less polished than she'd ever believed, or hoped.

Always count to five to give oneself proper time to formulate a proper reply. Everything was proper. Proper. Proper. Proper. Gently pushing aside her plate, Rowena counted to five, using that skill ingrained by Mrs. Belden. And suddenly, she wanted to scream at the constraints imposed on her. On all of them. Mayhap, Ainsley had the right of it.

"Are you counting, Mrs. Bryant?" Ainsley asked, scratching at her brow. She looked to her guardian.

He inclined his head. "It appears as though she, in fact, is."

"I am not counting," Rowena said evenly. She *had* been counting. Altogether different matter. "Furthermore, we were discussing language that is appropriate and language that is not," she informed, bringing them back to her earlier lesson. "I instructed Ainsley that it is impolite to go about cursing."

"Indeed," Graham agreed, having the decency to school his earlier amusement.

"And I believe it's unfair a man is able to go about cursing, while a lady is not permitted those same liberties," Ainsley countered, turning

Rowena's words back on her. In a show of protest, her charge took another large bite.

The servants' bodies shook with their amusement. It was all bloody well and...It was all *well* and good that they found amusement in the girl's spirit. It was not, however, in Ainsley's best interests.

"One can have no smaller or greater mastery than mastery of oneself."

Ainsley paused with the fork halfway to her mouth.

"Do you know who said that, Miss Hickenbottom?"

Her charge eyed her with a wariness of someone far more advanced in years.

"Your Da Vinci," Rowena neatly supplied.

"Are you using my Da Vinci against me again?" Outrage deepened the girl's freckled face.

"I'm using your Da Vinci to show you there is reason to be in control of yourself; from your words and your movements and your actions, for reasons that extend beyond societal dictates, and deal solely with the person we allow ourselves to become."

They sat locked in a silent battle until the young lady fell back in her seat. "Very well, Mrs. Bryant. I'll allow you your art lesson." She jabbed a finger in the air. "But only because it's in Hyde Park, and Hampstead can surely use some time out of doors."

That less-than-subtle scolding raised color to Graham's cheeks.

Goodness, the girl didn't need a companion. With her ability to scold a duke, she could oust Mrs. Belden from her post as headmistress.

"Shall we?" Ainsley asked, jumping up, with far more enthusiasm than one who'd been debating the merits of an art lesson only a moment ago.

At her unexpected eagerness, Rowena stitched her eyebrows and came to her feet alongside Graham. "Dip a curtsy to His Grace," she guided, demonstrating another one of those respectful movements. She watched Ainsley as she went through the stiff movements of a still painful curtsy...And then a slow understanding dawned—why Ainsley *wanted* an art lesson. In the short time she'd known the girl, she had gleaned Ainsley Hickenbottom was as proud as the day was long. Did she see her lack of ladylike skills as a testament of her failings when, in fact, there were no failings there? The failings belonged solely to the *ton,* which set the rules and standards as to what was important and who was of value. Invariably those calculated peers always found women such as her and Ainsley as inferior. That wasn't altogether true. There was one gentleman who never gave a jot about one's birthright.

"Well, Hampstead, are you accompanying us to this miserable art lesson?" Ainsley challenged.

Panic flared. "His Grace, I expect, is otherwise busy."

Instead, he remained standing. "I would not miss Mrs. Bryant's first art lesson for the world."

An afternoon in Hyde Park with Graham, even if his charge was there? Rowena choked.

Bloody hell.

❦

A short while later, Graham walked in a stilted silence beside Rowena. They trailed along behind a quick-moving Ainsley.

How did old lovers act around one another when they discovered everything, except for three fleeting years, had been steeped in lies and deception? What was there to say? Certainly not words that could ever make any of it right.

Ainsley skipped ahead along the graveled path with a joyful exuberance. Graham gazed on wistfully at Hickenbottom's daughter, who was near an age to Rowena when they'd first met. As a girl on the cusp of womanhood, she'd once been in possession of that same youthful innocence. They both had.

His smile crumpled. Then, he'd done as all dutiful second sons did and marched off to fight. He'd romanticized what war would be and donned his crimson uniform, only to return from war an empty version of the boy he'd been. How easily life altered a person, destroying that naiveté and leaving in its place a jaded person, rightfully wary of the world.

202

"You wonder that it was ever real," Rowena said softly, and he started. "You wonder if you merely imagined and dreamed that time in your life." Their thoughts had always moved in harmony. The spring breeze tugged and pulled at the hem of her woolen cloak. She shifted the sketchpads in her arms, and Graham reached for them.

Angling her body, she ignored his attempt to help. She'd always been proud. Too proud.

"Despite that innocence," he murmured, "she still bears the mark of life." Just as Rowena had, as a girl of fourteen. He'd, however, failed to see just how deeply she'd steeped herself in shame and sadness for having been born a bastard. Circumstances which said nothing of her great worth, and hadn't mattered a jot to him.

Rowena worried at her lower lip, as she was wont to do, in a telltale gesture that spoke to her concern.

"She will be all right," Graham said quietly.

"How can you be sure?" she countered, staring after the lady. Ainsley moved at a near-sprint for the lake, stocked with pink pelicans and swans.

Several passersby looked on with horror wreathing their features. The worry deepened in Rowena's telling eyes.

How much of herself did she see in the lady now in her care? "I am certain because she is strong," he said solemnly. "And because I'll stand beside her when she makes her entry into Society." *And I want you there with me, as more than a servant on my staff.*

A cinch cut off air from his lungs, trapping it in his throat. *I want to marry her.* Despite the fears of madness that dogged him. Where Jack had validated his worries of insanity and encouraged him to shape himself into a coldly reserved duke, Rowena matter-of-factly had refuted his madness. Instead, she'd challenged him, seeing his weakness not as insanity but a sign of his humanity. *Can I marry her? Can I, knowing every day, my nightmares could see her hurt at my hands?*

His mind in tumult, Graham glanced at her. Another breeze whipped about them, and it knocked her bonnet backward, loosening a curl in the process. She swatted it impatiently behind her ear. "You cannot protect her from hurt, Graham. You cannot make them accept her. If they find her lacking, they will never let her into their fold." Did she realize she spoke of herself?

"Then they can go hang," he vowed. It mattered not what Society believed about Rowena or Ainsley. It mattered who they were. And their happiness.

She gave him a sad smile. "The world is different for a duke than a bastard from scandalous origins."

"Here!" Ainsley's excited cry pealed through the park, attracting further looks from strolling passersby. She stood on the shore of the lake. Oblivious or uncaring of the disapproval around her, Ainsley lifted her arms above her head and waved.

The maid unfolded the blanket in her hands, and with Ainsley's help, they snapped the white fabric open and lay it down by the edge of the water.

Rowena rushed ahead and joined the pair. Graham followed along at a more sedate pace, taking in her movements. The way she spoke to Ainsley. The laughter that spilled past his ward's lips. How many of the ladies at Wilkshire's event had stared on, coolly derisive of the girl? People who sought to transform her and quash her spirit. Whereas Rowena sought to smooth Ainsley's way before polite Society, but retain the beautiful part of who she was inside.

She said something to the maid, and the servant dropped a curtsy and wandered off, leaving companion and charge alone. Opening a sketchpad, Rowena turned one over to Ainsley and retained the other. The young lady grabbed at it with a zeal that defied her protestations earlier that morn. Clasping his hands at his back, Graham continued to scrutinize them as they marked up their pages. An interloper in their moment.

With his father and brother's passing, he had ascended into a life he'd never wanted. His value to the *ton* had risen, his presence desired for his title alone. What he would not give for the simplicity of the life he'd dreamed of—married to Rowena, with a child at their side.

And God help him, he was selfish enough he'd ask her to risk all and be his duchess.

Why should she want to? Why, with everything that had passed?

Rowena glanced up, over Ainsley's head, and her gaze collided with his. She smiled, and motioned him over, a welcoming invitation that eased some of the tightness in his chest.

Returning that grin, his lips, for the first time in so many years moved easily into that expression of joy. Letting his arms fall at his side, he strode along the path; gravel crunched under his boots, and he came to a stop at the blanket.

Ainsley looked up briefly from her sketching. "Hampstead," she greeted, and then devoted her attention to the lines on her page. "Did you know Mrs. Bryant can sketch?" she asked, her question directed at her page.

Graham claimed the corner of the blanket and stretched his legs out before him, hooking them at the ankles. "I do. She excels in her mastery of the human form and..."

The girl again picked her head up, eying him peculiarly.

"Uh..."

"I told His Grace as much in my interview," Rowena neatly interjected and shifted her attention to the task at hand. Periodically she lifted her eyes from the page and gazed out at the lake. "When we sketch a landscape, we work in horizontal patterns, framing our work in a rectangle." She waited while Ainsley marked a dark pattern around her page. The lady looked up. "Next, you must have a focal point."

Ainsley chewed her pencil and scanned the horizon.

Graham leaned his weight back on his elbows as Rowena guided her charge. She was a master instructor, just as Mrs. Belden had pledged. In command. Confident. She was an older, more mature version of the girl he'd fallen in love with. There was something breathtaking in her absolute control. Ladies of the *ton*, like his own mother who'd died too young, hosted balls and soirees. They perfected pouring tea for guests. They neatly embroidered. And sang. Not a single woman he'd ever known, however, had managed to chart a future of her own. Working with her hands and mind to survive. And, though, she'd had little choice as a young woman but to march along this path, she'd not only survived but flourished.

The air caught in his lungs. And he loved her all the more for her strength.

"...And you must never make any two intervals identical," Rowena was saying. She glanced up, and a look passed between them.

"Your Grace."

And just like that the moment was severed. Graham whipped his head around. Then tamping down a curse, he climbed to his feet with Rowena and Ainsley following reluctant suit.

Lady Serena, on the arm of her brother, Lord Midleton, stared past her with bald interest. It was not, however, the woman Jack had handpicked for Graham's bride who held his notice. He frowned. Midleton's attention was trained on Rowena. A surge of irrational jealousy grabbed him in a tentacle-like hold.

"Lady Serena," he greeted, capturing her hand for an obligatory kiss, all the while Rowena's gaze bore into his back. "A pleasure as always." He lied. It had never been a pleasure. It had been a responsibility. A chore, given her cold ruthlessness. And yet, he, with Jack's urgings, had convinced himself that she was what he needed. How wrong he'd been.

"Hampstead," Midleton drawled lazily, with a slightly insolent bow.

Lady Serena continued to look past his shoulder. Graham couldn't make out anything from her cool expression.

Stepping out of the way, he revealed Rowena and Ainsley. "My apologies," he murmured. "You recall my ward, Miss Hickenbottom, and her companion, Mrs. Bryant?" God, how wrong that word sounded rolling from his lips, leaving bitterness in its wake. Rowena was so much more to him.

Rowena lowered her head deferentially and sank into a perfect curtsy. "My lady."

He balled his hands, hating that she should be subservient to people who were lesser in every way.

Lady Serena peered down her slightly up-turned nose. "Mrs. Bryant," she said softly. "How do you do?"

Ever polished and graceful, Rowena lifted her head. "Very well, my lady."

Surprise glimmered in Lady Serena's pretty blue eyes when she looked to Graham. "You accompany your charge on her lessons. How very *devoted* you are, Your Grace."

"Yes," the lady's brother continued in his bored tones, "how... *devoted.*" The slight emphasis made the words an accusation more than anything.

"This is his first time attending a lesson," Ainsley piped in, and Rowena's cheeks pinkened. "Since Mrs. Bryant's arrived, he's been far more devote—"

"We must return to your sketching," Rowena squawked, as the Montgomerys widened their eyes with warring expressions of curiosity and amusement.

Graham's fingers itched with the need to yank at his cravat. A drink. He needed a bloody drink. Nay, a bottle.

Lady Serena, however, proved even more tenacious and brave than he'd credited. "You have an affinity for art?" she asked the younger lady. Uninvited, she drifted over.

Ainsley pursed her mouth, but Rowena murmured something nearly inaudible that raised a sigh from his ward. "Hardly. Rather, I enjoy certain artists and certain subjects."

"Wouldn't that be tantamount to the same thing?" Midleton asked with a dryness that deepened Ainsley's scowl.

"*You* would think so." At that slight emphasis, the marquess opened and closed his mouth several times.

Graham's tamped down a grin, earning a sideways look from Rowena. "Miss Hickenbottom is working on a sketch," she provided.

"It is a swan," Ainsley clarified. "Do you know anything about swans, my lady?"

Lady Serena cocked her head. "Uh, no. Yes, well," she looked to Graham. "Would you care to join me, Your Grace?" The glint in her eyes spoke of her determination.

"He wouldn't," Ainsley called out, eliciting a series of shocked gasps.

"Ainsley." Graham and Rowena spoke sharply in unison, even as Midleton's bark of laughter filled the park.

Society would be eager to destroy Ainsley for her parentage. Any missteps on the girl's part would be fodder that fueled the unkind gossips.

"It would be my pleasure," Graham easily put forward, smoothing over his ward's awkward—if true—outburst.

Giving her brother a pointed look, Lady Serena looped her arm through Graham's and allowed him to lead her down the graveled path away from the pair he left at the blanket. Of course, Wilkshire's daughter would think nothing of leaving Rowena and Ainsley. To her, one was a servant, a suitable companion, and it hardly mattered if they were alone. Another wave of frustration at that station divide gripped him.

"She doesn't like me much," Lady Serena said tightly, and Graham slowed his steps at that unexpected honesty. "Your ward," she expounded.

And, he, wholly unflappable found his world upended again. Resisting the urge to tug at his cravat, he cast a look about. The marquess, sipping from his flask, remained at the tree beside Ainsley and Rowena. Graham frowned. Why in bloody hell was the man lingering with the unattended ladies? Except there could be no mistaking the wicked glimmer in his eyes.

"I at least expected you would deny it," Lady Serena said with an icy matter-of-factness, and his cheeks instantly heated.

"I assure you, Miss Hickenbottom"—he dredged up a lie—"respects you a good deal."

"Hmph," the young beauty on his army muttered non-committally. At the end of the trail, she slowed her steps and Graham was forced to either stop or drag her to the ground. Vastly preferring the spot where he still had view of Rowena and Ainsley now conversing with the marquess, he halted. The marquess's booming laughter filtered down the path.

"My father was quite certain I could bring you up to scratch," Lady Serena announced.

He stiffened. Now what to say to that? Mayhap it had been best he'd not allowed Jack to rush through a formal arrangement. For, with Lady Serena's boldness, she demonstrated she was certainly not the staid miss he'd taken her for. Then, it was certainly not the first time he'd been so wrong in his judgment of a person. "My lady?" he began slowly, trying to make sense of her serene features.

"Which is it?" she asked, curiosity coating her question. She lifted her chin in the direction of Ainsley and Rowena. "I've been unable to ascertain if you've gone and fallen in love with your ward or her companion." She paused. "Either is in bad form."

Graham choked on his swallow. *Undoubtedly.* "My lady, I…" Giving in, he pulled at his cravat hard. "I have no designs upon my ward, I assure you." She was nearly fourteen years younger than him and the daughter of a loyal, now dead, friend, and he had some scruples.

Lady Serena inclined her head. "Ah, the companion, then. How very…plebian of you, Your Grace." He tried to seek out a hint of recrimination there, but again the duke's daughter could have faced and beat any hazard partner.

Graham instantly shuttered his features. What she hinted at was the kind of scandal that would bring down not only Ainsley but Rowena, as well. "I've not confirmed your suspicions," he said tersely.

"With your adamancy of any interest in Miss Hickenbottom, you most certainly did." He winced at the accuracy of the clever miss. "Though…" She chewed at the tip of her gloved finger. "I didn't expect you were one who felt…*anything.*"

The feeling had been mutual. It was why he'd single-handedly picked her out as his future bride. "It's inappropriate for us to speak of such personal matters." He'd not, however, deny his affections for Rowena.

"*That,* I expected," she said with a sly smile that was gone as quickly as it had come. Lady Serena disentangled her arm from his and gave a quick snap of her satin skirts. "I promised my father I'd encourage your suit. That I would do everything within my power to see that you made a formal offer. Are you going to?"

Graham hesitated, and then gave his head a slight shake. "I can no longer do that, my lady," he said somberly. "It was not my intention to mislead you nor to toy with your affections."

She snorted and gave him a condescending once over. "*You* toy with *my* affections. Hardly, Your Grace. My father promised me my freedom of choice should I do everything within my power to encourage your suit." Lady Serena steeled her mouth. "And yet, I've too much pride to ever encourage a man whose affections and attention is reserved for another." The lady brushed an imagined speck from her puffed sleeve. "As such, I say I've fulfilled the agreement reached with my father." She arched a blonde eyebrow. "Have I not?"

He tried to follow this unexpected flow of discourse. "You…have, my lady?"

"Is that question?" With her ease at commanding a discussion and demanding answers, she was a duke's daughter in every way. Jack had been correct. With her domineering nature, she would have made a flawless duchess…just not in the ways either Graham or Jack had believed.

"You have," he countered.

A small smile, the first real one he'd ever witnessed from her, turned her full lips. "I wish you all the best, then."

With that, she yanked her skirts again, and wheeled off, calling after her brother. The marquess pulled his attention away from Rowena and Ainsley. Pocketing his flask, he rejoined his sister, and then they were off.

Graham stared after them, and a heaviness eased from his shoulders; a sense of rightness with his decision. Only, as he returned to his spot on the blanket, a thick tension clogged the air, killing the earlier joy. Studiously avoiding his eyes, Rowena periodically murmured instructions to her charge.

"*That* is the woman you intend to marry, Hampstead?" Ainsley demanded.

All the color seeped from Rowena's cheeks, leaving her an ashen version of her spirited self. And the sight of her hit him like a fist to the gut.

Wordlessly, he shook his head.

Fortunately, Rowena possessed far more dignity than he ever had. "You were working on your sketch, were you not, Ainsley?" Graham, however, heard the hoarse timbre to her voice, and the blade twisted all the deeper.

He cursed his inability to tell her all and refute the conclusions drawn by Ainsley. Conclusions that would have been accurate not even a week ago.

Ainsley continued working in silence, with Rowena occasionally interjecting guidance. Oblivious of the underlying tension, she snapped her head up. "I've finished," she said cheerfully, and turned the page around. He squinted, trying to make out the lines on the page. "It is a swan," she clarified. "Because everyone should have a swan." She tore the page out and handed it over to Rowena. "This one is for you, Mrs. Bryant. You deserve one of your own."

Rowena accepted the page, and as the wind tugged at the corner of the sheet, she smoothed her fingers over the corners. "It is perfect."

You are perfect. And Rowena Endicott deserved far more than a swan, and if she were willing, he would be the man to spend his life trying to earn her love.

NINETEEN

S prawled on her stomach in Graham's enormous library, Rowena rested her chin atop her folded hands and stared into the hearth.

Of course, it had been inevitable. A duke, with one of the oldest titles in the realm, he would honor that centuries old legacy. Yet, knowing it was so very different from witnessing it. In the middle of Hyde Park. With the lady he'd one day wed, staring baldly at her, and his too-clever charge watching.

As Rowena had looked on at the flawlessly beautiful and regal Lady Serena, she'd considered her own origins. They could not have been any more different than had they sprung from altogether different universes. She, a courtesan's daughter, had forever lived on the fringe of the world. When she was younger, she'd noted the sideways looks, but she'd been naively optimistic to imagine a world where people saw her as more than an extension of her mother. After Graham had left and his father had ordered her gone, her entire worldview had shifted. At that point on, she'd been forced to see that she was and would forever be different than members of the *ton*. Entering Mrs. Belden's Finishing School, she'd been fueled to prove her own self-worth. She'd fashioned herself into a driven, relentless instructor who'd labored over her lessons and worked to shape women into spiritless young ladies. Rowena's students had represented the possibility that one could be transformed into someone who was proper and in turn, into a figure whom polite Society respected.

Only realizing now...nothing she did, nor had, or accomplished would *ever* make her worthy in their eyes. Her students had been born to rank, and because of it, would always be afforded a respect that

Rowena would never earn. Could never earn. To those who moved in Graham's circle, she would only ever be lesser than the Lady Serenas of the world.

Rubbing her chin back and forth on her interconnected hands, she stared into the hearth. She braced for the same hurt, anger, and resentment that had riddled her for more than ten years when confronted with those reminders. Sentiments...that did not come. In the time she'd been here with Graham and Ainsley, she had been forced to look at Society in a whole new way...and more importantly, herself.

...You are far more worthy than any other woman, regardless of station...

She absently studied the fire's glow. Flipping onto her side, she touched her gaze on the two books resting spine to spine.

Proper Rules of Proper Behavior and Proper Decorum and *Da Vinci's Great Works.*

Rowena dusted her fingers over the faded words along Mrs. Belden's book, read so many times, she'd the lessons committed to memory. And yet, ones she'd read anyway because it had merely served as a vital reminder of who she should be...who she *needed* to be in order to be safe in the world. Sitting up, she flipped open the yellowed pages, marked in pencil along the margins.

Yet, it was who she'd thought she needed to be. All this time, she'd believed her spirit suppressed and dead and herself safe for it. Only, she'd not been living these past ten years because she'd never truly accepted herself with all her blemishes and imperfections. Just as Graham had shut himself away so, too, had she.

Setting aside the copy, she picked up the other, Ainsley's volume on artists and artwork. Rowena sifted through the unfamiliar pages, skimming her gaze over the artwork rendered there and the subtitles under them.

Riveted. With every inked word and underlined detail, awe filled her.

Rowena paused in the middle of the page, her gaze snagged on a heavily marked passage.

...The illegitimate son of notary, San Piero, and a peasant girl...

213

"A peasant girl," she murmured into the quiet. Not a marquess or duke's offspring like the noble peer Graham would one day wed, but someone with her bastard blood.

A log shifted in the hearth and the crimson embers snapped and hissed as though in fiery concurrence with her shock.

Ainsley, despite Graham's likening of the two, was not like her. Nor was Rowena truly like Da Vinci's mother. She was a whore's daughter, born of a nobleman whose identity could not truly be gleaned because of her mother's promiscuity at the time. For that transgression, she had been forever marked, and any hint of even a dream with Graham Linford, the now Duke of Hampstead, had been an impossibility.

Faced with the always-present reminder of her birthright, she'd shaped herself into the dragon that the students and Mrs. Belden had accused her of being.

She'd seen her value as a woman inextricably linked to her birthright. Just as Graham had accused; and despite her protestations on that muddied road, he'd been correct. She just hadn't allowed herself to acknowledge that truth until a seventeen-year-old lady had helped open her eyes even further.

You are far more worthy than any other woman, regardless of station...

She allowed the memory of Graham's quiet utterance to go through her.

Somehow, in being with him, and in his household, she remembered who she was. She spoke her mind and skipped and even now lay on her stomach in his library without fear of recrimination...and there was something so beautifully freeing in it.

Relinquishing the copy, she again picked up Mrs. Belden's book and turned it over in her hands. Rowena drew in a deep breath and tossed the leather volume into the hearth. It struck the top log. The orange flames licked at the corners of the book, curling them, and then it went up in a great fiery conflagration. She watched on wistfully as the pages that had guided her all these years quickly burned into nothing.

She briefly closed her eyes, and with a slow smile, she rolled onto her belly once more and recovered Ainsley's book. When had been the last time she'd laid on a floor? It was a minor triviality to some, but to her it was an act that would have seen her sacked at Mrs. Belden's. Reveling in the freedom found from that oppressive institution, she flipped through the book her charge was frequently studying.

Footfalls sounded in the hallway, and Rowena paused in her study. She arched her neck around, glancing at the open doorway. The heavy tread marked those steps as the male sort. Those footsteps paused at the library door, and she reluctantly looked back to the owner of them, and froze. Had she conjured him from her musings? A glass of brandy in hand, Graham eyed her through thick, dark lashes.

"Rowena." That husky timbre sent butterflies dancing in her belly. The darkness of the room concealed all hint of emotion from those eyes she knew better than her own. Green with gold flecks that danced when he laughed and turned dark when he covered her body with his.

I am my mother's daughter.

That truth would have weighted her with shame not even a week ago. Slowly, she was coming to see she was, as Graham had said, more than her birthright; and in this moment, she owned her desire for this man. Her mouth went dry, and she quickly stood.

"Graham." Her own wicked yearnings making her careless with propriety. But there was no helping it. Jacket unbuttoned, cravat now missing, the tall, muscle-hewn figure before her was, in fact, the same man who'd haunted her thoughts for more than ten years.

He rocked on his heels. "Unable to sleep?"

She gave a hesitant nod, and offered him only a partial truth. "I've been thinking of Ainsley's recital tomorrow."

"I have as well," he confided.

How singularly odd to think a man as unflappable and even as Graham Linford should be driven to restlessness with worries over a young lady's presentation to Society. It fanned warmth within her heart. This, however, was safe discourse. It didn't require mention of his Lady Serena or the future he'd have without Rowena in it. It required only thoughts and talk of the young lady who'd come to mean very much to her in a very short time. "I also had to finalize the scheduling of her lessons and appointments for the week."

He grunted. "I'll not have you losing sleep and devoting your every minute to work."

"That is my role here," she said gently.

"You are more than a servant."

More than a servant. Her heart kicked up a beat. That was the only purpose she'd served at Mrs. Belden's, and for so long. How unlike Mrs. Belden he was. Nothing like the monster she'd taken him for. Forcing her thoughts back to his order, she sank back onto the floor in a rustle of skirts. "It is work, but not *truly*."

Graham immediately fell to his haunches across from the untidy stack she'd been going through. Reaching out, he sifted through the pile, skimming titles.

"It began that way," she clarified. "Ainsley, she is unlike any lady I've worked with, and I learned she is fascinated by Da Vinci and his experiments with flight and astronomy, and so I began looking for ways to make those interests relevant to Society." For, she'd never given true consideration to why a lady must talk and walk simply to be a certain way, all to conform to Society's rules. Until Ainsley.

"She is a bluestocking," Graham said with a small trace of surprise.

"She is." Rowena nodded excitedly. She caught her lower lip between her teeth. "How do you explain to a young lady with a clever mind that she should conform? Unless you deceive her and destroy her spirit." As she had done to so many of her students. Guilt assailed her. "What reasons do you give that are truly meaningful?" she asked, more to herself.

Graham palmed her cheek, and she went still. "Is that what happened to you, Rowena?" he asked, hanging on to one part of her question. "Your spirit was crushed?" At his touch, her eyes slid briefly closed, and she leaned into his fleeting caress.

When was the last time she'd been held by anyone, in any way? And how very wonderful it was to take the warmth he now offered. It was dangerous, but there would come time for logic and reason when the sun rose, and they carried on in their separate ways. "It was," she confirmed, "because I allowed it to be." She firmed her jaw. "I do not want that to happen to Ainsley. I want her to be truthful to who she is, but also to know respecting certain social customs is not exclusive to one another."

Graham roved a path over her face with his eyes. "Your spirit was never truly crushed. I'd wager it's been dormant, but any woman to make her own way, despite all the world"—their families—"has thrown at you, could never be thought of as anything but courageous."

Those words were spoken with nothing more than a pragmatic delivery steeped in logic, and yet, for it, her heart sang. And with the shroud of nighttime privacy, all barriers came down between them. She was not a servant in his employ and he was not a mighty duke, descended from William the Conqueror. Rather, they were just a man and a woman speaking freely, with no constraints.

A look passed between them, weighted with charged emotion that had no place being breathed aloud. Graham was the first to glance away, but not before she saw the strain still present in his eyes, his nightmares so much darker and deeper than she could ever understand. She hated it was just one more thing that divided them. Wanted to know what those monsters were and help him slay them. He stood. "I should leave you to your planning."

Yes, he should. And yet..."Would you join me?" The offer spilled forth before she could call it back. She did not want to call it back. Rather, she wanted him to remain here, at her side. For a long moment, he stood there, frozen. "Never mind," she said finally. "I understand," she dangled the bait, in certain ways still knowing him better than he knew himself.

Graham arced a black eyebrow. "And just what does that mean, Mrs. Bryant?"

Mrs. Bryant. Did he deliberately draw forth the use of her surname, no matter how false it was, to convey his annoyance?

Rowena lifted her shoulders in a little shrug. "It means you are a duke and have no place designing lessons for..."

Graham reclaimed the spot he'd vacated. "Very well, madam," he drawled, dragging over a book. "Let us begin preserving Miss Hickenbottom's spirit, while preparing her for Society."

✍

A short while later, Rowena and Graham lay shoulder to shoulder in the same spot. The leather books she had plucked from the shelves and her own leather folios scattered about them.

"You are missing the point, Graham," she chided, turning a glower on him.

The proverbial *point* being the lessons which would most benefit Miss Ainsley Hickenbottom and smooth her entry into polite Society.

"Whether the lady can paint a watercolor or sketch a floral arrangement will not prepare her for the *ton*," he pointed out. There was no true preparation for the ruthlessness of that cold, calculated world. "Society will care that she can waltz, carry on a polite conversation," Rowena made to speak. "Without cursing." She immediately closed her mouth. "Tomorrow she'll be greeted by some of Society's leading matrons and their respective families." He grimaced. A guest list which included the Montgomery's and a no doubt livid Duke of Wilkshire.

"What is it?" Rowena prodded with a concerned thread to those three words.

Not allowing mention of Lady Serena to intrude on this shared moment with Rowena, he shook his head. "In time, you can cultivate proper interests in the lady." He was not the man his father was. He'd not seek to mold his ward into an emotionless version of every other societal lord or lady. "But her recital is tomorrow evening. I'd have you spend the day readying her." If one could ever be truly prepared for polite Society. "Instruct her again on respectable conduct." Or Society would eat her alive. As it was, they'd already met the girl with, at best, tepid unkindness.

She scowled. "What do you mean *proper* interests, Graham?" she demanded, focusing on the former part of his statement. "It is about finding who she is and accepting herself, finding pride in her accomplishments, despite what Society may say of her."

He angled his head to meet her gaze squarely and the challenge withered on his lips. The soft glow of the fire illuminated the earnest glimmer in her brown eyes. *In shaping Ainsley into a young lady both polished and true to who she was, Rowena seeks to regain what she'd lost.* Did the lady even realize it? "By your own words," he began gently, "the girl already indicated she detests art."

"Because she is focusing on the wrong subjects." She flipped onto her side and fished around for a sheet of parchment. Rolling back over, she waved it under his nose. "These are the interests Ainsley has expressed," she continued, pointing to the neatly compiled list. "As such, I believe the best place to begin would be art instruction. We have an obligation to guide her."

We.

How long it had been since he'd truly been with another person? The women he'd taken to his bed had been mere diversions with whom no real emotion had passed. Even his friendship with Jack these years had shifted where the strongest bond between them were his estates and Jack's assistance with his slipping sanity. He and this woman, who failed to see a monster, and only saw a man. Had life moved along differently for the both of them, it would mayhap even now be their own daughter they discussed and debated the merits of childrearing about. *We can still have all that, with a child of our own...* A calming lightness filled him. Healing with an absolute sense of rightness.

"Are you paying attention?" she asked, her voice rich with exasperation. Setting aside her list, she grabbed a book. "Here," she pointed, jabbing at the page. That slight shift of her hand sent the pages fluttering, and Graham reached a hand up, and held them in place as he tried to make out the words in the dark.

He squinted, taking in the lessons she wished to first pursue.

"She hates art, but she adores Da Vinci," Rowena persisted, releasing a frustrated sigh.

"And do you truly believe fostering a love of art will somehow make her inclined to follow societal rules?" He'd simply settle for a ward who did not hike up her skirts and curse like a sailor in the King's Navy. Or wear breeches. As much as he celebrated her spirit, he'd not see her hurt any more than she already would be by the *ton*.

"Keep reading," she ordered. "Aloud."

A half-grin snagged at the corners of his lips. "Are you instructing me, Mrs…"

She swatted his arm.

"Principles for the Development of a Complete Mind: Study the science of art. Study the art of science. Develop your senses—especially learn how to see. Realize that everything connects to everything else."

Before he'd finished speaking, Rowena was already scrambling up onto her knees beside him. "Everything connects to everything else, Graham. Don't you see?" She didn't await a response. "Ainsley despises conforming to the rules and dictates of polite Society because she sees no connection between them and anything else. She doesn't see how doing so can do her any good."

"And can there be?" he asked, pushing himself up onto an elbow.

"Developing an understanding of societal ways does not strip her of who she is…it helps her to develop a complete mind." As she spoke, a beautiful color filled her cheeks, so very different than the spirit-less women who'd clamored for the title of duchess. And he'd never wanted a woman more than he did this one in this moment, defending the education of a young girl. "Art can help her do that," she continued, when he sat up beside her. "As long as we do not expect her to lose who she is."

Rowena was magnificent. *How could I have ever considered wedding another?* And yet…he had. He'd resolved to marry, and had even been so emotionally cold that he'd let another hand-pick the woman who might be a match for him. Yes, Graham had handled all dealings with the lady and her family the way he did *every* business arrangement. In this instance, confronted with his past and realizing how very close he'd come to wedding Lady Serena for the Hampstead line, Graham didn't much like himself. There were too many crimes he was guilty of that could never be forgiven, truths that had at last been laid bare. He owed Rowena Endicott one more so that mayhap now there would be no more murky shadows between them. He stood and put several steps between them.

Rowena brushed a loose brown strand back behind her ear, and looked up questioningly. "What is it?" she asked cautiously, her earlier enthusiasm dimmed.

"I wanted to speak to you," he began, "about Lady Serena."

TWENTY

Rowena jerked, feeling burned. She'd been expecting it. Had anticipated that truth since Ainsley had uttered it, and yet, even expecting it as she had, it still knotted the muscles of her stomach. Hearing him refer to the lady not as the Duke of Wilkshire's daughter but by her Christian name deepened the realness of their connection.

With slow movements, she came to her feet. "You need not explain yourself to me," she said, calmly, even as her heart raced in an agonizing rhythm, wishing they could go back to the carefree talk of Ainsley's preparation for Society. Anything but…this. How quickly he'd thrown her life back into upheaval. That had always been the explosive effect he'd had on her. A volatile passion that flipped her world upside down.

Graham searched his eyes over her face. "I vowed to do right by the ducal line," he went on, relentless.

That all-important title had led his father to cut her from the thread of her own family. Peeling her lip back, she looked over at the broad desk owned by this man, and no doubt the one before him. He settled his hands on her shoulders, and she stiffened at that unexpected touch.

"Not because of the title," he said quietly. With his knuckles, he angled her chin up, forcing her gaze to his. "Because there are men and women dependent upon me for their livelihoods and security."

That had always been Graham. Always putting others first.

I don't want this discussion. Yet the question slipped forward anyway. "Is she…is the Duke of Wilkshire's daughter the woman you've selected as your bride?" Those words came out so very steady. How, when she was so taut inside one wrong word would snap her?

He hesitated. It was an imperceptible pause so small she might have missed it. But it was there. "She was. Jack identified the lady as an ideal match."

An ideal match? He spoke with such an emotionless detachment gooseflesh dotted her skin. Jack. That same man who'd known about Rowena's bastardy, and in the ultimate act of deception had asked for her hand and forced a kiss. Rowena folded her arms, and then rubbed the limbs in a bid to bring warmth back to them. "What made her ideal?" she asked, asking him to admit the truth. "Her lineage? Her impeccably blue blood?" How was her voice so steady when inside she was breaking?

He scraped his hand over his jaw. "I wanted to marry a woman who desired nothing more than my title." Odd, how that was the last thing she'd ever wanted or desired. Even in that, she could have never been a match for him. "Such a woman would not care that I am a monster, and Jack—"

She threw her hands up on a quiet cry. "Enough with Jack. *You* are not a monster." And Jack had proven even less of a friend to Graham than he had to her.

"He has been there since I returned." *I should have been there. It should have been me at your side.* "He knows what I battle and has helped me."

"Helped you?" she scoffed. "He's had you a recluse these years, Graham. He's kept you shut away and encouraged you to marry a woman you do not love. That is no friend," she said bluntly. *Tell him of that kiss long ago...tell him about that act of disloyalty...*Except taking in his grief-ravaged face, she could not hurt him with long-ago actions of a young, reckless man. *Or is it that you fear he'll again take the word of another over yours...*Filled with a restlessness, she looked around. "You have limited your interactions with people," she began again, returning her eyes to his. "Has that made the nightmares go away?"

Graham gave a brusque shake of his head.

"Because they won't," she said gently. "This is who you are now, and you cannot spend your life hiding or trying to shape yourself into someone else."

He turned shaking palms up, imploringly. "I don't want to be this person," he beseeched. His chest heaved with the force of his emotion, and her heart wrenched at the agony spilling from his eyes.

Rowena took a step over. "And I don't want to be *this* person," she said softly, drifting over to him. She stopped when only a handful of steps separated them. "I don't want to be a whore's illegitimate daughter, and yet that is what I am."

His face spasmed, and then he raked a gaze over her. A harsh, ugly, empty laugh ripped from his lips. "Do not profess to have peace with who you are when you continue to hide yourself away from everyone, including your family." He continued over her sharp, indignant gasp.

"How dare you?" Her family had sent her away. They'd taken coin to see her gone. He'd have her swallow the only thing she'd had these years, her pride, to search out the people who'd never cared to look for her. "You know nothing of—"

"I dare it because it is the truth," he said with a savage bluntness that made her flinch. "You still do not see your worth, madam, so do not profess to lecture me on my own."

"I am not having this discussion with you," she said tightly. "I have to see Ainsley is prepared for tomorrow's recital."

Graham positioned himself between her and the doorway, blocking her escape, and she frantically glanced around. Then with an infinite tenderness that threatened to shatter her, he took her shoulders in his hands. "I cannot do it," he whispered. She stiffened, trying to process. Trying to understand. "I cannot marry her. Not after you. Not after remembering what it is to feel and love."

Rowena closed her eyes and allowed those words to wash over her. She stood motionless as with his lips he trailed a searching path lower, over her cheek. The corner of her mouth. Then he kissed her. She paused, and then with a moan she parted her lips, allowing him entry. A bolt of desire ran through her. Angling her head, she reacquainted herself with the taste and feel of him. The hint of lemon and mint that clung to his breath, a sweet, intoxicating blend.

"Graham," she pleaded, as he shifted his attentions trailing his mouth down the curve of her cheek. A moan spilled past her lips as he nipped and teased the flesh where her earlobe met her neck.

I am lost.

With a moan, she met his lips. Tangling her fingers in his thick hair, she returned his kiss, parting her mouth, allowing him entry. Their tongues touched in a violent meeting of heat. Groaning, he caught her by the hips and guided her against the wall. "You are all I ever wanted," he rasped.

A wild heat burned slowly through her, warming every corner of her being, and she arched wildly in a desperate bid to get closer. Graham cupped her breast through the fabric of her nightshift in his large palm, and her head fell back on a tortured groan. He captured the nipple between his thumb and forefinger, and it sprung to life in his touch.

"Graham," she keened. It had been so long. So very long.

He jerked at the mention of his name and pulled back. With his chest moving in a rapid rise and fall, he stared back with horror wreathing his features. She resisted the urge to cry out when he took a lurching step backward. "Forgive me," he rasped. "I should not...you are in my employ," he whispered raggedly. "It is not my intention to—"

Rowena captured his face between her palms. Desire blazed in his eyes. "I have spent years believing I was a whore." He groaned, and she silenced his protestations with her fingers. "My mother may have been one, but I am not. Neither am I a child or an innocent. I am a woman of eight and twenty years, and in this moment, I'd take what we both want." She gripped his hair and dragged his face up for another kiss.

He briefly resisted, but she tugged free his lawn shirt, caressing his skin as she exposed it.

"I am lost," he groaned, his desperate entreaty an echo of her very thoughts, and so very right for it.

"We always were when we were together," she breathed against his lips.

They dueled with their mouths; a molten heat sang through her veins, as she pressed herself close to him. Together they worked to push his shirt up and Graham tossed the garment aside. The whorls of dark curls matting his chest, damp with sweat, tickled her peaked nipples, scorched her skin. A breathy laugh bubbled past her lips, and he swallowed that sound with his lips, fiercely stroking his tongue in and out of her mouth.

He tugged her wrapper off, and then expertly sliding the décolletage of her nightshift down, he exposed her to the night air. Her nipples puckered from the chill. "So beautiful," he whispered, worshipping one of those now-naked crests. Rowena's breath caught on a gasp. "You were always so sensitive here," he whispered, lavishing his attention on the beauty mark at her neck. "But never more sensitive than you were here." He reached between them and cupped her breast. "How perfectly you always fit in my hand," he murmured, continuing to caress that flesh. "As though we were made for one another." Then he dipped his head and captured one of the swollen tips inside his mouth.

Her moan echoed around the library and went on eternally as he suckled and tasted her. Never breaking contact, Graham brought her down slowly under him.

"W-We were," she whispered, as he shifted his focus to her other breast and lavished his attention on the previously neglected flesh. "M-Made for one another."

They had been...and they'd been separated not by life or by fate, but—Rowena thrust aside all resentment. She'd not allow it in this moment. An ache settled in her core, and she arched in search of his touch. He guided her skirts up, and the cool air slapped at her skin. Then he found her center, and there was only heat.

Biting her lip to keep from crying out, she splayed her legs, opening herself to him. Graham threaded his fingers through her curls, and then slipped a finger inside her wet channel. Desperate mewling whimpers escaped her as he continued his wicked ministrations. She panted, moving her hips in time to his strokes.

"I want you, Rowena," he rasped against her lips. "Only you."

Her heart quickened at his words, and not allowing herself to wonder or question what he was saying, she claimed his mouth.

A shuddery hiss exploded from her lungs as he parted her damp folds, and found the nub that was the source of all her pleasure. She bit her lip. She felt herself hot and dripping, and there was only pleasure and no shame as he stroked her. He paused, and she made a sound of protest and arched violently against his hand.

Graham slid an obliging finger inside, and her moan went on forever while he caressed her. "Tell me to stop," he pleaded, pressing a kiss against the place where her heart rapidly beat.

"Why would I tell you that when I want this so desperately?" she countered, her voice husky with desire, and with a groan, he released himself from his breeches. His shaft sprang free, and she reached out, stroking his member. "I have missed this."

He hissed, as his swollen flesh jerked proud and hungry against his belly. His brow beaded with sweat, Graham positioned himself at her entrance.

She splayed her legs wide, needing him. Just then, her origins, his title, their past, their heartbreak…nothing mattered—except knowing him in this way again.

"Rowena," he moaned, and then thrust hard and deep inside her.

She gasped and began to move, lifting her hips up in slow, searching movements. Matching his. Slower. Slowly building. And then they found a frantic rhythm as he pounded deep inside her. Gripping the generous flesh of her hips, he continued to thrust. Her sheath, wet with her desire, slicked the way.

"Come for me," he pleaded, increasing his strokes, as she panted and moaned beneath him.

Then her body went stiff, and he immediately captured her mouth, as she screamed her bliss. With a groan of surrender, he fell over the edge with her, and then with a quiet shout, capturing his weight with his elbows, he collapsed atop her.

Their breathing came in a like, frantic pace. Jagged spurts that fell together. He dropped his brow to hers. "Oh, God, how I have missed you. There has never been another like you."

They were at the same time the truest words. And the most wrong.

Sadness knifed at her heart. "But there were others after me."

At the agonized accusation, he jerked. For just like that…reality, as it invariably did, intruded. Everything that had come between them.

He rolled off of her, onto his back. Draping his forearm over his head, he stared up at the bucolic mural on the library ceiling "No one ever mattered more to me than you did," he said quietly. "You were all that kept me alive in the Peninsular. When the pain of my injuries drove me to plead for death, your face was there, pulling me back." Graham reluctantly pushed himself upright. Reaching for his jacket, he withdrew a kerchief.

An easy silence between them, he tenderly cleaned her and then himself. Readjusting his garments, he fixed her bodice and lowered her skirts. With every second ticking on the long-case clock across the room, the world outside reared its head, and the implications of what they'd done slipped inconveniently in.

"I should leave." His deep baritone rumbled in the quiet.

"Yes," she murmured. In being here, alone, as they were in dishabille, no less, they risked both Ainsley and Rowena's reputations. If she were a more honorable woman she'd insist he leave, and yet she ached for him to remain.

"I had no place making love to you here." He grimaced. "Not without the benefit of—"

Heart hammering, she held her hand up, stifling an offer that was not really an offer. Nor would she have it from him, and certainly not this way. "I didn't make love expecting anything, Graham," she muttered, grabbing her wrinkled garments. Shrugging off his attempt to help, she dragged her nightdress overhead, and then reached for her wrapper. Hugging herself at the waist, she took several steps back, placing much needed distance between them. "And I certainly didn't lay with you expecting an offer of marriage. I made love to you because I wanted to. You owe me nothing." And at the pregnant pause that developed, she gathered her books and papers—and fled.

TWENTY-ONE

Five hours

By Graham's calculations, that was the length of time he needed to endure a house full of venerated guests who'd come to gawk at and approve his ward.

The following evening, standing in the corner of the Gold Parlor, with his arms clasped at his back, he surveyed the guests assembled for dinner. Lady Serena's father glowered at him while the lady herself looked as icily indifferent as always. Graham continued past the Montgomery's. A nervous tension thrummed in his veins. Worry, not with the possibility of Ainsley's failure, but how she would be received.

Mayhap they should have waited for the girl's benefit. Members of the *ton* delighted in stumbles and went out of their way to push a person down on their face, so they might then gossip about it.

Ainsley sat on the edge of a gold satin sofa, her hands folded primly on her lap as she spoke to the Marquess and Marchioness of Waverly. Graham briefly focused his attention on that trio. Once friendly with the man when they'd been boys at Eton, he'd seen little of the marquess after that. However, when having to assemble guests for Ainsley's introduction, he'd summoned familiar names. And powerful ones. Ainsley said something, and Lord Waverly widened his eyes.

Stiffening, Graham took a step forward, when the husband and wife laughed. Some of the tension went out of him as the marchioness patted Ainsley's hands.

Rowena moved into position beside him. He stiffened, feeling very much like the uncertain boy he'd been years ago, when he'd first

229

made love to her. Only, she proved as undaunted now as she always had revealing not a hint of regret or embarrassment for what they'd shared. "She is going to be all right, Graham," she said reassuringly, her soft contralto barely reaching his ears. How harmonious their thoughts were. Had always been.

"I'm not worried about how they perceive me," he said from the corner of his mouth.

"I didn't think you were," she said softly.

He glanced at her; even in drab skirts, serviceable boots, and a hideously tight coiffure, there was not a lady more magnificent.

As if she felt his gaze, she looked up and gave him an encouraging smile. *We shouldn't be stealing glances and side conversations.* She should be on his arm, or wherever else she bloody wanted in the room, talking to whom she pleased, how she pleased. And as she looked out, he remained entranced. Unable to tear his gaze from her. The candle's glow bathed her heart-shaped face in soft shadows. Illuminated the dark burgundy hues of her deep brown tresses.

From across the room, Jack, in conversation with the Viscount Dailey and his spinster daughter, Miss Cornworthy, glanced over at him. A frown marred the other man's lips. The old viscount said something calling his attention back.

"Oh, yes," Ainsley was saying loudly. "Hampstead's a brilliant dance instructor, isn't he, Mrs. Bryant?"

All discourse came to a screeching halt, as every set of eyes swiveled to them. Probing eyes. Curious ones. Ones that searched for secrets and scandal. A dull flush climbed up Graham's neck, and he resisted the urge to yank at his too-tight cravat.

Rowena artfully drifted over to the trio. "His Grace was good enough to provide Miss Hickenbottom dance lessons," she explained to the room at large. The guests erupted into a smattering of sighs from the ladies present. And just like that, the guests were diverted from the hint of impropriety Ainsley had alluded to. Graham, an employer, waltzing his ward's companion about an empty ballroom, while laughter had trilled from her lips, that mirth contagious.

He stared on, riveted by the vision Rowena made. With her ease in speaking to the guests and her warm smiles for Ainsley, she radiated a beauty that robbed him of breath. Only hers was a beauty that moved beyond her delicate features and included her unwavering spirit, her strength, her courage. *She should be my wife...*She raised her head, and across the room, their gazes caught. A silent, charged awareness passed between them.

"This is going to be a bloody disaster." Jack stepped between Graham and his unobstructed view of her.

Silently cursing the shattered connection, he flexed his jaw. "She is doing splendidly," he argued in defense of the lady. And she was. With less than a fortnight under Rowena's tutelage, Ainsley had, though not perfected all societal customs, demonstrated grace and enthusiasm. It was infectious. When Jack made to speak, Graham interrupted. "And they can go hang if they take exception to the lady." His gaze landed on Lady Serena eying Rowena the way she might a rodent who'd scurried over her toes. "All of them," he added.

His friend tightened his mouth. "You should have delayed her entry into Society."

Momentarily diverted, he looked to Jack. "Is that what this is about? You are upset that I made a decision other than the one you urged me to make." At the stony glint in the other man's eyes, he realized he'd hit the mark. In the past, Graham had taken the man's professional stubbornness and meticulousness as signs of his acumen. Now, with him glowering on at Rowena and Ainsley, he saw a new glimpse of Jack. An ugly, unpleasant one, that forced Graham to reevaluate what he'd always believed about him. He motioned to a servant, and the liveried footman rushed off. "Relax, Jack," he urged. "If I'm not worried about the lady, you shouldn't be either." He slapped him on the back.

The matter was laid to rest as his butler appeared and announced dinner. As the guests paired off with their respective partners, Rowena said something to her charge, and with a nod, Ainsley skipped over.

She briefly noted Jack, and after a small, insolent curtsy, gave him the cut direct. "Well, Hampstead? Mrs. Bryant said you are to

231

accompany me for the meal. Or has Turner here commandeered your attention?" Again. The word hung, real, as if it had been spoken.

Ignoring the whispers from several ladies, Graham held his arm out. "Shall we, Miss Hickenbottom?"

The girl sank into a curtsy. A flawless, perfect dip, as though she'd been mastering them since she'd toddled out of her cradle and a sense of pride swelled...as well as something more...Regret that it couldn't be Ainsley's father here with her even now. As he and Ainsley led the way to the dining room, he ached to look back. Rowena should be at the front of this line. Not taking up the very last spot as a bloody servant.

"She's at the back," Ainsley whispered, startling him.

Graham coughed. "Beg pardon?" Surely, she'd not noticed—

"Mrs. Bryant," she clarified, too-loudly, and he stole a quick glance to determine whether anyone had ascertained her words.

"That is who you were looking for, was it not?" *Oh, bloody hell.* He'd lived alone for more than ten years, keeping largely to himself. He didn't know what to do with a far-too-clever young girl under foot. Particularly one who'd noted his interest in Rowena. "Or is it Wilkshire whose been glowering at you all evening?" the girl prattled on. "Always better to keep an eye on an enemy."

"Er..." He made a clearing sound and looked around desperately. Alas, there was no rescue coming. Not for the first time, he damned the distance between him and Rowena.

"Very well, Hampstead," Ainsley said placatingly and patted his hand. "No need to speak about it." They reached the dining room. "Unless you wish to."

He stifled a groan. "I assure you I do not."

Her eyes brightened, and he damned his slip of the tongue which had only confirmed her accurate supposition. "That is," he clarified. "There is nothing to speak about. I'm not looking for anyone in particular." Had he always been this rotted of a liar?

You're a miserable liar, Graham Linford.

Rowena's voice from long ago trilled around his mind. They entered the room and took their places at their respective spots. With the Marquess of Waverly positioned on one side and Graham the other,

Ainsley slid into her chair. The young lady gathered her napkin, and with precise movements, unfolded the fabric and placed it on her lap. She looked down the end of the table to where Rowena sat.

A pride-filled smile turned Rowena's lips up, and she lifted her head in acknowledgement of the girl's accomplishment.

Just then Rowena's dining partner said something, commanding her attention. Grabbing his wine glass, Graham scowled into the contents. How in blazes had the Marquess of Midleton come to maneuver the spot beside her? Then, Graham himself a former rogue, nothing should surprise him. Lady Serena's brother dipped his gaze to Rowena's décolletage. Graham gripped the stem of his drink so hard, it nearly snapped. He forced himself to relax his hold. Some of the fury eased, when the gentleman finally pulled his gaze upward—only to ogle her damned mouth. A mouth Graham had kissed, and—with a growl he took a healthy swallow.

"Why in blazes did you seat her beside that rogue, Hampstead?" Ainsley hissed.

"I didn't," he muttered under his breath. "I didn't even know he'd be in attendance." What bloody rogue attended recitals and card parties? Poor excuses of ones, those were the kind.

"You didn't know?" Ainsley demanded on a whisper that earned her several curious looks. "Who in blazes put your list to—" She narrowed her eyes. "You let Turner, didn't you?"

"I made some suggestions," he mumbled, feeling very much like the scolded lad in the schoolroom.

"But not enough to leave off a man so easily able to wring a blush from Mrs. Bryant?"

His ward sounded on the cusp of bloodying his nose for that offense. Graham thinned his eyes into menacing slits. Why, the gentleman was, in fact, saying something close to her ear that earned one of those smiles that had only belonged to him.

"Well, I don't like him," she said, grabbing her fork as a plate was set before her.

And as Graham suffered through the inanity of the polite dinner party, he found he rather hated the blighter, too. He gave thanks when the meal had finally concluded and the guests were led to the recital room for the evening's performance.

Soon, Ainsley would perform for the invited members of the *ton*. And then the whole infernal affair would be blessedly concluded. As they reached the music room, his ward dug her heels in, and he was forced to either stop or drag her forward. "What is it?" he asked quietly as the collection of guests filed into their seats.

"I need a moment, Hampstead," the young lady said bluntly, and then without awaiting permission, darted off.

He searched the gathering for Rowena and found her on the fringe, surveying the guests. Graham stood, watching her, studying her.

She should have been my duchess long ago. She should be here, sitting at my side, dressed in the softest silks and satins.

And instead, she hovered, waiting for her charge to walk the narrow aisle and perform for the leading peers of the *ton*.

A viselike pressure coiled around his lungs and squeezed off his ability to draw in an even breath. She sat there, because of lies told by his father and her mother...and because of him. After he'd visited her mother and found Rowena gone, he had owed it to her to find where she'd gone and have the words from her own mouth. His throat worked, and he took a swallow of his champagne. For what did it say about a man who'd had so little faith?

He'd wronged her in every way a man could wrong a woman, and for it, they'd lost countless years together. She'd lost her happiness and he'd lived a shiftless life, carousing and womanizing as she'd first accused. Shame slapped at his conscience. For who he'd let himself become. Rowena had deserved more than his faithlessness. She deserved a man who would have stood at her side and loved her and matched her in strength and courage.

He wanted her. All of her. In his arms. In his bed. In his life. Forever. But he'd forfeited all rights, long ago. Too many years had passed and, in that time, they'd both changed. He was scarred in his mind and soul from horrible deeds he'd committed in the name of war. And Rowena? She'd fought her own battles of life, and in the wary set to her eyes and hesitant smile, she'd been forever marked. Because of him.

At the noisy whispers and chattering of guests, she glanced around at the collection of lords and ladies, and then their stares met.

He expected her to quickly yank her focus elsewhere, but the faintest smile hovered on her lips, and his heart doubled its beat the way it had in his youth. For that faint smile gave him…hope. Hope that what they'd shared in one another's arms last night had been more than sex. That it had been the joining of hearts and souls. *I want forever with her…*

Then, the moment was shattered. Rowena stood, and made her way from the hall. Uncaring of how it might look, Graham quickly followed after her. He studiously avoided the determined matchmaking mamas attempting to gain his notice. His gaze remained on a single woman.

I do not envy you being a noble born, but I do envy that I'll never attend a ball.

Of course, you shall, love. You'll attend every event as my wife.

The peal of their innocent laughter echoed around the chambers of his mind, fresh now as when they'd been children, already dreaming of a future together.

Graham quickened his pace. With her hurried movements, a number of locks revolted from that miserable coiffure and sent hair spilling from the tight knot at the base of her skull. Those chocolate brown strands cascaded about her waist and held him immobile. She was a brown-haired Athena, and he'd never wanted a woman more than he did her.

Reaching for those loose strands, Rowena stole a horrified glance about. Alas, the whole of the *ton* was too bloody foolish to see her standing there in all her beauty.

Never taking his gaze from the determined path she set, he followed. She exited the ballroom, and he increased his stride, coming up quietly behind her. "Rowena," he murmured quietly. A small gasp escaped her and she swung around.

"Graham?" she whispered, blinking madly. "What are you—?"

He pushed open the nearest door and pulled her inside a parlor, closing the oak panel quickly behind them. The room, bathed in darkness but for a handful of sconces lit, cast eerie shadows off the walls. "I would speak to you," he murmured in hushed tones.

"Your Grace," she whispered, a plea underscoring the impropriety of the moment.

"Graham," he implored. Wanting to be more than a bloody employer to her. Wanting to have a future with her, even as she deserved so much more.

"There is your ward. It is time for me to collect her for her appearance. And if we are discovered, I will be ruined."

She may as well have run him through with the stark reminder of the gulf that Society placed between them. The lords and ladies and all their rules and opinions could go hang. And yet, it mattered to her. To her, they risked ruin. A young woman who served as an instructor at a finishing school had nothing more than her reputation.

He would give her everything, if she'd but let him.

When he said nothing, she stamped her foot in an endearing show of frustration. "I do not have the luxury afforded me that I can simply—"

He cupped his palm about her neck.

"Wh-what are you doing?"

That her voice emerged as a breathless whisper, absent of any outrage, encouraged him. He dipped his head lower, giving her time to draw back. And then he claimed her mouth. Their lips met in a fiery explosion, and he caught her as she went limp against him. Their tongues dueled, while their hands explored one another as they had a lifetime ago. As they had again last night.

Fueled with the memory of the feel and taste of her, he filled his hands with her full buttocks and dragged her closer. She moaned into his mouth and undulated her hips in a helpless, hopeless searching rhythm.

"Graham," she pleaded, as he trailed his lips down her neck and lower to the swell of her modest décolletage. Then he stopped.

Her heart pounded solidly and loudly against her breastbone. He turned his ear, resting his head to the sweet beat of her heart. How many times had they lain in the Wallingford countryside in this very repose, staring up at the sky?

"What are we doing?" she whispered, stroking her fingers through his hair.

He forced himself to draw back and with slow, precise movements, he put her hair to rights. "Marry me."

Her body turned to stone in his arms. "What?" she asked, her voice a threadbare whisper.

"I said marry me, Rowena."

She scoured his face with her gaze. "What game do you play, Your Grace?" she hissed, pushing herself from his arms with such alacrity that he stumbled.

Graham frowned. "Do you think this is a game?"

"No," she said, fear flashing in her eyes. "This is my life."

"And I want to share it with you." It had always been her. It had been her since she was a girl of fifteen who'd moved into Wallingford and stolen his heart. "Because I love you." How easily those words spilled free, and he should be fearful of everything entailed in spending forever with this woman, given his moments of madness, but there was no fear. Not anymore.

Rowena's eyes formed horrified circles, and she clutched at her skirts. Was the idea of a future with him so repugnant to her? A blade twisted in his chest, and he avoided her gaze. "If you do not wish to wed me because you fear me…"

"Fear you?" she asked perplexedly, swiftly dropping her arms. "Oh, Graham," she said gently, caressing her fingertips over his cheek. "Long ago, I hated you for doubting me and sending me away, but I never feared you."

He motioned to his throat and then hers. "I am not the same man I was."

Understanding lit her eyes. "My rejection of your suit…" He winced. "It has nothing to do with *fearing* you. It was impossible years earlier when you were a duke's second son, and it is even more impossible n-now," she said, her voice breaking. Her words pierced his heart. "Don't you see?"

He'd have shed his title and worked the land with his hands if that would bring her happiness. "I only see you," he put in.

She stalked away from him and began to pace. "You are a duke, and I'm a whore's daughter."

His gut churned. "How can you see good in me, with the madness I carry, and not see it in yourself?" His words halted her mid-stride. "I would have you as my duchess." He braced for the fear that request would bring. For twelve years, he'd vowed to live a life alone. Now, he asked Rowena to enter his world and spend her days with him, forever.

"Is this because of your father?" she asked bluntly. "Because, I'll not have you make an offer out of some misbegotten sense of guilt."

He deserved her mistrust, and her hatred, and doubt for his love. She'd been his friend and he should have fought to find her. "This isn't about my father or guilt or what we did last night." Which he did feel for the hardships she'd known in his absence. "This is me, loving you, and wanting to own the next eleven years and beyond, together."

Rowena blanched and held her palms up. "I don't want to be a duchess, Graham," she said, her voice a threadbare whisper that carved a hollow hole in his chest. The irony was not lost on him: he'd been searching for a wife who wanted nothing more than his title, and the only woman he could envision taking as his bride didn't want him because of that rank. She continued, "I don't want to be part of a world where my life's purpose is that of tea-pourer and hostess." A panicky laugh burst from her lips. "I'd make you a rotten duchess."

Her words jolted him into movement, and he strode over to her, hovering, at sea. "You can hold no teas or a thousand," he said gruffly. "Let us begin again."

"We can't, though." She looked about the room, her gaze distracted. "There can be no going back."

He moved quickly away from the door and over to where she stood, and then stopped, hovering, uncertain. "Then let us go forward," he pressed. He'd lost her once on a lie. And to lose her again would rob him of his every happiness. There was no joy without her in his life. *What about what she wants?* He shoved aside that niggling voice.

Her lower lip trembled. "Do not do this, Graham," she begged.

He lowered his mouth once more, and she placed her palms on his chest. She turned her head, so his kiss grazed her cheek. "Please." That was it. An entreaty that was a denial. She staggered away from him and reached for the door handle. "There are guests," she pleaded, looking past him.

I am not enough for her.

Oh, God. He would rather face a charge of French soldiers battling up the hillside with their bayonets drawn than this potent rejection. He managed a jerky nod. "Of course. Forgive me," he said, proud of that smooth deliverance when he was breaking from the inside out. Graham stepped away and Rowena fled from the room.

Silence hummed in the empty room as he stared at the oak-paneled door.

TWENTY-TWO

Rowena fled through the halls. Her pulse pounded loudly in her ears as his words rang around her mind.

He wants to marry me.

After all the years apart and the lies that had divided them, he offered her his name...uncaring of her bastardy.

She caught the inside of her cheek between her teeth, strangling a sob. And what weakness was it of her character that with his vow of love and his promise of forever, she'd wanted to forget the years of heartbreak between them, abandon her hatred for polite Society, and take everything he offered? To take it and hold on to it, as the hopeful girl she'd been, clinging to forever.

A figure stepped into the hall, and she skidded to a stop. Her heart knocked hard against her ribcage. Jack passed a disdainful up and down look over her person. One would never guess that this same man begged to court her all those years earlier. The man who'd vowed his love and implored her to forget Graham and marry him instead.

"Mr. Turner," she said tersely. "If you'll excuse me. I have to find Miss Hickenbottom."

He remained rooted to the spot, blocking her retreat. "You could not stay away. It mattered not that it was best for him."

She steeled her shoulders. "Move out of the way." She owed this man no explanations. Mayhap, long ago. No longer.

"Graham will want you gone when he knows all." He wrapped those last words in an icy condescension that set her teeth on edge.

Drawing on years of cruelly mocking students, she cast a bored glance over her shoulder. "Graham already knows everything." *And he wants me anyway.* To him, her parentage did not matter. He'd been the one person who'd not cared that her mother was a courtesan…and he'd taught her there was no shame in her origins.

All the color leeched from the other man's cheeks. "E-Everything?" Ah, so he wondered if she'd told him of the last visit he'd ever paid her. As though he'd followed the silent path her thoughts had wandered, Jack tightened his mouth, his arrogance returned. "If he loved you, he would have found you years earlier. Let him go, Rowena."

Did he expect those words to sting? At one time, they may have. No longer. She was no longer the pathetic girl cowering before him or anyone. She stole a glance about, searching for interlopers, and strolling forward, she spoke in hushed tones. "And what would you have me do, Jack? Leave, so there is only you here to convince him he's mad?" she said with a perverse delight. His confidence wavered, revealing hesitancy in his hard features. "I'm not going anywhere. Not because you ordered me gone. Not because Graham wishes me here. But because I choose to be here. For Ainsley."

She started around him, and gasped when he shot a hand out, closing his fingers around her upper arm. "Did you tell him?" he demanded harshly. There was a harsh desperation lining that question.

When she remained silent, he tightened his grip. She winced. His hold strong enough to leave marks, she felt the first stirrings of fear since he'd come upon her. Rowena searched around for a hint of Graham. A servant. Anyone. *Why…why…he is terrified.* "Did I tell him what, Jack? That you were disloyal in his absence?" she tossed back. "Do you fear he'll sack you if he learned how you pressed a kiss on me and urged me to break the vow I'd made to him?"

All the color leeched from the other man's cheeks, and he suddenly released her. "I was young, foolish. It was a lifetime ago." He sneered, giving her a quick once over.

She shot her chin up. "Do you believe that will matter to Graham?"

"He'll never trust you," Jack snapped. "Not over me. He didn't trust you all those years ago, and he won't now." Rowena curled her hands into tight, painful fists. The movements left marks on her palms. She'd be damned if she let this monster know his jibes hit like well-places arrows. "You were purged from his memory," he continued, with a triumphant grin. Nonchalant, Jack flicked a speck of dust from his puce coat sleeve. "And me, I was given the trusted role of man-of-affairs."

"Ah, but he knows who I am," she said with a perverse delight. His face fell, revealing hesitancy in his hard features. "He knows that my letters were never delivered. And do you know, Jack…" She curled her lips up into a hard smile. "Someday he will learn just what you are. A cold, heartless, disloyal bastard."

Graham had not doubted her since they'd discovered the evil enacted against them, and should she tell him about Jack's advances, he'd not doubt those, either. Such an understanding came from knowing her since she was a girl of fifteen and he a boy of seventeen, counting stars in the night sky when they should be abed.

He gave his head a faltering shake. "He won't believe the daughter of a whore."

She arched an eyebrow. "Ah, but would I be here even now serving as a companion for his ward if he didn't, at the very least, trust me?" Love had been ruined by time, but it was still there and, now, a fragile, but real, trust. Then she froze, as his words settled around her mind. "What do you know of my mother?" Her voice emerged breathless as her mind raced. Had Graham confided that in this man before her? As soon as the thought slid in, she thrust it aside.

Jack's Adam's apple bobbed. "It does not take much to deduce she was a whore," he said sharply, faltering with that deliverance.

She staggered back. Why was she shocked? *Then, I didn't truly know the ugliness in Jack's soul until the day he visited when Graham was gone.* How could Graham, then, see anything but good in a man he'd known since they were children of seven? "I am telling him, Jack," she said softly, setting aside her earlier jeering. "I am telling him what you did."

"By God, you bitch," he hissed, "The moment you reentered his life, I knew you would set out to destroy the life and reputation I've built. One of us will fall, Rowena, and I'll be damned if it's me."

She gave her head a pitying shake. "Your life and reputation are built on a lie of false goodness and friendship." And with Jack Turner choking in her wake, she marched on, head held high.

"Do you truly believe Miss Hickenbottom's reputation is safe as long as you are her companion?" he called after her.

An eerie chill scraped her spine. Not pausing to look back, she continued on, in search of her charge. As soon as she rounded the corner, she layered her back to the wall, borrowing support, as she attempted to right her world.

"Mrs. Bryant."

Rowena shrieked and spun around. "Ainsley," she managed faintly. Her mind raced, and she searched the girl for a hint that she'd over-heard the volatile exchange between herself and Jack.

Ainsley hovered, a tense smile on her face. "Are you nervous as well, Mrs. Bryant?"

The frantic beat of her heart slowed. Nervous?

"I was hiding," the girl whispered.

Rowena's heart pulled, and thoughts of Graham receded. "You're going to do splendidly," she assured her charge, taking her hands and giving a faint squeeze.

"It will not be fine. I lied to His Grace," Ainsley whispered. Guilty splotches of red suffused the young lady's cheeks.

Volatile exchange with Jack forgotten, Rowena picked her way through her words. "What do you mean?"

"I told you both I played the pianoforte." Ainsley yanked her hands free. "I did not want you or Hampstead to believe I had *no* skills," the girl said, her voice, desperate. "And now, he's assembled a room full of Society's leading members to hear me and…" And she could not play a note. The muscles of her throat moved.

Oh, dear. I allowed this. Rowena stole a look toward the recital hall. *This is what Society makes of women—even bold and proud ones like Ainsley.* She knew all too well the sense of being on the outside, of wanting approval. She reclaimed Ainsley's hands. "Look at me." With a reluctance she'd never witnessed from the girl, Ainsley lifted her eyes. "Playing pianoforte poorly or as a virtuoso does not make you who you are. Your strength and courage and intellect do." Ainsley's eyes widened. "And do not ever let anyone diminish your sense of self-worth." *As I have done.*

243

"But what shall we do?"

Her mind raced. "Run abovestairs. I will find His Grace and speak to him." And then they would proceed from there.

"Thank you, Mrs. Bryant," the girl whispered, bussing her on the cheek. With that, she darted off.

Rowena hurried to the recital hall. How to explain to a room full of guests about to meet the Duke of Hampstead's ward there would be no performance. There would of course be whispers. There always were. Regardless of the type or depth of scandal. As she stepped inside the room, she was met with loud whispers and horrified stares. A frisson of unease rolled through her.

It is all my imagining.

"...Whore..."

"...Mother was a..."

Nausea roiled in her belly as the loud whispers reached her ears. They spoke of someone else. What notice would these people dare pay her? Still, she looked about the recital hall for Graham, foolishly searching him out, needing the comforting reassurance of his presence. Instead, her gaze landed on a familiar woman seated amongst the other guests. The same one who'd been scrutinizing her at Lord Wilkshire's. Rowena froze as recognition slammed into her at last.

A dragon.

Mrs. Munroe, an instructor sacked by Mrs. Belden for filling the students' heads with scandalous works. And that fellow dragon now looked back at her with a knowing...and a pitying look. Rowena clutched at her throat. What was happening? Why was everyone staring at her?

Graham stopped before her. "Come," he said sharply. His face, a cool ducal mask of arrogance and strength, restored some of her strength. He held out his arm to her and she immediately put her fingertips on his sleeve.

"I don't..." And then she *knew.*

"...Courtesan's daughter serving as a companion..."

Oh, God.

They knew. How could they? Then, *he* stepped into her line of vision. Jack Turner lifted his head in a mocking greeting. He'd made good on his pledge. Her knees went weak, and she dimly registered Graham shooting an arm about her waist and the explosion of shocked gasps at that boldness.

"I can walk," she said, her tongue thick. But he retained his hold, guiding her from the room.

"Rowena," Graham said quietly.

"Please, don't," she begged.

"We need to speak," he said as they reached his office. She briefly eyed the opposite end of the hall, and then followed him inside.

Not another word was spoken until he'd closed the door behind them.

She lingered at the door, contemplating escape. Cool as only a duke could be, he crossed over to his sideboard and poured a brandy. He came over and handed her the drink. "I don't drink spirits," she said stiffly as he pushed the glass into her hand.

"Some days you need to. This is one of them."

Rowena hesitated, and then raised the snifter to her lips. She took a swallow and promptly choked as the liquor flooded her throat.

"Small sips," he instructed. "It becomes easier with each one."

She took another small, experimental one and grimaced. It was rotten stuff, and yet, with each small drink, a soothing warmth filled her. Mayhap Graham had been right after all.

"They know," he said quietly, an apology there for a crime that was not his. Not this one.

And mayhap the liquor was grander stuff than she credited for the heady effects of the spirits dulled the potent shock his words should bring. She pressed her eyes closed. "How?" Jack's venom-filled face crept behind her vision. It was him...and yet, how had he come to know? Her mind attempted to put to rights something that could never be clearly sorted through. Had it been Graham's father. A panicky half-laugh, half-sob spilled from her lips. Then, did it really matter who had revealed her secret?

Taking the glass from her grip, Graham set it down with a loud thunk. "It does not matter what they believe," he insisted, claiming her hands. He gave them a firm squeeze, in a reassuring touch that forced her eyes open.

Oh, Graham. As a duke he could not see. A companion must be above reproach, for one's reputation was linked to the child in one's care. For Rowena, that child was no mere stranger…it was Ainsley. Ainsley whose life had already been difficult, and would continue to be so, without compounding Rowena's past to her existence.

"Know," she whispered. "It is what they know, as fact." A person's birthright, whether Graham wished it another way, determined who they were before Society, and even with his rank, a step below royalty, he could not force their acceptance. Wary, she moved out of his reach and folded her arms close. Society's hatred mattered little to her when presented with the girl who'd been placed in her care. "I have to leave," she realized aloud.

A violent curse exploded from his lips, halting her distracted movements. "That is rot. You do not have to go anywhere."

Poor Graham. She stopped and wheeled slowly to face him. A sad smile played on her lips. "You truly believe that." It was a statement, and nonetheless, he nodded.

"What of Ainsley?" she gently pressed. For though she despised agreeing with Jack about anything, he'd been correct in this.

"Marry me. Be my duchess, and we will weather this together." Her palms moistened. His duchess. How very easy he made it sound. Only, as a duke's noble son, Graham could never know what it was to be an outcast amongst Society. To know the pain that came from derisive sneers and from being the recipient of heartless words. She, however, knew. It had been a lesson learned as a small girl in London, who'd had the word 'whore' pounded into her vernacular by the unkind nursemaid assigned her.

"Marry me," he repeated, with a quiet resolve to that request.

Again, he sought her hand, and once upon a lifetime ago, there had been nothing she'd wanted more in life than to be his wife. But that had been before. When they were young. When he'd not been a duke, and she'd not have to spend the remainder of her days filling that esteemed, unwanted role. A life where she'd forever be reminded by cold, unfeeling people around her about her origins, and that she didn't belong because of them. She pressed her fingertips against her temple and rubbed. She'd spent her life making decisions with the purpose of avoiding scandal. She'd not bind either of them together for all eternity because Society had discovered her secrets.

She loved him, but she could never marry him. To live here, amongst the *ton*, would crush her spirit and reduce her to the scared girl she'd once been. *I cannot go back to that.* But at least, she could, before she left, give him the truth. "You do not wonder how my secret was revealed?"

Rowena spoke with a finality that sent his heart racing into the same panic it had known just before the calls were raised for battle. It did not escape his notice that she had again failed to answer his plea. Now, she'd pose a question.

I am going to lose her. Panic spiraled through him, and he searched for the words to keep her at his side. Instead, he fixed on her question. He shook his head befuddled. In the mayhem of the moment, he'd thought of nothing but getting her away from societal scorn. He'd not given thought to who had been in possession of her secret and revealed it before his guests. He mentally ran through the list of visitors who even now sat in his recital room.

Rowena wandered over to his desk and trailed her fingertips along the edge of the surface, studying those digits as though she could divine the meaning of existence from them. He stood stock still, taking in her every movement. "It was Jack who revealed my secret, Graham."

He opened and closed his mouth several times. Trying to make sense of that and wholly unable to.

"It was Jack," she repeated. Her soft-spoken announcement sucked all the life from the room and left him in this netherworld of doubt and shock. The three of them had been closer friends than the *Les*

Trois Mousquetaires. As those useless to their family as second and third-born sons, he and Jack, boys from neighboring estates, had formed a fast friendship. The day they'd come upon Rowena on the hillside, she'd become one of them.

"Jack?" he echoed.

Rowena inhaled. "When you were gone, Jack paid a..." She grimaced. "A call to me. It was the same day your father ordered me gone." Her eyes took on a dark, distant, haunted look that knifed at his insides. What memories did she live? Only ones of pain, and always because she'd made the foolish mistake of loving him. Loving him when he'd never been deserving of that gift.

A fist was being squeezed about his heart, breaking an organ that had only ever belonged to this woman as her words drew forth images that had once been real moments in her life. Ones that had seen her alone, unguarded, but Jack had been there. Why hadn't Jack helped her? Unease skittered along his spine.

She stared at those white-knuckled digits, and fear turned his mouth dry. He didn't want to know the rest, didn't want to know where her words would lead him.

"My family was in the gardens and Jack came." Rowena angled her body, presenting herself in profile, and she hugged her arms to her waist. "He asked to speak to me. Alone. Insisted I should marry him." Graham jerked. Marry him? His heart thudded to a slow stop, and then resumed a quickened pace, knocking against his ribcage. Jack. The man he'd called friend had offered her marriage in his absence. "He told me you were dancing attendance on French beauties all over the Continent," Rowena said softly.

"Never." The denial ripped from deep inside where truth dwelled. "I never betrayed you." He winced. "Not in those days." After. After he'd returned, and risen from his bed broken-hearted, attempting to drive the memory of Rowena Endicott from his head. Oh, God. *I'm going to be ill.* He and Jack had vied for her affections, but when she had ultimately professed her love for Graham, the other man had ceased trying to woo her. He'd believed Jack had accepted her decision. Believed he'd set aside his stalwart intentions. Graham gripped the top of his head hard, attempting to squeeze out rationale thought. *I asked him to look after Rowena in my absence.*

Jack couldn't have betrayed him...He...

Graham looked up. By the wariness in Rowena's eyes, she expected his doubt. And he could not. She would not lie to him. Her eyes were windows to her soul, a soul that shared the same vicious agony at Jack's treachery.

She wetted her lips. "He held me while I cried." *It should have been me who held her. Nay, she should have never been reduced to that misery because I should have been there protecting her from my father's evil.* Shame and regret twisted inside. "And then asked that I marry him. When I said no..." Her gaze took on a vacant quality.

Graham glanced frantically about, wanting to escape the darkness hovering on those unspoken words. "What did he do?" The question ripped from his throat, and he drew in a breath, forcing himself to ask the question that needed to be asked. "Did he put his hands on you?" Dead. He would kill Jack with his bare hands, then reassemble him and kill him all over again.

Her eyes formed wide circles. *She expects I'll doubt her.* God, how he hated that he'd given her no reason to trust his word or his worth. "He kissed me," she said, her voice devoid of emotion. "Touched me..." She brushed her fingertips over her breast, creating an image of Jack forcing his kiss on her.

An animalistic growl better suited for an untamed beast thundered around the room and Rowena drew in a breath. "I wrested myself free, and that was the last I saw of him...until I returned to Wallingford Castle. You were home, and he greeted me in the foyer as though he owned it," she spat. "And then left me alone with your father."

I trusted him. I entrusted him with caring for her in my absence. His gut roiled. He'd called Jack friend, and all this time, he'd kept secret after secret. Withholding the single most important detail that would have saved Graham from madness. Rowena had come to him. He closed his eyes and concentrated on his breathing to keep from throwing up. "I made him my man-of-affairs," he said hoarsely. Invited him into his home even now.

Rowena lifted her slender but strong shoulders in a shrug. "You trusted him." He flinched. She shot her eyebrows to her hairline. "I did not mean—"

He waved off any apology she would make. He was wholly undeserving of it. She'd been the only one wronged. If he spent the remainder of his life trying to right the past, it still would not be enough.

Energy thrummed through his veins, rolling together regret, hatred, horror, and love—love for this woman who'd been all he'd ever wanted in a partner. With a violent curse, Graham stalked over to the sideboard. He spread his hands on the smooth surface and leaned over it, taking in her words that lingered in the air and his own pain. "I would have never sent you away," he said, unable to open his eyes. "I loved you. I never stopped loving you." Though she, with every justifiable reason, had stopped loving him. Why should she accept his offer of marriage? He opened his eyes and forced himself to face her.

She stood stoic, her body erect, like a warrior princess. How strong she was. He and the men who'd fought years to defeat Boney hadn't an ounce of her courage. "I did not tell you this to make you feel guilt, for there is nothing to feel guilty of." And his father. "I told you this," she said calmly, "so you know who he is. He is no friend, Graham. He is a man who would have you hide from the world." And a man who'd betrayed him, countless times. "I cannot stay here."

That unexpected pronouncement jolted him back, and he stared blankly at her. "You can." It emerged as a plea.

"I cannot," she repeated with quiet insistence.

Why should she wish to remain? He'd cut her from his life and trusted another...a man who'd been privy to the truth of her birth and bandied that story inside his own home to ruthless strangers. He had no right to her. He never had. "Where will you go?" he asked, his voice hoarse.

Rowena wetted her lips. "I don't know."

Graham eyed her blankly. Surely this discussion, with talks of partings and the end of any future between them, belonged to someone else? He stood, a silent observer in his own misery.

She hesitated. And for one breathless moment where hope dwelled, he thought she would give him words of love and give the possibility of them together a chance.

Instead, she bowed her head and left, closing the door behind her, leaving him alone with the tortured truth of lies unveiled too late.

TWENTY-THREE

"**Y**ou are going to leave, aren't you?"

From the windowseat overlooking the Mayfair streets, Rowena shifted her attention to the young lady who occupied a nearby shell-back chair. "I—"

"You've only just arrived, you know," Ainsley pointed out.

Had she? It felt like she and Graham had never parted, and this fortnight together rolled neatly into all the times they'd once shared. But, at last, they had honesty between them. All truths had been revealed, and though there could never be the loving marriage they'd dreamed of as children, there would be peace. Her lower lip quivered and she bit it hard. There would be no peace. There would never be anything more than the regret for what could have been. "I am afraid I must go," she said when the girl stared at her expectantly.

Ainsley dropped her chin into her palm. "Where will you go?" The girl's question, an echo of the very one Graham had put to her, raised a slight smile.

"I..." Do not know. What was there for her in that small country cottage on Graham's properties other than memories of all that had been and would never be? Mrs. Belden's was no longer possible. For if word had not yet reached the esteemed headmistress, it soon would, and then Rowena would be thrown out on her illegitimate arse.

A knock sounded at the doorway and they looked up. "Mrs. Bryant, you've a visitor."

The gold floor-length mirror from across the room reflected her and Ainsley's equal shock. Swinging her legs over the side of the bench,

Rowena climbed slowly to her feet and moved toward Wesley who held a silver tray.

She plucked the card from it. Her heart dropped to her stomach.

"I've taken the liberty of showing her ladyship to the Blue Parlor."

With a murmur of thanks, Rowena continued to study the card. The butler rushed off. What need did any of the nobility have with her?

"Do you know where it is?"

She shot her head up.

"The Blue Parlor," Ainsley clarified, hopping up. "I will help show you there."

In her tenure at Mrs. Belden's, she had been the object of scorn and ridicule by young ladies who treated her with disdain for nothing more than their elevated statuses. Never, in the nearly eleven years of employment, had she known the kindness Ainsley had shown her over the course of even a single day. "I would appreciate that very much."

Together, they started for the Blue Parlor. "The peculiar thing about it," Ainsley prattled, blessedly filling the quiet. "Is that the duke has a blue parlor, a pink one, a green, and gold. And do you know, not a single one bears upholsteries or curtains in those respective shades," she groused, startling a laugh from Rowena. Oh, how she would miss this girl. Flinging her arm around Ainsley in a move that would have shocked Mrs. Belden, Rowena gave her a quick hug.

And again, she would be forever grateful to Ainsley for that brief distraction that made her march to her meeting bearable.

They arrived at the Blue Parlor, and with a grateful smile, Rowena forced herself to enter. She located the marchioness at the hearth, staring down into the empty metal grate. With the comforting presence of Ainsley gone, the same sick dread of having her secrets and life bared before all rushed forward.

"My lady," she said quietly, and Lady Waverly spun about. Her skirts whipped noisily at her ankles and the fabric tightened across her slightly rounded belly. A horrible, vicious envy twisted inside, stunning

Rowena with the depth of her own selfishness. "Forgive me," she said quickly, rushing over. "Would you care for refresh—?"

"No. No refreshments are necessary, Mrs. Bryant. Please." The marchioness motioned to the brocade sofas. "I hoped we might speak."

This from the woman who'd served at Mrs. Belden's, whom Rowena had also caught carefully studying her. "Speak," she echoed dumbly. Other than berating her for creating a stir at the recital last night, what could they have to talk of?

"Yes," the lady repeated. "Talk."

Springing into movement, Rowena, wholly out of her element, found a seat, with the marchioness claiming the wingback Bergere chair. "Perhaps I might get precisely to the reason for my visit." The golden-haired woman spoke in purposeful tones, drawing off her gloves. "I recall you from Mrs. Belden's. You were a dragon."

"Am a dragon," Rowena instantly corrected. Her gaze fell involuntarily to her lap. Or she had been. How quickly did such news travel to a finishing school? Or mayhap the *ton* wouldn't bother with mention of her when she was gone. Or mayhap pigs would fly over the skies of London.

A gentle hand covered hers, and Rowena snapped her head up. "Is it still as miserable there as it was when I was there?"

"More so," she muttered. The frank honesty pulled a laugh from the marchioness. With the old headmistress' passing years, Mrs. Belden grew stodgier and more demanding.

"And do you wish to go back?"

I'd rather pluck my fingernails out one by one. Rowena rested her hands on the arms of her chair and curled her fingers into the cherry wood. "I expect I'll not truly have a say on it either way now." Except, where that prospect had filled her with terror in the immediacy of the scandal at Ainsley's recital, she had a peculiar...peace. A peace she'd not had since Graham had left for war. One in which all lies had been, at last, revealed, with a heart now able to heal.

The marchioness edged her chair forward, scraping it along the floor. "But would you?" she persisted.

"It is the only place I've known for ten years," she settled for.

"Very well. What is your opinion on Mrs. Belden's instructions?"

"Truthfully?"

The other woman inclined her head.

"If you'd asked me that question not even a month ago, I would have praised her methods of instruction. I would have applauded the efforts to shape ladies into proper ladies with a respect for decorum."

The marchioness leaned forward. "And now?" she asked, hanging on to Rowena's words.

"I've learned how wrong I was. Mrs. Belden's methods are archaic," she said automatically. "I believe desperate young women take on work as instructors in her *distinguished* institution because we have no choice. And in that desperation, we sell a piece of our soul for security, by transforming young women into empty shells of who they once were."

Lady Waverly nodded slowly. Then said softly, unexpectedly, "I have a finishing school."

Rowena tipped her head.

"Mrs. Munroe's Finishing School. I am searching for instructors. I'd like to offer you a position."

Rowena's mouth fell agape. "But…but…you do not even know me."

A twinkle lit the other woman's eyes. "I've seen you with Miss Hickenbottom." At Lord Wilkshire's. So that accounted for the lady's staring. "And I saw you at Hyde Park." Rowena blinked. She'd seen her? "Miss Hickenbottom was sketching and skipping." She smiled. "It was the skipping which confirmed the rightness of my decision." She held her index finger aloft. "Furthermore, any young woman who can survive eleven years inside Mrs. Belden's, and then enter the miserable world of London is a woman of strength and character."

A woman of strength and character. For more than eleven years, she'd only seen her own weaknesses. She'd viewed her mother's past as their family's weakness. Only to find it was, as she'd said to Ainsley…It mattered not what your birthright was or the blueness of your blood. It mattered the courage one showed through the uncertainty that was life. Her mother may have once been a courtesan. But she'd survived.

And she'd transformed her life to make a better world for her daughter. Just as Rowena had sought and attained some control of her own existence. Not everyone, however, was of like mind. Certainly, not one of the nobility.

She folded her hands primly in her lap. "I thank you for your... offer...but I am not a lady. I'm a bastard. My mother was a—"

"Do you know who my father is?" the marchioness cut in.

Puzzling her brow, she shook her head.

"My father is the Duke of Ravenscourt. I, too, am a bastard. Judged by Society for my birthright. My school is one that serves ladies like ourselves." Ourselves. Even though she had ascended to the rank of nobility, she would place Rowena into her own category? "It caters to the illegitimate children of noblemen. Merchant's daughters. Families who've faced scandal and want better lives for their girls." In short, everything that Mrs. Belden's was not, nor would ever be.

The marchioness dangled a beautiful gift before her. A promise of a future not built on fear. A new beginning where no one knew who she was or would care, either way.

A life without Graham.

Grief scissored her heart. Could she let him go and begin again without him? "Why would you do this?" Rowena asked hoarsely.

"Because we all require a bit of help sometimes, Mrs. Bryant."

"Rowena," she swiftly corrected and held her fingers out. "My name is Rowena."

The young marchioness smiled. "And you must call me Jane. Will you accept my offer?"

If she took this, she would never again see him. There would be no reason or need for their lives to intersect. They would continue on as though they'd never been. He would eventually find a dignified English miss with blood to match his own. The truth knifed around at her belly and she had to press her hands to her stomach to blot the pain.

It was as she'd said to him last evening, however. Too much had come to pass. Too many mistakes that could never, ever be undone. Forcing a smile that she did not feel, Rowena nodded slowly. "I will."

❧

She was going to leave.

He was going to lose her, all over again. And the pain of her absence this time would gut him in ways it hadn't before. Since Rowena had reentered his life, Graham had learned to again laugh and smile and tease and feel. And see himself not as the madman he'd believed but as a man who carried the invisible reminders of what he'd seen and done.

And with her departure, she'd take all of that.

Seated in his office, he examined the stack of ledgers on his desk, those meticulous books kept by his late father's man-of-affairs. To keep from thinking of the agony tearing away at him, Graham absently flipped through the pages of the old ledger. He turned another. And then stopped. Heart hammering, he looked back at the previous page. The earth froze upon its axis as Graham sat frozen, staring at one specific column: 30th of June 1814.

Two months after Graham's father had passed. "No," he whispered.

It couldn't be. There had to be a reason those fifteen pounds had been paid out, two months after the death of his father. Those funds had gone to something else. Someone else. *God, no.* And he knew. Knew it because of the treachery Rowena had opened Graham's blind eyes to. That damning unmarked column with fifteen pounds recorded told him everything. The truth that she'd come to Graham all those years ago, and Jack had never uttered a word of it.

And now this. Jack had known of Rowena's past, and the sum settled on her by the late duke, and he'd continued to pay that silencing money.

He closed his eyes tight and fixed on his breathing to rein in the violent fury simmering under the surface. What a bloody fool he'd been. Graham's first order of business after his father died had been to replace the late duke's loyal man-of-affairs with his own, trustworthy, honorable *friend.*

That same *friend,* who, in Graham's absence, attempted to woo Rowena and forced an embrace upon her.

Bile stung the back of his throat. When they were young men competing for her affections, he'd never questioned Jack's loyalty. Instead, he'd believed Jack had accepted her decision. All these years, however, that friendship been just one more lie in a quagmire of them.

Graham picked up the book, taking note of details he'd never even given a cursory thought to. But now seeing it with new, open eyes.

A knock sounded at the door and Graham glanced up. Punctual, as he'd been since the day he had hired him. Professional in every way. The bloody traitor. "Enter," he called out.

Folios in his arms, Jack stepped inside. "Hampstead," he greeted, strolling over to his usual seat with a marked calm.

Foregoing pleasantries, Graham searched the smooth planes of the other man's face for a hint of guilt. Regret. Something. *Anything* that proved he was human. Proved that he felt some compunction at having destroyed his life and Rowena's reputation.

"I have brought the forms for you to sign, solidifying your business arrangement with the Duke of Huntly," Jack said, after he'd claimed his seat. Setting his burden on the edge of Graham's desk, the other man briefly froze, and surveyed the stack of older ledgers. "Huntly would like a meeting," he continued, returning his attention to his papers. Jack rifled through his leather folio, searching around for papers that did not matter, with business that was irrelevant.

With a violent hatred poisoning his blood, Graham stared at his bent head. How many times he'd sat across from this very man, trusted him with his secrets, and all along he'd committed the ugliest act of treachery.

"I have the paperwork in order for the steam investment," Jack said in his perfunctory businesslike tones. He withdrew a stack of documents and set them on the desk before Graham.

"Why did you do it?"

The other man furrowed his brow. "You asked me to pursue the venture with the Duke of Huntly—"

Gathering his late father's ledger, he slid it over to Jack.

The traitorous bastard hesitated, and then taking the book, scanned the pages. "What am I looking for?" he drawled with such boredom, Graham's fingers twitched with the need to bury them in his face.

"The thirtieth," he replied with a frosty calm that gave the other man pause.

Giving that page a cursory look, Jack lifted his shoulders. "I don't know—"

"What were the fifteen pounds for?" he interrupted harshly.

A beleaguered sigh escaped the other man. "This again?" he drawled, leaning back in his chair. He hooked his ankle across his bent knee with an infuriating detachment. "I already told you. You are focusing on numbers kept by your father's—"

"They are yours." Graham's quiet interruption froze the other man mid-speak. "They are your accountings," he repeated. Jack's mouth fell open, but no words came forth. Violent energy hummed in his veins, and the need to destroy the fiend opposite him called with a greater intensity than had ever struck on the fields of battle. "Rowena told me everything."

All the color bled from the man's face in a damning testament of his guilt. Then, in a remarkable show, he smoothed his features into a bored mask. "I don't know what you're talking about."

God, did Jack think him for a bloody lackwit? Except, he had perpetuated a lifetime of lies Graham had readily believed. Layering his palms to the desk, he leaned forward. "I'd think carefully in how I respond."

Swallowing loudly, Jack nodded. "I was acting on your behalf," he said, that slight stammer hinting at his fear, and Graham reveled in it. He should be afraid. Graham had only done harm to those enemies he'd faced on the battlefield, but in this, he wanted to gleefully take this man apart limb by limb. "He asked that I see a final payment settled on her family."

Oh, God. He'd known. Of course, he had. It was the only thing that made sense. And yet, all these years, Graham had believed him loyal, only to find, he'd been a part of the puzzle keeping him and Rowena apart. "You spread the word about her parentage around my home." His own voice came as though down a distant hall.

Crimson splotches slapped the other man's cheeks. "I do not—"

"Do not lie to me," Graham thundered, and surging across the desk, he dragged the other man out of his seat and shook him. "I told you, Jack, I know all. She told me."

"She is a goddamn liar," the other man said, desperation underlying his charge. Graham leveled him with a solid fist to the jaw.

Jack crumpled in a heap. Ignoring the other man's piteous moan, he came around the side of the desk and dragged his limp form up so he met his gaze squarely. "How dare you?" Jack cried, his nose leaking a slow trickle of blood. "You would doubt *me*? I, who stood by you when she broke your heart? She did."

"You offered her marriage. Kissed her," he growled. In breathing those words aloud, the ugly visited upon Rowena that day in her cottage took on a realness that shattered his control. Fury pumped through his veins all over again, and he dealt Jack another punch.

Panting, Jack collapsed to his knees. "She wanted it. Begged for— *eek*." His words ended on a sharp cry as Graham gripped him by his throat. Squeezing Jack's neck, he drove him backward into the wall, slamming him with a solid *thunk*.

He loosened his grip, allowing this man he'd called friend to suck in a gasp of air. "You are a liar. You stole eleven years from Rowena and me. Why?" he pleaded, taking him by the shoulders and shaking him. "Why?"

"B-Because you had everything." Jack's threadbare words barely reached his ears. "Because you had everything." His lips peeled back in an ugly snarl that revealed the inner ugly of his soul.

Flexing his fingers, he released the man he'd called friend. Sucking in slow, gasping breaths, Jack borrowed support from the wall.

Graham dragged a hand through his hair. *How did I fail to see this? How was I so blinded?*

"You were a duke's spare and you were even lucky enough to have your brother die for you." A cold went through Graham at the empty, maniacal laugh that bubbled from Turner's throat. "You had Rowena and love. Why did you deserve to have everything?"

My God. All these years he'd believed himself mad, and all along it was Jack whose brain had been destroyed. "You are sick," Graham breathed.

"Mayhap." In a show of brazen stupidity, Jack grinned, a cocksure smile full of evil. "But I wrote the note that cost you Rowena and her love."

Jack had written the note. That forged scrap of lies.

Graham stood motionless, and then swung his arm back and leveled his fist in the other man's face. Shrieking and wailing, Jack crumpled in a heap and Graham came down over him. Chest heaving from his tumultuous emotion and exertion, he drew back to bloody him once more—and stopped. He looked at Jack, sniveling before him, and then suddenly released him. Beating the other man would not right Jack's evil or his own wrongs. Wiping a tired hand over his face, he slowly stood. "Get out," he ordered. When Jack remained curled in a ball at his feet, he yanked him to an upright position and shoved him toward the door. "Never come back. If you breathe a word about Ainsley or Rowena, if you so much as go near or mention even her family, I will end you."

Tripping over himself, Jack rushed from the room.

Footsteps sounded in the hall and Graham spun.

Rowena lingered in the entranceway. "May I come in?" she asked hesitantly.

He blinked slowly. "Yes, of course. Come in." His heart thundered as she drew the door closed behind her. Graham motioned her to one of the chairs at his desk. With her gaze, she did an inventory of the papers strewn about the haphazard furniture. He quickly righted the other seat.

"You didn't have to do that for me."

So she knew? How much had she heard at the doorway? "I had to do that for us." For all they'd lost, which could never be restored.

She lingered at the chair, not sitting but hovering like a scared bird about to take flight. "I am leaving." She confirmed that she was, in fact, that bird.

His heart stopped.

"I received a visit from the Marchioness of Waverly a short while ago. She has a finishing school."

"A finishing school," he repeated when she just stared at him.

"Her Ladyship extended me an offer of employment." She held his gaze squarely. "And I accepted."

How was he still standing and breathing? How, when his heart was withering and dying slowly in his chest, leaving in its place a dark, empty void? "I see." His voice emerged garbled to his own ears. "And this is what you want?" *Please tell me no. Please tell me I'm all you want. A future with us, together.*

Rowena folded her arms close. "Every decision I've made in life had been thrust upon me. From my mother's decision to move to Wallingford with my stepfather to your father sending me on to Mrs. Belden's." Graham wanted to drag the old bastard from the grave and kill him dead all over again. "Neither of those decisions were mine. I worked and survived, but I was only there because of him. And now here." She motioned to the room. "I'm here, employed, because of you." What in blazes was her point? He could see nothing through this thick haze of madness. "If I marry you now following the scandal…it will be no different than a decision that was thrust upon us. I need to do this…for me."

For me.

Not us.

Rowena reached inside the front pocket sewn on her skirts and withdrew a small sack. She handed it over to him. Next, came a heart pendant. With stiff, aching movements, he looked inside the purse. "There is fifty pounds there," she answered. She'd had a small fortune. Instead of using even a pence, she'd toiled and worked for everything she'd earned. God, how was it possible to find with each passing moment he loved her more and more? "I never touched a coin."

This is what his father had given her. This final nail that had severed her faith and love in Graham. *Nay, I did that all on my own…*With unsteady fingers, he set down the purse and necklace. "Please, don't go." He dropped to a knee beside her, and a single tear streaked down her cheek, blazing a lonely trail. "Stay with me. Marry me."

"I need to leave." The weakening of her whisper stirred the embers of hope.

"You do not," he entreated, gathering her hands.

"For Ainsley. For me." Those last two words ripped a hole through his already shattered heart. Tears hung on her lashes.

"The *ton* doesn't matter. None of this does." How could he make her see? "Only we together matters."

Another tear trailed down her cheek, followed by another and another, until her eyes were soft, shimmery pools of brown sadness. "Oh, Graham." She caressed his face, and he leaned into her touch, the warmth of it healing. And then she spoke. "Don't you see? Nothing but darkness exists when our worlds are combined. Together, we love, but we bring heartache. I do not want this life. If it was you and nothing else…" His dukedom. "…we could be, but the divide between us matters. Your father knew that. My mother knew that. And, in time, you will, too." She opened her mouth as though to say more, but then she dropped her hand to her side and left him just as he'd been for the past eleven years: alone.

TWENTY-FOUR

One month later
London, England

Seated at his desk, with his new man-of-affairs going through his weekly reports, Graham only partially listened. Instead, his gaze kept straying to that small book tucked in the corner of his desk; to the same spot it had occupied for the past two months.

She'd been gone one month. And not a single bloody moment of the day passed when she did not occupy his thoughts. Was she happy? That was the most important question filling him with a longing to know. He had a desperation for her to miss him as he missed her.

He closed his eyes—

"Ahem..."

And then swiftly opened them. Blinking slowly, Graham stared at Roarke, a master of numbers and business who'd replaced Turner, and who now sat staring at him expectantly. "As I was saying, Your Grace, the Duke of Huntly requests a meeting to discuss the partnership. May I set it up for..." He examined a book on his lap. "Sometime next week?"

The inanity of those business deals. "Yes." Going through the motions was how he'd existed since Rowena had left. Of life. Of business. Everything. "That will be all for the morning," he said dismissively, and the other man nodded and rose to his feet.

The servant with graying hair at his temples collected his belongings, and then left Graham to his own musings.

Silence ringing in the room, he leaned forward and picked up the small book that was always close at hand. *Da Vinci's Great Works.* That copy she'd pored over with an animated light in her eyes, as she'd challenged him on everything he'd thought he'd known about propriety and the way a person ought to conduct oneself. And, yet, whenever he held the leather tome, whenever he glanced upon it, memories of lying beside Rowena on the library floor flooded him. He fanned the pages as he so often did, and a thick sheet of vellum slowed his perusal. Graham paused, transfixed by that hated note he'd stuck in the middle. That note had single-handedly decided and destroyed their future, that last mocking testament left of his father's evil.

They had been robbed of their happiness. Nay, that wasn't altogether true. Even now, the lady might be blissfully happy in her new role. His stomach muscles contracted. For what kind of selfish bastard was he that he wanted her to be as empty in this moment as he himself was? Sucking in a breath, he drew the book close to his face. Missing her. Wanting her. Needing her. Loving—

"Hampstead?"

Swiftly lowering the book, he looked up to find his ward, Ainsley, at the front of the room. God how he hated how she'd taken to calling him Hampstead. It was a title that served as a horrid reminder of the man who'd sired him. "Ainsley," he called and came to his feet. With Rowena's absence, a new companion had been sent by the Marchioness of Waverly. The young woman, Mrs. Dubois, who now served in his employ had come to them from the same finishing school where Rowena now worked. And he hated the new companion's very presence here for her connection to the place he'd lost Rowena to.

Ainsley strolled over and plopped into the leather winged chair. "Well?"

"Well, what?" In the time he'd navigated through his household with his charge underfoot, one thing he'd learned about the girl was that she was a master of confusion with words. He'd read complex battlefield plans that were easier to sort through than her ruminations, most times.

"Dukes don't sulk."

Sulk? "I'm not sulking," he mumbled.

Ainsley scoffed. "And dukes certainly don't mumble, either. But you've done a good deal of both." She winged an incredibly mature eyebrow up. "Since Rowena left, that is."

Despite the misery he'd lived for the past month, a grin pulled at the corners of his mouth. "You know so very much about dukes."

"I know very much about all number of topics."

And he decidedly did not want to know anything about what those topics might be. "Is this about your recent companion?" They'd gone through two since Rowena had departed. Not a woman had an ounce of her spirit or skill. But more, she'd been a lady who'd not entered this household to quash a girl's spirit.

"Yes, well, I *do* miss her as a companion," Ainsley conceded, draping her right leg over the arm of her chair. "But Mrs. Dubois and I get on well enough." When the girl was not hiding from the lady. Graham knew better than to say as much. "But I'm not one who worries only for herself. I'm more worried about the sulking, mumbling, and sniffing."

He puzzled his brow.

"You are often sniffing that book." Ainsley pointed to the object in question, still clutched damningly in in his hands.

Neck heating, he quickly set it down. "I was not *sniffing* it." Sometimes he brought it to his nose for the hint of her. This, however, had not been one of those times.

"May I speak freely?"

"Do you ever not?" he asked wryly, enjoying the break from his usual grief.

"Mrs. Bryant loves you and you love her. I really do not see the need for all this maudlin business." She slashed the air with her hand.

"It is...complicated." It was too many years of broken dreams and promises that Rowena believed could not be fixed. And certainly not words he'd share with this young lady who'd been tasked to his care, only after her rakehell father and reprobate guardian had gone and died on her.

"Complicated?" Ainsley snorted. "You do understand I'm a ward of nearly seventeen and not seven? You, sir, found your swan and you let her go."

Graham scratched his brow.

With a frustrated sigh, Ainsley pointed her eyes to the heavens. "Your muted swan." She flapped her arms in what he expected was her attempt at a birdlike gesture. "They partner for life, and build nests together, and mate…"

Choking, he yanked at his cravat, and his ward let those words thankfully go unfinished.

"Yes, well, they do everything together," she settled for. "And you were Mrs. Bryant's swan. I wish you'd both get on with your happiness instead of lamenting the past." She hopped up. "That is all."

That was all?

"Go to her, Hampstead," his spirited ward called, not bothering to look back, "and get on with…" He emitted a strangled laugh. "*Nest*-building." Shooting him an insolent last glance, she winked.

Go to her.

Rowena had been clear she wanted a new life without him in it. *Or did she worry that a future between us is impossible because of all that had come to be?* Graham raised her book to his face and inhaled deeply. Sniffing books, indeed. He set it down hard. He needed to see her one more time and attempt to convince her they were one another's swans.

With a renewed purpose, he climbed to his feet.

It was not that Rowena wasn't happy at Mrs. Munroe's. Her charges were kind and clever girls. Her dwellings were cheerful. The food was palatable, which was a good deal more than one could say for the rubbish served at Mrs. Belden's.

And yet, in the time since she'd been here, a hollow emptiness remained in the place where her heart was. She missed him. She missed everything there was to miss about him. She'd believed she would be better off alone than living amongst the ton as Graham's duchess. She'd convinced herself that taking employment at the marchioness' school was safer, and that Rowena would be spared the risk of any further hurt.

How very wrong she'd been.

This time being apart was no less painful than the ten years they'd been separated. Graham was the other half of her soul. Be it now or all those years past when they were not together, an ache existed in the place where her heart should be.

Only, this had been her choice. This was what was best for her and him. It was…Seated at her desk, Rowena banged her head slowly on the surface. Why did it feel as though with each passing day she sought to convince herself of the rightness in her decision?

Why could she not be happy? She lifted her head and looked about at the cheerful, now quiet rooms, where she delivered her instruction on *Mrs. Wollstonecraft's Works*. She had security and independence and cheerful charges and…

She covered her face with her hands. And she was bloody miserable. Though contented, she was no happier here than she'd been at Mrs. Belden's. She wasn't, because her happiness and her heart were inextricably linked to a man she'd loved since she'd been a girl of fourteen…mayhap, even longer.

The frantic beat of footsteps passed her door. Followed by another set. And another. Until a loud stream of giggles and whispers echoed down the corridors.

Such displays of exuberance were not uncharacteristic in a school that did not seek to stifle young ladies' spirits.

"What in blazes?" A cry went up and Rowena surged to her feet. For such panicky shouts from fellow instructors were unheard of.

She rushed to the door and pulled it open just as another handful of ladies went passing by. "What…"

"Do not go outside," the young headmistress, Mrs. Devon, shrieked at the charges bypassing her.

Rowena cringed at that blatant disregard for the unusually frantic young woman, who was wholly out of her element. "He is a madman," the headmistress cried. "Mr. Davenport," she screeched for the stable master.

Feeling her first real stirrings of interest, Rowena quickened her stride and followed the bustling activity. She squeezed her way past girls rushing from their rooms to the open door at the front of the establishment. She lifted her hand to shield her gaze from the late morning sun and blinked to adjust to the brightened light. "What is it?" she asked a nearby instructor, Lenora Lovel, who stood with her hands propped on her hips, peering in the distance.

"There is a madman fighting with birds," a nearby student supplied for her.

"I say he's far too splendid to be a madman," one of the other giggling girls said in return.

Creasing her brow, Rowena stalked forward, and then stopped abruptly, her heartbeat following a like movement. She touched a hand to her breast.

Four carriages sat, with their doors hanging open. Graham frantically dashed back and forth over the immaculately tended grounds… guiding…her lower lip trembled.

"Blast it, Hampstead," Ainsley shouted directions from within one conveyance. "You're letting them escape."

"They aren't birds," a student corrected from beyond her shoulders. "They are—"

"Muted white swans," she whispered. With Ainsley still barking orders to the frantic Graham, Rowena abandoned the cluster of curious girls and onlookers and continued walking. Calls of worry went up, but she ignored them. With every step, Graham's muffled cursing and mumblings reached her ears. He remained intent in his pathetic attempt at herding those recalcitrant creatures to the lake.

A large white swan cut out and charged at his legs. He stumbled and tossed his arms wide in a bid to keep from falling on the bird. He soundly landed on his buttocks. Ainsley covered her face in her hand with a furious groan. "Bad form, Hampstead. Bad form, indeed."

A laugh escaped Rowena, and she rushed forward in a flurry of lavender skirts. "Graham?"

From around the swarm of white swans that surrounded him, he peeked his eyes up at her.

"What are you doing?" she asked, shaking her head in abject confusion. *He is here. Why is he here?*

"Rowena Endicott, the woman who never required more than two names because you were always perfect as you are," he called loudly, climbing to his feet. Her heart pulled at that long ago lamentation she'd made to him about her lack of a second name. "I am here to again ask you to marry me. As I should have done before I went to war." Her heart jumped. "As I should have done when I returned. You, madam," he barked, jabbing a finger in her direction, "are my swan."

Her lips parted on a whispery soft exhalation. And throughout the grounds, but for the collective sighs that went up, the students and instructors fell silent.

"And if you must stay here," he gestured to the modest stone establishment at her back and the cluster of onlookers, "then, I would stock this lake with white swans, so every day you wake up, and every day you look out that window and remember, I am yours." Tears flooded her eyes. "And you are mine. My partner for life. The woman I'd build a nest or a castle for, if you'd but let me."

Rowena blinked back the crystalline drops, attempting to bring his beloved face into focus, but the tears continued to come. "Graham—"

"Tell me where you wish to be and let me be there with you. Because you are home. We are home, together. And—" Another angry swan charged at his legs once again and he grunted. "And...and...I expected this would be a good deal easier," he boomed, fending off another attack from several other swans. "Vastly different than sheep." Giggles echoed about the grounds, followed by loud shushing from the instructors. "Not that I would not climb into the heavens and grab you a star if you so wished, because I would," he added. "But—"

"Graham—"

"It would be vastly more romantic if I wasn't getting..." He winced, dancing out of the way of one of the fowls. "...For the love of God..." Rowena's lips twitched. "Pecked to death by angry swans, who should really quite figure that the water is right over there, and a good deal more—"

"Graham," she cried, cupping her hands around her mouth and bringing an immediate cessation to his words. "Yes," she said softly.

He tossed his hands up. "What?" And then his arms fell to his sides.

Rowena nodded. "Yes," she repeated. She walked quickly, her legs eating away the distance as she cut a swath toward him, scattering the swans. She stood before him and angled her head back to meet his gaze.

"Yes?" His throat bobbed.

"Yes, I will marry you. I love you, Graham Linford with so many names, and I never stopped. I never can stop. I—"

"For goodness sake, Hampstead. Kiss the lady already," Ainsley wailed.

To the shocked gasps and romantic sighing, he claimed Rowena's lips. Her eyes slid closed as heat burned through her like the high sun. He drew back and her lashes fluttered open. "It is fortunate I am a duke and not a shepherd, or we would be penniless."

Several swans flapped their broad wings in apparent fowl-agreement.

Rowena's lips twitched, and as she leaned up on tiptoe so their noses brushed, she said, "Ah, but that is where you are wrong. You may not move a muted swan about with much success, but my heart will go wherever your heart is."

Graham stroked her lower lip with his thumb. "My heart is wherever you are. Let us find that home, together."

He kissed her, once more, in a kiss that promised forever.

The End

BIOGRAPHY

C hristi Caldwell is the bestselling author of historical romance novels set in the Regency era. Christi blames Judith McNaught's "Whitney, My Love," for luring her into the world of historical romance. While sitting in her graduate school apartment at the University of Connecticut, Christi decided to set aside her notes and try her hand at writing romance. She believes the most perfect heroes and heroines have imperfections and rather enjoys tormenting them before crafting a well-deserved happily ever after!

When Christi isn't writing the stories of flawed heroes and heroines, she can be found in her Southern Connecticut home chasing around her eight-year-old son, and caring for twin princesses-in-training!

Visit www.christicaldwellauthor.com to learn more about what Christi is working on, or join her on Facebook at Christi Caldwell Author, and Twitter @ChristiCaldwell

For first glimpse at covers, excerpts, and free bonus material, be sure to sign up for my monthly newsletter! Each month one subscriber will win a $35 Amazon Gift Card!

OTHER BOOKS BY

CHRISTI CALDWELL

"To Enchant a Wicked Duke"
Book 13 in the Heart of a Duke Series

A Devil in Disguise

Years ago, when Nick Tallings, the recent Duke of Huntly, watched his family destroyed at the hands of a merciless nobleman, he vowed revenge. But his efforts had been futile, as his enemy, Lord Rutland is without weakness.

Until Now...

With his rival finally happily married, Nick is able to set his ruthless scheme into motion. His plot hinges upon Lord Rutland's innocent, empty-headed sister-in-law, Justina Barrett. Nick will ruin her, marry her, and then leave her brokenhearted.

A Lady Dreaming of Love

From the moment Justina Barrett makes her Come Out, she is labeled a Diamond. Even with her ruthless father determined to sell her off to the highest bidder, Justina never gives up on her hope for a good, honorable gentleman who values her wit more than her looks.

A Not-So-Chance Meeting
Nick's ploy to ensnare Justina falls neatly into place in the streets of London. With each carefully orchestrated encounter, he slips further and further inside the lady's heart, never anticipating that Justina, with her quick wit and strength, will break down his own defenses. As Nick's plans begins to unravel, he's left to determine which is more important—Justina's love or his vow for vengeance. But can Justina ever forgive the duke who deceived her?

"One Winter with a Baron"
Book 12 in the Heart of a Duke Series

A Clever Spinster
Content with her spinster lifestyle, Miss Sybil Cunning wants to prove that a future as an unmarried woman is the only life for her. As a bluestocking who values hard, empirical data, Sybil needs help with her research. Nolan Pratt, Baron Webb, one of society's most scandalous rakes, is the perfect gentleman to help her. After all, he inspires fear in proper mothers and desire within their daughters.

A Notorious Rake
Society may be aware of Nolan Pratt, Baron's Webb's wicked ways, but what he has carefully hidden is his miserable handling of his family's finances. When Sybil presents him the opportunity to earn much-needed funds, he can't refuse.

A Winter to Remember
However, what begins as a business arrangement becomes something more and with every meeting, Sybil slips inside his heart. Can this clever woman look beneath the veneer of a coldhearted rake to see the man Nolan truly is?

"To Redeem a Rake"
Book 11 in the Heart of a Duke Series

He's spent years scandalizing society.

Now, this rake must change his ways.

Society's most infamous scoundrel, Daniel Winterbourne, the Earl of Montfort, has been promised a small fortune if he can relinquish his wayward, carousing lifestyle. And behaving means he must also help find a respectable companion for his youngest sister—someone who will guide her and whom she can emulate. However, Daniel knows no such woman. But when he encounters a childhood friend, Daniel believes she may just be the answer to all of his problems.

Having been secretly humiliated by an unscrupulous blackguard years earlier, Miss Daphne Smith dreams of finding work at Ladies of Hope, an institution that provides an education for disabled women. With her sordid past and a disfigured leg, few opportunities arise for a woman such as she. Knowing Daniel's history, she wishes to avoid him, but working for his sister is exactly the stepping stone she needs.

Their attraction intensifies as Daniel and Daphne grow closer, preparing his sister for the London Season. But Daniel must resist his desire for a woman tarnished by scandal while Daphne is reminded of the boy she once knew. Can society's most notorious rake redeem his reputation and become the man Daphne deserves?

"To Woo a Widow"
Book 10 in the Heart of a Duke Series

They see a brokenhearted widow.

She's far from shattered.

Lady Philippa Winston is never marrying again. After her late husband's cruelty that she kept so well hidden, she has no desire to search for love.

Years ago, Miles Brookfield, the Marquess of Guilford, made a frivolous vow he never thought would come to fruition—he promised to marry his mother's goddaughter if he was unwed by the age of thirty. Now, to his dismay, he's faced with honoring that pledge. But when he encounters the beautiful and intriguing Lady Philippa, Miles knows his true path in life. It's up to him to break down every belief Philippa carries about gentlemen, proving that not only is love real, but that he is the man deserving of her sheltered heart.

Will Philippa let down her guard and allow Miles to woo a widow in desperate need of his love?

"The Lure of a Rake"
Book 9 in the Heart of a Duke Series

A Lady Dreaming of Love
Lady Genevieve Farendale has a scandalous past. Jilted at the altar years earlier and exiled by her family, she's now returned to London to prove she can be a proper lady. Even though she's not given up on the hope of marrying for love, she's wary of trusting again. Then she meets Cedric Falcot, the Marquess of St. Albans whose seductive ways set her heart aflutter. But with her sordid history, Genevieve knows a rake can also easily destroy her.

An Unlikely Pairing
What begins as a chance encounter between Cedric and Genevieve becomes something more. As they continue to meet, passions stir. But with Genevieve's hope for true love, she fears Cedric will be unable to give up his wayward lifestyle. After all, Cedric has spent years protecting his heart, and keeping everyone out. Slowly, she chips away at all

the walls he's built, but when he falters, Genevieve can't offer him redemption. Now, it's up to Cedric to prove to Genevieve that the love of a man is far more powerful than the lure of a rake.

"To Trust a Rogue"
Book 8 in the Heart of a Duke Series

A Rogue
Marcus, the Viscount Wessex has carefully crafted the image of rogue and charmer for Polite Society. Under that façade, however, dwells a man whose dreams were shattered almost eight years earlier by a young lady who captured his heart, pledged her love, and then left him, with nothing more than a curt note.

A Widow
Eight years earlier, faced with no other choice, Mrs. Eleanor Collins, fled London and the only man she ever loved, Marcus, Viscount Wessex. She has now returned to serve as a companion for her elderly aunt with a daughter in tow. Even though they're next door neighbors, there is little reason for her to move in the same circles as Marcus, just in case, she vows to avoid him, for he reminds her of all she lost when she left.

Reunited
As their paths continue to cross, Marcus finds his desire for Eleanor just as strong, but he learned long ago she's not to be trusted. He will offer her a place in his bed, but not anything more. Only, Eleanor has no interest in this new, roguish man. The more time they spend together, the protective wall they've constructed to keep the other out, begin to break. With all the betrayals and secrets between them, Marcus has to open his heart again. And Eleanor must decide if it's ever safe to trust a rogue.

"To Wed His Christmas Lady"
Book 7 in the Heart of a Duke Series

She's longing to be loved:
Lady Cara Falcot has only served one purpose to her loathsome father—to increase his power through a marriage to the future Duke of Billingsley. As such, she's built protective walls about her heart, and presents an icy facade to the world around her. Journeying home from her finishing school for the Christmas holidays, Cara's carriage is stranded during a winter storm. She's forced to tarry at a ramshackle inn, where she immediately antagonizes another patron—William.

He's avoiding his duty in favor of one last adventure:
William Hargrove, the Marquess of Grafton has wanted only one thing in life—to avoid the future match his parents would have him make to a cold, duke's daughter. He's returning home from a blissful eight years of traveling the world to see to his responsibilities. But when a winter storm interrupts his trip and lands him at a falling-down inn, he's forced to share company with a commanding Lady Cara who initially reminds him exactly of the woman he so desperately wants to avoid.

A Christmas snowstorm ushers in the spirit of the season:
At the holiday time, these two people who despise each other due to first perceptions are offered renewed beginnings and fresh starts. As this gruff stranger breaks down the walls she's built about herself, Cara has to determine whether she can truly open her heart to trusting that any man is capable of good and that she herself is capable of love. And William has to set aside all previous thoughts he's carried of the polished ladies like Cara, to be the man to show her that love.

"The Heart of a Scoundrel"
Book 6 in the Heart of a Duke Serie

Ruthless, wicked, and dark, the Marquess of Rutland rouses terror in the breast of ladies and nobleman alike. All Edmund wants in life is power. After he was publically humiliated by his one love Lady Margaret, he vowed vengeance, using Margaret's niece, as his pawn. Except, he's thwarted by another, more enticing target—Miss Phoebe Barrett.

Miss Phoebe Barrett knows precisely the shame she's been born to. Because her father is a shocking letch she's learned to form her own opinions on a person's worth. After a chance meeting with the Marquess of Rutland, she is captivated by the mysterious man. He, too, is a victim of society's scorn, but the more encounters she has with Edmund, the more she knows there is powerful depth and emotion to the jaded marquess.

The lady wreaks havoc on Edmund's plans for revenge and he finds he wants Phoebe, at all costs. As she's drawn into the darkness of his world, Phoebe risks being destroyed by Edmund's ruthlessness. And Phoebe who desires love at all costs, has to determine if she can ever truly trust the heart of a scoundrel.

"To Love a Lord"
Book 5 in the Heart of a Duke Series

All she wants is security:
The last place finishing school instructor Mrs. Jane Munroe belongs, is in polite Society. Vowing to never wed, she's been scuttled around from post to post. Now she finds herself in the Marquess of Waverly's household. She's never met a nobleman she liked, and when she meets

281

the pompous, arrogant marquess, she remembers why. But soon, she discovers Gabriel is unlike any gentleman she's ever known.

All he wants is a companion for his sister:
What Gabriel finds himself with instead, is a fiery spirited, bespectacled woman who entices him at every corner and challenges his age-old vow to never trust his heart to a woman. But...there is something suspicious about his sister's companion. And he is determined to find out just what it is.

All they need is each other:
As Gabriel and Jane confront the truth of their feelings, the lies and secrets between them begin to unravel. And Jane is left to decide whether or not it is ever truly safe to love a lord.

"Loved By a Duke"
Book 4 in the Heart of a Duke Series

For ten years, Lady Daisy Meadows has been in love with Auric, the Duke of Crawford. Ever since his gallant rescue years earlier, Daisy knew she was destined to be his Duchess. Unfortunately, Auric sees her as his best friend's sister and nothing more. But perhaps, if she can manage to find the fabled heart of a duke pendant, she will win over the heart of her duke.

Auric, the Duke of Crawford enjoys Daisy's company. The last thing he is interested in however, is pursuing a romance with a woman he's known since she was in leading strings. This season, Daisy is turning up in the oddest places and he cannot help but notice that she is no longer a girl. But Auric wouldn't do something as foolhardy as to fall in love with Daisy. He couldn't. Not with the guilt he carries over his past sins...Not when he has no right to her heart...But perhaps, just perhaps, she can forgive the past and trust that he'd forever cherish her heart—but will she let him?

"The Love of a Rogue"
Book 3 in the Heart of a Duke Series

Lady Imogen Moore hasn't had an easy time of it since she made her Come Out. With her betrothed, a powerful duke breaking it off to wed her sister, she's become the *tons* favorite piece of gossip. Never again wanting to experience the pain of a broken heart, she's resolved to make a match with a polite, respectable gentleman. The last thing she wants is another reckless rogue.

Lord Alex Edgerton has a problem. His brother, tired of Alex's carousing has charged him with chaperoning their remaining, unwed sister about *ton* events. Shopping? No, thank you. Attending the theatre? He'd rather be at Forbidden Pleasures with a scantily clad beauty upon his lap. The task of *chaperone* becomes even more of a bother when his sister drags along her dearest friend, Lady Imogen to social functions. The last thing he wants in his life is a young, innocent English miss.

Except, as Alex and Imogen are thrown together, passions flare and Alex comes to find he not only wants Imogen in his bed, but also in his heart. Yet now he must convince Imogen to risk all, on the heart of a rogue.

"More Than a Duke"
Book 2 in the Heart of a Duke Series

Polite Society doesn't take Lady Anne Adamson seriously. However, Anne isn't just another pretty young miss. When she discovers her father betrayed her mother's love and her family descended into poverty, Anne comes up with a plan to marry a respectable, powerful, and honorable gentleman—a man nothing like her philandering father.

Armed with the heart of a duke pendant, fabled to land the wearer a duke's heart, she decides to enlist the aid of the notorious Harry,

6th Earl of Stanhope. A scoundrel with a scandalous past, he is the last gentleman she'd ever wed...however, his reputation marks him the perfect man to school her in the art of seduction so she might ensnare the illustrious Duke of Crawford.

Harry, the Earl of Stanhope is a jaded, cynical rogue who lives for his own pleasures. Having been thrown over by the only woman he ever loved so she could wed a duke, he's not at all surprised when Lady Anne approaches him with her scheme to capture another duke's affection. He's come to appreciate that all women are in fact greedy, title-grasping, self-indulgent creatures. And with Anne's history of grating on his every last nerve, she is the last woman he'd ever agree to school in the art of seduction. Only his friendship with the lady's sister compels him to help.

What begins as a pretend courtship, born of lessons on seduction, becomes something more leaving Anne to decide if she can give her heart to a reckless rogue, and Harry must decide if he's willing to again trust in a lady's love.

"For Love of the Duke"
Book 1 in the Heart of a Duke Series

After the tragic death of his wife, Jasper, the 8th Duke of Bainbridge buried himself away in the dark cold walls of his home, Castle Blackwood. When he's coaxed out of his self-imposed exile to attend the amusements of the Frost Fair, his life is irrevocably changed by his fateful meeting with Lady Katherine Adamson.

With her tight brown ringlets and silly white-ruffled gowns, Lady Katherine Adamson has found her dance card empty for two Seasons. After her father's passing, Katherine learned the unreliability of men, and is determined to depend on no one, except herself. Until she meets Jasper...

In a desperate bid to avoid a match arranged by her family, Katherine makes the Duke of Bainbridge a shocking proposition—one that he accepts.

Only, as Katherine begins to love Jasper, she finds the arrangement agreed upon is not enough. And Jasper is left to decide if protecting his heart is more important than fighting for Katherine's love.

"In Need of a Duke"
A Prequel Novella to The Heart of a Duke Series

Years earlier, a gypsy woman passed to Lady Aldora Adamson and her friends a heart pendant that promised them each the heart of a duke.

Now, a young lady, with her family facing ruin and scandal, Lady Aldora doesn't have time for mythical stories about cheap baubles. She needs to save her sisters and brother by marrying a titled gentleman with wealth and power to his name. She sets her bespectacled sights upon the Marquess of St. James.

Turned out by his father after a tragic scandal, Lord Michael Knightly has grown into a powerful, but self-made man. With the whispers and stares that still follow him, he would rather be anywhere but London...

Until he meets Lady Aldora, a young woman who mistakes him for his brother, the Marquess of St. James. The connection between Aldora and Michael is immediate and as they come to know one another, Aldora's feelings for Michael war with her sisterly responsibilities. With her family's dire situation, a man of Michael's scandalous past will never do.

Ultimately, Aldora must choose between her responsibilities as a sister and her love for Michael.

"Once a Wallflower, At Last His Love"
Book 6 in the Scandalous Seasons Series

Responsible, practical Miss Hermione Rogers, has been crafting stories as the notorious Mr. Michael Michaelmas and selling them for a meager wage to support her siblings. The only real way to ensure her family's ruinous debts are paid, however, is to marry. Tall, thin, and plain, she has no expectation of success. In London for her first Season she seizes the chance to write the tale of a brooding duke. In her research, she finds Sebastian Fitzhugh, the 5th Duke of Mallen, who unfortunately is perfectly affable, charming, and so nicely…configured…he takes her breath away. He lacks all the character traits she needs for her story, but alas, any duke will have to do.

Sebastian Fitzhugh, the 5th Duke of Mallen has been deceived so many times during the high-stakes game of courtship, he's lost faith in Society women. Yet, after a chance encounter with Hermione, he finds himself intrigued. Not a woman he'd normally consider beautiful, the young lady's practical bent, her forthright nature and her tendency to turn up in the oddest places has his interests…roused. He'd like to trust her, he'd like to do a whole lot more with her too, but should he?

"A Marquess For Christmas"
Book 5 in the Scandalous Seasons Series

Lady Patrina Tidemore gave up on the ridiculous notion of true love after having her heart shattered and her trust destroyed by a black-hearted cad. Used as a pawn in a game of revenge against her brother, Patrina returns to London from a failed elopement with a tattered reputation and little hope for a respectable match. The only peace she finds is in her solitude on the cold winter days at Hyde Park. And even that is yanked from her by two little hellions who just happen to have a devastatingly handsome, but coldly aloof father, the Marquess of Beaufort. Something about the lord stirs the dreams she'd once carried for an honorable gentleman's love.

Weston Aldridge, the 4th Marquess of Beaufort was deceived and betrayed by his late wife. In her faithlessness, he's come to view women as self-serving, indulgent creatures. Except, after a series of chance encounters with Patrina, he comes to appreciate how uniquely different she is than all women he's ever known.

At the Christmastide season, a time of hope and new beginnings, Patrina and Weston, unexpectedly learn true love in one another. However, as Patrina's scandalous past threatens their future and the happiness of his children, they are both left to determine if love is enough.

"Always a Rogue, Forever Her Love"
Book 4 in the Scandalous Seasons Series

Miss Juliet Marshville is spitting mad. With one guardian missing, and the other singularly uninterested in her fate, she is at the mercy of her wastrel brother who loses her beloved childhood home to a man known as Sin. Determined to reclaim control of Rosecliff Cottage and her own fate, Juliet arranges a meeting with the notorious rogue and demands the return of her property.

Jonathan Tidemore, 5th Earl of Sinclair, known to the *ton* as Sin, is exceptionally lucky in life and at the gaming tables. He has just one problem. Well…four, really. His incorrigible sisters have driven off yet another governess. This time, however, his mother demands he find an appropriate replacement.

When Miss Juliet Marshville boldly demands the return of her precious cottage, he takes advantage of his sudden good fortune and puts an offer to her; turn his sisters into proper English ladies, and he'll return Rosecliff Cottage to Juliet's possession.

Jonathan comes to appreciate Juliet's spirit, courage, and clever wit, and decides to claim the fiery beauty as his mistress. Juliet, however, will be mistress for no man. Nor could she ever love a man who callously stole her home in a game of cards. As Jonathan begins to see Juliet as more than a spirited beauty to warm his bed, he realizes she could be a lady he could love the rest of his life, if only he can convince the proud Juliet that he's worthy of her hand and heart.

"Always Proper, Suddenly Scandalous"
Book 3 in the Scandalous Seasons Series

Geoffrey Winters, Viscount Redbrooke was not always the hard, unrelenting lord driven by propriety. After a tragic mistake, he resolved to honor his responsibility to the Redbrooke line and live a life, free of scandal. Knowing his duty is to wed a proper, respectable English miss, he selects Lady Beatrice Dennington, daughter of the Duke of Somerset, the perfect woman for him. Until he meets Miss Abigail Stone...

To distance herself from a personal scandal, Abigail Stone flees America to visit her uncle, the Duke of Somerset. Determined to never trust a man again, she is helplessly intrigued by the hard, too-proper Geoffrey. With his strict appreciation for decorum and order, he is nothing like the man' she's always dreamed of.

Abigail is everything Geoffrey does not need. She upends his carefully ordered world at every encounter. As they begin to care for one another, Abigail carefully guards the secret that resulted in her journey to England.

Only, if Geoffrey learns the truth about Abigail, he must decide which he holds most dear: his place in Society or Abigail's place in his heart.

"Never Courted, Suddenly Wed"
Book 2 in the Scandalous Seasons Series

Christopher Ansley, Earl of Waxham, has constructed a perfect image for the *ton*–the ladies love him and his company is desired by all. Only two people know the truth about Waxham's secret. Unfortunately, one of them is Miss Sophie Winters.

Sophie Winters has known Christopher since she was in leading strings. As children, they delighted in tormenting each other. Now at two and twenty, she still has a tendency to find herself in scrapes, and her marital prospects are slim.

When his father threatens to expose his shame to the *ton*, unless he weds Sophie for her dowry, Christopher concocts a plan to remain